W9-BKA-822

One Perfect Shot

Books by Steven F. Havill

One Perfect Shot

A Posadas County Mystery

Steven F. Havill

Poisoned Pen Press

Poisoned Pen Press
6962 E. First Ave., Ste. 103
Scottsdale, AZ 85251
www.poisonedpenpress.com
info@poisonedpenpress.com

Printed in the United States of America

Acknowledgments

Special thanks to David Gallegos, Jack Polen, and Henry Smith for their comprehensive tour of the Whittington Center's Cat road grader.

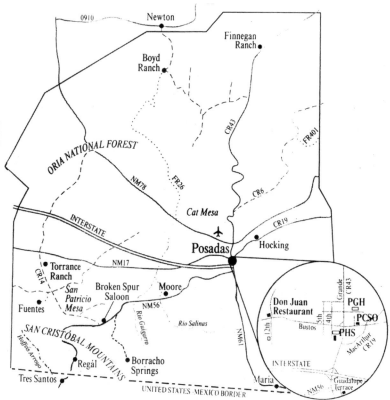

Posadas County, New Mexico

Chapter One

"I thought he was asleep," Evie Truman whispered. She stood with her arms crossed over her ample chest, shoulders hunched so far forward that the outboard ends of her clavicles were in danger of touching. Her feet, shod in simple house slippers, shuffled in the red dust of Highland Avenue. Her lower lip quivered. No one is ever prepared to be a witness, to be the first to arrive on a nasty scene.

Evie didn't need to whisper. There we stood in the hot sun of that late August Tuesday afternoon with no one within a hundred feet to overhear our conversation. The insects and songbirds continued their enterprises as if nothing humans did surprised them. Evie's broad face crumpled a little more as she watched the bulky red EMT rig approach, its gruff diesel muttering.

Farther down Highland Avenue, Deputies Robert Torrez and Tom Mears discussed with Posadas Coroner Dr. Emerson Clark how the elderly medical examiner might clamber onboard the towering road grader without risking damage to his arthritic, creaky body. Dr. Clark had wasted no time responding to our call. He hadn't been deep in some patient's bowels, or off at Elephant Butte fishing. But the old man didn't look eager.

For her part, Evie showed no inclination to trudge back and join in that discussion with the coroner. She didn't want another look at the limp, bloody corpse. I didn't think she had much more to tell us. Other than promoting community relations,

I wasn't accomplishing a whole lot by standing in the hot sun digging at sand chiggers who migrated up my socks and commiserating about how miserable it was to discover a corpse cooking and bloating in the hot sun.

As if sensing that I was about to walk off and leave her stranded, Evie sniffed and said, "I saw him earlier this afternoon, Bill. I did. I told you I did. He was working the bar ditch all along here, and everything was just fine. I can't believe it. What a horrible, horrible thing."

Sure enough, the fragrant soil had been graded up out of the ditches, deposited in a precise, laser-straight windrow on the unpaved street. To finish the job, the operator of the Posadas County Highway Department's road grader would stroke lanes down the side of the dirt street, creating a smooth, perfectly crowned finish bordered by straight, open ditches. Larry Zipoli was deft with the grader. Hell, he was better than that. He was an artist with the blade. He'd had thirty years practice with the highway department, and I doubted that there was a foot of roadway anywhere in Posadas County that Larry didn't know down to the last pebble.

But Larry hadn't finished his artistic grading job on the primitive lane on the north border of the village of Posadas. Half of Highland Avenue was finished, half was untouched, hard, pothole pocked and washboarded. Before he could finish, someone had put a high-velocity rifle bullet through the cab of the county road grader and through Larry's skull. There the big machine sat, diesel engine idling, for most of the afternoon until sixty-one year-old Evie Truman made her run into town and discovered that Larry Zipoli was well beyond snatching a quick nap.

"You went to the school shortly after noon?" I asked. One of the issues most fascinating to a cop is finding out precisely when a corpse *became* a corpse. Freshly graded though it was, Highland already showed a plethora of car tracks. Evie wasn't the only person to have driven Highland while Larry's blood leaked unreported.

She nodded vigorously, and the nodding morphed into a sad side-to-side shake. "I left my grade book at school, and thought I'd want it for later. We have that all-day faculty meeting tomorrow, you know. Now, he was just turning his grader around down there by the intersection with Hutton, and we both waved. He had to wait for me to go by."

"And then you discovered what happened on the way home from that errand?"

"No, no." Her response was immediate and snappy, a tone that would work with a recalcitrant eighth grader. "It was most likely around three o'clock. I needed to do a little shopping, and I thought, well, certainly, he would have finished grading that little street by now. And of course, there are any number of other ways to go into town. See, I had this nagging thought that there was just *something* that I had forgotten at school. Anyway, there he was, parked right along the side of the bar ditch."

Her hands fussed. "I don't know why I even noticed him, Sheriff. I mean, what business is it of mine? But what did they do to him? I mean, so much blood." She gulped a breath. "I think I looked more closely because the machine was idling, you know. It's so loud. But his head was back against the window, and I was sure he was asleep. Until I looked closer." Her hand fluttered up to cover her mouth.

It was painfully obvious what had been done to Larry Zipoli. At a glance, he looked asleep, until you saw that blood had flowed down from his left eyebrow to the hollow of his eye, and then down the fatty cleft beside his nose, across his parted lips, and then down chin and neck to matt on the front of his grubby t-shirt. His heart had stopped and blood pressure had dropped before enough blood had been pumped to form a puddle on the floor. But there was plenty spread across his enormous belly. His head rested back against the cab's rear window, jaw slack, eyes half-lidded.

Having no doubt heard her share of all the old, lame jokes about highway department employees slumbering on the job, I could imagine that Evie Truman might have thought Larry was catching himself an afternoon nap, all warm and toasty with the August sun streaming through the glass of the grader's cabin. A little too toasty, maybe. The center portion of the windshield was canted open from the bottom a couple of inches, with the left-hand door wide open, latched back against the cab frame.

"We'll need a deposition from you, Evie. As much detail as you can remember, starting with the first time you drove by. What you did, what Larry did. Who you saw."

"I'm going to have nightmares about this, Sheriff. I mean, I didn't see anyone in the area, no one at all. But if I had come along a little earlier…" Her face started to crumple again, and I patted her substantial shoulder.

"One of us will walk you through it. I can either swing by your house later this evening, or you can come down to the office at your convenience. If I'm not in the office when you stop by, the sheriff will be, or one of the deputies."

Evie took a deep, shuddering breath. "May I bring Carl for moral support?" Before I could answer with more than a nod, she reached out a hand and touched me on the forearm. "Larry's family…"

"We'll be contacting them first." Marilyn Zipoli worked at Posadas State Bank as a cashier, and her day was about to fall to pieces. "At this point, Evie, I'd rather that you didn't talk to anyone else about the incident. Sometimes it's hard to tell in the beginning what's important and what isn't. Carl understands that." Her husband of decades had been a Game and Fish officer before ruining a spinal disk while unloading one of the department boats at Elephant Butte.

I watched Evie retrace her steps to her Mercury, and then rejoined the party. Bob Torrez had worked a pair of cotton gloves over his huge hands. On down the road, just beyond Evie's car, the EMT unit had rumbled to a stop beside Deputy Mears' Bronco, effectively blocking the street. They'd sit there until we waved them in. To the east, Highland was blocked by Torrez's own patrol unit, pulled crosswise in the road beside mine.

An orange county truck had stopped behind the deputy's car, and I recognized Tony Pino, the county's Highway Superintendent, and his foreman, Buddy Clayton. They made their way along the bar ditch, in no hurry to see what they had to see.

"So." I made no move to climb up on the grader. I'd already done that and seen all I needed to see. Besides, one person in that tiny cab was a crowd. But I wanted a second opinion of the scenario before I had to explain to Tony Pino how one of his best men had come to die on this quiet afternoon.

"One shot, sir." Deputy Torrez stood below the grader's doorway, one boot on the blade and one on the first rung of the two-step ladder, perhaps ready to catch the elderly coroner should Dr. Clark inadvertently step backward through the doorway. The deputy pointed up at the windshield. Sure enough, the hole through the dusty safety glass was big enough to poke a pencil through, immediately beside the center stud that attached the windshield wiper rubber to the wiper arm. The deputy tapped his own forehead above the left eye.

"Through and through?" I stepped around the end of the blade, moving back to the first of the two mammoth rear tires. The cab window behind the driver showed no holes, no explosion of brain and skull against glass.

"No, sir." Torrez sounded a little surprised. I stood with my hands in my pockets, looking up at the hole in the windshield, then pivoted and gazed off down Highland Avenue, trying to imagine where the bullet had come from. To the southwest, the nearest house was three hundred yards away on Hutton Circle, with nothing north of that. Highland Avenue, a grand name for the lane-and-a-half cow path through the cacti and chamisa that Larry Zipoli had been grading, marked where the village of Posadas met prairie. Within a quarter mile of this lonesome spot, dozens of folks might have heard the gun shot. And enough tracks marked the freshly graded surface that a dozen folks might have driven by, perhaps laughing at the notion of another public employee snoozing on the job. It had been Evie Truman's misfortune to be so observant.

Dr. Clark stood in the grader's doorway, both hands on the frame. The climb up had been hazardous for the old man, and I had told him not to bother. It was clear to me that Larry Zipoli was as dead as dead can ever be, and any other mysteries would be solved on the autopsy table. But the good doctor had persisted, perhaps more out of professional curiosity than anything else. He had stepped up first onto the blade's support structure, and from there across to the first chain step. Torrez, who was tall and powerful enough to have lifted Dr. Clark up into the cab, had supported him from behind, not in the most dignified fashion for the old physician.

Now, Dr. Clark lowered himself with exaggerated care, taking time to place each polished shoe, both hands gripping the hand rails with white knuckles. Safe on the ground, he snapped off his rubber gloves, scowling as he did so.

"I don't think he moved one iota after being hit," he announced. "You see the way his hands are?" Larry Zipoli's arms hung limp, his hands open, the back of his right hand settled against one of the control levers beside the seat. "Dead before he knew what hit him. His hands aren't even bloody. He never grabbed his head, or anything else. No particular cadaveritic spasm." He pointed at the floor where the remains of a stogie rested between the victim's feet. "Smokin' a cigar, didn't even spasm to hold on to that."

"It's dead out," Torrez offered. "The cigar, I mean."

The elderly physician looked sideways at me. "You knew Larry about as well as I did. Who'd want to do a thing like this?"

I didn't reply to the rhetorical question.

"Yesterday morning he was gradin' the shoulders of McArthur right in front of my place," Torrez offered.

"You talked to him?"

"Nope."

Out of habit, my right hand explored my shirt pocket, scouting out a cigarette. The pocket was empty, though, my latest effort at quitting now three days old. I took a step or two toward the front of the machine, partly out of curiosity, partly to put a few feet between my nose and that fragrant cab.

The grader's long prow, with the large blade resting on the ground and the two front wheels cocked at an absurd angle, held all of the hydraulic guts of the machine, and I stopped by the end of the blade, touching it with the toe of my boot.

A dozen feet ahead of the blade, a stain on the reddish earth spread wide just inboard of the left front tire. Keeping one hand on the frame beside my head so I wouldn't crack my skull, I knelt beside the tire and touched a finger to the sand, then smelled it. A spray of hydraulic fluid had soaked the ground. The nearest line ran down from a junction box on the frame, out along the axle beam to the hydraulic ram that steered the front wheel. The spurting fluid had soaked the old yellow paint, and I could see where it had run down around the hydraulic piston, aiming for the ground. Most of the maze of hydraulic lines on the machine were Cat yellow. This one immediately above the leak was obviously new, a nice clean black, with wrench marks on the fitting at each end.

"I've done all I can do here," Dr. Clark called to jar me out of my reverie. "Looks like Tony wants to talk to you. It's odd…" He stood back and regarded the mammoth machine.

"What would that be?" I asked.

"Whoever fired that shot must have been a ways off," Clark said. "Could have been damn near all the way down Highland, here. The bullet hits the windshield and then him, all pretty much in a straight line. The gunman didn't stand right down here on the roadway, or even in a truck that stopped by. He took his shot dead on, from the front." He took a deep breath. "That's my take on it, and now I'll shut up and get out of your way."

"You'll let us know ASAP what you find in the prelim."

"Don't I always," the old man growled. "What more there'll be, I couldn't guess, except the bullet that sure as hell killed him is still lodged in his brain. Kind of odd entrance wound, no exit." He shrugged and removed the stethoscope from around his neck, absently straightening out the rubber tubes.

"I'll have the details for you, but I can tell you right now, there's not much mystery about that part of this deal. You can take the rest of your pictures now, and then tell the kids to get him out of there." He turned and waved a hand at Deputy Torrez, grimaced again at the road grader and raised his voice for emphasis. "And thanks for shutting that damn thing down, Bobby. My God, some peace and quiet is nice. I couldn't hear myself think."

Deputy Torrez, just coming on duty that afternoon, had been the first on the scene, with me following. The grader had been running when we had arrived, and neither of us had been in any hurry to shut it down. Once a crime scene is tampered with even in the most insignificant way, there's no going back. But when we'd seen most of what we were going to see, even heard the last thing Larry Zipoli might have heard after the snap of breaking glass and the bolt of destruction through his brain, we needed some peace and quiet. We might be content to shout at each other, but Dr. Emerson Clark wouldn't have been.

Torrez had slipped a leg past the victim's slumped corpse, and planted his heel on the kill pedal. The diesel sighed to blissful silence.

That simple motion added another piece to the puzzle. Larry Zipoli, facing a threat or even an innocent conversation with someone, had but to shift his right foot an inch or two to do the same thing. He hadn't done it. He either hadn't felt the need, or hadn't had the time.

With the coroner satisfied, and with a hundred photos shot by Deputy Tom Mears and myself, it was time for Larry Zipoli to make his last trip. Rigor hadn't yet set in. A damn good thing, too. We'd have needed a sky crane or a chain saw, or both. The 'kids', a couple of county paramedics neither of whom had yet enjoyed a thirtieth birthday, still would have had a struggle with Larry Zipoli without Bob Torrez's help. Zipoli was a big fellow, huge of belly and thick everywhere else, probably topping two-fifty. There was no graceful, dignified way to hoist him out of that cramped little cab. He came out feet first, with Torrez holding him under each arm and the rest of us down on the ground to add support. By the time the EMTs had their grim cargo stowed in the ambulance, the rest of the troops had started to arrive.

Tony Pino and Buddy Clayton, understanding how we worked a scene, hadn't just barged in after they had arrived. They patiently stayed a couple dozen yards away, smoking and talking in hushed tones as they watched us work, not eager to move a step closer to the blood and smell. I beckoned, and they approached with trepidation, as if they were trying to walk on eggs.

Chapter Two

Before Pino and Clayton reached us, Sheriff Eduardo Salcido's black Impala nosed to a stop, and he hadn't pulled his bulk out of the car before a state police cruiser joined us. Highland had become a parking lot. The sheriff cocked a pistol-finger at the state officer before they shook hands, and the two men stood by their cars for a moment, hopefully figuring out how they might approach without planting size twelves all over the crime scene. I waved them toward the far shoulder of the road.

"Tony, I don't know what to tell you," I said to the highway superintendent. "Someone put a shot right through the windshield. It appears that Larry was parked right here."

"Jesus," Tony whispered. "Not Larry. My God." He stepped closer to the framework below the cab, putting him at eye level with the floor of the grader's cab.

"No one witnessed it. Evie Truman happened by and found him. She's the one who called us."

"He's dead?" That seemed so obvious as to be comical, but what the hell. When we don't want to believe the ugly way things are going, we're apt to say silly things.

"Yes, sir. Probably never knew what hit him."

"My God."

"I'm going to get together with you later, Tony. We're going to need Larry's schedule, things like that. What he was doing this morning, and so forth."

"Yeah, sure." Pino's voice was distant. He gazed up at the bullet hole through the windshield. "Why…accident, you think?"

"I have no idea, Tony. None. We'll be working on that."

I turned as Sheriff Salcido approached. He walked with his hands on his rump, fingers in his back pockets, head down to watch where he put his feet. Although he was a couple of months younger than me, I still looked at Eduardo Salcido as an older man—at least until I happened to look in the mirror. Over the past ten years, after I was named undersheriff, Salcido had become less a hard-riding lawman and more of a comfortable bureaucrat, perfectly willing to turn the responsibility of day-to-day operations of the Posadas County Sheriff's Department over to me.

By no means a lazy man, Salcido simply redirected his energies as the years crept up on him. I suppose I did the same thing without ever noticing. He was good at dealing with the county commission. I wasn't—and didn't want to learn. He could give a lively, amusing talk to the Kiwanis Club, while I fumbled and stumbled. He enjoyed talking to a classroom of sixth graders. I'd rather drop rocks on my feet. I preferred long, quiet ambles through my county at any time of day or night, windows down, listening, watching, even smelling that wonderful prairie. And most of the time I did that while the rest of the county was snoozing.

"Who we got here?" Salcido asked when he was within easy conversational distance. His accent was heavy, musical, even soothing. He could thicken it, or dilute it, depending on the circumstances. He reached out a hand and shook hands with each of us in turn, his grip like squeezing a concrete block.

"Larry Zipoli. One shot, from the front." I pointed at the windshield.

"For heaven's sakes." The sheriff's frown darkened. He stood four-square, a few pounds heavier than me but four inches shorter than my five foot ten. If he had a neck, it grew buried under muscle somewhere on top of massive shoulders. For a while, he'd sported a droopy mustache, but then abandoned it, claiming it made him look like "something from one of those movies."

Bob Torrez waited patiently off to one side. Deputy Tom Mears had trudged west on Highland, seeking a panoramic photo of the crime scene. Salcido shook his head wearily and made a point to shake hands with Torrez who, at six four, towered over him. If Sheriff Salcido left the scene for ten minutes and then returned, we'd be treated to the same handshakes, except it wasn't token. Eduardo Salcido kept his circle connected.

For a long moment, the sheriff said nothing, taking in the mountain of machinery parked in the sun, the obvious insult of it all. He stretched, rubbing the right side of his upper belly where I knew his cranky gall bladder fussed. Kindred spirits in that regard, the two of us.

"You got tracks down there?" He pointed with a little nod toward the west, where Mears was making his wide-angle survey. "Freshly graded like that," he added. "Something will show."

"Sure enough," I said. "He was about half finished. So this lane is hard-packed. Not much is going to show unless they drove in the fresh stuff."

Salcido squinted up at the cab. "*Por díos,* this is *no* good." He turned and looked back down the road, trying to make the geometry work. It was a good hundred yards west to the intersection with Hutton, maybe a hundred and fifty. The rifle shot could have come from across the intersection, anywhere out on the prairie. Dips, arroyos, brush—there was plenty of cover. I had only a general working knowledge of how much a high velocity bullet dropped at various distances, but at a hundred yards or so, a couple of inches would cover the mid-range trajectory. I was uneasy about that, since a heavy caliber rifle bullet should have popped through both the windshield and Larry Zipoli's skull, perhaps even out the back window. To stop short, somewhere in his brain, had to be telling us something.

"To clear all the gear in the front of this rig, and then go straight into the cab? That's interesting, don't you think?" The sheriff reached out and took Bob Torrez by the elbow as if expecting the deputy to say, "Yes, I *do* think it's interesting."

"The bullet's going to tell us a lot," Torrez said instead. "It ain't no .22, I can tell you that much."

"You keep after it, Bobby." The sheriff turned and gazed down Highland, lips pursed. Without looking, he reached out a hand and touched my shoulder, as if he had to have physical contract in order to talk to someone. "This is bad, *jefito*." I didn't respond, and Salcido obviously didn't expect an answer. I didn't mind his slang nickname for me. He'd called me what translated as 'little boss' since the day he'd hired me, although I was neither. He glanced at his watch. "Have you talked to *la esposa?*"

"That's next on my list," I said.

Salcido shook his head. "Let me do that. I have to swing back that way anyway. I'll find his pastor, and we'll go on over." His hand reached out to Tony Pino. "You'll go with me?"

"Sure, Sheriff. You bet. Jesus, I hate this. What the hell are we going to tell her?"

"What we know," Salcido shrugged. "Right now, she needs to go down to the hospital to be with Larry." He turned to me. "You need any more hands to get this measured up?"

"We're set."

"Wrong spot at the wrong time," Salcido mused. He reached out to make contact with State Patrolman Frank Aguilar. "This guy here…he can hold the idiot end of the tape measure, you know." The sheriff grinned and flashed some gold. "You gotta wonder…" He let the thought drift off. "Somebody had to see or hear something. They got to come forward."

"We can hope so." I didn't feel particularly optimistic. "Evie Truman found him and called us. That gives us a time window. She saw him alive just after noon. If anyone else drove by, he didn't stop. It was shortly after three o'clock when she drove by the second time and found him dead. That's three hours of opportunity."

"Well, then, we talk to people," Salcido said. "Somebody knows something. He didn't have time to radio in, did he? I mean back to the maintenance barn." He turned to Tony as he said that, and Pino shook his head.

"He had trouble with the rig this morning, I know that. He had it back at the yard right around lunch time." Pino said.

"And still some trouble." I nodded toward the hydraulic leak up front. I ushered them to the spot, and for a long moment, Tony and Buddy squatted under the rig, examining the new hose.

"He blew that this afternoon," Tony said, and stood up with a grunt. "He radioed in. I know that. Who brought him the new one, Bud?"

Clayton wiped his mouth. He looked as if he'd been considering throwing up ever since he'd watched Larry Zipoli sag down out of the cab, dead face covered in blood.

"Jeez," Buddy allowed. "Who was that? I don't know. One of the boys in the shop. I know that Zip called in on the radio and told 'em what he needed."

"No big deal to change that?" I asked.

"Nah. Easy. *That* little one is easy." He turned and patted the big yellow frame beside his head. "Break one up inside, and it's a pain in the ass."

"Does he have to shut down the machine to do that work?" Salcido asked.

"Don't have to, but I guess he *would.*"

Blow a hose, call for help, wait for the replacement, take the old one off and put the new one on, I thought. Then fire up the machine and back to work. But before he can put the machine into gear, *blam.* He's dead.

Tony kicked a boot in the dirt in frustration. "Shit, I don't know. I was out most of the morning."

"After the shot, he sure as hell didn't radio anybody. What we know for sure is that when he was found, he was sitting in the seat, stone dead. The engine was idling, the gears in neutral, blade down. Beyond that, we don't know diddly," I said.

The sheriff shook his head sadly and thrust out his lower jaw as if loosening a necktie. "You let me know what you need." He nodded toward the state policeman. "If we need to ask for more help, we will." He paused. "I didn't know this Larry too well. I see him around, you know. But beyond that…" He shrugged and then brightened with another thought. He stepped away from the group and took me by the elbow, walking me toward the rear of the machine.

"I interviewed a friend of yours this afternoon. A young lady that I think we should hire."

"There aren't a whole lot of young lady friends in my life at the moment," I laughed.

"Reuben's grandniece?" The sheriff's eyes twinkled.

My mind went blank. Reuben Fuentes was a basically good-natured old codger who enjoyed a wonderfully casual relationship with the law, often fueled by excessive bouts with the bottle. A stone mason gifted with remarkable skill and artistry, he had relatives a few miles south in Mexico, and pretty much ignored the line in the dust drawn by the Border folks when he needed to haul rocks or cement or bricks from job to job. I found him immensely likeable, had bought him lunch on several occasions, and had made a trip or two with him south of the border—more than once to make sure that he didn't end up a permanent resident of a Mexican prison.

"I don't know the grandniece."

"Oh, sure you do. I want you to talk with her, too. I set it up for tomorrow. She'll come in first thing."

"Does this grandniece have a name?"

"Estelle Reyes? Teresa's adopted kid down in Tres Santos? Fresh out of school. She'll be a good one."

The memory flooded back, but it was of an eleven year-old urchin playing under the cottonwoods in Tres Santos, Mexico. Reuben had introduced me first to his aging niece, Teresa Filipina Reyes, a woman who eked out a living teaching school in the tiny village, and then to the skinny little twerp whom Teresa had adopted from the church orphanage a decade before. Reuben and I had had other issues to attend to that day, but I knew that a few years later, when the child turned sixteen, she had come across the border to live with Reuben and attend Posadas High

School. Maybe she'd come across legally, but knowing Reuben, ceremony perhaps had not been stood upon.

I knew *about* her during her two years at the high school, but not much else. She'd been in classes once in a while when Salcido or I had given guest talks during career day, but managed to get through her two years of public school without showing up on law enforcement radar. As far as I knew, no raucous parties, no lead foot, no experiments with alcohol or weed, despite her guardian's propensity for sauce. And then she'd gone off to college. Since Reuben Fuentes wasn't the sort to blab about his relatives, the girl had dropped off my planet.

"I didn't even know she'd sent in an application to work for us," I said. Most of the time, such things would have crossed my desk, but Eduardo Salcido was Eduardo, after all, operating under the *patron* system more often than not. "There hasn't been a background check, has there?" I'd had my share of challenges trying to convince Eduardo Salcido to join the twentieth century in a lot of ways. Now, in the late summer of 1987 with technology in full bloom, using formal background investigations remained an issue between us.

Eduardo tended to hire either people he knew, or people about whom he felt comfortable. He asked enough questions on the first face-to-face meeting to satisfy himself, bedamned what some "fancy computer" might reveal. To my knowledge, he'd never ordered up a background check when he'd hired me. We'd interviewed, and while I answered his questions, I recall that those dark eyes of his had never wavered from mine, as if he were x-raying my brain. He'd read through the paperwork I'd offered him, and nothing beyond.

"Is she even a citizen?" What an interesting can of worms *that* could turn out to be. I knew that plenty of people served in the armed forces on a visa, but as a cop?

"Last year," Eduardo said. "She told me that she started the process when she turned eighteen, and took the oath the week that she graduated from university. You'll like talking to her.

A most articulate young lady." He said the four syllable word with relish.

"Well, all right, then. And by the way, Evie Truman will be working on her deposition. I'll be caught up with that, too, unless you want to work with her on it."

He frowned and rubbed his belly. "When you have a chance, see what you think. Have the young lady sit in with you, then. See how she responds. I told her she'd have to catch you on the run."

Having a civilian in the room during an official activity like a deposition wasn't the usual policy—probably not even a *good* policy—but I didn't argue. Eduardo Salcido had his way of doing things, and I respected his judgment. Right then, a new hire was the last thing on my mind, even though our small sheriff's department stretched desperately thin. But hell, that was normal.

Chapter Three

The holes in the county road grader's windshield and Larry Zipoli's skull didn't offer much of a datum line. Deputy Mears conjured up a duct-tape and pencil solution to secure the contractor's foundation twine to the inside of the windshield. From there, the line was strung forward over the seventeen feet of the grader's big yellow prow, off into the hard, sinking sun. I stood on the blade, one hand on the cab, with Tom Mears gingerly sitting in the driver's seat. Tom was slight of build, perhaps five-eight, with a short torso.

Larry Zipoli had been at least six feet tall, long of torso. To hit him in the eyebrow would have meant that the bullet was angled slightly upward—exactly what made sense to me. The bottom of the cab door was about sixty inches from the ground, another three or four feet up to a spot even with the victim's eyebrow. Fired from in front, the bullet would naturally angle upward, unless the shooter had either scrambled aboard the grader's nose, or had set up a stepladder in the middle of the road.

"How curious," I muttered. Torrez was obviously excited by the whole thing, though, like figuring out the perfect five hundred yard shot on a trophy antelope. If there was something about firearms, shooting, and hunting that he didn't know, I hadn't stumbled across it yet.

I trudged out a couple of yards in front of the grader, where Torrez stood, string in hand. "What's all this tell you?" Down the road a bit, Trooper Aguilar waited.

"The main thing is that it wasn't real high velocity, sir. Pretty stout bullet that wasn't goin' fast enough to break up. Pretty good sized." He raised his voice, calling back to Mears. "I'm going to be pullin' hard on the line, so make sure that thing is secured."

We then walked down Highland, away from the grader, the twine spinning out behind us. We reached a point about a hundred feet in front of the grader. By then, when Torrez held the twine at shoulder height and pulled on it until it twanged, he could sight along the slight sag, all the way back to the grader, clearing its massive snout, to Deputy Mears' forehead.

"Somewhere right around here," Torrez said. "If the shooter was shorter'n me, then on down the road a bit." If we continued westward on Highland, we'd cover a couple hundred feet before reaching the intersection. Had the shooter parked on Hutton and then walked toward his target? That was coldly calculating. Had Larry Zipoli seen him advancing down the lane weapon in hand, and wondered what the hell was going on? Had the gunman fired, then walked forward to gaze up into the grader's cab, admiring his handiwork? Had he first driven *past* the grader, made sure of his target, and then returned? Tracks weren't going to offer a convenient answer, since the dirt of the ungraded portion of Highland was hard as concrete.

"That's a good shot, though," I mused. "To place it like that."

"A hundred feet? Nah. You could do that with a rock."

"*I* couldn't." But I knew what Torrez meant. A skilled *rifleman* could place an easy shot like that, and that told me something else. This didn't look like a snap, panicky shot taken by a shaking amateur—no "buck fever" involved here, and that would be what Bob Torrez was thinking. I imagined that the shots *he* took during his hunts were coldly calculated, too. He didn't need a trophy. He wanted to fill his freezer, and would place a careful, confident shot to do the trick.

He traced a line through the air. "It's going to matter what kind of gun it was, sir." I noted the trace of satisfaction in his tone. He held the string motionless while Mears took a roll of film from every angle possible. "I don't think the shooter was standing any farther out." Without releasing his hold on the string, Torrez turned and nodded westward. "The angle says that ain't likely. Then there's that arroyo on out there where a lot of folks go and shoot, but it's deep enough that a bullet isn't going to stray this far unless the shot is deliberate."

"Ricochet?" I prompted, even though I could see for myself that the bullet that had killed Larry Zipoli was no errant fragment.

"A ricochet ain't going to drill a straight hole like what we got here. And it's far enough away that a deliberate shot from the arroyo would have to cover five or six hundred yards. That's a whole different thing for the shooter. There ain't many people who can shoot at those kinds of ranges."

I looked down Hutton. A couple of cars had parked across the field, driven by curious onlookers who had the sense not to approach any closer.

"Somebody drives up, stops about here, and takes one shot." The freshly graded surface on the south half of Highland included a fair collection of tracks that were going to take a careful inventory to sort out. It would have been nice to see a clear trail of shoeprints, but in all likelihood the shooter had skirted the freshly graded side. We hadn't had time to complete a formal, complete survey, but nothing obvious had jumped out at us. No tracks, no stash of fresh butts, no shiny shell casing—no nothing.

"All right," I sighed. "I want Highland closed from one end to the other, Roberto. Nothing missed."

"I'd like to have that shell casing," Torrez said.

"Maybe we'll get lucky. That's more than Zipoli got."

Chapter Four

By the time darkness made more work at the scene impossible, we had a disappointingly short list of evidence. I didn't want the grader moved until we'd had time for a fresh survey in the morning, and there was a single good shoe print and tire mark that I wanted to cast off the north shoulder.

A yellow crime scene ribbon wouldn't be adequate to keep the curious at bay, and believe it—when word spread, half the town would take a drive out to the site, hoping to catch a glimpse of some blood and the gruesome bullet hole. Maybe we could boost the county budget by charging admission…maybe for an extra contribution we could even include a stop by the morgue.

I left Deputy Scott Baker at one end of Highland Street with village part-timer J. J. Murton at the other. I promised Baker that he'd have relief, but Murton could sit there all night as far as I was concerned, a job just about perfectly matched to his skill levels.

While Mears processed film, Bob Torrez hung over Dr. Clark's shoulder waiting for the rifle slug to be removed, and Deputy Howard Bishop led Evie Truman through her formal deposition, Sheriff Salcido and I cruised the neighborhoods off Hutton that evening, doing what both of us did best.

Only four houses graced Hutton on the outer fringes of the village, and of the four, only one resident had been home. Julie Sanchez worked the night shift at the Posadas Inn down by the interstate, and she rented the little bungalow on Hutton because it was cheap and far from the roar of interstate truck traffic. She hadn't even noticed the road grader, hadn't heard its gutteral diesel, hadn't heard a gunshot. Loud as either might have been, a radio or television on inside the house would blanket the sound. Our luck didn't improve, even when we scouted through the modest little homes east of Hutton, or south toward Twelfth Street. That left all the neighborhoods to the south, to Blaine and beyond.

"You know how much noise a high powered rifle makes?" Salcido asked rhetorically. "And *por díos,* not a soul hears it." He shook his head in wonder and popped his seat belt off so he could stretch his burly torso. He preferred to ride, and I didn't mind being chauffeur. As we drove south on Twelfth, he nodded at the parking lot of the Don Juan de Oñate restaurant.

"I'll buy dinner," he said. "You got to take advantage of that." The offer wasn't unusual. One of Eduardo's favorite management techniques was taking his people out to dinner or lunch. One on one with a deputy was good strategy. *"You're the one I really want to talk to,"* was the obvious message. *"I want to hear what you have to say."*

"You're standing Maria up again?"

"She's in Cruces with our oldest daughter. Another baby, you know. I'm a grandfather *again.*" He shook his head in wonder. "That's number six for those two." He looked across at me. "Like *rabbits.* You think they'd figure out what causes that *condition.*" He accented each syllable of the word in the most Mexican way and then laughed gently. "Six, now. *Bautizos,* birthdays, Christmas...*Jefito,* they're going to break me."

Not many folks shared our enthusiasm for such a late dinner, and the restaurant was nearly deserted. The booth's bench suspension was comfortably broken down, and we settled in with the mammoth basket of chips and salsa that Arlene Aragon presented.

"You two are out on the town?" she quipped, and the sheriff wagged an eyebrow at her.

"What time do you get off?" He tried to sound lecherous but managed instead to sound more like a concerned grandfather.

"Midnight," Arlene laughed. "That's way past your bed time, *viejo.*" All she needed was a nod from us both to take the order. Years before, it was Eduardo Salcido who had introduced me to the Don Juan's flagship offering, the *Burrito Grande,* one of those nonsensically-named dishes that could put you right under the table if not approached carefully. The "big little burro" had been my favorite ever since. It helped me think, and if I hadn't been such a damn insomniac, it might even have helped me sleep. It had certainly padded my waistline.

Salcido regarded a chip critically. He nibbled off one corner so he could dip it in the salsa without breaking it. "Me and Tony spent half an hour over there with Marilyn. She's having a hard time."

"I would think so."

"She couldn't give me a single idea about what happened. She said Larry hadn't argued with anybody…nothing."

I didn't reply, and Salcido added, "They have four grown kids, you know. All over the place. Just like you."

"They'll be able to come home to be with her?"

"I think so. Her youngest daughter was coming in from Albuquerque tonight."

"And not a thing that she could think of, eh? Larry had anything going on in his life that she knew about? You said no arguments, but Christ, everybody has *something* in their life that's rubbing 'em the wrong way."

Salcido made a face. Maybe the salsa wasn't hot enough. My forehead was popping out in beads of sweat, but the sheriff seemed immune to the potent *chile.*

"She's not in condition to even think about it right now," Salcido said. "This thing really came out of left field, Bill. That's my *impression.*" The sheriff loved to linger his tongue around those syllables.

"A random potshot."

"Hell of a *potshot, jefito*. Somebody that would do a thing like this…they're sick in the head. " Arlene Aragon reappeared, but not with our dinner. She held spread fingers up to her ear to indicate telephone, and then pointed at me.

"We've been found," I groaned, and slid out of the booth.

"Over under the register," Arlene instructed. She didn't tell me who it was. Neither the sheriff nor I had told dispatch where we were, one of those liberties you take when you're the stud duck. But anyone with half a brain would know.

I picked up the receiver. "Gastner."

"Sir, we got something kind of interesting goin' on." Bob Torrez's quiet voice prompted me to shift the phone a little so I could hear him. "When you're finished up there, were you planning to stop back here for a few minutes?"

"*Here* being the office? Yes, I was. The sheriff and I are feeding our faces."

"No rush. We'll be here."

"What did you find?"

"We got the bullet, sir. It penetrated the victim's skull for about seven inches. Didn't touch the bone at the back. It's .308 caliber and used to be a flat-nose 170 grainer. That last is kind of a guess, but that's what I think it was."

"All right. That's common enough, unfortunately." The .308 diameter included a vast gamut of rifle cartridges, from the ubiquitous .30-30 on up through all the .308's, .30-06's, and the plethora of .30 caliber magnum cartridges. Dozens of the pesky things. Life was never simple.

"Not like this one, sir. We got a slug that doesn't show rifling marks. Not a lick. And it was yawing like crazy."

"Yawing?"

"Yes, sir."

"How would that happen?"

"Don't know."

"Old and worn rifling, I suppose?"

"That was my first thought. But this one has *no* rifling tracks on it. Like it was fired from a smooth-bore. Like a shotgun."

"Really. You know of such a thing?" A blizzard of questions fogged my brain, but a public phone in the restaurant wasn't the appropriate place to pursue them.

"Nope. I'm workin' on the possibilities."

"Good enough. Give us a few minutes."

It's possible to gobble down a *burrito grande* in "a few minutes," but the results wouldn't be pretty. The sheriff and I made good use of the time and the calories to mull every possibility we could think of. Nothing made sense.

Chapter Five

A chunk of misshapen brass and lead lay under the old stereo-scopic microscope. I'd picked up the microscope during a garage sale of surplus junk over at the high school years before. Why the microscope was no longer adequate for ninth graders to spy on the critters in swamp water, I didn't know, but it was just what we needed at times like this.

I fiddled with the sloppy adjustment knob until I had a clear picture. "For sure a jacketed rifle bullet." The words were scarcely out of my mouth when I realized how dumb that sounded. "As opposed to a handgun of some sort." I looked some more. "And I can see how the forward portion is mushroomed backward." With a pencil point, I nudged the slug this way and that under the objective. "I *can't* see that it was a flat-nosed bullet. But that's what you're guessing, right? Tell me why."

For a moment Bob Torrez didn't reply, and I glanced up from the microscope.

"Just a guess." He looked uncomfortable. "There's a little bit that isn't so badly deformed, like it was already yawing a little bit when it hit the glass."

"Keyholing, they call it?"

"Yes, sir. Not a lot, but some. And the bullet does have a can-nalure around it, but that don't mean shit one way or another. Some manufacturers press crimping cannalures into just about every bullet they make, others just cannalure the bullets meant for tube feeders, where the cartridges have to sit nose to tail."

"So tell me what we *do* know," I said. "What's this fragment weigh now?"

"Right at 163 grains."

"That's where you came up with the 170 figure for the original, then. It could have been 165, maybe 168."

"Could."

I sighed and looked at the nasty little chunk some more. "Through glass that already had plenty of age cracks in it, then through a tough part of the skull and a few inches of soft brain. And then comes to a stop. Interesting."

"What we want is something that narrows this down," Eduardo said. He'd commanded one of the lab stools—also a reject from the high school—and sat with boots on the bottom rung, arms folded over his gut. He'd taken his turn at the microscope, and had only a shrug to offer.

"The unusual thing is the lack of rifling marks," Torrez said. "I don't get it."

I turned and gazed at him, waiting to see if he intended to elaborate. If there was something about guns and ballistics that Bobby Torrez didn't *get,* I hadn't run across it—at least until now. I looked through the microscope again. The base of the bullet was undamaged, and offered a brass palette for marks, even the most faint. For a quarter of an inch forward from the base, the brass was clean and unblemished, other than some of the straight line scuffing normally expected when a new bullet was pressed down into the shell casing during the manufacturing process, or blown back out of it when the powder ignited. I saw nothing that I would guess to be a sharp rifling cut—certainly not a mark that we could imagine was a spiral track.

Just behind the cannalure, that belt-like grove pressed into the slug's carcass to give the brass casing something to grip, a scuff mark marred the bullet's brass surface. Forward of that, the rough mushrooming impact damage began, more on one side than the other.

"How much would smacking through the glass upset the bullet?"

"Don't know," Torrez said after a pause. "If the bullet hit at an angle, we could expect a bit of deflection, slow as this was goin'. If it was startin' to yaw, there's just no way to predict. The entrance wound in Zipoli's skull?" I nodded and waited. "It wasn't regular by any means. Almost twice as long as it was wide, so that bullet was kicked over to one side pretty good." He held out his hand, then cocked it sharply at the wrist.

"How do you know *slow?*"

"'Cause if it wasn't goin' slow, it'd fragment and be *all* torn up. High velocity bullets sometimes leave brass all along the wound channel, especially if they hit bone. And if it had been truckin' right along, it would have blown the back of his skull all over the back window…and then gone on through *that,* too. We wouldn 't be lookin' at it now."

"What I guess I meant was how much would the bullet *mushroom* going through the glass? How soft is that lead up front?"

Torrez shrugged slowly. "Some, I guess. We'd have to try it."

"Do that," I said. Eduardo nodded silent agreement. "And we need to work on some theories about *why* there are no rifling marks." I turned to the sheriff, who was keeping his own counsel, one index finger hooked over his mouth as if he needed to keep the zipper tight. "What do you think, Eduardo?"

"You know," he said slowly, "I saw a guy once." He stopped as if that explained everything, and both Bob and I waited patiently. "I was elk hunting up north, and there's this big shooting range up there? Just south of Raton. We were camping there, and did some sighting in with our rifles one morning. There was this guy there trying to shoot some targets, and his rifle brass was just blowing up, you know. He'd shoot, and man…" Eduardo's head shook in wonder. "I looked at the fired casing, and it was split open all along the neck in about five places. Just blown out. You know why?"

"I'm afraid to ask," I said.

"He had a .300 Weatherby Magnum rifle, you know. A *nice* gun. And you know what he was shooting in it? He had a box of *.270* Weatherby Mag ammo. At a hundred yards, he was getting a group like this." Eduardo held his arms in a circle a yard across. "That was good enough for him."

"An idiot," I said. But Eduardo wasn't reminiscing just to waste time. "So you're saying that maybe a .27 caliber bullet skipping out the barrel of a .30 caliber gun wouldn't be marked up much by the rifling?"

"I wouldn't think so. I mean why would it be?" The sheriff's deep shrug was eloquent. "We didn't recover the bullets he was shooting, but he used up a whole box. I can't think why they would be marked, can you?"

I looked back at our specimen. "So if this passed out a larger barrel—something larger than .308—it wouldn't be marked. That's what we're saying? I have just one problem with that theory. This bullet," and I jabbed a finger toward the microscope, "shot a really tight one shot group, Eduardo. Damn tight. Right through the middle of the grader's windshield, and right through Larry Zipoli. One perfect shot. If that's what the shooter was aiming at, he sure as hell didn't have a group the size of a bushel basket."

Eduardo nodded judiciously and shrugged. "I'm just saying… that's one way to explain why no rifling marks."

"I'd like to see that," I said. "Most of the time, I wouldn't think the wrong ammunition would even chamber in a gun."

"That's true only some of the time," Bob Torrez said. "But any cartridges that share the same parent case could." He shrugged. "A .270 is just a necked down .30-06. The ass end of the cartridge case is common to both. A .270 slips right into an '06." He almost smiled, hilarity for Bob Torrez. "Not vice versa, though. You can't put an '06 into a .270."

"I'd like a list," I said. "And a list of theories. I mean, there's *something* here. Rifles have rifling, don't they. That's why they're called *rifles*. Smoothbores that are actually *meant* to shoot jacketed rifle bullets could be counted on one hand, right?"

"I would think."

"I want a list," I repeated.

The sheriff looked at his watch and grimaced.

"And there are some sabots bein' experimented with," Torrez offered. He pronounced the word *sabeau,* and the French sounded odd from a guy for whom slang formed the foundation of his vocabulary. "There's a nylon sabot that covers the bullet and pulls it out the barrel. That would give you a .25 caliber bullet comin' out of a .30 caliber gun, or a .22 out of a .30, even. I don't know anybody who makes one for a .30 caliber bullet out of something bigger, unless it's something the military is workin' on."

"A sabot. That's high tech, sort of. Uncommon, anyway." I sighed. "And something to pursue, then," I said. "Come day light, we need every set of eyes out on Highland. Right now, we have no witnesses, no definitive tracks, no diddly squat." I stabbed a finger at the specimen under the microscope. "*That's* what we have. One God damn bullet." I looked at Bob Torrez, expecting him to offer up a simple answer that I would believe. He remained silent.

Chapter Six

I had a list of things to do a yard long, but a little Post-it note on my desk blotter drew my attention. *Marilyn Zipoli would like you to stop by.* Dispatcher Marcus Baker, Deputy Scott Baker's brother, had taken the message at 7:33 p.m. The sheriff had taken care of family notification earlier, and I had seen no point in duplicating his efforts until I had something definite to tell the grieving widow.

Eduardo, Bob Torrez, and I had dithered and talked the evening away, and now it was pitch dark and 9:05. I would have gone home, but to do what other than drink too much coffee and wish I had a cigarette, I didn't know. I dialed Zipoli's number and waited for seven rings before a voice answered that sounded as if the young lady was standing ten feet from the phone.

"Zips...this is Rori." *Zips?*

"Rori, this is Undersheriff Bill Gastner. May I talk with your mother for a moment?"

"Sure. Just a sec, sir. She's outside talking to somebody." The phone clattered on a hard surface before I had a chance to say anything else, and I listened to various background noises for a moment. A door slammed, and I heard footsteps and then a scuffling as the receiver was picked up.

"This is Marilyn." She sounded out of breath.

"Marilyn, Bill Gastner. I know it's late, but I wanted to get back to you."

"Late, my heavens, what does the time matter?" she said. "Unless we can turn the damn clock back."

I didn't know Marilyn Zipoli well, just as a pleasant face and name behind the counter at the bank, doing her part to keep the community moving forward. I was able to remember her well enough to recall the brilliant flash of her smile with which she favored each customer, no matter how cranky we might be. And somehow, she didn't seem the perfect fit for Larry Zipoli—but who's to predict chemistry. And the Marilyn I knew wouldn't talk about a "damn" anything.

"The sheriff was out to see you earlier," I said. "I apologize for not coming over myself."

"Yes, and I know that was hard for him. Tony came too. I appreciated that." Something interrupted her. It might have been a tissue to the nose, or a heavy sigh that threatened tears, maybe a little niece pulling at her skirt. "Is there any chance that you can break away from what your doing and come over for a few minutes?"

"Of course. How about right now?"

"I wouldn't ask if it weren't important."

"I understand that. Give me five minutes." I hung up and sat for a moment, deep in thought. "Huh," I said aloud. There's a statistic somewhere—if I rooted through the files long enough, I'd find it—where the folks who collect such data claim that the majority of homicides involve family members. Domestic disputes turn ugly, and somebody steps in front of a bullet or knife or tire iron propelled in anger. And if we spread our definition of "family" just a little bit to include the loose groups of punks, gang bangers, border-ducking hoodlums or just drunken thugs, the net catches the majority of folks who belong behind bars.

I was willing to bet my paycheck that Marilyn Zipoli hadn't taken the family rifle in the closet, driven out to where her husband was grading Highland Avenue, and fired at a puzzled Larry as he sat in the big Cat. But something was niggling at her, and she obviously felt that I needed to know. Why she hadn't told

Eduardo Salcido when she had the chance was another puzzle, but evidently she was comfortable talking with me.

The Zipolis lived in a neat place on north Fourth Street just beyond the intersection with Blaine Avenue. "For Sale" signs had started to crop up as the last cleanup crews at Consolidated Mining finished buttoning up the hard rock mine up on the mesa flank.

I pulled the LTD to a stop at the curb behind a long-of-tooth Datsun B-210 and alerted Dispatcher Baker.

"Three ten will be ten-six on Fourth," I said when he came on the air. The folks who spent time listening to police scanners didn't need to know that I was going to talk with Marilyn, but Marcus Baker would figure it out.

"Ten four, three ten." He sounded enthused.

It appeared that Marilyn managed the family coffers as carefully as she managed my money at the bank. The Zipoli corner of the world was neat and tidy, a brick-fronted home that looked to be a standard three-bedroom affair. The front yard was xeroscaped except for a narrow flower bed that separated the property from the neighbor to the north. A fat-tired three-quarter ton Ford pickup parked on the left side of the wide driveway carried a massive cab-over camper. Slipped into the space between the garage wall and the property boundary was a hotrod ski boat on a trailer.

Every light in the house was ablaze, and I suppose that friends and neighbors had been doing their thing, covering every flat surface in the kitchen with food platters. The thought brought an automatic hunger response from my undisciplined gut, which should have been content with that *burrito grande* for the evening.

For a long moment, I stood on the sidewalk and listened to the neighborhood. An old yellow dog across the street stood by the curb and watched me. He wasn't on a leash, and he looked like he owned the turf. Apparently I wasn't worth a single bark. None of the other dog neighbors had noticed my arrival. Somewhere down Blaine Street, a Skilsaw shrieked and I wondered what home builder was working at this time of night. When the saw finished its cut and the night fell quiet, I could hear the regular flow of traffic on the interstate, a mile south.

The night before, with the weather a carbon copy of this evening, had Larry Zipoli paused in his front yard to listen and enjoy the peace and quiet? Probably not. Assumption drives our days, and one of the most comforting assumptions is that tomorrow we'll still be here.

I took a deep breath and walked to the Zipolis' front door. I didn't need to knock. When my boot touched the first concrete step, Marilyn Zipoli opened the door.

"I saw you drive up." She held the screen open for me, but paused as if having second thoughts. "The old guy across the street doesn't bite, by the way."

"My stealth approach," I said. "I figured he didn't. Just watching takes most of his time and energy."

Marilyn hesitated, still blocking the door. "Maybe we could take a little stroll. It's so nice out, and it's so *stuffy* inside. If the phone doesn't stop ringing, it's going to drive me insane."

"That would be fine. Whatever you want."

She sniffed something that I didn't catch, and slipped past the screen, closing it carefully. "What I want isn't going to happen," she offered. I fell in step with her. At the sidewalk, she turned north. For a block, she said nothing, and I didn't prompt her. We reached Blaine, and she stopped, gazing off into the darkness of a vacant lot. That lonely, desolate spot seemed to suit her, and she turned to face me, arms folded tightly across her chest. Enough light from the street light across the way illuminated the tears on her cheeks.

"I try to imagine how…" She managed that far and stopped. "Sheriff Salcido said that Mrs. Truman found him?"

"Yes. She was running an errand into town."

"Tell me how it happened. Neither the sheriff nor Tony seemed to know very much." *Or wanted to say the ugly words.*

"We *don't* know very much, Marilyn. Someone fired a shot that hit the grader in the windshield. The bullet passed through and struck your husband. He never moved from his seat."

A yelp escaped from her lips, and she pressed a hand over her mouth, turning away. I started to reach out, to put an arm around her shoulders, but she turned back, both hands held up as if to block the scream of a jet engine. "And if it was…if it was *intentional?* The sheriff wouldn't say. But how could it be anything else? My God. That's all I've been able to think about. How something like this could have happened."

"The bullet could have come from farther out, from out by the arroyo. Lots of folks shoot out there. We just don't know yet."

She looked at me, making no effort to wipe away the flood of tears. "Is that what you believe? I mean, how could that *happen?* You would have to *aim* right over that way. You'd have to *want* to shoot that way. Was it just some vandal who saw the county grader and decided to pop one over at it? Couldn't he see that Larry was working?"

"I would think that he could, Marilyn, but we can't be sure. That time of the afternoon, the sun would be on the glass of the grader's cab. Whoever it was might not have known Larry was inside."

"Anybody up that way would have *heard* it, sheriff. "That old thing is awful. Anyone would have heard it."

"Maybe so. Maybe not." Sharing an investigation closes some doors, and I didn't want that to happen. So I settled for the lame platitude. "We're going to find out. One way or another, we'll find out exactly what happened. Did you have something in particular that you wanted to ask me? Or tell me?"

"Mostly I was just frustrated that the sheriff couldn't or wouldn't tell me very much. And he asked me if Larry had had any arguments recently. I wasn't thinking."

"Did he?"

She struggled with that for a moment. "I want…I want you to talk with our neighbor." With that said, she ducked her head and looked back down the street as if expecting a response.

"Which one?"

"Just next door. Mr. Raught. The fellow with all the cacti."

"Raught." The name rang only the faintest of bells. It always surprised me when I heard of a county resident whom I *didn't* know, the busy-body nature of law enforcement being what it is. "Mr. Raught has information we should know? Or you have information about him?"

She drew a great, shuddering sigh as if uttering the words were going to cost her a great deal. "He threatened Larry."

"Really. Threatened how?"

"Well, he's *always* ready with something snippy." She wiped her eyes. "Always. Some snippy comment. Larry would stop home for lunch once in a great while, and if Raught was home and saw the county pickup truck in the driveway, he'd make some snide comment about taxpayers paying for lunch. That sort of thing, just constantly. He complained when he saw a drop or two of oil from the boat on the driveway—and it's *our* driveway, after all. Just every opportunity. He threatened to call the cops when Rori had a birthday party, and one of her friends parked for a few minutes in front of Raught's house, with his car radio a little bit loud. Just no end to it."

"Complaints aren't threats, Marilyn. You said that Mr. Raught *threatened* your husband."

"Oh, that was the most recent thing. You're not going to believe this, Bill. You know where the boat and camper truck are parked? The west side of the drive. And then there's that narrow little border flower garden? Larry put up one of those decorator fences, one of those little plastic things that's just a foot high or so? Right down the property line between us and Raught's. And of course, wouldn't you know, Mr. Raught complained about *that*. Last week, he just pulled it out and tossed it on the lawn between the flowers and the driveway."

"He pulled it out? Without asking first? What was his problem with it?"

"He says that he can't maneuver around his gardens with that fence there."

"The fence would be on your property, wouldn't it? You said that Larry put it in, right?"

"Of course it was," Marilyn said. "But Mr. Raught said that it wasn't, and that it prevented him from taking care of his own yard. And he said it was ugly. So he just pulled it out."

"And Larry put it back," I guessed. That seemed predictable somehow. We had a couple little kids at work here, arguing in their sand box and smacking each other with plastic shovels.

"He did, and he even moved it a couple inches our way, too, so Mr. Raught wouldn't have anything to complain about."

"But he complained anyway?"

"He pulled it out again, sheriff. I couldn't believe it. That's so *childish*. And he didn't just pull it out. He broke it up and threw it in the dumpster in the alley. He said the next thing he was going to do was rip out the flower garden, since most of it is on his property anyway."

"And is it?"

"No, it's not on his land. Good heavens. Larry was so angry, I thought he was going to have a stroke. The two of them had words, and Larry asked Mr. Raught how he'd like to have the cops come and check out his back yard."

"Ah. Do I want to know about this?" From plastic decorator fence to World War III. The old dog across the street must have had quite a show.

"That's when Mr. Raught started talking about *real trouble*. I told Larry that he just needs to forget all about it. Just pretend that *no one* lives next door. You know," and she rubbed her nose, searching for a tissue with the other hand, "sometime that man is going to need help from somebody, and *nobody* is going to come to his aid. That's not very Christian, I know. But that's how I feel."

"So he promised what you're referring to as 'real trouble.' When was this last confrontation?"

"Yesterday morning. That's when we found the fence had gone missing, and we found it in the dumpster. And now, Larry …" She closed her eyes. "I'm sure Mr. Raught had nothing to do with Larry's accident. But the coincidence of it all was on my mind, and I needed to talk to someone." She tried a smile. "You know, one of these days, I'm going to come face to face with that man and he's going to say something nasty about Larry, and I'm going to punch him right in his fat nose. And it's going to feel really *good*." She reached out and touched my arm. "Just so you know it's coming, sheriff."

"Marilyn, I can't imagine that an argument over a foot high border fence resulted in shots fired, but you're right to mention it." Well, yes I *could* imagine it. I'd responded to fights that had started over far less, but Marilyn didn't need to know that. "We're looking at every angle, talking to everyone we can think of. I'll add your neighbor to my list, sooner rather than later." I took her by the elbow and we started to wend our way back down the sidewalk.

Marilyn Zipoli stopped in her tracks, and looked up at me through her tears. "Larry's always saying that the man probably has a backyard pot farm, what with all his walls and security. I mean, that's *exactly* what Larry thinks he's growing back there. Mr. Raught said it was just Virginia Creeper, and Larry thought that was the funniest thing he'd ever heard. 'Virginia Creeper, my ass,' he'd say. 'Not in this country.'"

"Be interesting to check that out," I said. I had a tough, valiant Virginia Creeper vine trying to survive on the back of my old, shady adobe on the other side of town, so it was certainly possible.

"Oh, let it go," she said, and that surprised me. "I don't care what he's growing. I know that he was a thorn in Larry's side, and that they'd had a confrontation, and it seemed to me that maybe that was important. And now I'm thinking I probably shouldn't have mentioned a thing. It's hard to keep things straight at a time like this. Someone to blame. That's what it is, I think. Someone to blame. Something so stupid, so senseless…"

I sidestepped a bicycle that lay half in the gravel of a front yard and half on the sidewalk. I'd ignored it when we'd passed by before, but now I took a moment and nudged it out of the way. "The neighbor kids must have a good time with this Raught fellow, if he's as contentious as you say. He'd be easy to bait."

"I don't know about that. I suppose he keeps pretty much to himself. I mean, *we* don't see Mr. Raught all that often."

I glanced sideways at Marilyn Zipoli. Conflicted and confused, she was a bundle of contradictions. Was Raught a neighborhood curmudgeon, or was he a recluse? Did he make a hobby of confrontations, or did he remain in the shadows? Marilyn changed course.

"You know, Larry spends a lot of time with the neighborhood kids. He works with the scouts, you know. And with the 4-H, especially when Rori was active. And there's always a group ready to go fishing or water skiing. You'd think we had ten kids, instead of just the one daughter home now." She stopped as if she'd walked into a stone wall. "I just don't know," she murmured. "I don't know what we're going to do now."

We had reached their property, and I glanced at the narrow flower garden sandwiched between the driveway and the neighbor's property. In the dark with just a distant street lamp for illumination, the narrow garden didn't look like much, but I could see where the spread of neat cactus gardens and arrangements crept right to the property line. Working in the Zipolis' little flower garden would have been risky. Stumble and fall into the neighbor's yard and you'd end up a pincushion. A fence might have been a good idea.

Raught's home was dark, with one of the bedroom windows open on the street side. No doubt he could hear every word we were saying.

"Would you like a cup of coffee or something?" Marilyn offered. "We have a houseful of food, and my sister brought over that big coffee maker from the church." She shook her head wearily. "Oh my."

"Thanks, but I have some things that need tending to." I gripped her shoulder and rocked her a bit, making sure I had her attention, and spoke just above a whisper. "We're going to get through this, Marilyn. That's the extent of what I know at the moment. We're going to find out exactly what happened to your husband. Somewhere, somehow, somebody knows something. It's just a matter of putting all the pieces together. If you happen to think of anything else—any little bit, no matter how insignificant—be sure to give me a call. Don't hesitate."

"And I know what I said, but I don't blame my neighbor." She glared toward Raught's house. "Really, I don't. I hope you don't think that I'm just looking..."

"That's the whole point, Mrs. Zipoli," I said. "We *are* looking. Under every rock, in every dark corner. Tomorrow afternoon, when you've had a little time to rest, one of our officers will be by to chat again. As I said, we'll explore every avenue. I'll come by myself and talk with Raught. Even if the argument didn't go anywhere, he might have heard something, somehow. Something useful." I rocked her shoulder again. "And don't worry. I certainly won't tell him that you complained."

"Oh, he'll know." She looked numb from fatigue and the emotional drain of this impossible day. I watched her go into the house, and then walked back to my county car. The old yellow dog stood so still he might have been a statue.

"What do you know?" I asked. He didn't answer.

Apropos of nothing, I realized that in all the years I'd lived and worked in Posadas, in all the years I'd known who the Zipolis were, in all the years I'd had the opportunity to perhaps greet one or the other on the street or in the bank, in all those years, I had never seen them together.

Chapter Seven

I didn't give much thought to what Marilyn Zipoli had told me about Mr. Raught. Gossip about neighbors was not generally reliable…certainly not the stuff of court testimony, which is where all this would end up eventually. You see the old lady digging in her iris bed, and it's obvious as hell that she's burying body parts that used to belong to her husband because, when you saw her, that's the creative daydream that shot through *your* head. Surprise, surprise. She was burying iris bulbs. Marilyn Zipoli wasn't thinking straight, and I wasn't about to go charging into a man's life based on her wandering statements.

Maybe Jim Raught did have a marijuana plant in his back yard. Maybe his idea of happy hour included a big fat reefer. I didn't care. Some cops would, and I probably *should* have, the law being something that I was sworn to uphold. What he did with his weeds in the privacy of his own home was up to him, until he sold some of it to a neighbor kid, or baled it to take to Albuquerque.

I didn't care what arguments Jim Raught had had with Larry Zipoli, either—unless the argument turned violent. I *did* care that someone had put a high-powered rifle bullet through a seated, defenseless victim. That was the work of a warped and twisted sniper, and the idea that we might have one of them living in our little village was enough to massage my natural insomnia.

At midnight, the county building was like a tomb. Two trustees were currently in residence, and both would be asleep upstairs in the lockup, so there was no gentle swishing of the mop on the entryway tiles, no monotonic whistling as Benny Vasquez dusted everything with a treated cloth—he'd even dust *me* if *I* held still long enough. The sheriff's wife drew a pittance salary as the department's chief matron, and she made sure the trustees—never would she use the word 'prisoner'—were well fed and comfortably housed. My own theory was that Benny enjoyed his lodging just a little too much. Locked up with Benny was Todd Duncan, a long-haired dope-sniffing loser who was basically good-natured enough, and enjoyed washing county vehicles. Todd enjoyed our hospitality for short stretches every couple of months.

Even the dispatch center was quiet, and Ernie Wheeler, just now coming on for his shift, would be hard pressed to stay alert through the night. A rookie dispatcher himself, Ernie would have help from Eddie Mitchell, a young deputy who had joined us the spring before from the metro department in Baltimore, Maryland. Why Eddie had given up on the east coast, why he had embraced our hot, bleak little county in southwestern New Mexico, was his business. I couldn't argue his decision, since I had been bread and buttered in North Carolina, and now couldn't stomach the thought of a hundred and ten percent humidity and mosquitoes playing the role of state bird.

And sure enough, the radio came to life as Mitchell fired a license number for an NCIC check. When times were dismally slow, several of the deputies took a moment to swing through the parking lot of the big motel down by the interstate. They'd run numbers until both they and the dispatcher grew weary of the exercise. Once in a rare while, there'd be a hit, and the traveling felon would be just as surprised as the deputy.

In another hour, the bars would close, and there'd be a little flurry of activity as the last patrons tried to figure out how to drive home without being nabbed for DWI.

I leaned on the counter until he'd finished with the NCIC check and radioed the news back to the Deputy that the blue older model Olds 98 didn't belong to a fleeing Bonnie and Clyde.

"Quiet night, sir," Ernie said as he swiveled his chair to glance my way. Just twenty-one, Ernie was one of those twenty-one going on fifty fellows, already steady and unexcited by life. I could imagine that in twenty years, Ernie would still be sitting in that chair, working the day shift so he could go home to his comfortable wife and four kids. Neither the wife nor the kids had materialized yet.

"That's a good thing." Now that I had a comfortable perch, elbows resting on the old, polished oak of the divider, I felt no huge inclination to do anything constructive.

"The new hire is going to be workin' graveyard?"

"When we *have* a new hire, sure enough." That's what new hires did, after all. Sheriff Salcido and I were in agreement that we wanted no part of those torturous rotating shifts, where employees worked a few weeks on days, then went to swing, and then to graveyard. The brain never quite caught up and adjusted, and everyone ended up cranky and tired. It had been our experience that there were plenty of people who *wanted* to work midnight to eight, or who *wanted* the adrenalin rush of the rowdy four to midnight shift, or who enjoyed toasting in the sunshine of broad daylight. That worked for us. The sheriff worked mostly days, and I worked mostly whenever I wanted to. I didn't count the hours.

"So," I said to Ernie, "Tell me everything you know about a guy named James Raught. He lives over on north Fourth, just a half block off Blaine."

"I don't know him, sir."

"You know the Zipolis? Larry and Marilyn?"

"I know that Marilyn is one of the cashiers at the bank. I don't know her husband. A nasty deal, sir."

"Nasty indeed. Keep your eyes and ears open, Ernie. The truth of the matter is that someone is out there with a high-powered rifle. Don't go sending the deputy into deep water without everybody being heads up."

"Eddie was reading the case folder before he went out. He was going to swing by Highland and talk with Scott Baker from time to time. And with Murton." The deputies and part-time village officer were talking, and nervous. That was as it should be.

I regarded the battalion of heavy filing cabinets across the dispatch island. I knew that Jim Raught had no record with us. I didn't have to paw through miles of file folders to tell me that. Until today, no folder had carried the name of Lawrence E. Zipoli, either.

With a couple raps of my Marine Corps ring on the divider, I straightened up and nodded at Ernie. "I'll be out and about," I said. "The pumps, please." He reached over and flipped the switch that powered the fuel island outside, and I trudged back out to 310. Fueled, fat, and happy, I idled the car out onto Bustos, in no hurry to go anywhere in particular. With all four windows rolled down and the radio turned to a whisper, I could mosey along and listen to a quiet county, letting the sweet air flow through the car.

Bustos Avenue cut through the village east-west, and I headed east, driving past the two car dealers and turning on Camino del Sol, a short spur street whose pavement soon gave way to gravel and County Road 19. The Drive-in theater had seen the economic slump coming, and when Consolidated Mining announced that it was shutting down its Posadas operations, the owners of the drive-in jumped ship. Now the parking lot sat empty, the speakers removed, the ocean-wave humps studded with row after row of naked steel posts, a wonderful attractive nuisance for ATV and motorbike riders.

I shot the spot light across the lot, and bounced it off the towering screen. I was waiting for one of our knucklehead gang-bangers to figure out a way to climb up and spray-paint his turf mark on the face of the old screen. Motorbike tracks criss-crossed the lot, and for the young and reckless, I suppose it was a hoot to ride across the rows of swells, dodging the speaker posts.

Beyond the drive-in, the mobile home park was quiet. I swung in and maneuvered down the narrow center lane, head-lights off so the beams wouldn't blast through bedroom windows. After the final reclamation at the mine was finished, I wondered how many empty slots there'd be. Three "For Sale" signs already were posted and more would sprout.

In several units, I could see the spot of color from the television as someone watched the late-late show or an early morning movie. Swinging around the loop end deep in the park, I stopped for a moment and shut off the engine, listening. It's amazing how sound travels, particularly at night. I could hear the murmurs of the various television sets, and off to the left, a dog inside the last trailer had taken offense at my presence, and yipped up a storm. The door opened and Vernon Chambers stepped out onto the narrow porch. He wore a pair of colorful boxer shorts and no shirt, but didn't let that stop him. He approached, his slippers scuffing the parking lot.

"You lost?" He bent down, leaning on the window of 310. The slight breeze washed his too-scant deodorant and body odor into the car, and I was tempted to zip up the window.

"Vernon, how the hell are you?" Scrawny to the point of emaciation, Vernon managed to look as if he were in the last stages of chemotherapy. He'd looked that way for the fifteen years I'd known him. His trailer court hosted its share of domestic disputes.

"Well, I'm fine. What's the law up to?" He asked the question and then I saw his jaw drop a little as the memory hit him. He lowered his voice to a hoarse whisper. "Say, I heard about what happened down on Highland. What the hell was that all about, anyways?"

"That all depends on what you heard." One of my life's ambitions when I retired was to write the definitive textbook on *Rumor and the Pathways of Community Intelligence*. A bestseller, for sure, except maybe it's *Unintelligence*.

"Somebody shot Larry Zipoli?"

"Yes."

"Hooooly shit. You're kiddin'."

"Nope."

"Accident, you think? I mean, how in the hell…I mean, *who* in the hell…"

"We don't know yet."

"I heard he was workin' with the grader. Is that right?"

"It appears so, Vernon."

"Some one just drove by and took a shot? That's what I heard."

I shrugged expansively as if to say *That's all we know.* I let Vernon fill in his own interpretation. "Look, if you happen to hear something about all this, I'd like to know."

Chambers straightened up and rubbed a hand across his shrunken, hairless belly. "Shit," he said, "he was gradin' the road out front just yesterday. I mean just yesterday."

"Is that right?"

"Just yesterday." He hitched up his boxers again, not having the butt or the hips to keep them in place.

"Did you happen to talk with him?"

"Nope. I went to town just after lunch, and he was makin' a pass up along the bar ditch. And then a little later, he was on up past Hocking's place. I don't know if he had a breakdown, or what. He was down off the grader, talkin' to a couple kids on bikes. Don't know who they were, didn't think nothin' about it."

"And why would you." Another little piece—Bobby Torrez had seen the grader and its operator down on McArthur in the morning, and now we knew that Larry had tackled the larger county road in the afternoon. I surveyed the double row of blunt-snouted trailers. "Are you losing a lot of folks with the mine gone?" I knew the answer, but it was always interesting to hear Vernon's take on things.

"Oh, God. Got three gone now, another couple before the end of the month. This is going to be a damn ghost town, sheriff."

I sighed. "I guess." I didn't add that a good many folks had lived in Posadas before Consolidated Mining arrived to gouge out the mesa flank north of the village, and a good many would remain after the mine had finished reclamation and locked the gates.

"Folks run out of work, they either leave or start causin' trouble. Drink too much—don't know how they afford it." He rapped 310's door sill. "Don't guess you folks will ever run out of work, eh?"

"Unlikely, but we can always hope." I took my foot off the brake and 310 edged forward. "I need to get," I said. "You take it easy, Vernon."

"No other way. Not no more." He lifted a hand in salute.

The tires rustled along the freshly graded lane as I worked around the east end of the mesa before skirting the county landfill and then joining the state highway out of the county. Far in the distance, a tractor-trailer on the interstate hit its jake brake to take the Posadas exit, the percussive sound carrying easily on the soft air. The radio mumbled as Eddie Mitchell called in another license number, and I nodded in approval. It was possible, I suppose, for the beat to be so quiet, so muted, that cops just stop looking, relaxing out of sheer boredom. And that's when it turns and bites. I couldn't remember the last domestic dispute I'd responded to during the bright, cheerful sunshine of mid-morning. Night time brought out the kinks in human behavior.

The dash clock said 1:21 a.m. when I turned onto the smooth pavement of County Road 23 and circled back toward town. Deputy Mitchell had stopped a truck south on State 56. That highway encouraged lead feet, and all the critters who slipped through the right-of-way fence and wandered out onto the warm asphalt gave the speeders an obstacle course to enjoy.

Through the middle of town, I turned north on Twelfth Street and passed the quiet neighborhoods. Hutton Street and its offshoot Hutton Court marked the northern boundary, with Highland just beyond, the first street actually in the county's turf.

The village had its own tiny department, and the other Eduardo, Chief Eduardo 'Danny' Martinez, welcomed our efforts. But he and two full-time officers couldn't provide 24/7 coverage, and the chief didn't pretend that he could. He concentrated on school zones and helping stranded travelers, and that was fine with us. Once a decade or so, a good bank robbery might keep them sharp. And they got lots of practice responding to the ubiquitous domestic disputes.

A man who hated to think ill of his friends and neighbors, Chief Martinez might be able to give me a different slant on Jim

Raught. But he was off in Albuquerque on some family errand, so he was missing all the fun.

As I drove out Twelfth to Hutton Street to Hutton Court, I punched the lights out and let 310 drift down to a gentle walking pace. Up ahead, starlight glinted off J.J. Murton's village unit. He was parked facing north, his back to the village, blocking the intersection with Highland. The laid-back police chief was a forgiving boss, but even Eduardo had avoided hiring J.J. Murton as anything more than part-timer.

I knew that Murton wanted to work for us in the worst way—and would, when hell froze solid. I'd kicked Murton off the interstate once, after he'd decided, as a part-timer with a month's experience, to work radar there. One of the state police officers had seen him swaggering toward a vehicle he'd stopped, walking on the pavement with his back to traffic, ready to get himself killed.

The state officer had hauled around and come up behind Murton, giving him unrequested back-up. And then the officer had stopped by our office and chatted with me. I'd driven out and had a chat with Murton at Chief Martinez's request. I guess he understood me. I never saw him on the interstate again.

He still hadn't learned about facing a probable threat. On this dark night, if Murton was watching in his rearview mirror, he would have seen the shadow of another car sliding up behind him, head lights off. That alone should have kicked his pulse up a notch. But there was something about the odd tilt of the officer's head, something about the absolute quiet of his patrol car, that gave me pause. All the worst thoughts paraded through my head as I took my time getting out of the LTD. There was a likely possibility, of course, so I didn't slam the door.

Ten feet from the driver's door, I could hear it. The simple son of a bitch was snoring. I admit to a wave of relief—no one had snuck up on Murton and blown out what few brains he had.

Sure enough, Murton's head was relaxed back against the door post and headrest, jaw slack, breathing deep and evenly, a little trail of spittle on his chin catching the starlight. For a long moment, I stood by his driver's door, regarding the sleeping beauty. A whole gallery of possibilities presented themselves. I could just do the brotherly thing by reaching out and shaking him a little by the shoulder. I could return to my car and hit the yelp on the siren, sending J.J. through the headliner. I could call car-to-car on the radio and let him try to cover for his inattention. But sometimes, it's more fun to be nasty and juvenile.

I reached in and slipped my finger behind his badge, pulling it gently forward so I could toggle the clasp. It released easily and I straightened up, dropped the badge in my shirt pocket and left Officer Murton to his dreams. I let 310 idle backwards a ways so I wouldn't awaken the sleeping beauty, and a quarter mile down the road, I keyed the mike.

"Three oh six, three ten."

"Three oh six, go ahead." Deputy Scott Baker's response was instant and alert. *He* hadn't been snoozing, even though he was off-shift and earning himself some overtime.

"Things quiet?"

"That's affirmative."

"Be aware that you don't have coverage on the west end," I said, and let Baker puzzle about that for an instant or two. Somewhere in Posadas County, someone with too much free time would be listening to his scanner, and he could puzzle too.

"Ah, ten four, three ten. You want me to swing over that way?" He was probably sitting up straight, trying to see through the half mile of darkness to where J.J. Murton was parked.

"Negative. Just be aware. He'll wake up after a bit."

That earned a moment of silence. "Ten four."

"PCS, three ten is ten eight."

"Ten four, three ten." Dispatcher Ernie Wheeler wasn't sleeping, either, and I could almost hear the pucker of Ernie's forehead.

The rest of the night was silent, nothing but the coyotes yipping and more vehicle registrations being checked. I accomplished nothing else. It would have been nice to say that by dawn, we had answers. But we didn't. By three I'd had enough

of being vertical, and went home to try for a few minutes sleep.
I left J.J. Murton's badge with dispatch. Murton probably had
a more restful night than I did.

Chapter Eight

The Don Juan de Oñate opened at six, but the Aragons were always there early, and they never grumbled when I slipped in the back door. They probably enjoyed the rapture on my face when the first aroma of good stuff hit my nose. Some folks can't function first thing without coffee. I had to have food, and at 5:15, I was wrapping myself around a gorgeously presented smothered breakfast burrito, the aroma of the green chile already loosening up the nasal floodgates. By 5:45, stoked by a short nap and now high octane fuel, I was set to face the day.

Eddie Mitchell's grin—a rare thing—greeted me when I walked into the office.

"J.J. picked up his badge," Ernie Wheeler offered. "He was pissed."

"Well, good for him," I said cheerfully. "Pissed but well rested."

Ernie leaned back in his chair, clasping his hands behind his head with grand satisfaction. "First he thought it had just slipped off somehow, but Scott told him that he might want to check with you. He picked it up a little bit ago. Didn't seem to want to stay around and gab, though."

I nodded, thinking of the day's challenges, all of them far more important than the village idiot. The staffing calendar told the story, and I grimaced. I needed about fifty people, and had a handful. "We're going to do another sweep of Highland this morning, so I need every available body." I hesitated. If I could round up half a dozen, I'd be lucky.

Both Ernie Wheeler and Deputy Mitchell would go off duty in a couple of minutes, but they weren't clock-watchers. If there was something that needed doing, they'd do it. "When Barnes comes in, you want to work on this?" Ernie looked sincerely eager. The county manager wouldn't be eager when he saw the overtime chits, but he didn't have a corpse on his hands.

T.C. Barnes had managed to smash himself in a Highway Department accident years before, and joined us to work dispatch instead of sitting home. He had a casual attitude about clocks—to him, six a.m. meant anything 'six-ish'—but Ernie never complained when his relief for the day shift showed up ten minutes late.

"I want to meet out on Highland at 7:30 on the button. Anybody you can find—I don't care who, as long as they know how to take simple orders."

"You want J.J.?"

"Sure. Why not?" I heard the front door open, and expected to see T.C. Barnes limping in to work. An attractive young woman—well, to me she looked about one click beyond a teenager—approached, and it wasn't until she was within a dozen feet that I recognized her.

"Good morning," I said. "I'm Undersheriff Bill Gastner. I understand you've talked with the sheriff."

"Yes, sir. I interviewed with him yesterday."

"You're out and about early." I offered a hand, and found Estelle Reyes' grip firm, perhaps a little reserved. She'd come a long way from the little tyke I'd first met in Tres Santos, a long way from the last time I'd seen her at the high school. Rueben Fuentes' grand niece had matured into a poised young lady. Rich olive skin set off a set of enormous, bottomless, black eyes. She'd cut her hair since the last time I'd seen her, now keeping it short and elegant. As if headed for a job interview, she wore a tan pants suit, the creases in the trousers military sharp.

"We were going to meet at nine?" I glanced at the wall clock.

"Yes, sir." She didn't offer an explanation of why she'd arrived at 6:07 a.m.

"How about now, then," I said. "We're going to get busy here in a few minutes."

"I thought that might be the case," she observed. She included both Eddie Mitchell and Ernie Wheeler in her greeting. I wasn't surprised that Mitchell responded only with the briefest of nods, but Ernie looked uncomfortably flummoxed. One of those gangly young men who was easily embarrassed, his eyes were locked on Ms. Reyes as if she'd just stepped off the pages of a calendar or from the silver screen.

In my office, I hooked a chair out of the corner and slid it closer to the desk for her, then settled in my own creaky swivel chair. "So...I haven't seen Reuben in a couple of weeks. How's the old badger been?"

"He's all right, sir. The usual old age complaints."

I nodded. "And your mother?"

"She's just fine, sir."

Finding her file in the right hand drawer of my desk took a moment, and she waited patiently, hands relaxed in her lap. I cut to the chase. "Why ever would you want to work for us?" An intelligent young lady, on the gorgeous side of beautiful—working as a deputy sheriff for $19,000 a year in one of the smallest, most isolated rural counties in New Mexico—it didn't make stereotypical sense. But my guess, from what little contact I'd had with this first child and now young lady, was that there was nothing stereotypical about Estelle Reyes.

"It's an interesting area. And close to home."

"Oh, we're *interesting,* all right. What draws you into law enforcement?"

She hesitated for a moment, her dark eyebrows knitting. "The puzzles, sir." A trace of a smile touched her face. "You spoke at school once, and I remember you saying that." She made a circle with her hands. "That a difficult case begins with bits and pieces, and the challenge is to make them coalesce into something that makes sense." She spoke in measured tones as if working hard to control a strong accent. And not many folks could use words like "coalesced" and make them sound natural.

"I see that I need to be careful about what I say." I laughed, relieved that she hadn't claimed the need to "help people," the usual unthinking response. Her résumé was mercifully brief. "An associate's degree in criminal justice from State. That helps. Planning on continuing with school?"

"Eventually, sir. When I can afford it."

"On what we pay, that might be a while. But there are lots of scholarships out there. Many go begging."

"Yes, sir."

I looked down her transcript, and saw a humbling array of A's. If chemistry or anthropology or statistics had given her any trouble, there was no evidence of it. There was a minus sign after one of the A's. "What happened in osteology? That's not a course in the associate's program, is it?" She'd need about seventy credits to fulfill the associate requirements, and her transcript displayed a hundred and two.

"No, sir. That's a basic course in the pre-med program that they let me take. I had the flu and missed a lab practical."

"Slacker." I grinned at her and was rewarded with a tiny twitch of the corner of her mouth. "So, with this many credits, you're not far from your bachelor's."

"No, sir."

"It'd be a shame to let it slide." I sighed. "And speaking of school, the next session of the state law enforcement academy begins in September. You have any problems with attending that next month?"

"No, sir. That will be fine."

I leaned back. "The sheriff explained something of our way of doing business?"

"It's my understanding that if hired, I would start in dispatch, doing office work, general duties like that, then the academy, then rookie assignments."

"And you're all right with that?"

"Certainly, sir."

"Not even *in* dispatch, Ms. Reyes. You'll spend time observing dispatch during all three shifts. A rotation sort of deal. Your training officer would give you a schedule that takes you through weekends, days, swing, graveyard. It's a grind. We'll do that for eight or ten hours a day for two weeks, and toward the end of that time, when you're familiar with the lingo and the procedures, you'll be in the chair yourself—with a full-time dispatcher in the room with you at all times." I hooked my hands behind my head. "Absolute, deep, depressing boredom. That's what it is, most of the time. We find things to do to keep us sane. Filing, typing, waxing the floor, washing the windows, changing the oil on the cars." I grinned. "You'll have to get proficient at all that important stuff."

"I can do that, sir."

She seemed so serious that I had to chuckle. "I'm kidding, of course. We don't want to put our trustees out of work. Anyway, after that, off and on, you'll be assigned to ride with a deputy. You'll do a couple of weeks on days first, to learn the community better than you ever thought possible. Every street, every back alley, every county road and two-track. Then we'll put you in swing and graveyard. Now, I won't kid you. Some of the road deputies won't mind a passenger, but I know one or two who *will* mind, since you'll be excess baggage, Ms. Reyes. Although you might carry a sheriff's commission card and a badge, you *won't* be certified as a police officer. That comes only after successful completion of the academy and various other qualifications. We cut lots of corners with other things, but not with that."

"What the sheriff calls the hoops."

"That's exactly right. Now tell me...why ever would you want to do all that?"

"It suits me, sir. You've been with Sheriff Salcido for seventeen years, sir. You wouldn't have stayed if there wasn't something satisfying—something that suits you."

I smiled at her, and wondered at the same time how much more about us this young lady had researched. I leaned forward and folded my hands on top of her folder. "You know, I'm used to hearing that people want a job as a cop because they want to help people."

"That's probably possible sometimes, sir. I'm not sure."

"Really." I waited for a handful of seconds for her to elaborate, but she didn't. "Is there anything about the job that you don't look forward to?"

"The deep, depressing boredom, sir." Her eyes twinkled. "I would think that part of the challenge is making sure that doesn't happen."

"I wonder…" I started, then paused. "I wonder if you've given any thought to some of the other challenges that you'll face."

"For example?"

"For example, this is hardly a woman's world, Ms. Reyes. At the moment, other than the sheriff's wife who acts as our jail matron, we have one part-time female employee. Gayle Sedillos works relief dispatch from time to time. You know her?"

"Yes, sir. She was one year ahead of me in high school."

"There you go. So when somebody leaves for greener pastures, she'll swing in to full-time. She has no ambition or desire to be a road deputy, and at the moment, we don't have one. Not a single female road deputy. And there are some folks out there who believe there shouldn't *be* a single one."

"I'm sure there are, sir."

"Is what they think going to matter to you?"

"Only if it prevents me from doing my job, sir. They're free to think what they like." Those black eyes didn't exactly smolder, but they reminded me of Katy Jurado's expression when she bites her immature boyfriend's head off in the '50's film classic *High Noon.*

"It wouldn't bother you to be the first one to walk into a saloon, looking to break up a bar fight?"

"That would be a good time to request back-up before the fact, sir."

I laughed gently. "Which we don't have most of the time."

"Then I do the best that I can."

I had no doubt that the combatants would instantly stop fighting at her entrance, probably hold out their wrists and say, "Cuff me…please."

"Should things work out, when are you available to start? Did Sheriff Salcido ask you about that?"

"He said that would be up to you, sir. But he got the preliminaries out of the way."

"Meaning…"

From her blouse pocket she drew out a small white card, and the deputy sheriff's commission carried Eduardo's signature and yesterday's date. I examined it, amused. Maybe I should have been irked with the sheriff's pre-empting my decision, but I'd been in both the military and law enforcement long enough to know that the guy at the top of the chain of command is free to act his conscience.

In this case, I knew what statistics predicted. Estelle Reyes would work for us for a year or so, then either be headhunted away by a better-paying job, or be swept away by a husband. We were a stepping stone on that path for her, but it made no sense not to benefit from her skills while we could.

"How are you with a camera?" Her résumé reported that her high school experiences included membership in the photography club, but what that accomplished was anyone's guess. Her college transcript included two courses specific to forensic photography.

"It's one of the tools of the trade," she said. "I'm comfortable with a camera, sir."

"Darkroom?"

"Yes, sir. I've processed film at school. Only black and white, never color."

"Which is fine, since we don't have color facilities. Yet." I closed her folder and leaned back. "So explain chain of evidence to me."

"Sir?"

I handed the commission card back to her, worth no more at the moment than such a card given by the sheriff as a courtesy to a county commissioner. It was a long way from that to responding to an incident as a trained, certified police officer. "If you did a ride-along with me today, out at the homicide scene we've got going on, what's the issue with you taking photos? Even if you have a talent that way?"

She hesitated, and I noticed that she didn't ask, "*What* homicide scene?"

"Well, for one thing, I'm not a member of the department, sir. If I were to take a photograph that later might be useful in court, and the attorneys could prove that at some time in the process, the photos had been out of the department's possession, that would be an issue. You couldn't say beyond any doubt that when the material was out of your possession, the photographic evidence had not been tampered with or altered. The photos could be called into question if that were the case. The chain of evidence would be broken because at some point, the evidence was not in your possession or control."

I nodded, impressed. "So you see the issues."

"I think I do, sir."

I pushed myself away from the desk and turned to one of the heavy filing cabinets. It took me a moment to fumble the correct key, and Estelle Reyes waited patiently. In the center drawer I found the box I wanted and slid the top off. "Pick a number. I have eleven, twelve, twenty-seven, and thirty."

"Twenty-seven, sir." She didn't ask why.

I picked up the heavy brass seven-point badge with the colorful enameled state seal in the center. "Let me have your commission card back for a moment," and when she handed it to me, I wrote her badge number in black ink in the appropriate space, then handed both badge and card to her. "Congratulations, young lady. Make us proud." I shook her hand, and her smile was radiant. "You were already sworn in when you signed that commission card with the sheriff. And you'll be sworn in a couple more times before you're through with all the ceremony. And…" I heaved a heavy sigh. "You have a ton of paperwork to complete, or the county won't pay you. Later today, see Sandy

Bacher over in the main county offices, and she'll skate you through the payroll hoops. And after that, you could stop by the Department of Social Services and apply for food stamps, since with what we pay, you'll probably qualify."

I watched as she tucked the badge into her slender black purse. "You know, we've never established a uniform for female officers, but I would suggest that your first move is to get rid of the purse. That's an extra nuisance that might get in your way." I smiled. "The pants suit looks just fine. We don't stand on much ceremony around this joint. It's not quite as simple as the days when you were handed a badge, gun, and the reins to a county horse, but damn near. I'll talk to Eduardo and see if he has something in mind for a uniform. But I doubt it."

Holding up an admonishing finger, I added, "Now tell me why you don't wear that badge in public, or flash it around."

She hesitated, then said, "After the paperwork, I'm a member of the staff, sir. But not being a certified officer, I wouldn't want a misunderstanding with the public. For all legal purposes, I'm as much a civilian as anyone else on the street. I can't respond to an incident as a certified officer would."

I nodded. "That's right. All it says is that you work for us in some capacity. That's all. You don't use it to try and dodge speeding tickets, or restaurant discounts, or anything like that. The appropriate place is in your wallet. Have you ever been sued, by the way?"

"No, sir."

"Understand that when you make mistakes, or even when you don't, you'll be a favorite target for all the wackos who want to make a quick buck at the government's expense. We try *not* to do stupid things to encourage litigation. Walking into situations without preparation, backup, or even proper authority is one way to encourage the wackos. We have a wonderful county attorney, but he can't work magic if you don't use your head."

"Yes, sir."

I surveyed my desk. "So...that's enough yakking. We have a long day ahead, and contrary to what I just got finished explaining, I'm not going to have you sit in dispatch today. We have too much to do, and I'm about fifty bodies short of what I need. And this is too good an opportunity for you to miss. Are you ready to go to work?"

"Yes, sir."

"Good. By the time the day's over, you'll be royally sick of hearing me talk. I like to preach when there's somebody to listen. Most of the time, I'm talking to myself. You've had breakfast?"

"Yes, sir."

"Good, because in this business, you'll never be sure where your next meal is coming from." I started toward the door, then stopped. "One more thing. At *all* times, what you think is important to me, and to the sheriff. Don't keep ideas, or intuitions, or hunches, to yourself. Share, share, share. Use your own judgment for when and how to do that. I'll want to see how you make those decisions. We're a team, Ms. Reyes. Yes, there's a chain of command, but since I'm your training officer for the next few weeks, not to worry about that. What you need to know is that we're not in competition with each other. And that starts today."

Chapter Nine

By 7:45 a.m., we had a dozen folks at Highland Avenue, each with a fistful of yellow surveyor's flags. We fanned out in a line and tramped through the mounds of weeds for the entire length of Highland, from the intersection with Hutton at one end to the intersection with County Road 43 on the other. Five passes offered a walk of about two miles. We moved slowly, eyes locked on the ground. Every time a treasure was discovered, an evidence flag sprouted if in the officer's judgment the item could be of interest to us.

I kept the search and seize instructions simple. An old, sun-bleached beer can wouldn't be much of a find. A fresh can or bottle ripe with fingerprints might be. An old, weathered shot shell casing wouldn't matter, but a fresh, shiny .30-06 casing damn sure would. A rotted cigarette butt didn't count for much, but a stash of fresh butts demanded scrutiny. And so on.

The catch with all this, of course, was that after a dozen sets of size 12's had walked through the area, not much that might be evidence would be left. So we had to get it right the first time.

After five passes—two down each side of the roadway and one right down the middle—we had a mediocre collection of flags growing. Satisfied, Sheriff Salcido and I excused everyone except Bobby Torrez, Tom Mears and my ride-along.

With the traffic gone and the prairie quiet, we visited each flag site in turn. The list of interesting tidbits was depressingly short. One set of tire tracks marked the soft, ungraded shoulder eighty-five yards directly in front of the parked Cat. It appeared that someone had swung off the road far enough that when they did so, their vehicle would have pitched sharply. A moment's inattention, perhaps, quickly corrected.

"Not a chance." Tom Mears shook his head. "A cast would be a waste of time. All we can get is a measurement of the width of the tire, and even that's more of a guess."

"I'll take it," I said. "Any little piece." We added a pop can so fresh that the remains of the half ounce of liquid inside still showed traces of carbonation. That interested me, since the soda hadn't been finished before being flung—and whether or not that meant anything was any one's guess. It went into an evidence bag, with Estelle Reyes watching our every move.

Fifty-five yards in front of the road grader, and within five feet of the roadway itself was a nest of .22 casings, fresh enough that even I could smell the burned powder—or maybe it was the clump of desert yarrow in which the casings had landed. We had the bullet that killed Larry Zipoli, and it sure as hell was no .22. We bagged the .22's anyway.

Thirty feet in front of the Cat, eight feet from the roadway, we picked up a handy lug wrench. That's certainly something I always do after I change a tire—fling the wrench off into the desert. Not far from that was a nest of two quarters, three dimes, and two pennies. How one goes about losing eighty-two cents out in the prairie would be interesting in and of itself.

All in all, we found absolutely nothing of significance—nothing we could look at and say, "Ah ha, *this* fits!"

Sheriff Salcido stood in the center of Highland Avenue and watched Tom Mears take the last of the documentary photos.

"I don't like this," the sheriff said. "We don't have *nothing.*"

"Half an ounce of Pepsi and eighty-two cents," I said. "That's more than we often get for a day's work."

He mopped his forehead and resettled his Stetson. "Why would anybody do this. Just for kicks, you think?" He pronounced it *keeks,* with a grimace.

"At this point, we can't know," I said. "The only thing we *think* that we know is that the shooter fired from somewhere between here and the intersection with Hutton. If we knew the height of the shooter, from ground to rifle barrel, a little trigonometry would tell us how far he stood from the grader. We're going to have to go with averages."

I dug a toe of my Wellington boot into the dirt. "The list of what we *don't* know is much, much longer. Were there other shots fired that didn't hit the grader? What kind of gun was it? Did the victim know the shooter? Hell, did the shooter know who the hell he was shooting at? Or that *she* was shooting at? We could go on and on with questions, like the basic one...*why*."

Salcido reached out and took the bundle of unused flags that Estelle had collected. "I'd like to have that list," he said. "You're assuming it was no accident."

"I don't believe it was," I said. "I hope I'm wrong." I turned to Bob Torrez. "Today I want to know everything there is to know about that recovered bullet, Bobby. That's a start. That's something we *have*. I want a firmer handle on the trajectory. That would be your best guess how far away the shooter was standing, if you take five feet from ground to rifle barrel as an average."

I turned to the other deputy. "Tom, the thought occurred to me that you could borrow a laser from one of the county surveyors and shoot a beam to establish a trajectory. Hell, I don't know. Maybe that wouldn't work. Lasers don't drop over distance, bullets do...and there's the issue of deflection when the bullet hit the glass." I waved a hand, orchestrating frustration. "Hell, I don't know. But try it. Try anything."

Tom Mears nodded as if he perfectly understood my ramblings. I glanced at my watch. "I'm headed over to the county yard to talk with Zipoli's supervisor. Tony didn't have much to say about any maintenance issues, or with something broken on the grader, but if there was, they'll have some record of it. He'll have scouted that out. Somebody will remember something. I want to know what Larry Zipoli was doing when he was shot. The grader was running, but the transmission was in neutral.

Go figure that one. He wasn't stopped to talk with someone, not with that noisy diesel running. So why? And it's a start with one fundamental question...does anyone have a single notion about why somebody would *want* to shoot Larry Zipoli."

"Would *want* to?" Salcido frowned.

"Sure as hell, would want to," I replied. "If it's not an accident, then the shooter has to *want* to pull the trigger. That's not rocket science, is it. But it gives us a trail to be followed. And I had an interesting conversation with Marilyn Zipoli last night. Her husband had some issues with a neighbor. We'll see about that. I'll talk to that neighbor today and see where that takes us." I slapped my belly. "I wish my gut told me something intuitive, but it doesn't. So we plug along, check under all the rocks and in the dark little corners."

"And my gut...I wish it would go away." The sheriff rubbed his girth. "This neighbor...you're talking about Jim Raught?"

"That's the one."

"I don't know him very well." But obviously he *did* know Raught, after a fashion. Eduardo Salcido probably knew ninety percent of the Posadas County residents.

"I don't either, Eduardo. But we're *going* to know him."

Salcido laughed ruefully. He regarded Estelle Reyes for a moment with an expression of almost paternal pride. He knew Estelle's great uncle Reuben better than I did, enough to consider him an old friend. "Are you ready for all this?"

She didn't just belt out a chirpy, enthusiastic, unthinking "Yes, sir." Instead her face darkened a bit, eyebrows knitting. "No one should get away with something like this," she said.

"*Más sabe el diablo por viejo que por diablo,*" the sheriff murmured, and Estelle smiled.

"That's one of my mother's favorite sayings," she said.

"Well, you listen to her. And you listen to this one." He nodded toward me before starting to turn away, then paused. "We all pay attention, and the son of a bitch *won't* get away with pulling that trigger."

Eduardo Salcido didn't cuss much, but he was as frustrated as I was. He settled his Stetson again and nodded at the young lady. "And my best wishes to your mother."

"Thank you, sir."

He grinned at me and pulled his Stetson down the military two fingers above his eyes. "I heard about last night," he said. "With *Officer* Murton." Again, he enjoyed each of the three syllables. I'm not sure what kind of *off-i-cer* he thought Murton to be. "Those badges...they sometimes take a walk, don't they."

"Minds of their own," I replied.

"I'm going to work this section of the village." Salcido swept a hand to include the houses just to the south of us, where he and I had spent time the evening before. "One at a time. Somebody heard something, you know. You can't fire a high-powered rifle this close to houses and not hear it. All those folks yesterday who claimed not to hear nothing...maybe they've had time to think it over." He turned back with a look to include us all. "Anything at all...I want to hear about it sooner rather than later."

As he trudged back toward his car, I turned to Estelle. "What's the *dicho* mean?" I didn't know much Spanish—what three years in a North Carolina high school forty years before could teach. I didn't mind when others settled into their home language, leaving us gringos behind. After all, it was *my* choice to remain so clumsy and inept in that language of the border.

"Literally, 'the devil knows more because he's old than because he's the devil.' A colorful way to say that experience is the best teacher."

"Ah. Well, we'll see. Right now, I'm feeling just this side of stupid." I sighed. "Are you ready to meet some people who may not be so excited to meet us?"

"Yes, sir." No hesitation there.

Chapter Ten

The Posadas County maintenance barns were on north Third Street. If Third had crossed the big arroyo that scarred the north side of the village, it would have intersected Highland in a quarter mile or so. The county barns and bone yard were close enough to Highland that anyone working outside should have been able to hear a rifle shot clearly.

But this was the rural southwest. Shooters abounded, whether slaying beer cans on the mesa, rattlesnakes invading the yard, or ravens ravaging a song bird's nest. No one took particular notice of gun shots. *Shots.*

This had been, as far as we could tell, a *single* shot, in my book one of the most lethal sounds. One bullet was all it took if the shooter knew what he was about and conditions were right. During hunting season, if I heard *blam, blam, blam, blam,* I could guess that the deer or elk or antelope had probably escaped unscathed, the flurry of bullets kicking dust. But one, solitary, definitive *blam*… that was a different scenario. A critter dropped in his tracks. Or Larry Zipoli dead before he could move a hand to the gearshift, or duck to safety.

I swung 310 through the boneyard's generous gate in the chain link and razor wire boundary fence, and drove cautiously through all the junk before reaching the maintenance office, housed at the north end of a long, steel building with four gigantic bay doors. Two were up, two down. In one, a twin-screw dump truck was resting on jacks, its hind-most differential in a thousand pieces. One of the county pick-up trucks was backed into the other open bay.

Parking directly in front of a single door marked *Office*, I lowered the front windows on both sides, then nodded at the mike without reaching for it. "PCS, three ten is ten six, county barn."

Without hesitating, Estelle slipped the mike off its hook and repeated the message, her tone measured and pronunciation distinct without being exaggerated.

"Three ten, ten four," dispatcher T.C. Barnes responded immediately.

"Most of the time, we want dispatch to know where we are," I said. "There are times when we don't, too. Half the goddamn county is listening to what we say, so we want to think before yapping. It's a balance between staying safe and staying discreet. I keep badgering the sheriff to put mobile phones in each car, so we can stay off the radio waves entirely. No *dinero*. And radios are a tradition, stupid as that sounds."

I hadn't made a move to get out of the car yet, and took a moment to make a notation in my log...a document I cheerfully ignored most of the time. Now that my every move was under scrutiny by my ride-along, perhaps it behooved me to do things properly to start her off right.

"We want to talk first with Tony Pino. He's bossman. He was out at the crime scene yesterday, and he's shaken by all this." I paused. "By way of historical interest, Tony's grandfather was the first mayor of Posadas. Between Eduardo Salcido and myself, we could devise a hell of a trivia game about this little corner of the world—and what I find interesting is that sometimes, that makes folks nervous, thinking we know something about 'em that we shouldn't. That can be to our advantage."

I glanced at the steel office door, ajar just enough that anyone inside would have heard the crunch of our tires. "There will be lots of questions. Yesterday when we were buttoning up Highland, we had something of a crowd watching, although watching what I don't know. Tony's foreman was there too—Buddy

Clayton. They're going to have questions, and the trick is to make them feel included without giving anything away." Looking sideways at my passenger I saw the look of noncommittal interest on her pretty face. My lectures hadn't driven her over the brink yet.

"At this point, they don't need to know what we know—which I'm sorry to say is diddly squat. But they don't need to know that." I slid the aluminum clipboard that included my log sheets under the pile of junk that threatened the center arm rest. "The base line is this: *somewhere* out there is someone with a high powered rifle who picked an easy target. We need to remember—*always* remember—that that son-of-a-bitch is still out there, still watching. We don't get complacent, we stay sharp, we look and listen and watch. Okay?"

"Yes, sir." Flat, noncommittal. Her fingers didn't even stray toward the door handle. Maybe she expected more lectures.

"And that's whether you're riding with me or anyone else. And while you're at it, ponder this cheerful thought. It might be quiet as a tomb in Posadas County for days on end. But we're just off the interstate, and that connects us to the world. Some creep might have killed a dozen people in Terre Haute, Indiana, and be fleeing west…right through here. Or some hijacker slips custody in San Diego and heads east. Or some dealer is heading north with five hundred pounds of cocaine from downtown Mexico. Here we sit, hopefully not half asleep. It might be quiet here, but elsewhere, maybe not. And we're all connected."

"Yes, sir."

"Let's see what they have to say." I popped the door, at the same time noticing the lithe, effortless, almost anti-gravitational way that Estelle Reyes moved. Oh, to be twenty-two again. What interested me even more was watching her close the car door. Not a slam, just a gentle nudge against the latch. And all the while her eyes were roaming the boneyard, inventorying who knew what.

I rapped a knuckle on the office door and pushed it open. Two steps and I was greeted by a belly-high counter. A heavy-set woman sat at the first desk, the surface more cluttered than my own, a vast sea of requisitions, time sheets, phone messages, blueprints, job or parts—all the things that keep a busy department busy.

"Well, good morning." Bea Summers spoke without any of her usual bounce or sunshine. "Tony was trying to call you earlier. I think he talked to Sheriff Salcido."

"I've been out and about," I said, without adding that I hadn't checked my answering machine in the past couple of hours. I took a deep breath and let it out in a long, heart-felt sigh. "I'm sorry about all this," I said. "Rough time."

"Is there any news?"

"I wish there were. There are a number of things we need to find out from you, if we might." *If we might.* I couldn't imagine that Bea Summers would hesitate to cooperate in any way we asked, but sometimes folks hesitate when it's the privacy of their turf that's being violated. We'd find out what we needed to know whether Bea, or even Tony Pino, was agreeable or not, court orders being what they are.

"And by the way, Bea, this is Estelle Reyes. She's a new hire who's spending some ride-along time with me this morning."

Bea didn't rise from her swivel chair, but favored Estelle with a polite smile. "I know her great uncle, Reuben Fuentes."

"Ah," I said. Interesting that Bea hadn't directed the comment to Estelle, instead speaking as if the girl were a piece of furniture. Maybe the grudge against Reuben extended to the next generation as well. Bea no doubt knew that over the years, Reuben had swiped more base course gravel from county and state piles than anyone else, and had been caught a time or two. I guess that when the crusher fines were stockpiled right beside the highway, the temptation was too strong to ignore. That might be what Bea was remembering.

"So…first I need to talk with Tony. He's buried under paperwork?"

"Actually, he went over to Marilyn's for a little bit this morning. Bill, this is all so *terrible,* so *senseless.* Tell me it didn't really happen."

"I wish I could. Maybe you'd give Tony a shout and see when he'll be able to break loose. And if it's not a good time, I would think that you're going to be able to help us as well or better than anyone else." She was the office czarina, after all, with her finger on the Highway Department's pulse.

She nodded and picked up the radio microphone, turning up the volume a little as she did so. "Base to one. Copy?" Silence ensued and she repeated the message without success. "He's not in the truck. Should I call the house?"

"Well, we hate to interrupt 'em. But look, two things right away, and as I said, you know as much or more than anyone else. Larry's personnel file. We're going to need a look at that." I knew that was thin ice, and Bea's reaction was immediate.

"His *personnel* folder?"

"Or whatever version of that you have in this office. There'll be something in the county manager's office too, but I need to see anything you have."

"*Personnel?*"

"Yes, ma'am. I don't think that we'll need to take it out of the office." Bea could figure out for herself that Larry Zipoli's life was about to come under the microscope.

She pushed herself to her feet, closing the center drawer of her desk tightly as if concerned that I might peak at *her* secrets. "This is just so awful. What else will you be needing?"

"It's my understanding that Larry took one of the department trucks home at night."

"Yes." She frowned. "He's one of the senior men, Sheriff. He needs to be able to respond during emergencies." Her tone said clearly, with just a touch of petulance, as if somehow I might be judging her department's procedure, "*You already knew all that.*" She stepped over to the window and pointed. "The white Dodge Ram, over by the fence. That's Larry's."

"Out at Highland yesterday—he didn't have the truck out there with him."

"Well, no. I mean, it's what, a few blocks? In the morning, he was out on 43, and drove back to find a part before going out

Highland. The lower muffler clamp had burned through. He fixed that just before lunch, and that darn old thing *still* broke down on him and blew a hydraulic hose. One of the boys ran it out to him after lunch."

"Do you remember the time?"

"Oh, maybe two o'clock or so."

"As early as one-thirty?"

"Not that early. Maybe even two thirty. Louis had to make one up real quick, and that took him a few minutes, then to run it over." She nodded. "No, I'd say closer to two-thirty."

"This is Louis Duenas?"

"Yes…but now wait. Louis made up the hose, but he's busy working on the truck. I think Mike ran it out." She nodded. "I'm sure he did."

"Mike Zamora?"

She nodded.

"We'll need to talk with him, Bea."

"Oh, my," she sighed, and turned to scrutinize the large white board on the wall behind her desk. "He and Dougy Burgess went to Deming to pick up a whole raft of parts from Pitts Diesel. They'll be back this afternoon. I gotta tell you, *none* of us are real excited about working today. This whole thing has been such a shock. I mean, *Larry?* My gosh, I've known him and Marilyn for Lord only knows how long. I don't know what she'll do now."

"Bad times," I said sympathetically. "We'll all do what we can. I'll catch up with Mike later, when he gets back. You have the keys to Larry's truck?" There had been a set of keys that went into the evidence envelope along with the rest of the items on the victim's person, and I assumed they included one for the Dodge.

"I'll have to find the dupes." But Bea made no move toward where the duplicates might be kept.

"If you'd do that, I'd appreciate it. We'd like to take a look inside the truck while you're finding the personnel files." That stirred her into motion, and in a moment she returned from one of those walk-in vault closets with a single key and tag on a chrome ring. "I believe this is to his vehicle," she said, handing it to me. "Now listen…I'm going to have to talk to Tony about those records."

"Whatever it takes, Bea. Thank you. We'll be back with these in a few minutes."

She nodded and offered Estelle the ghost of a smile. "Nice to see you again, young lady. I hope you enjoy your stay."

Enjoy her stay? However brief? Not, "Welcome aboard, we look forward to working with you?"

If Estelle caught the nuances, which I'm sure she did, she replied graciously, "Thank you, ma'am. I'm sure I will."

Outside, the sun was brilliant, the earth of the bone yard fragrant with oil, diesel, and a dozen other nifty chemicals. Larry Zipoli's white Dodge three-quarter ton was backed tight against the fence, nose out, ready to go. I took my time crossing the parking lot, watching where I put my feet. Estelle kept stride, and I wondered what thoughts were occupying her, at the same time thanking my good fortune that she wasn't a compulsive chatterbox.

"Most of the time, they trail the truck behind the grader out to the job site," I said. "But for little jobs around the perimeter of the village, he's just going to drive the grader."

I tried the door handle, and was surprised to find it locked. In a secure bone yard, fenced with razor wire and lighted with sodium vapor lights to noontime brightness all night, what was the point of locking a work truck? Habit, perhaps.

The key turned easily. This old monster, government low-bid specs anyway, didn't feature niceties like electric door locks or electric windows. As it opened, the door squalled against slightly bent and dry hinges. An effluvia of odors flooded out, mostly stale tobacco in a variety of forms. Smoke residue blued the glass, and a nifty little cup holder hung from the driver's side door, nestled in which was a coke can with the top sliced off. It was half full of tobacco juice. The ash tray was pulled out, stuffed with butts. Larry's tobacco habit spanned the gamut from generic cigarettes to chaw to stogies. The cab's aroma, exacerbated by the sun through the glass, was ripe.

A thick log book rested on the seat, and I flipped it open to the last page of notations. Larry had pumped 22.1 gallons of diesel into the Dodge two days before, noting the mileage as 177,671.9. I inserted the ignition key and turned it until the dash lit up.

"So he's driven eighteen miles in two days, more or less." I turned and grinned at Estelle. She was standing at junction of cab and bed, watching my performance. "And that tells us... only that. If it read that he'd covered two hundred miles in a county this small, we'd wonder, wouldn't we."

Another aroma had interested me from the moment I opened the door, and I turned my attention to the modest lunch cooler that rested on the passenger side floor. I couldn't reach it by stretching across, so I slid out and trudged around to open the passenger door.

"Interesting that he didn't take his lunch with him on the grader," I mused. Estelle's left eyebrow raised about a sixteenth of an inch. "Or not," I added, and opened the cooler. "Well, hello there."

Chapter Eleven

Larry Zipoli's lunch was well balanced: four empty bottles of dark beer, two empty micro bottles of good bourbon. The cooler still contained two full beers and one unopened whiskey sampler. The blue freezer cube was still cool to the touch.

"Well, now," I said. "That's quite a diet." I didn't touch any of the bottles, but could read the labels well enough, and saw a price tag on one of the samplers. "He liked the good stuff."

"Do you suppose he had a sack lunch with him?" It was her first question of the morning, and until that moment, her reticence had been striking.

"He might have, but we didn't find anything on the grader, and he didn't toss the remains out the window along Highland. He was back here at the barns over the lunch hour, we're told. If he was brown-bagging it, then he had ample time to eat here. And these puppies?" I reached out and tapped one of the whiskey bottles with the tip of a pencil. "Motorists toss these out the window all the time. Take a mile walk along any highway, and you'll find 'em."

"But he kept the empties in the cooler."

"And why would he do that, I wonder? I mean, the county doesn't condone employees drinking their lunch, especially *in* a county vehicle. He didn't want to risk being seen dumping cans and bottles in the dumpsters here?"

"Did Mr. Zipoli have a record of DWI?"

"I don't think so. I don't recall that *I've* never stopped him, and usually if deputies stop one of the town fathers, or a village or county employee, they talk about it among themselves, generally with some self-righteous delight. I don't recall any of the deputies talking about Larry Zipoli."

The young lady was standing beside Zipoli's truck, gazing across the bone yard. "If he sat in his truck way over here out of the way, he'd be safe enough to enjoy his lunch," she said. "If somebody starts to walk toward him, he's got time to slip the bottle back in the cooler."

"If that's what he did." I snapped the lid on the cooler shut and lifted it out of the truck. Other than the log entries and the booze, the Dodge offered nothing that jumped out at me and cried, "Look at this!"

I stashed the cooler in the trunk of 310, and then settled in the driver's seat, turning the air conditioner up to high for a few minutes.

"So, now we know something else. Our man has a significant drinking problem if he downed four bottles and two samplers in just one day. Of course," and I shrugged, "that might be a week's supply. A bottle of dark beer one day, a whiskey the next—or any combination of the above."

"Reuben is an alcoholic," Estelle said quietly.

I looked at her. "I know he is," I said. "And he has been for years, at least ever since I've known him."

"When I was little and he'd visit Tres Santos, I used to think it was his cologne," she mused. "I could tell when he had been in my mother's house. The smell lingered for a long, long time. If Mr. Zipoli had consumed all that alcohol for lunch, I would think that the cab of the road grader would have smelled like a brewery."

"Mostly the cab smelled like a body too long in the sun, and stale cigar. All that overlaid over the grader's own body odor—oil, grease, hydraulic fluid." I paused, the image playing in my mind. There Larry Zipoli sat, perhaps half buzzed, reflexes slow, big stogie clamped in his mouth, the thick smoke clinging to his skin, clothing, and every surface of the Cat's cab.

"So, was this a one-time thing, or a constant problem with him? If it's a beer a day or so, that's one thing. If Larry Zipoli was chugging through a six-pack and three samplers every day, then that's another story." I chuckled at the image. "How the hell could he grade a straight line? Maybe that's where we need to go." I tapped a little tattoo on the steering wheel. "This is a doorway of sorts, Deputy Reyes." I turned and looked at her, and her expression was intense. She was a listener, not a talker, and I liked her all the more.

"We go through the door, or we don't. That's the first choice. Well, of course we do. We welcome any doors, painful as they might end up being for somebody. A good share of the time, there's a causative link between the victim and the killer." I shrugged. "Now, sometimes there isn't." My door was ajar, and I lowered my voice so there was no chance of the sound carrying across the boneyard to Bea Summer's keen ears.

"Let's say the killer sees the grader parked along Highland, with the sun maybe on the windshield. He can't tell if someone is in it or not, and doesn't bother to check. Maybe he assumes the machine is untended. Those guys do take work breaks after all. Standing some distance away, maybe the shooter can't hear the grader idling. And at idle, there isn't much smoke out the stack, not until the throttle is cracked. So he takes a shot just for the hell of it. A vandalism kind of thing. He figures the operator will come back, see the bullet hole, and freak out." I shrugged again. "It could have happened that way."

"In that case, it doesn't matter whether or not Mr. Zipoli drinks his lunch, or is an alcoholic, or not."

"That's exactly right. And that's why we go through that door carefully and discreetly. Nothing is gained by spreading Larry's bad habits all over town. Those who know him well enough, already know that he had a drinking problem. That's the thing about alcoholics. They don't think anybody is going to notice. They'll go to elaborate lengths to hide the habit. The efforts are a waste of time. You can't hide it, not the smell, not the behavior, none of it."

I switched off the car. "End of lecture. Let's take a look at the files, if Mrs. Summers has those records for us." I hesitated. "And I hope I don't have to tell you how confidential all of this is. It's between you and me. You don't even discuss any of this with *anyone* else, unless the sheriff himself has questions for you. Whatever Eduardo Salcido wants to know, he *gets* to know. But not with the other deputies, not with anyone."

"Yes, sir."

"You have a boyfriend you talk with?"

Her frown was instant but fleeting, as if I'd stepped on her foot and then as quickly recovered.

"Yes, sir."

"Be very, very careful. What's he do?"

"He's a fourth year medical student at Baylor, sir."

"Ah. *That's* a long hard road. Local young man?"

"His family lives in Las Cruces and in Mexico."

"Well, good. Anyway, confidential, just like between him and his patients." She nodded and followed me out of the car, taking just a moment to tuck in her blouse and straighten her summer weight cotton jacket.

My hand was on the office door knob when a late model pickup came through the bone yard gate without slowing a lick and managed to stop beside my patrol car without spraying gravel against the building. Tony Pino was behind the wheel, with his foreman, Buddy Clayton, riding shotgun.

"I was hoping Bea would be able to reach you," I said, and extended my hand. Tony's grip was a single, perfunctory, limp pump. Buddy managed a little better. "This is Deputy Estelle Reyes," I said, and let it go at that. Buddy gave her a thorough head-to-toe survey, looked like he wanted to say something cute, and bit it off. Tony had other things on his mind, and got right to the point.

"We was just over talkin' to Marilyn Zipoli," Tony said. "Christ, what a tough time."

"Yes, it is. "

"You got any new ideas since yesterday? Who mighta done something like this?"

"That's why we're here this morning, Tony. I need to know from you exactly what happened yesterday. From the first time you saw Larry yesterday morning until late in the afternoon. And I understand that Mike Zamora ran the new hydraulic hose out to him. I'll want to talk with him."

"He's in Deming, I think." Pino grimaced and glanced at the blinding blue sky. "Let's go inside, then," he said. The cramped office became a crowded place, all of us under the watchful eye of Bea Summers. Before I forgot it, I handed the keys back to her, and then we headed to Tony's dark little cave of an office. I noticed that Bea didn't offer me the personnel file. She'd let Tony field that one.

Buddy Clayton appeared intent on joining the party, but I stopped him at the office doorway with a gentle hand on the shoulder.

"Let us catch you in a little bit, Buddy," I said, and he shot a nervous glance at his boss. Tony waved an impatient hand at him, and I moved a floor fan so that I could close the door. Estelle moved to one side, taking the corner by a filing cabinet that offered handy support for an elbow. Before we were finished with this day, it would be a wonderful test of her discretion, but I had little reason to worry. So far that morning, I had been absolutely unable to judge just what she was thinking at any given time. She could have taken up a career as a professional poker player.

"Let me tell you what it looks like to us." I tried to find a comfortable spot on the metal folding chair. "One rifle shot, fired directly from a point in front of the road grader, the shooter standing some indeterminate number of yards west on Highland, or maybe even beyond somewhere. You saw what it did. The slug blew through the center of the grader's windshield right beside the windshield wiper, and struck Larry in the forehead, just over his left eyebrow." I paused. "That's it. You know as much as we do."

Tony Pino's face paled another shade, and he swallowed hard. "Jesus, Bill." For a moment, he didn't know what else to say, and I sat in silence, letting him work on it.

"There's kids out at the arroyo all the time, shootin' and stuff. There's this one place out west of Highland where the arroyo is pretty deep, man. You know all about it. That's where they go. Most of the time, we don't have so many problems."

"Most of the time." The arroyo was just outside the village limits, and a sore point with some of the commissioners. Shooting there was legal, since it was a fair distance from the nearest dwelling, and if the shooters stayed down in the arroyo, the steep sides provided some barrier. Some.

"You thinking that's what it was?"

"We're exploring a couple of different avenues," I hedged. I'd known Tony for years, and thought of him as an honest, hard-working village employee. But sometimes it was hard to tell what the connections were. "Tony, this is hard for you guys, I know. But I asked Bea if we can take a look at Larry's personnel files."

"Jesus, Bill, I can't let you do that," Tony replied without taking a moment to think it over. Well, he *could,* of course, but I hadn't used all the keys yet to open that door. "I mean those files are confidential." I nodded as if that was that, giving myself time to mull my options. I hadn't said "warrant" yet in this conversation, and once I did, there was no going back. I was convinced that the shot that killed Larry Zipoli had not been an errant slug from across the arroyo.

"Does...*did*...Larry have much of a drinking problem on the job?" The blunt question might as well have been a ball peen hammer between the eyes. I saw the blood rush up Tony's dark face, and he blinked half a dozen times, digesting the question.

"What?"

"There's some indication that Larry liked his booze, Tony."

"I...I don't know anything about that. Larry's been working for us for Jesus knows how many years. He gets the job done, just like he's paid to do. Hell, Bill, you've known him as long as

I have. Where'd all this come from? Did Marilyn say something to you about him drinking, or what?"

"He had the remains of a pretty good party in the cooler in his truck," I replied.

"You were in his truck?" Why that would have surprised Tony, I didn't know.

"Sure enough. His daily log doesn't show many miles, and we need to know what he did yesterday, Tony."

"Jesus," Tony muttered. "We got to get into all this?"

"Yes." If not now, then on the witness stand under a D.A.'s grilling, I thought, but spared Tony Pino that worry so early in the game. "He started work at the usual time?"

"Left the yard with the grader right around 8:15," Tony snapped, his turf thoroughly stepped on. "He was workin' up on Nineteen the day before, and yesterday he was going to catch up on some work up on Highland. That last frog strangler we got? Did some damage up there. He went out in the morning, and had some damn problem with the exhaust stack, so he brought the grader back before lunch, and he worked on it for an hour or so right here in the yard. And then he went back out and right away blew a hydraulic hose. Louis made up a new one, and got Mike to run it out."

"What time was that?"

"Maybe Bea could tell you. I was down in María most of the morning. Buddy or Louis might know. They spent most of the morning on that twin-screw that we got in shop."

"So Larry would have eaten lunch here in the shop?"

"I guess so. Hell, I don't know. He might have drove down to the Don Juan. Sometimes at the Country Club. Maybe he went home."

"And then over to Highland after lunch sometime."

Tony nodded, thinking it through. "What time are you thinkin' that all this happened?"

"The original call to 911 came at seventeen minutes after three. The grader's engine was running but in neutral. No sign that Larry ever had a chance to move an inch."

"Jesus. This is a crazy world. Something like this happening *here*, for God's sakes. I mean in the big cities, you know. But here?"

"We have our moments," I said. "Did Larry have any arguments with anybody here at work? Were you aware of any friction between him and, well, anyone else?"

"Larry minded his own business," Tony said. "He can drive anything with wheels, and is the best heavy equipment operator we got. He can grade a dirt road so it feels like you was drivin' on pavement, for Christ's sake. He don't give a hard time to any of the kids we got workin' for us now. Some of the young bucks can do some pretty stupid things, you know. Larry, he just laughs it off and does his best to keep 'em on the straight and narrow." He held his hands parallel. "I can't even imagine who'd do a thing like this, Bill."

"Anything you can tell us is a help," I prompted. "Anything at all. Did you and Cheri get together with Larry and Marilyn much?"

Tony took a moment before answering. "Not so much, no. They're always here when we have some special thing, you know. But other than that, we kinda…"

"Keep to yourselves?"

"That's right."

"In the past few years, did Larry have any disciplinary actions against him for anything?"

"What sort of things do you mean?"

"Anything at all. Any infraction that you noticed. Any unexplained absence from work. Drinking on the job. Money problems. Anything."

"That's all his business, don't you think?"

I took a long, deep breath. "Tony, Larry was a county employee. He was killed while on the job, in the most cold-blooded way I can imagine. We're going to find out who did this thing, believe it. And I'll do whatever that takes, Tony. One of the first things I want to establish is a victim profile. Like anybody, I'm sure Larry Zipoli had his share of secrets." I paused, then decided to hell with it. "In a homicide investigation, we'll look for links where ever we can, including all the demons in the closet."

Now that the word was out, floating around the office while Tony Pino tried to cope with it, I pushed him just a little. "We need to see his personnel records, Tony."

"Marilyn don't deserve any of this," he said quietly.

"No, she doesn't. And neither did Larry, for that matter. But some son-of-a-bitch doesn't get to pull the trigger on him, and then just walk away. That isn't going to happen."

"Jesus."

"If you want, we'll go through the records here in the office, but it would be a whole lot better if we could take them over to our *casa* for a thorough review."

"I just don't think I have the authority to do that."

"Well, you do, Tony. You're the boss."

"If I don't give you the records, you'll get a warrant?"

"Yes."

"Then I guess that's what should happen, Bill. You know, I hate to play hard-nosed about this, but we should probably follow all the rules." He shrugged. "Maybe by tomorrow, then?"

I smiled good-naturedly, as if that was all just fine with me. "May I use your phone for just a moment?"

Tony reached out and shoved the multi-buttoned console toward me. "Any line that isn't lit," he said, and I nodded my thanks. T.C. Barnes in dispatch answered promptly.

"T.C.," I said, "ask Sheriff Salcido to give me a call ASAP." I gave him the Highway Department's number. "If he's out in the car, have him either call me, or stop by. If he's out of reach somehow, have one of the deputies track him down."

"I think he's over off Hutton talking with folks," Barnes said. "I'll reach him somehow."

"ASAP," I reminded Barnes. "Send someone over there if you have to. I'll be at the Highway Department until I hear from you." I replaced the receiver gently.

"I hate to be a prick," Tony said with a regretful shake of the head. "But I'd tell Eduardo the same thing. The personnel records are confidential…"

I held up a placating hand. "Not to worry, Tony. The sheriff is not going to argue with you. Either he or I will go for the warrant, and we'll get all this moving on down the road."

"You don't have to do that."

"Well, we do. We need to look at the records, the sooner the better. You're absolutely correct, Tony. A warrant is the proper way to make sure all the i's are crossed and the t's dotted. That lets all of you off the hook." He didn't look amused or mollified.

"We can get all that stuff together for you," he said again. "Whatever you want." Somehow, Tony Pino didn't understand that *tomorrow* wasn't good enough.

"That's okay. I'll wait." I didn't bother to explain that I wanted the records untainted by helpful, editing hands. I'm sure he was smart enough to figure that out.

Chapter Twelve

I'd never earn that sunny smile from Bea Summers again. She struck me as one of those fine women who was a jewel until crossed, and then your name was forever engraved on her shit list. The eyes went glacial, the glances toward Estelle Reyes and me were fleeting and cold. Apparently the issue wasn't so much an urgency to explore every avenue in the life of Larry Zipolil, even if that was what was necessary to find out who killed him. But nobody likes to be strong-armed. The gray filing cabinet that held the personnel records was *their* turf, not mine. Bea Summers wanted me to know that.

My hand-held radio squawked, and I pulled it off my belt. "I'll take it outside," I said to Estelle, and she understood and settled into one of the gray metal chairs just inside the office counter. I didn't mind her overhearing my conversation, but I also wanted her eyes glued to those filing cabinets during my absence. Not that I didn't trust Bea or Tony, of course. But turf is turf.

"Go ahead," I said into the radio as soon as I cleared the door and switched to channel three, our most restricted, car-to-car frequency.

"Bill, what do you have going on over there?" Eduardo Salcido's tone was its usual sing-song, even over the radio waves.

"We're going to need to look through Larry Zipoli's personnel records, Eduardo. " Despite the restricted radio channel, I didn't want to go into details of our discovery in Larry's truck. "Can you talk a warrant out of Judge Smith?"

"Tony won't give you the records?"

"Reluctantly, at best. I don't want to argue with him and make an enemy. He'll feel better with paper. So will the DA when all is said and done."

"You want that now?"

I chuckled. "Yes. I don't want there to be an opportunity for anything to go missing, Eduardo."

"Oh, they're not going to do that."

You gentle old soul, I thought. "When you drop the warrant off, I'll show you something interesting," I said, adding some additional bait so he didn't sink into *mañana* land.

The sheriff had his thumb on the transmit button quickly enough that his sigh came through loud and clear. "Ten four, then. I'll see what I can do."

"Thanks. We'll be waiting."

Back inside, Bea Summers was trying to find something on her computer, and I leaned casually on the counter, watching. "Are most of the department's records computerized now?" I asked, going for my most pleasant and innocuous tone.

"I wouldn't trust these things with a birthday party invitation." Bea's tone was brittle, but she glanced my way and the corners of her mouth twitched. "We hard-copy everything, just like B.C."

"Who's B .C.?"

"Before Computers, sheriff."

"Oh, well of course. We do too."

"I should think so."

Tony appeared from his office, hesitated, and then beckoned. "Let me talk to you for a minute, Bill," he said, and his invitation was singular. Estelle heard it and stayed where she was.

Back in the office, Tony closed the door carefully and took his time settling back in his chair.

"You reached the sheriff?"

"I did. He's on his way, so we're all set." Whether the lugubrious Judge Everett Smith would get his ass in gear was another issue.

Tony fell silent, and I let him think uninterrupted.

"Look, Bill, we've known each other a long time."

"We have indeed."

"This is just between you and me, now."

I held up a hand. "I'm here in an official capacity, Tony. If something you tell me has a bearing on this particular case, that information will go into the hopper along with everything else. You need to understand that."

"Shit, man, I know all that. I'm just asking that you keep this under your hat. That's all." *Ask me once, no. Ask me twice, yes?* My kids used to play that game, and it didn't work then, either.

"I understand." I smiled sympathetically. "What I'm telling you is that any information we gain will be used as we see fit. You're just going to have to trust my judgment."

He signed and regarded his desk blotter.

"Look, Larry had his share of troubles, you know? Now, I don't know everything, but I know a little. Money's tight for them."

I nodded. On an equipment operator's salary, even coupled with a bank cashier's wages, a nice house, nice family, nice boat, nice truck and camper ate up a budget. And that was just if all those nice things sat unused. A weekend trip to Elephant Butte to enjoy fishing, camping, and water skiing took another big chunk.

"You know what I think?" Tony asked rhetorically. "I think Larry was maxed out."

"You mean money-wise."

Tony nodded. "You know, last week, he won five bucks in that scratch-off lottery? First thing he did was buy ten more tickets." He smiled ruefully. "None of them were winners, so he's further in the hole than before."

Money troubles that can lead to depression can deepen to suicide, but Larry Zipoli hadn't offed himself from eighty yards away. "He drinks a lot? Sometimes that can really screw things up."

"I think so. No," and he waved a hand impatiently. "I *know* so. He thinks those damn cigars of his hide it, you know. Well, they don't."

"He drank on the job?"

Tony reared back in his chair and hooked his hands behind his head. He gazed at the water stains on the ceiling tiles for a few seconds while he made up his mind. "Yeah, Bill. Couple of times."

"A couple?" The cooler left in the pickup cab didn't suggest a *couple.*

"'Look,' I told Larry, 'look, man, you can't be doin' this. You can't be takin' the booze with you on the job.'" Tony's hands waved in frustration. "He'd say, 'Yeah, yeah. I not doin' that.' But he was, Bill. He was. And you know, I got to protect the department. So that's what you're going to find in the files.

"I wrote him up a bunch of times. The last time was just a week ago. Something like that. I said, 'One more time, Larry. One more, and we got to let you go.' And I meant it, too."

I didn't believe that for a second.

Tony shook his head sadly. "Last week, over on Nineteen, he hooked the blade on the end of a culvert. He never would a done that before. Took us the rest of the morning to fix what he done. And yeah. I wrote him up."

I hadn't taken any notes, hadn't had a tape recorder running, and apparently Tony Pino took some comfort in that. "So what now?"

"Just what I said before, Tony. We see what comes out of all this. There's three routes this can take." I held up two fingers. "One, his death is an unfortunate, unthinking, careless accident. Somebody let fly from across the way, and Larry was sitting in the wrong place at the wrong time. Two, it was a deliberate act of vandalism, and maybe the shooter didn't know Larry was sitting in the machine. The angle of the sun, all that." I took a deep breath and held up the third finger. "And three, someone shot Larry Zipoli deliberately. One shot."

"Who would do a thing like that?"

"I have no idea. If I did, I wouldn't be sitting here, enjoying your hospitality."

"All this drinking business…that comes out, it's going to be hard on Marilyn, you know."

"Of course. Right now, it's anyone's guess whether anything about Larry's personal life is connected to his death."

Tony shook his head and expelled a long, heart-felt sigh. "I sure wouldn't want your job right now."

"Sometimes I don't want it either."

His philosophical expression brightened. "The young lady you got riding with you…she's a looker. She living out there with old Reuben?"

"Actually, I don't know where she's living." I realized as I said that just how little I actually *did* know about Estelle Reyes. What was supposed to be a simple across-the-desk interview with a new hire had turned into something else, but I was okay with that. I was finding out far more about the young lady than any conversation would offer.

Despite the logistical problems of finding a judge and talking him into executing a warrant with short notice, Eduardo Salcido managed the challenge in less than an hour.

He didn't exactly say, "I don't want to know" when he delivered the warrant, but he didn't get out of the car or offer to come inside and commiserate with Tony and Bea. "I got some things on the burner," he said, and let it go at that. "What are you diggin' up?"

"Larry was into the sauce, Eduardo. To the point he was carrying both beer and whiskey in his county truck." I nodded across the bone yard at the orange Dodge.

The sheriff's face scrunched up in genuine sadness. "What makes you think…" He hesitated and looked up at me with one eye comically closed. "So what's the connection?"

"Damned if I know. But it's something to follow up on. I want to see his files. Tony tells me that he wrote Larry up a time or two for drinking on the job. I want to see just how many times."

"Why didn't Tony just fire him?" Salcido asked in wonder. "What's so hard about that? Well, don't answer that...I know how hard it is."

I straightened up. "It's just somewhere we need to go, Eduardo. You never know."

"No, you never do." He nodded. "You do what you think is best, *jefito*. I got somebody over on Hutton who heard the shots, by the way."

"*Shots?* Plural?"

"That's the story. We got one neighbor who heard one shot, another who heard more." He shrugged and pulled the car into gear. "We ask ten people, we'll have ten stories. You know how that goes. Let me know when you're back at the office." A slow grin lit his heavy, dark features. "How's our young lady doing?"

"Just fine. I'm impressed so far."

Eduardo laughed gently. "Tongues are going to wag, the two of you driving around town." He looked up at me. "But that's good, no? Good exercise for those tongues. Maybe they'll tell us something we need to know."

"Thanks for this," I said, rapping the warrant on the window sill.

The car started to drift backward, and then he spiked the brakes. "Bobby is up to something. I don't know what. Something with a rifle."

I made an umbrella in the air with both hands. "We'll cover it all. Something will turn."

"Talk to me later." Eduardo nodded at the warrant. "Judge Smith said to be careful with that."

A few minutes later, the heavy drawer of the security file glided open, and Bea Summers ran her hand over the tops of the folders. "Now exactly what did you want?" she asked pleasantly enough, but the implication was there: *and nothing more.*

"Larry Zipoli," I said, but her hand had already stopped in the thin Z section. She pulled out his folder and laid it on top of the others. Her hand stayed there, flat and protective on top of the folder.

"I just don't like this, sheriff," she said.

"I don't either."

"Larry was a *good* man, Bill. A good man. And Marilyn is just a doll. They don't deserve this."

"I appreciate your sympathy, Bea." I slipped the thick folder out from under her hand.

"That shouldn't leave this office."

I reached across to her desk and picked up the warrant and handed it to her. "You'll find a paragraph in there that talks about taking into custody all pertinent materials and documents, blah, blah, blah. I'll make sure it all comes back to you in one piece. Would you like a receipt?"

She took a few seconds to decide whether or not to huff. "No…I don't think that's necessary. I hope you have what you want now."

"Me too. If not, we'll be back. Thanks, Bea." I turned to thank Tony, but he'd disappeared into his office and closed the door behind him.

Despite sounding like a soft-spined schmoo, Tony Pino had not been unaware that there was a problem with Larry Zipoli. He'd reprimanded Larry Zipoli formally five years before for the first time, including a letter in his file that forbade possession of open alcoholic containers at any time on or in county property or county vehicles. It appeared that incident had followed a citizen's complaint that Larry had been slow to move his machine out of the way so the motorist could pass.

I had no intention of sitting in the car, pouring through the file while the hot sun baked us through the county car's untinted glass, but a quick look was enough to satisfy my immediate curiosity.

"We go through this one word at a time at our leisure," I explained to Estelle, who had made no comment after we left the Highway Department offices. "I don't know what I'm looking for, and I don't know if there's anything in this file that might help. It's a slow, plodding process." I grinned. "Not like the movies. We spread it all out on the table and comb through. I'll welcome any flashes of inspiration or intuition."

She didn't respond to that, and I glanced over at her as we left the county bone yard. "We're going to do that eventually, but my next stop is over at Jim Raught's. I want to see if there's any mention of a complaint involving him in Larry's folder." She made no comment, but at least I earned a nod out of her.

"So tell me what you think," I prompted. "You've hiked around in the hot sun, helped collect garbage, sat in the corner of an office for an hour and listened to some good folks worrying about protecting themselves…that's about as good as it gets in this line of work."

"People's motives are interesting," the young lady said carefully, but her smile was warm.

"Yes, they are." I wondered if we would have had to bother with a warrant if I had let this new kid talk to Bea or Tony first.

Chapter Thirteen

I glanced without much interest at Jim Raught's front yard as I walked by, then paused for a second look, taking in details that hadn't been apparent during my earlier visit. The collection of cacti was impressive enough that no one would take shortcuts across his yard. The plants were content and well fed, the beavertails flush and fat, the spines on the cholla long and lethal. Near the door, Raught had several species that I'd never seen growing wild in Posadas County—surely visitors from much farther south.

The house itself was brick with window frames painted turquoise to high-light the red in the bricks. The off-white metal roof was a neat cap, avoiding the maintenance that the roasting sun demanded from composite shingles. A hail storm must have sounded interesting.

I had given Estelle Reyes a sketchy background briefing that included Marilyn Zipoli's complaints, and the young lady was doing a good job inventorying the property as we approached. The general character of the street first, then eyes roaming over Jim Raught's neat but spiny yard, assessing and absorbing. When she'd read her forensic text book, she'd paid attention to the paragraph that suggested general to specific as a *modus operandi*. Think the big picture, then go microscopic.

"I haven't actually *met* Mr. Raught formally," I explained as we strolled up the front walk. "I would recognize him if I saw him—he usually attends County Commission meetings. Maybe he always does. I don't know. On the rare occasions that I've attended, Mr. Raught has been there, too. I remember him addressing the commission once after Sheriff Salcido made a report. I don't remember what the issue was, if any. So, that's what I know, and it ain't much."

Estelle nodded and fell back a step when I approached the front door. *J. T. Raught.* Nice script letters in Mexican tile, mounted in a hardwood frame screwed to the cross beam of the front storm door with brass screws. Simple yet elegant, a cut above the usual wooden sign with stick-on letters from the hardware store. Jim Raught's place didn't look as if it had suffered much wear and tear associated with a houseful of active kids— no toys scattered out in the yard, no tears in the screen door or windows, no smudgy handprints on the painted wood trim.

She stood to one side, watching first the side window and then the door itself. I heard footsteps inside, and a voice said loudly, "Just a second!" The three words sounded friendly enough.

Eventually the door knob turned and the door opened, creating enough suction that the screen door pumped inward a bit. The house was as tightly sealed as it appeared.

Jim Raught peered out at me, his steel-gray hair wet and disheveled. He carried a towel in one hand, and when he had donned a t-shirt, he'd been wet enough that the shirt had blotched. His neatly creased khaki shorts were water-spotted as well.

"Well, hello there." He cranked a corner of the towel into his left ear, opened his mouth wide, and when he was sure his Eustachian tubes were equalized, he shook his head hard, the sort of thing a movie starlet might do to settle her hair. It didn't do much good.

"How's the esteemed undersheriff this fine morning?" He grinned at that, a nice smile that lit up his pleasant features. Probably going on sixty-five, maybe a little older, he was a fine-looking senior citizen—fit, lightly tanned skin that somehow had avoided those nasty age spots that give us away, pleasant strong features, and a melodic voice just on the upside of baritone.

"I hope we didn't catch you in the middle of something," I said.

He made a face. "Just a cold shower, undersheriff. The nice thing about showers is that they're easily interrupted." He mimed turning off a water valve, then squiggled the other ear with the towel, peering at Estelle. "And who might *you* be?"

"Estelle Reyes," my companion said, and let it go at that.

"Well, Estelle Reyes, I'm Jim Raught. My pleasure." The screen door remained between us and a handshake. He looked back at me. "This is about yesterday, I take it?"

"Yes, sir. Do you have a few minutes?"

"Of course I do. How about if you come inside out of the hot sun." He snapped the lock button on the heavy screen and swung it open. "I happen to have some world class ice tea. May I tempt you?" Holding the storm door with one hand, he shook my hand with the other, a damp, cool grip.

"You may indeed," I replied promptly. He raised an eyebrow at Estelle, who evidently had more self-discipline than I did. She accepted the handshake, but not the offer of tea.

"No, thank you, sir."

"You're sure? You don't know what you're missing. Traces of mint, just a hint of rock sugar, sun brewed. Thin shaved ice that brings the glass to a proper sweat." He laughed, a deep, pleasant burble. "Listen to me."

He waved a hand toward the living room, off to the left. "Take a seat wherever. I'll just be a moment."

I didn't take a seat, as attractive as the heavy wood and leather furniture was. Instead, I ambled after Raught, which took only a couple of steps before I was standing in the kitchen archway, the living room behind my back. I watched as he selected two tall amber-colored glasses from the upper cabinet to the right of the fridge. Nice cabinets, too, the clear-pine doors and framework a soft honey—custom, not off the shelf from a box store. Mexican floral designs curled on the doors and around the window frames, hand done by someone with obvious talent.

"Really a terrible thing," Raught said when the ice maker was finished with its automated crushing. He glanced back at me. "Next door, I mean. Hell of a thing."

"Yes indeed."

"Are you making progress?" He set the glass he was holding down on the tiled counter and held up a hand. "I know...I know. I don't get to ask about an ongoing investigation." He shot me that warm grin again. "Well, I can *ask*. That's about as far as it goes."

"As it happens, we are making some progress," I said. "Some."

"Well, that's good." The ice snapped and popped as the brilliantly clear tea flowed over it, and with his left hand, Raught reached out and selected a small spray of mint from a colander by the sink. "Ah...perfect."

I accepted the glass and congratulated myself on accepting bribes so easily. After all, the perfect glass of iced tea is to be cherished. He watched as I took a tentative sip.

"Need sugar?"

"No, sir. This is perfect." I watched as he fixed his own, and then he gestured toward the living room, where Estelle waited. She was standing in front of the fireplace, looking at a spectacular triple *retablo* displayed over the heavily carved mantle. One saint stood in each panel, but the background behind them flowed from one panel to the next, a floral garden of tendrils and blossoms and unlikely birds, all executed in powerful, vibrant colors.

"*El Jardin do los Tres Santos,*" Estelle said.

"Easy for you to say." I stepped onto the tiled hearth for a closer look. I was no fan or patron of religious art, but even I could see that this piece was exquisite. Each *retablo*—each saint in his garden background—was eighteen inches tall and a foot wide, the entire triptych framed as a single work of art, touched here and there with what appeared to be gold inlay.

"San Mateo." She indicated the figure on the left, whose expression suggested that he was stepping on something sharp.

"San Juan in the middle, and," she leaned forward a bit, cocking her head. "San Ignacio." The other two saints didn't look especially content, either.

"Now, I'm impressed," Raught said.

I stepped off the hearth onto the saltillo tile of the living room floor, watching where I put my feet and keeping a tight grasp on the sweating tea glass. The floor tile was polished to resemble old leather, a deep rich brown touched with a scatter of finely woven rugs. Stepping through Jim Raught's front door was like stepping into the heart of downtown Mexico, from the tile floors to the nichos in the walls and spread of spectacular artwork both secular and religious, right up to the hand-adzed ceiling beams.

"Quite a collection," I said.

"Perhaps beyond a passion," Raught laughed. "Closer to obsession."

"You've lived in Mexico?"

"Two years," he said. "I worked for Honda in Ohio for a lot of years, and then did a gig down in Mexico for them, setting up one of the new parts plants. That job didn't last long enough by any means, but I make frequent trips. Just whenever I can." He grinned. "Which, now that I'm retired, is whenever I please."

I turned a slow, full circle, taking in the Mexican sanctuary. "I gotta ask. How did Posadas reach out and grab you?"

Raught laughed. "Ever lived through an Ohio winter?"

"Can't say as I have."

"I thought about retiring to Mexico, but you know, when you get used to the infrastructure this country enjoys, and then you look at theirs…some things are hard to give up." He turned to Estelle. "You probably know what I mean. You could be courting a job with the *federales,* but you chose the esteemed Posadas County Sheriff's Department instead."

"Yes, sir."

He regarded her for a moment over the top of his glass. "Not long in this country, am I right?"

Estelle took her time. "Long enough to feel at home, sir."

"Green card or naturalized?" The question was blunt, but offered with such off-hand, non-judgmental curiosity that I let it go, wondering how Estelle Reyes would react.

"I don't think that my citizenship status is germane at the moment." She said it without bark or umbrage, just a gentle statement of fact. Raught's left hand fluttered up to his chest, as if his heart might be considering a little fibrillation.

"No, no," he said, holding out a reassuring hand. "I don't mean to pry, young lady. I just get so curious about this world and what wags it. That's all. I mean no offense. Here thirty miles south of us, we have that line in the sand to make our lives interesting. I meant no offense."

"None taken, sir."

"But look," Raught said, "I'm sure you didn't come here to talk about my life at Marysville, or to be grilled by me about what's new at the Sheriff's Department." He kept talking even as he walked into the kitchen, returning immediately with the glass tea jar. I held out my glass for a refill, he followed with his own, and returned the jug to the kitchen. "What do you need to know?"

I took another long sip of the tea. "As you know, Larry Zipoli was killed yesterday while he was out working on one of the county roads," I said. "At this stage, we're developing a profile of the incident, learning what we can about Mr. Zipoli and his activities leading up to the incident."

"I see." His tone said, "*More, more.*"

"It's standard procedure to talk with neighbors, to talk with whomever we can."

"I understand that. What can I tell you?"

"Actually, as the crow flies, you're only a quarter mile or so from the scene," I said. "Maybe a touch more than that. I'd be interested to know if you heard any gunshots yesterday."

"Gunshots? No, I think not. Fire crackers, yes."

"Fireworks…you're sure?"

"Oh, perfectly sure. One of the kids across the street—" He pointed diagonally toward the north. "He had what sounded like M-80's. Is that what they call 'em? Those firecrackers that are just a bit *too* big for the average kid? *KaBOOM!* He let fly about four of them, and I thought the Sandoval's old dog was going to go into orbit. I don't know what the lad was blowing up, but he seemed to be having a good time."

"That was what time?"

Raught frowned and looked at the immaculate tile under his bare feet. His face suddenly brightened. "That had to be just around noon or so. Maybe a little before. I happened to glance out the window—I was curious about what gangster was practicing to blow up the bank, you know. Larry Zipoli's truck came around the corner just about then, and the kid took off. Don't know why Zipoli would care about fire crackers, but the kid evidently thought he would."

I paused a moment, sifting through some mental files about who lived where before I came up with a name. "The Arnett youngster, no doubt." Mo Arnett was one of the Posadas Jaguars benchsitters. I cruised the village often enough to have seen him trudging home from school, megaton backpack sagging his pudgy shoulders.

"Indeed. I certainly don't want to get anyone in trouble for a few firecrackers."

"Not likely. So…Larry Zipoli came home for lunch *yesterday?*"

Raught nodded. "Well, maybe not to eat lunch. I heard him drive off just a couple of minutes later. Marilyn wasn't home, so maybe he just had to pick something up. He was only here for a couple of minutes."

"You're here all day most of the time?"

"Well, more or less. This is my own private Eden, you know. I've seen the rest of the world. Now I'm ready to be a hermit, Undersheriff."

"Marilyn Zipoli often comes home for lunch?"

"I wouldn't say *often*. Once in a while. Once in a while one of them, once in a while both. You know," and he sipped his tea. "I really don't make a point of monitoring their habits." He frowned and played with the sprig of mint on the edge of his glass, then, as if the thought that had wandered into his mind was inappropriate, shook his head quickly.

"In the past few days, did you have occasion to talk with Mr. Zipoli?"

"No, I haven't."

"No neighborly chats, no property line disputes, nothing like that? No noisy children? No issues of any kind?"

Raught's eyes narrowed a little with amusement. "You sound as if you've heard something, Undersheriff." He set his glass on an end table with great care, then clasped his hands between his knees. "The last time I actually spoke to Larry Zipoli was…was." He shrugged. "Was sometime. I would be making something up if I tried to pinpoint a time. This is one of those interesting neighborhoods where everybody keeps pretty much to themselves, Undersheriff. We don't do community barbecues. I've never been in Zipoli's home, or the Sandoval's across the street, or in Mrs. Fernandez's next door the other way, or the Arnetts'. And they haven't been in here." He sawed his hands back and forth. "Separate lives, so to speak."

"I know exactly how that works," I said. I would have been hard pressed to remember the last time someone had stepped across the threshold of my old adobe on the south side of town. "A quiet neighborhood where everybody minds his own business. Still, Mr. Raught, we hear things." I slipped two fingers into my pocket and drew out the little business card wallet. "Do you remember what the discussion was about?"

"Actually, I do. Larry stuck one of those ugly little plastic fences in his front yard—a boundary marker, I suppose. In my usual tactless fashion, I told him it was the ugliest thing I could imagine, and that we could probably work out something more artistic." He shrugged helplessly. "He didn't like that."

"And that's as far as it went?"

"Well…I suppose not."

"Which means what?"

"Not only was the fence ugly, he didn't install it properly. The first wind gust grabbed it, and there you go. The next day,

I found a piece in the middle of one of the cactus beds. I tossed it back in his yard."

"You had words over that?"

"No. Apparently they got rid of it."

"You didn't throw it away?"

"Now why would I do that? I tossed the one piece—what, they're about six feet long? I tossed it back into their yard."

"This was recently?"

"No. Several days ago, I guess."

I handed a business card to him. "If you happen to think of anything else, give me a call. I'd appreciate it."

"I can't imagine thinking of *what,* Undersheriff. Sure enough, sound carries easily. Last night was pretty grim. You know, I enjoy swimming. But I couldn't last night. Marilyn Zipoli was in a way, let me tell you. My God, this must be hard for her. I crawled back into my cave so I didn't have to listen…just heart wrenching."

"And during those evening swims, when both Marilyn and Larry were home, you didn't hear any ruckus of any kind in the past few days?"

"No." He looked sideways, maybe a trifle embarrassed. "You know, I moved in here about seven years ago. I hadn't been here for more than a *month* when Marilyn Zipoli made a forward pass. At *me,* if you can imagine. I sure as hell don't want to encourage that sort of thing, so maybe I take to an extreme this keeping to myself business."

He stood up and beckoned. "Let me show you something." He included Estelle in the invitation. We followed Raught through the house, out into the back yard—a place to take the breath away. The yard, perhaps a hundred feet wide by eighty feet deep, was an incredible accomplishment, but this time, from the oriental corner of the world. Totally out of place in Posadas, New Mexico, the plantings heavily favored sculptured oriental evergreens, dense bushes the like of which I hadn't seen since my brief military posting in Korea. And rocks, rocks everywhere, gorgeous sandstone things with *more* exotic plants tucked in crannies.

One long back wall was home to half a dozen grape vines, their tendrils winding and entwining, fruit already heavy by late summer.

The central feature of the yard was a redwood gazebo complete with high-end teak garden furniture, looking out across one of those narrow lap pools that jet a raging river so that you either exercise wildly to stay afloat or end up smashed against the downstream end, a drowned rat. Jim Raught's physique said that he swam miles and miles upstream.

"An amazing place," I said. "Congratulations."

"I have photos of what it looked like when I first moved in," he replied. "Lots and lots of desert weeds."

"That's what I specialize in," I laughed. "You know, it's amazing. I can drive up the street and never know this little paradise is here."

"And that's the whole point, I suppose," Raught said. "I can enjoy old Mexico inside, and then duck outside for a touch of Japan." He grinned "Visited there half a dozen times for Honda." He nodded toward the east, toward Zipolis. "They took out a scruffy old elm that died a good number of years ago. I was using some of the dead limbs that spanned across the fence as part of the artwork, so I'll have to work on that a bit now. It looks kind of bare."

It didn't to me, but then again, bare to me was clean gravel or sand. The wall separating the neighbors was a full six feet, concrete block plastered adobe color, supporting redwood lattice panels. There was so much vegetation on Raught's side I could spot the wall only as a shadow in a few places. Interesting. I would have been able to stand in the Zipolis back yard and not be able to see anything of Jim Raught's place...certainly not enough to be able to see a purported marijuana plant growing up his back porch.

I turned in place. Like everything else, the back porch was designed to blend with the entire motif. Very Architectural

Digesty. Or Better Japanese Gardens. Lots of redwood, stout vertical lines that somehow managed to look airy and light, latticework that wasn't just the cheap stapled together stuff from the home improvement center.

And sure enough, a hale and hearty Virginia Creeper grew up the side of the house, softening the abrupt corner, a transition of sorts from one dimension to another. A Virginia Creeper might be mistaken for marijuana, but only by one of those numb folks who have blown or snorted enough stuff to addle their brains.

I pivoted and looked back across the yard. How the hell did Larry Zipoli find a spot to peer into this enchanted place? Did he have a small step ladder on far side? Is that how he got his jollies? Well, he'd really have to work at it. Or had Marilyn been spying on her buff neighbor as Raught took his laps?

Raught spread his arms wide to encompass the little paradise. "This is my hobby, Undersheriff. If Posadas ever runs out of water, I suppose it'll go back to desert." He looked wistful. "It'll be Mexico outside, as well as in."

"You miss Japan?"

"Well…sure, in some ways. But it's a very small island, Undersheriff. Very small. With *lots* of people." He took a deep breath. "You know what's nice? When I step out here at two in the morning and slip into the water, the only sounds are the coyotes out on the mesa. All the televisions are off, the kids are asleep, most of the dogs have shut up. Have you ever stood on a Tokyo street at two in the morning? Ye Gods." He grinned benignly at Estelle, like a father proud of his daughter. "Rural Mexico, or the big metro areas? I would guess rural. Am I right?"

"Tres Santos."

His head cocked to one side as if he'd been poked, but then he nodded in familiarity. "Well, it's hard to be more rural than *that.* You would know what I'm talking about, then. The deep, deep quiet." He took another deep breath. "Gotta have it. My drug of choice."

He patted the redwood railing of the gazebo, brow furrowing. "I don't know what else I can tell you folks. The Zipolis kept to themselves, and as far as I'm concerned, lived a nice quiet life. Nice kids. No loud pets. Some weekend outings that appeared to involve just about every youngster in the neighborhood. The Butte is one of their favorite spots, as I understand it. They invited me to go along once or twice, but I declined. Noisy ski boats, party-hearty teenagers, hot sun, hot sand, and murky Rio Grande water aren't my idea of paradise, as you might assume by visiting here. Crowds don't light my fires, Undersheriff. But around here? I can't imagine who got crosswise with Larry Zipoli."

"Did he have an alcohol problem?" The blunt question prompted a raised eye brow.

"That would be entirely none of my business, Undersheriff. Obvious it's *your* business, but not mine." He held out both hands, palms up. "Nothing I can tell you there. If I did, I'd just be making something up." He looked at first me and then Estelle expectantly. As far as he was concerned, our conversation was over.

I offered my hand, and his grip was firm and brief. He made a point of shaking Estelle's hand, too.

"I hope you enjoy your new adventure," he said to her. A logical guess must have been what it was, but I was impressed never the less.

"Thank you, sir," Ms. Reyes replied quietly.

Raught followed us back through the Mexican living room, and then out to the front yard deep in the Sonoran desert. If a kid lost his tricycle in there, it'd be gone forever—maybe the kid, too. "Folks, if there's anything else you need from me, don't hesitate. I'm here most of the time."

I thanked him, and moseyed out to the sidewalk and 310. Raught's front door closed out the sun and heat. Estelle Reyes read my hesitation correctly, and was in no hurry to slip into the car. I walked east a few feet, and looked at the small flower garden that edged the property boundaries. I didn't see any stake holes that would indicate the presence of a little decorative fence, but those were so easily obliterated…and would have been by someone with a fetish for making every aspect of his yard just so.

Chapter Fourteen

"So." I settled into the almost comfortable seat of the Crown Victoria. Its idle became a bit ragged as I kicked in the air conditioner. "We have about a million conversations like our little chat with Jim Raught for every stand-off with an armed and dangerous bank robber." I looked down the quiet street. Two blocks away, a trio of little kids—maybe still too young to be excited about school looming on the immediate horizon—played with a lawn sprinkler. I could hear the kids' chirps and screams.

I looked across at Estelle. "And what do you think about all this?"

She didn't answer immediately, a characteristic reservation I was coming to accept as ingrained. "I can't imagine Mr. Raught killing Mr. Zipoli out on a hot, dusty road with a lucky shot," she said eventually. "It's too messy, too inconsistent with the way he controls his universe."

"His universe," I repeated. "I would be willing to bet that if we opened his garage, we'd find a neat little imported car, something on the luxurious side, like a BMW or Porsche. It would be spotless, waxed, perfect. The garage would be a showplace, with even the paint arranged on the shelf alphabetically by color."

"Something very like that, sir." She watched the neighborhood slide by. "I picture James Raught as coldly calculating, should the need arise. I don't picture him doing something as risky, as *untidy*, as what happened to Mr. Zipoli. I don't picture him flying off the handle in a screaming rage over a little garden fence."

"Believe it or not, people have been killed over less."

"*Sin duda,*" she said, and just as quickly translated. "Without a doubt. But I would imagine that if the need arose, Mr. Raught would use some kind of distilled venom drawn from the pectoral fins of an oriental rock fish."

I laughed loudly. "Maybe that's what happened to his wife."

"I didn't see any family photos on display in that house."

"Nope. And I didn't ask. I *assumed,* based on what Marilyn Zipoli said. And that's not very smart. We'll have the chance to correct that." The dash clock read 10:03. As we eased out on Grande Avenue, I reached out and slid the mike off the hook. Force of habit brought it toward me before I remembered, and handed it to the young lady. "I need to know what Bob Torrez has on his plate right now." She took the mike, thought for five seconds, and then keyed it.

"Three oh eight, three ten. Ten twenty?"

The airwaves simmered in the August sunshine as the seconds ticked by. I couldn't remember listing off deputies and their car numbers to my ride-along, but it's something she had had the opportunity to pick up during the course of the morning's activities. I glanced at her, impressed. She was gazing out the window, perhaps counting the appropriate number of seconds before repeating the message.

"Three ten, PCS." Dispatch was paying attention.

"PCS, go ahead."

"Three ten, be advised that three oh eight is ten-six with MacInerny."

I nodded to assure Estelle that I understood, but before she could acknowledge, Torrez's voice, so quiet he might have been inside a church, came on the air.

"Three ten, three oh eight. I'll be here for a bit."

"Three ten's ETA is twelve minutes," I prompted, and Estelle relayed the message.

"Ten four." Torrez's response was entirely unexcited.

Anyone who had spent significant time listening to the Sheriff's Department radio chatter had no doubt been able to crack our sophisticated code. Dale and Perry MacInerny, of MacInerny Sand and Gravel, owned a gravel pit that was unused at the moment, as the family outfit was occupied up at the Consolidated Mine, part of the reclamation effort. While they were thus occupied and their big pit east of town was quiet, we used a portion of it as a shooting range.

I turned south on Grande, heading south-east on State 61. In five miles, we would reach the dirt road that took off straight to the east, a road packed hard by constant heavy truck traffic. The gravel pit turn-off was still two miles ahead when we rounded a gentle curve and saw the late model Cadillac pulled off the side of the road. Well, half pulled off. The ass end of the big barge draped out so that the back bumper hung over the white line.

We hadn't had any rain lately, so the shoulders were nice firm sand, and the back tires were still on asphalt. After turning on all of my own emergency lights, I idled 310 up close behind the Caddy.

"Go ahead." I nodded toward the radio mike. How many times had this young lady called in a plate? Maybe never? She'd had the opportunity to hear others do it during the past few hours riding with me. But radios find the tongled tangs among the best of us, and rookies are sure fodder for tales from the air waves.

"PCS, three ten," she said, and released the mike key, about as excited as we sound when we say, "Hi, how are you?" to a stranger we meet while passing through the automatic doors at the grocery store.

"Three ten, PCS."

"PCS, ten twenty-eight three-niner-seven Romeo, Alpha, Mike."

"Ten four, three ten. Ten twenty?"

Yes, soon-to-be-officer Reyes. Where the hell are you? The request for a twenty came out clipped and fast enough that I knew Dispatcher Barnes really wanted to add, "Don't make me have to ask, damn it." He would already be typing the plate number into the computer as he spoke.

"Three ten is just beyond mile marker four, State 61."

"Tennnn four, three ten," Barnes drawled. His tone gave me the impression that he'd have taken delight in giving the young lady a hard time had he not known she was right seat with me.

I hadn't even noticed the mile marker post, although I would hope that I knew where I was without it. "Ten six," I prompted, and Estelle relayed the message that the officer would be busy with 397RAM for a few minutes.

"So why did he park half on the roadway?" I asked, in no hurry to get out of the car. I recognized the big sedan, and that in itself was a puzzle, since Jack Newton, with his wrecked knees, bad hip, and bunions, wouldn't have hoofed back into Posadas. Jack wouldn't hoof anywhere.

"I think he's lying across the seat," Estelle said quietly. "I saw his hand as we approached."

I looked across at her with keen interest. "His hand?"

"Yes, sir. As if he were lying across the seat, and raised his arm up in the air for something. Just for an instant."

A sage nod of agreement was the thing for that moment. Hell, I hadn't seen any hand wave at us. Maybe I'd been busy looking for damage as we rolled up, or traffic coming up behind us, or for Jack's body slumped in the thorny weeds along the shoulder. Jack Newton was at least seventy-five, and his body was no longer eighty percent water, or whatever that figure is supposed to be. He was too thin and emaciated for that.

"Three ten, PCS. Be advised that three-niner-seven Romeo Alpha Mike should appear on a 1983 Cadillac, color maroon, registered to a John R. Newton, 41 Third Street, Posadas, New Mexico. Negative wants or warrants."

"Ten four."

"I'll be but a moment," I said. "Stay in the car." Sure enough, Jack Newton was stretched out across the back seat of the Cadillac. The back seat. His keys hung from the ignition, and his wallet appeared to be resting in the center console, along with a pair of sun glasses and a Styrofoam cup. When I opened the passenger side door, the effluvium charged out, thick and sweet with a hint of tangy gut juice.

A 750ml bottle lay on the floor, just a swallow or two left. Normally, Jack Newton kept his drinking inside his modest little mobile home on a quarter lot on Third Street. I'd never arrested him for DWI, and couldn't remember the last time one of the other deputies had.

His wrinkled old face was flat against the Caddy's fancy seat cushion, a trail of spittle running out of the corner of his mouth to stain the fabric.

"Jack, you with us? It's Bill Gastner." I swung the door as far as it would go and ducked inside far enough to be able to put two fingers on the side of his withered old neck. His pulse wasn't paying much attention—a wandering beat just waiting for an excuse to lurch to a halt from the alcohol poisoning. And add a match and his breath would have made a cutting torch. He snuffled and jerked, and for a moment it appeared that he wanted to open his eyes.

A small man, Jack fitted neatly on the seat. Had I left him there, he no doubt would snooze the day away, or perhaps give it all up when some tired portion of his system collapsed. Or a semi might drift over a bit and smack the Caddy into the cacti. In the worst case scenario, Jack might awaken late in the afternoon, disoriented. He'd fumble behind the wheel again to weave his way home—and smack head-on into a station-wagon carrying the eight member Johnson family from Terre Haute, Indiana.

I sighed and glanced back. Ms. Reyes had stayed in the car, but her door was open.

"Oh," Jack groaned, and a hand flopped unerringly toward the bottle.

"We're going to get you out of here, Jack," I said.

"I don't feel so good," he mumbled.

"I'm sure you don't, Jack my friend. But you can't sleep it off here."

"Nicky…"

"Nick will come and pick you up," I said. "Just hang in there, Jack." His long-suffering son managed Posadas Auto Parts, and would be just delighted to break away to tend to his old man. Just delighted. The open bottle of bourbon on the floor, the Caddy skewed on the shoulder, the keys handy in the ignition… all those things sealed old Jack's unhappy fate with this particular stunt. Nick would be doing a *lot* of waiting on this old man.

I hustled back to the car and settled behind the wheel.

"National Drunk Week. It's not my favorite time," I said to Estelle Reyes. "But I guess no time is a good time for Mr. Newton. He's passed out on the back seat, and he's got a pulse that would make a doctor go pale." I keyed the mike.

"PCS, ten fifty-five this location. One adult male. Intoxication poisoning."

"Ten four, three ten."

"And expedite that," I added. "Then call Nick Newton at Posadas Auto Supply and have him make arrangements to fetch the vehicle this location." I saw the hand appear as Jack Newton tried to swim up from his alcoholic bog.

"Ten four, three ten." We were three miles south of town, and it would be a couple of minutes before we had company. I watched a truck approach from behind us, and the driver swung all the way into the far lane to give us lots of room. Even so, his bow-wave rocked us. "We need to get Mr. Newton's car off the highway," I said. "The keys are in it, so as soon as the ambulance picks him up, we'll move it. If we're lucky…if *Jack* is lucky… we won't have long to wait for transport."

Back at the Caddy, I saw the restless, waving hand that said the old man was still trying to keep in touch. Mr. Newton probably weighed maybe a hundred and twenty pounds dripping drunk, and was as fragile as a sack of dishes. Leaning both hands on the Caddy's roof, I chatted with him as if he was perfectly cogent. There would have been a time, I suppose, when I would have hauled his old butt out of the car, slapped the cuffs on him while spreading him over the trunk lid, and then marched him back to the patrol car for the ride back to town. But Jack

Newton didn't have that kind of reserve. We'd wait, and let the tax payers fork out a few extra bucks.

I reached out and checked his neck pulse again, grimacing at the aroma from inside the Caddy. As I straightened up, I heard approaching traffic slow abruptly.

The black and white Chevrolet Impala pulled off the highway and parked directly behind my unit, red lights winking. J.J. Murton got out of his patrol car without so much as a glance toward traffic that might be approaching from behind him. As he walked the length of my county vehicle, his eyes were locked on the passenger in 310. He nodded at Estelle Reyes as he passed.

The old man groaned again, and I eased him upright on the seat so that his head was cradled back. He couldn't hold his mouth shut, and a string of drizzle escaped and ran down his chin.

"Oh, what have I been doing," Jack moaned.

"Just take it easy now," I said. Murton approached hesitantly, not sure if he should grab hold of something or someone.

"Dispatch said you might need an assist?"

I hadn't asked for assistance, and dispatch hadn't put out the call…I would have heard the radio call. Murton had no reason to wander outside the village, either. But his intentions were good, so I didn't bite his head off. "We're just waiting on the ambulance," I said, and about that time I could hear the siren in the distance.

"You want me to transport?"

I wasn't sure that it was possible to educate J.J. Murton, but I made a stab at it. "No. He's old and frail and seems to be suffering a little cardiac distress. The last thing you want is for him to crap out in the back seat of your patrol car."

"Well, you got that right, Sheriff," Murton replied.

"If you'd manage traffic for the ambulance, I'd appreciate it. They're going to want to park right here." I nodded at the southbound lane immediately beside the Cadillac. "You take north, I'll take south."

Murton nodded vigorously, perhaps a little relieved that I wasn't going to go Marine Corps Sergeant on him. "You do the breathalyzer already?"

"No. He's so high he'd probably break the scale. We'll wait for the hospital to stabilize things before the law lands on him with both feet."

"Damn good thing he pulled off the road when he did," Murton observed. "Mighta killed someone."

"True enough. His lucky day." Lucky day or not, Jack's tortured gut gave up just then. He managed to twist sideways just enough that when he tossed his cookies it didn't spray all over the inside of the Cadillac—which meant that most of it was aimed at Murton and me. I danced sideways, damn near knocking Murton ass over teakettle. Then I just had time to dive forward and prevent Jack from collapsing headfirst out of the car.

"Oh, Jeez," Murton bleated, making ineffectual little swipes at his trousers. His face had gone pale. Apparently he was one of those guys whose own stomach starts to gyrate with the permeating aroma of vomit.

The ambulance eased to a stop on the highway, a veritable eruption of colored lights.

I waved Murton away. "Take the highway," I said, and he did so with alacrity.

I'm sure that handling drunks isn't high on an EMT's list of favorite things to do, but these two were too experienced to complain.

"Erratic pulse," I explained to Jesse Tarrantino, and that was all the explanation the EMT needed. He and his partner, Mary-Anne Buckley, packed up old Jack Newton with tender concern, taking half a second to clean his face first with an alcohol wipe before putting on the oxygen, talking to him all the time.

They lifted him out of the back seat as if he were a bundle of feathers, and had an IV going faster than I thought possible.

"I would guess that he consumed most of a 750 of bourbon," I said, and Jesse grimaced. "I don't know what his health issues are, but I think he needs the ride."

"We'll get him all straightened out," Jesse said. He reached down to pat Jack's thin shoulder even as they started to lift the gurney.

MaryAnne Buckley, a heavy-set girl with pleasant features, offered a smile as she passed. "Thank you, sir." She sounded as if she really meant it.

"Lots of fun, huh," I said. In a moment, Jack was all packaged, and the big diesel rescue vehicle eased away, found a wide spot in the road, and U-turned back toward town. I watched J.J. Murton officiously wave the ambulance by, and then he sauntered over toward me.

"He sure as hell stinks." He shook his head in wonder.

"Drunks do that."

He leaned a little closer, and the wash of his powerful aftershave smelled as if he'd walked into a bed of Pacific kelp. He jerked his head toward my car, and he couldn't quite keep the leer off his face. "She ridin' with you all day?"

"I'll know that at the end of the day."

Murton nodded sagely. "New hire?"

"Probably so." I knew that in all likelihood J.J. Murton would have given his left nut to work for us—and just as likely that Sheriff Eduardo Salcido—or I—would shoot him before allowing that to ever happen. 'Thanks for your help, J.J." He looked as if he wanted to say something else, but evidently thought better of it

"Catch you later, sir," he said, and walked back to his patrol cark, rubber-necking the attractive young lady in my county car as he did so.

As I slid into the driver's seat, I grinned at Estelle. "This is a glamorous job, sweetheart." The words were no sooner out than I realized that I had to be a little more circumspect in this new age of correctness, even if she was the grandniece of an old friend. What the hell. Let her sue me for discrimination. The smile of sympathy that I earned *was* entirely sweet, and she was young enough to be one of my daughters.

"*Now,* fates willing, we see what trouble Bobby Torrez has managed to get himself into. Notice how we're able to stick with one thing from start to finish without interruption in this job. You'll get used to being peripatetic."

I started to pull the car into gear and just as quickly reversed the process, grumbling with impatience as I opened the car door. "Give 308 an update. ETA about eight minutes." It took only a moment to start old Jack's Caddy and ease it far off onto the flat of the shoulder, well away from the pavement. I locked it and pocketed the keys.

Back in the car, I took time for a long sigh. "Go ahead and tell dispatch that we're ten-eight and that I have the keys to the disabled vehicle. I'll drop them off at Nick's place on the way back in. Probably an hour or two."

She nodded and did so while I made a quick log entry.

"How will the legal process go with all this?" she asked.

"You mean will Mr. Newton be charged with DWI? That's absolutely what will happen. But first, we take care of *him.* That's the interesting thing about all this. You can chase the worst goddamned felon half way across the state, but when you have him in custody, you then become his guardian. You take *his* goddamn welfare in your hands, regardless of what he might have done, what pain and suffering he might have inflicted on others." I shrugged and put the log book away. "In Mr. Newton's case, we make sure that nothing we do contributes to his physical distress. That's why he ended up in the ambulance and not in the back of my car. When he's sober, when the docs are sure that he's not going to drop dead in front of us...well, *then* we take up the legal issues."

"They'll revoke his license?"

I snorted with derision. "What the *courts* do, my friend, is another matter. My cynical guess is that Jack Newton will be behind the wheel of his car and making a stop at the liquor store so fast it makes our heads spin. That's the way the system works."

The car tires chirped as I pulled back out on the pavement. "What kind of doc is your fiancé studying for?"

Ms. Reyes didn't correct my word choice. "Vascular surgery, sir."

"Ah. Well, that's good. Lots of plugged pipes around, my own included. He—what's his name?"

Her natural reticence prompted a slight hesitation. "Francis Guzman." Her delightful accent put the emphasis on the final syllable.

"Does young Doctor Guzman want to stay in the southwest?"

"Yes, sir."

"You said he has relatives in Mexico?"

"Yes. His entire family. Down in Veracruz."

"No intentions of going back, though?"

"I don't think so. He wants a small town practice, somewhere near the border."

"Well, that's us. You've met Alan Perrone yet?"

"I have."

"Maybe he can link up with Alan. Who knows what lies ahead." I turned the county car off the pavement, following a dirt road pounded to brick by heavy trucks. The sign for McInerny Sand and Gravel Products had been painted sometime in the past decade, and served as well as a sporting target for shooters too lazy to get out of their cars.

Another mile, and the chain-link fence with razor wire on top hove into view. The gate was closed but unlocked, and before I had a chance to unbuckle, Ms. Reyes had bounded out of the car and done the honors. Just as she slid back into the car, the gate closed behind us, a loud gunshot peeled out.

"Genius at work," I said. "There's a set of ear plugs in the center console under all my shit. Dig 'em out." Around a massive pile of gravel and a fleet of decrepit ore trailers, I saw Bob Torrez's Bronco in one of the alcoves, the quarry banks towering twenty feet over his head. No bullets were going to escape from this place.

Deputy Torrez hefted a single-bit axe and aligned the blade with the top of a large chunk of pine about a foot long and as much in diameter. He then picked up a three pound hammer. He didn't glance up at us, but concentrated on the task at hand—a most methodical, craftsman-like way of splitting firewood.

The yule log resisted a few blows, but then crackled and yawned, and the deputy pried it open.

"Ah," he said with satisfaction.

"We have a regular bullet trap back at the office," I said.

"Didn't want to wait," Torrez said, and stood up. He held half of the twelve inch diameter log in one hand, and offered it to me. "This is just an experiment, anyways." The splitting process had been dead-on accurate, and I reached out and took the rifle bullet that had been jarred loose from the wood fibers. The nose was mushroomed nicely, the jacket and lead core deforming all the way back to the cannalure. That wasn't what I found interesting.

I adjusted my bifocals and peered more closely. The brass jacket toward the rear of the slug was bright and shiny. Not a trace of rifling marked the slug.

Chapter Fifteen

"So how did you do this?" I asked, and passed the bullet to Estelle Reyes. It seemed a natural enough thing to do. The deputy beckoned toward the back of his Bronco. The tail gate was open, and the mess inside was typical Bob Torrez. No doubt—well, *maybe*—he knew where everything was, but his organization was a private affair.

Two rifle cases rested close at hand, and he opened the nearest one and retrieved what anyone who had watched television westerns or had even a faint interest in firearms would instantly recognize as a Winchester lever action carbine. He jacked the lever open and handed the weapon to me. It appeared to be pristine, without a scratch on the wood or the bluing.

"All right," I said, and peered at the legend on the barrel. "A .32 Winchester Special." I nodded at the bullet that Estelle still held. "And that?"

Torrez opened a tool box full of gun stuff—patches, oil, screw drivers, rods and hammers, even a stopwatch. He opened an ammo box and held the cartridge out to me.

"Thirty-thirty," I read off the headstamp, and then made the connection. "You're telling me that you fired this in… that?" I looked with suspicion at the .32 Winchester, warm in my hands. "You're telling me that the .30-30 will chamber just fine in the .32?"

"Sure enough."

"And that's what you shot into the log."

"Yes, sir."

"Huh." I rolled the cartridge between my fingers. "From how far away?"

"A yard, maybe."

"Okay."

"You want to follow with me on this?" His tone said that I didn't have much choice. Excited in his own quiet way, Torrez was sniffing hard on a trail.

"Sure."

He retrieved a roll of qualifying targets and peeled one off. I'd probably shot half a thousand of the B-27 human silhouette qualifying targets in my career. Featuring a full-sized human head and torso on a 24 x 45 inch sheet of paper, it was an absurdly easy target to hit, mainly because it didn't shoot back.

"I have a stand," Torrez said.

"I hope so, 'cause *I* ain't going to hold the target for you," I quipped. We watched him staple the target on the light frame, supported by a pair of steel feet. Satisfied, he walked the target stand out perhaps fifty feet, in front of the sloping back wall of the gravel pit.

"Ears?" he asked.

I nodded at Estelle, and she dug out the set of ear plugs. The deputy handed me a set of the department's fancy schmancy ear muffs.

"I just get one?" I said as Torrez rummaged and then handed me a single cartridge. I glanced at the head stamp and saw that it was a .32 Winchester Special, the right ammo for the right gun.

"Go ahead, sir," he said.

"Range is hot," I mumbled and stepped forward, glancing at my two companions to make sure ears were covered. A quick glance along the rim of the quarry assured me that no youngsters had sneaked up to watch. The cartridge slipped into the chamber effortlessly and I closed the lever. Fifty feet isn't much of a challenge with a rifle, so I aimed for the head. What the hell. Why not grandstand when given the chance. The light rifle's sights were clear, the stock comfortable.

The report was a muted bark, the recoil a good stout punch. With the sun as it was, even my sorry eyes could see the light streaming through the hole right in the center of the felon's forehead.

"Nice rifle," I said. "I should own this."

"George Payton can make that happen, sir." Torrez referred to one of my oldest friends, owner of the Posadas Gunnery.

"He let you walk out with this?"

"Sure." He handed me another cartridge. "Try it again."

Not the dullest tool in the box, I saw that the cartridge had come from another box, a .30-30. From neck down, it looked exactly like a .32 Winchester Special. The only difference was from the neck up—a slightly smaller bullet at .308 rather than .323.

"Well, this is going to be fun," I said, and suddenly the rifle felt awkward. A lifetime of gun handling, without a single incident of jamming the wrong cartridge into a weapon, made the whole process just feel *wrong*.

I glanced back at Torrez and Estelle Reyes, both of whom waited expectantly.

Loaded and locked, a thoughtful exhale, just the right sight picture, my index finger *so* smoothly increasing pressure on the heavy trigger. The rifle bellowed again, bucked against my shoulder, and I saw dust fly.

The felon stood in the sun, a single hole in his forehead. I lowered the rifle and peered more closely.

"Must have gone through the same hole," I laughed. "The old Robin Hood splitting the arrow trick."

"Do it again," Torrez said, and this time he handed me five rounds. "Just shoot until you have a group."

One after another, I fed the five rounds into the carbine's magazine. And one after another I let fly at the target. With the first shot, a hole appeared near the bottom edge of the human figure, right under the belt buckle. The second and third kicked dust, no where near the damn paper. Round four blew off the felon's right ear, and the fifth and final shot exploded a chunk of target frame just above the steel feet. "Oops," I said, and lowered the carbine, its barrel warm. "Well, *that's* impressive shooting," I said. "Did you do any better?"

He beckoned and I took the opportunity to stow the rifle in the case. The target he unrolled showed a tight group of five rounds, slightly above and to the right of the X in the center chest. Torrez came as close to a laugh as he ever did. "This five shot group is with the correct ammo, sir. The other group is with the .30-30 stuff."

"I see no other group."

He reached across and pointed at the hole right beside the lower right staple that secured the target. "I made one." He took his ballpoint pen out of his shirt pocket. "And this is what's interesting." He lightly circled the irregular hole.

"It's keyholing," I said. "At what, only fifty feet?"

"Yes, sir."

I turned away and walked out to the target stand. The hole through the forehead was true, but the other two were skewed, indicating that the bullet had wandered and slapped through the paper obliquely, damn near sideways…reminiscent of how the single slug had smacked Larry Zipoli just above the eyebrow.

"That's half of it, sir," Torrez prompted as he saw me settle into a quiet moment of reflection. He pointed at a cardboard box. "I ran both guns through my chronograph." I knew that the little gadgets used two sensors triggered by the shadow of the bullet as it sped by. Simple stuff for the electronic chips inside the machine to compute velocity in feet per second.

The deputy pulled a small notebook out of his pocket. "The .30-30 cartridges, fired from a standard .30-30 Winchester," and he jerked his chin toward the second rifle case, "worked out to an average velocity of 2270 feet per second. That's an average. They were pretty darn consistent."

"And so?" I relaxed back against the narrow shelf of the bumper.

"When I fired the .30 caliber ammo in the .32…" He held out the notebook. "Take a look at these." The velocity of each of five rounds was recorded in Torrez's block printing. The shots ranged wildly, the slowest at 1712 feet per second, the fastest hitting 1925.

"So," I said, "not only is the damn thing grossly inaccurate, not only does it throw bullets sideways, but it's also slowed way down. Not fast enough to pass through both the windshield and Larry Zipoli's skull. What did you get for penetration in that block of firewood? About five inches?"

"Give or take."

I let all that digest for a moment. I had to admit that the little butterflies of excitement were starting to flutter in my gut.

"That could be how it happened, sir."

"Yes, it could. You have the right ballistics to match the penetration, you've got the yaw of a sideways strike, you've duplicated the lack of rifling marks." I grinned up at him. "Nice work, Deputy. Only one thing's wrong with this whole scenario."

"Yup." Torrez pocketed the notebook. "With the wrong ammo in the gun, we can't hit shit."

"How many rounds did you fire at the target?"

"Same as you, sir. Five rounds. One hit. The rest just splattered. The one hit was dumb luck."

"Not much of a batting average." I regarded the gravel at my feet. "I've got this image of the gunman walking toward Larry Zipoli. He's carrying the rifle, and Larry puts the grader into neutral. What, we're going to have a little show and tell? Someone's bought a new rifle and he's going to show it to Larry? But then the guy stops some X number of feet in front of the grader and throws up to his shoulder. Larry's got time maybe to think, 'Oh, shit,' and the round comes through the windshield and nails him in the forehead."

"Maybe." The tone of his voice said that he didn't believe it for a second.

"So the statistics say, Roberto. But are you going to go assassinating with a rifle that hits the target only one time out of five? And that's at only fifty goddamn feet. I don't think so. I mean, *none* through the center. *None* where we aimed. Only a moron would try that. Hell, big and pugnacious as Larry Zipoli might be, he'd have had time to jump down and bury a lug wrench in the guy's head." I shrugged.

"And we even found the lug wrench this morning," Torrez reminded me.

I looked across at Estelle. "Remember what I said about puzzle parts, young lady?" She nodded. "We're ready to hear ideas."

Again, she took her time. "It would be helpful to know how many shots people heard."

I laughed and stood up. "You and me both. And suppose that two reliable witnesses...and isn't *that* a goddamn oxymoron—suppose that two people heard a total of *ten* shots. Are we supposed to think that Larry Zipoli was so stupid that he just sat there smoking his cigar as thirty caliber bullets went zinging all around his cab? And not one of those bullets even grazes the grader...not a goddamn one...until the fatal shot hits dead center?" I shook my head in frustration.

"Except that it's possible that the *first* shot just happened to be the successful one," Estelle Reyes said quietly. She didn't amplify the comment. I could figure out the one-shot scenario for myself, but I didn't believe it for a second. I guess I out-waited her, since eventually she added a statement of simple statistical fact.

"The first shot can just as easily be the one bulls-eye as the fourth, the seventh, or the tenth...or the hundredth."

"Yup," Bob Torrez said. After all his work, of course he wanted that to be true.

"Pretty goddamn undependable way to kill somebody," I said.

Chapter Sixteen

My brain was a whirl of disconnected thoughts on the short ride back into town. A tractor-trailer rode up on our back bumper for a while, and I realized that I was putting along, not much more than thirty-five miles an hour in a sixty-five zone. After a few seconds of that, the trucker grew impatient and thundered by, cop car or not. His plates were Texan, his mud flaps big, waving promos for Tyler Trucking in Kansas, his trailer hauling something under the banner of Merlin Foods out of Denver, the cab door bearing the logo for Dutchess Trucking headquartered in Phoenix. That potpourri of places might have made me curious if I hadn't been distracted with other issues.

He blew through the first speed zone on the outskirts of Posadas, then braked hard to catch the westbound ramp for the Interstate, where he'd be someone else's problem.

I was about to comment that with all the curious geography displayed on his truck, the driver might have been more careful about basic things like signaling his turns so he didn't attract undue attention. Had I just been cruising, I would have stopped him for a chat.

My radio chirped even as other concerns rumbled through my brain. Larry Zipoli's personnel records remained untouched. I needed a quiet corner to settle in and catch up on my reading. I didn't need another interruption.

Without being told, Estelle Reyes palmed the mike like a veteran. "PCS, three ten."

"Three ten, contact Dr. Perrone at Posadas General reference your previous stop," the dispatcher said. Estelle glanced at me and I nodded.

"Ten four, PCS," she said and hung up the mike.

"We'll swing by the hospital on the way," I said. "We need to do that anyway."

I saw one of her shapely black eyebrows drift upward and knew what she must be thinking...*on the way where?*

"I want to chat with Marilyn Zipoli again. A couple of things keep nagging me. Something doesn't quite fit, and I don't know what it is." I paid attention to traffic for a moment—elderly Theodora Baca's huge sedan pulling across my lane to enter the Posadas Inn's parking lot. Perhaps it was their iced tea that beckoned her—the only recipe on their little restaurant's menu that wasn't close to poisonous.

"And before we do that, I need to spend some time with Zipoli's records. It'll be interesting to see what Marilyn has to say about all that. I mean, how could she not know that Larry had a drinking problem. No way she wouldn't know. Not someone as sharp as she is."

We passed through the intersection with Bustos, then turned east on the little spur of North Pershing to the Posadas General Hospital parking lot. I parked in one of the slots marked *Emergency Vehicles Only*, and saw the white Dodge van with the Posadas Auto Parts logo on its broad flank. The keys to old man Newton's Caddy were still in my pocket.

"Unfinished business," I said. "When young Nick went to work this morning, he thought this was going to be a normal day. And then it went to shit."

Despite its interesting collision of aromas, the hospital could be a comfortable spot on a hot summer's day, and my pace slowed a little to enjoy the ambiance. The sign requested that all visitors report to the receptionist out by the lobby, but she didn't need to deal with us. The emergency room was empty, and I headed down past radiology toward the new ICU wing—"wing" a grand term for two new rooms and an exterior doorway that led to a tiny sun-dappled courtyard.

Nick Newton sat outside on one of the courtyard's concrete benches in a shady corner dominated by a fountain based on the *Zia* symbol. The water pump wasn't quite up to the task, and the creation managed to look more like a bad leak than an arty fountain. Smoke wafted up from Newton's cigarette. His forearms rested on his knees, his head hanging as if he wasn't sure about his stomach's ability to hold down lunch.

He looked up as we entered the courtyard.

"Sheriff." He shook my hand without much enthusiasm.

"This is Estelle Reyes," I said, and Nick Newton's gaze flickered to the young lady with little interest. "How is your father?"

"Not so good. He's across the hall in the ICU. What the hell happened anyway? You stopped him out on 61?"

"Actually, Nick, I didn't stop him. He was parked with the ass end of his car hanging out in the traffic lane. He was semi-conscious in the back seat."

He muttered an oath. "He probably would just sleep it off if you left him alone."

"Maybe he would have. Or a semi might have rear-ended him, or he might have come to and fumbled and stumbled his way into an accident. What's Dr. Perrone say?" I glanced back through the double doors, but couldn't see beyond the tinted glass across the hall.

Nick waved a hand impatiently. "Some mumbo-jumbo about his heart and liver. Hell, there's never been anything wrong with him that a little common sense wouldn't cure." It sounded more like a father talking about a wayward son than vice versa. "So what's the deal? I mean when he gets out of here. Is he in trouble with you guys? You charge him with DWI, or what?"

"I haven't charged him with anything yet, Jack."

"*Yet*," he snorted. "You know, all he's got is Medicare, sheriff. You have any idea how much this is going to cost?"

He's got you, I wanted to mention, but that wasn't any of my business. I managed to look suitably sympathetic.

Nick lit another cigarette. "I don't know. I just don't know. Take his car keys, I guess. And *then* what."

"Speaking of which," I said, and dug out the key ring. "The car is pulled well off the highway and locked. You can pick it up any time. The sooner the better. It's a tempting target out there."

He looked at the collection of keys, leafing them one by one around the ring.

"So what's the deal, then?"

"The deal is that right now, you take care of your dad," I said. "When he's clear-headed enough that we can talk with him, then we'll see." I knew damn well what the District Attorney's attitude would be. "Make sure he doesn't get behind the wheel, Nick. Keep those keys out of his reach until we straighten all this out."

"'Preciate it, sheriff." He nodded first at me and then at Estelle Reyes. "You're with the department now?"

She nodded. "Yes, sir."

"And what's this deal about Larry Zipoli?" Nick asked me. "I'm hearing all these weird stories. Like he got shot somehow and fell right out of the county grader he was driving?"

"That's one version I hadn't heard," I replied. "We're investigating, Nick."

"Christ, ain't that a kick. You think suicide maybe?"

"As I said, we're checking out everything. Did you have the chance to talk with Larry recently?"

Nick took a deep drag on the cigarette. "I saw him yesterday, as a matter of fact. He come into the store to pick up an ignition switch." He frowned at the memory. "He was pretty steamed about the latest county snafu. You probably run into it. About no open purchase orders? You need somethin' simple—hell even a new double-A battery or a new screwdriver—you got to have it approved by the department supervisor? In *writing?*"

"I think that order is one of the things that the sheriff threw in the trash," I laughed. "But it'll catch up with us, I'm sure. So all in all, Larry seemed all right to you?"

"Well, sure. I mean, how's a guy to know, after all," Nick said. "I don't think he felt all that hot, if you ask me. His back was giving him hell." He was tactful enough not to say any more about that—I was fully aware that my own ample gut, although not in the same class as Larry Zipoli's gigantic, pendulous belly, put plenty of strain on my spine. "How's Marilyn takin' it all?"

I shrugged noncommittally and Nick seemed satisfied with that. He nodded toward the door, and I turned to see Dr. Alan Perrone. The physician held the door open for us. Nick Newton took the opportunity to light up again, in no hurry to go back inside to the atmosphere of chemicals, clicking machines, and hushed voices.

"How are you doing, Bill?" the physician asked as we stepped inside. I suppose he had reason to ask, since he'd been in charge of my innards for quite a while and knew where all the leaks, creaks, and odd noises lurked.

"I'm dandy," I replied. "This is Estelle Reyes."

Perrone grinned at her. "We're acquainted." He didn't elaborate but shook her hand, adding a genteel bow of the head at the same time, then turned back to me. "I left a message for you with dispatch. Look, it's highly unlikely that Jack Newton is going to pull through. I mean, miracles do occasionally happen, but I would be surprised this time."

"You told Nick?"

"Yes. I don't think he was in the mood to hear it. I understand that you were the one who stopped the old man?"

"No. He was pulled off the road, passed out on the back seat. Ms. Reyes and I happened by."

"Ah. Well lucky for him. The *back* seat, you say. That's interesting." Perrone heaved a deep sigh. "Look, his liver is shot, he has an enlarged spleen, and fluid is collecting in his lungs. The old heart just can't manage it all. Half a bottle of alcohol wasn't just what he needed, although at this stage of the game, I don't suppose it matters much. Anyway, I wanted to touch bases with you, since the whole thing entered the system as a complaint from your department."

And who the hell knew how the "system" that Perrone referred to would have reacted had we cuffed and transferred Jack Newton to the back of J.J. Murton's patrol car, and then had the old man expire hours later in the drunk tank. His son could have had a field day at our expense.

"Keep me posted, doctor. I do need to know when he's out of your custody."

Perrone's smile was pained. "I don't often think of my relationship with patients as 'custody', Sheriff." He nodded again to Estelle. "My best wishes to your fiancé, young lady."

Now, how the hell did *he* know Estelle Reyes' boyfriend who wasn't even out of school yet? Perrone's web of informants was damn near as effective as mine—maybe better.

I stood in the sun outside the cool chemical world of the hospital for a moment, leaning against the comfortable fender of the county car. Off to the north, the buttress of Cat Mesa heaved up against a scattering of boiling cumulus, and at that moment I would have welcomed an hour or so sitting in the shade of a piñon, listening to the jays discuss the quality of the current pine nut crop.

"I'm ready for great thoughts." I looked over at Estelle.

"If I had them, I'd share them with you, sir."

"The first thing I want is an endless pot of fresh coffee," I said. "Then we'll see what the personnel files have to say."

Chapter Seventeen

If the young lady wanted to be a cop, she would have to learn to like coffee. That seemed only logical to me. There was something about that first snort of caffeinated fumes that jolted the brain into gear—especially if amplified with a little nicotine. I sighed with regret.

Estelle Reyes settled into the chair across from my desk without so much as a drink of water, completely comfortable, completely at ease. My over-weight, over-caffeined, over-nicotined, under-exercised fifty-eight-year-old body could have used some of her discipline.

I passed paperwork across to her as I read through Larry Zipoli's file, keeping my thoughts to myself. A half hour later, I tossed the folder toward her so she had someplace to put the stack of papers that she'd accumulated on her lap.

"None of this leaves the room," I said. "Ever. Not to anyone." Her nod was almost imperceptible, and I suppose I had no reason to be concerned. The day I'd spent with her hadn't featured much more conversation than if I'd been driving around Posadas County by myself.

I folded my hands across my gut and relaxed back, closing my eyes. "So here is a man with a dozen infractions," and I paused and looked at the note pad on my blotter. "Eleven separate incidents over the course of fifteen years." I held up my hand and ticked fingers. "He wrecks a county dump truck and that's put down to a 'shifting load' by the investigating sheriff's deputy—who died of cancer a dozen years ago, by the way. You got to wonder how a few cubic yards of gravel *shifts* suddenly, but there you go. But Larry earns a letter of reprimand from Everett Carlyle, who was superintendent then, a year before Tony Pino got the job." I closed my eyes again, seeing the parade of paper work as it drew a picture of an employee who might be a wizard with machines when sober, but a genuine liability when soused.

"Tony Pino is covering his own ass," I said. "That's what it amounts to. Ten of those incidents were on his watch. He sticks a letter in the file, but beyond that, what does he do? Does he turned Zipoli over to the county manager? To personnel? To any goddamn body? No."

"Is he required to, sir?"

"I don't know the answer to that," I said. "Common sense would say 'yes.' But Tony never does. Larry Zipoli wrecks a truck, a couple of years later parks his county pickup in a bar ditch, ruins a taxpayer's culvert with the road grader, is reported by a concerned citizen for drinking beer during his lunch hour—and we could fairly ask how many incidents there might have been that didn't earn the goddamn letter from Pino."

"Why didn't he fire Zipoli long ago, sir?"

"Good question. The reason might be as simple as Tony Pino's will power. Firing a long-time employee for something like this is damn hard to do…at least for some folks it is. 'Well, he's learned his lesson.' That sort of thing. Except alcoholics *don't* learn any lessons until tragedy forces the necessity. Zipoli could work magic with a road grader or back hoe even when half sauced. It could be as simple as that. Pino is short-handed, and can't afford to lose an experienced employee. So he turns his back on all this stuff." I waved a hand at the stack of papers. "No major catastrophes in the record—just a potpourri of little incidents."

"It's interesting that Mr. Pino continues to document all the incidents even though he's disinclined to do anything further," Estelle said. I enjoyed hearing the way her melodic Mexican accent touched the syllables. It made an awkward word like "disinclined" sound damn poetic. "I would think that puts considerable liability on him."

"One would think so," I agreed. "A lawyer would have a field day with all this during a trial for civil damages." I stretched back. "You know what's interesting? We don't have a damn thing on Larry Zipoli in our department files. Not a damn thing. That's how lucky he's been—or how lucky the unsuspecting public has been." I straightened the folder. "Going on twenty years on the job, and not a single ticket or violation. That's a talent all by itself."

For a long moment, I remained silent, staring at the front cover of Larry Zipoli's personnel folder. "I need to talk with Marilyn Zipoli again." I rested my hand on the folder as if it might levitate off the desk. "This is the kind…" I stopped when Eduardo Salcido appeared in my office doorway. His expression was one of resignation.

"I'm tired of talking to people who don't know shit," he said, and the mild profanity surprised me. He leaned against the door jamb, his hands thrust in his pockets. "I got *two*—two people who agree on what they heard or saw."

"That's better than none, I suppose."

"How can you shoot a high-powered rifle in a quiet neighborhood and not have half the town hear it?" A bemused grin lit his features. "I tell you, *jefito*—we got to let people know when something is going to happen…tell them when they're supposed to pay attention, so they can be good witnesses." His frustration was understandable, of course. Nothing is more infuriating to investigators than witness behavior—those witnesses whose senses are simply turned off as they cruise through life, or those on the opposite end of the scale, who invent juicy tidbits in their eagerness to be of help to the police. And every shade in between.

"Who are the two?"

"You know the Deckers?"

"Sure." Hugh and Tody Decker were active members in the Posadas County Sheriff's Posse, a group of civilians who liked to dress up and ride horses in parades. The posse hadn't chased a killer on the lam since the 1890s, but they were handy for managing traffic control during the Posadas County Fair.

"Tody says that her husband had just gone outside for something, I don't know what. He came back in the house complaining about the shooting."

"The shooting?" I asked incredulously. "You mean he claims he saw it?"

"No. He told his wife he heard a shot." He nodded at my expression of skepticism. "Well, that's what he said. He looked off that way, and claims that he saw a person walking toward a car parked right at the intersection of Highland and Hutton."

The sheriff wagged an index finger. "Tody says she remembers exactly when that was, because Hugh had a dentist's appointment in Deming, and she was worried about him being late. She looked at the kitchen clock while Hugh was fussing around trying to find his binoculars."

"He found them, I hope."

Salcido held out both hands in disappointment. "He saw the person get into his car. That's all. He decided it was someone taking a shot at a coyote or snake or something."

"He saw the gun?"

Salcido shook his head.

"Make and model of car?"

"A small sedan, he said it was."

"That's a goddamn big help."

"Well," Salcido sighed, "it's something, you know. It rules out all the pickup trucks with the gun racks in the back window. That's half the town, *Jefito.*"

"What time was all this? What did Tody say?"

"She said it was just after two. If she's right, that cuts down the window of opportunity."

"Huh." I rested my chin on my fist. "But Hugh never saw the gun? That's what he says?"

"That's what he says."

"Did Tody hear the gunshot as well?"

"She says she did. A single *crack*. That's how she described it."

I rose from my chair and walked across the small office to the two framed maps on the wall—one of Posadas County, the other the village itself. "The Deckers live right about there." I jabbed a finger at the intersection of Sixth and Hutton.

"On the west side," Salcido added.

"Right. He goes outside, looks to the north," and I stroked a finger across the short distance toward Highland. "If the shooter was about here…" Both Salcido and Estelle Reyes let me muse with the map without interrupting my chain of thought.

"No one else saw a thing?"

Salcido hooked one of the military surplus folding chairs with his toe, turned it around and sat down with his arms folded across the back. He drew a small note book out of his shirt pocket and used his thumb to push through the pages. "There are a total…" he lingered on that word… "a *total* of seven people who heard shots. And the number varies, *Jefito*. From one to a whole string. Some heard a loud boom, like maybe a shotgun. Some heard what they assumed were firecrackers." He looked up at me, the crow's tracks at the corners of his eyes crinkling. "Now if you hear *one* rifle shot, how do you translate that into a *whole string*?"

"Inventive," I said. "I don't know. I need to talk with Hugh. He saw the road grader working?"

Salcido shook his head. "Tody didn't know. Hugh wasn't home when I stopped by." He made a spinning motion with one hand. "He has this rototiller that he's trying to make work. He's in and out all the time."

"I'd like to talk with him," I said, and turned to Estelle. "You ready to roll?"

"Yes, sir."

Salcido laughed gently. "Quite a job interview you're having today." He regarded Estelle critically. "Did he find a vest that fits you?" This was one of those occasions where it's *do as I say, not as I do,* since in all the years I'd known him, I'd never seen

Eduardo Salcido wear a protective vest. Maybe it was vanity—a vest would plump out his already blocky shape and make him resemble a gourd—or just the discomfort of the thing, stiff and hot under the shirt. Those were my excuses, anyway.

In this case, any idiot could see that someone with Estelle Reyes' body shape wasn't going to enjoy the unyielding discomfort of the Kevlar body armor.

"I think we're going to have to order for you," I said.

"Sooner rather than later," Salcido added gently. "She needs to observe in dispatch in the meantime." He pushed himself up from the chair.

"That's one of the goals for this afternoon," I said. "I'll come up with a schedule for her."

"This afternoon," Salcido chuckled. I could see it for myself, that inexorable advancement of the clock when Larry Zipoli's corpse now lay on a slab at Salazar's Funeral Home while his killer kept a sharp eye over his shoulder. The passage of time was the killer's ally.

"You be careful out there," Salcido said as he read my mind. "You're going out to see the Deckers?"

I nodded. "And then I have a few more questions I want to ask Marilyn Zipoli." Settling on the corner of my desk, I patted the personnel folder. "Pino had every reason over the years to can Zipoli's ass. There are a dozen letters of reprimand in his records. And no action taken other than that, Eduardo. Just letters."

That earned the familiar "oh well" expression from the sheriff.

"It's almost as if Pino was afraid of him. Or at least afraid to face up to him and straighten things out."

"Lots of folks find that hard to do," Salcido mused. "It's just easier to let it go. As long as nothing happens, you know. I don't think it's an issue of fear, *Jefito.*" And I was willing to bet that the sheriff knew exactly what the issue was. I was also willing to bet that Larry Zipoli's drinking on the job was not the motive for his murder.

"I would hope not. Tony Pino certainly would have the county attorney on his side if he wanted to make an issue of personnel matters. And by the way, I talked with Jim Raught earlier. *He's* an interesting fellow."

"He is that," Salcido agreed. "Keeps to himself. That's what *I* know about him."

"We're stumbling around in the dark," I said. "I find it hard to believe that Larry Zipoli's drinking on the job had anything to do with his death, and I don't believe that a little argument with a neighbor did."

"There's something that we're missing, then," Salcido said, echoing my own thoughts exactly.

Chapter Eighteen

Hugh Decker was glad to see us. Just in case we might decide to pass him by, he dropped the rag he'd been using to polish the engine housing of his rototiller—something I would certainly want to do should I own one—and made for the curb to head us off. The Deckers owned the cleanest, most meticulously maintained tiller in Posadas County. Exactly why blow sand needed tilling was a mystery to me.

I parked in the shade of an enormous cottonwood whose roots had to be sucking water from five neighboring yards.

"Keep a straight face," I ordered.

Hugh waddled across to us, his thin shorts more like cut-off pajama bottoms and threatened by gravity at each step. His sleeveless T-shirt was inadequate for its task, and hairy pink flesh bulged in some unattractive places. Enormous flat feet splayed his sandals.

"Tody said you were by," he rumbled in greeting, and he mopped his forehead with a mammoth wrist.

"The sheriff was," I corrected. And who knew. With Hugh's damaged eye-sight, he might well have mistaken Eduardo for me, or vice versa.

"Well, lemme show you something," he said, and then stopped short as he caught sight of Estelle Reyes. "And who are you, young lady?"

"This is Estelle Reyes," I said. "New with the department."

Hugh thrust out a huge paw, and Estelle's hand disappeared for several pumps. "Good to make your acquaintance," he said. "Where do you hail from?"

"Posadas, sir."

Hugh looked puzzled. "Do I know your folks?"

"I would doubt it, sir." A safe enough assumption, since Estelle herself didn't know her folks.

"What's to show us?" I prompted, and Hugh nodded vigorously and beckoned for us to follow him around to the back of the house. The place was tidy. The garage door was open to reveal a late-model Ford LTD with Sheriff's Posse license plates and two whip antennas sprouting from the trunk. In the back yard, half a dozen dwarf fruit trees were making a valiant effort.

"Oh, hello!" Tody warbled, sticking her head out the back door. "Hugh, remember that you have a doctor's appointment this afternoon."

He waved a dismissive hand. "Goddamn doctors, excuse my French. They're never satisfied." He grinned at me and punched his glasses back up the slope of his fleshy nose. "I expect you've had your share." Not waiting for an answer, he walked to the back block wall and pointed. Over the four-foot barrier, the open prairie stretched uninterrupted to the north. A view of the streets was impossible, the vegetation in the back lots just high enough to block the road surfaces and bar ditches from view, but I could just make out the stop sign at the intersection of Hutton and Highland—and only then because I knew it was there.

"Car parked right at the intersection," Hugh said, affecting an officious, clipped delivery. He swept his arm to the east. "Now, the road grader would have been right about over there. The guy I saw was walking *back* to the car."

"Holding something?"

"I couldn't swear to it, sheriff."

I leaned an elbow on the top row of blocks. "How far do you suppose that is, from here to the stop sign at the intersection."

"Two hundred yards, maybe three."

"Two or three football fields," I translated. "Close enough that if the wind was right, you could hear voices."

"Didn't, though."

"Could you hear the road grader?"

"Not when it was just idling. When he was actually grading, I could catch snatches of it."

"You heard a gun shot?"

Hugh held up a single finger. "One. Just one. At three minutes after two." He held up his left wrist to display the impressive, multi-functioned watch. Again, he adopted the officious tone. "I hear a shot, I look at the clock."

"We're glad that you do," I said. "When you heard that one shot, where were you?"

He turned and pointed across the yard at the chaise lounge. "Right there, letting lunch settle."

"So you heard it—at three minutes after two—and got up to see what's what."

"That's exactly what I did. Every once in a while, you know, somebody gets itchy on the trigger just a little bit too close to dwellings. And I tell you…" He stepped closer and lowered his voice. "Old war time thing—you hear a whole mess of shooting, not to worry. You hear *one* shot, it's time to worry. Somebody bought the farm."

"Exactly," I agreed, and Hugh nodded sagely. "You heard the shot, checked the time, and walked over to the fence?"

"Yes. And I saw one figure—I would guess it to be a man—walking back to a car by the intersection."

"The grader was sitting still at the time?"

"It was."

"Running?"

"I couldn't swear that it was."

"Couldn't see an operator moving around?"

"Hell, I couldn't even tell if there was anyone on board. My eyes aren't what they used to be."

"Ain't that the truth. As the man—woman, whoever—walked back to the vehicle, how would you describe his pace, Hugh. Hustling, trotting, sprinting?"

"Walking. As best I could see. Just walking along."

"And carrying..."

"Nothing that I could see. 'Course, if he was right-handed and held the rifle in that hand, it'd be hidden mostly by his body."

"True enough. You watched him get into the vehicle?"

"Well, sort of. I mean, it was a small car, you know. We got a lot of weeds and desert shit between here and there. Couldn't see much."

"Heard one door slam?"

"Didn't hear *any* door slam," Hugh corrected. "Too damn far for that."

"You watched him drive off?"

"I did. He turned around in the intersection and drove back down Hutton into town."

"Speeding? Big dust plume?"

"Nope. Just normal." He looked askance at me. "You thinkin' that wasn't the shooter, then?"

"I don't know."

"Well, like I told Eduardo, I don't see how it *couldn't* be. And that says to me that you've got one cool cucumber."

I turned around and regarded the house. "Where was Tody, then?"

"At the kitchen sink, right inside." He pointed. "See that window that's a little higher than the others? That's right over the counter top beside the sink."

"She has a minute?"

"'Course she does."

Tody Decker looked like the nurse that she'd been for thirty years, neat and cool in shorts and polo shirt, fighting the battle of the waistline with a moderate paunch, legs a little heavy from years spent working on both the hospital and the high school's unyielding concrete floors.

"This is just the most awful thing," she announced after pumping our hands. "I mean in our little neighborhood. I told Sheriff Salcido the same thing. I just can't believe it." She leaned forward and stared at Estelle Reyes as if maybe she'd missed her at the handshake. "My word, *you're* a gorgeous young lady," she blurted. "And we know each other somehow."

"Mrs. Decker, you were our school nurse when I was at the high school." Estelle offered a warm smile.

"Well, that hasn't been so long. My word, my old memory is *so* full of holes."

"Tody," I said, not wanting to settle into a round of reminiscence, "after you heard the shot, you looked outside?"

She pointed back at the kitchen. "I heard the shot and then Hugh got up and I heard him say, 'Now what the…are they shooting at?" She smiled demurely and glanced affectionately at her husband. "I won't tell you what he *actually* said. And then I looked out across the field. I remember that there was a road grader out there. That's all I saw."

"No car, no one walking?"

"Sheriff, I'm not saying there wasn't someone. It's just that the screen over the window makes it hard. I think that I saw the car, but it was a little thing."

"A compact, maybe?"

"No, I mean at that distance, it's just too far to see clearly."

"Well, *I* saw the Goddamn car and the guy walking back toward it."

I gazed off to the north, trying to form the image. "So…and this is important, Hugh." With one arm, I pointed at the spot where the car would have been parked. With the other, I made an angle back toward the road grader. "I want to know how far the man was from the car at the very first instant you saw him. How far did he have to walk to make it back to the car?"

Hugh frowned, the expression producing a rumple of his massive forehead. He turned, and held up his own arms, mimicking my geometry. "My guess…my guess is that he was maybe a hundred feet from the car when I caught sight of him. And he was already walking back toward it." He swept one arm to the east and sighted along it. "So right about there. Yeah, that would be about right."

I wondered what he could see through his thick and not entirely clean glasses.

"See there's a good-sized group of tumble weeds just past the little dip there?"

The "tumble weeds" could have been long horn steers as far as Hugh was concerned. "So he actually had to walk a little bit to reach the car. I mean, as much as twenty or thirty paces."

"That's a fact. I had time, thinkin' about it now, to watch him walk for a little bit. I was wondering if he was the one who had fired the shot, and at what. See, the road grader was way the hell over there," and he nodded eastward.

"And you couldn't hear it or see the operator."

"That's right. You know, sheriff, it don't sit just real good with me knowing that Larry Zipoli was just lying out there, shot dead, while I sat here drinking iced tea." He shook his head. "What time was he found?"

"He'd been there a while," I offered. "But that's the way these things go. Someone might have driven by and never noticed him."

"Could have, I suppose." He slid one huge arm around his wife's shoulders, waiting for the next question. But I didn't have any. The Decker's portrait of events did nothing to alter the chilling image of the scenario that I imagined. Step out of the car, maybe walk as much as a hundred feet or so, take aim and fire at a defenseless man. And then stroll away.

Chapter Nineteen

"You see the problem?" I asked Estelle Reyes. She'd been taking a slew of notes in a small spiral notebook. I didn't wait for her to read my mind. "On the one hand, Hugh Decker hears one shot, and then sees a man…a person…walking back to a parked car." I held up an index finger. "If we take him to be the shooter, then he's as cold and calculating as they come. No rush, no fuss. He shoots *once,* doesn't check his target, and saunters away. Once he's back in the car, he doesn't even drive down Highland to see what damage he's done." I shrugged. "Now tell me how that jibes with Bobby Torrez's experiments."

"Do you trust what Mr. Decker claims to have seen, sir?"

"Now that's a question." I swung the car onto Hutton, and we approached the intersection with Highland at a sedate ten miles an hour. For a moment, neither of us said anything, both of us looking off to the east along Highland, trying to imagine circumstances on that quiet day. To the south, I could see the back of the Deckers' house, squat and secure among a half dozen other homes, the big cottonwood dominating their double lot.

"Let me put it this way. Were I a defense attorney, I'd be ecstatic to see Hugh Decker as a prosecution witness."

I stopped the car, hunching forward over the steering wheel, linking the fingers of both hands. "Most of the time, something breaks for us. Some insignificant little thing pops its head up. If we stay receptive, maybe we see it." I shrugged philosophically.

"We're coming at this thing from several directions. We keep at it, and something will break."

The young lady was an easy passenger to talk with—well, *to*. She didn't blab pointless theories, or push an opinion based on nothing. She appeared to absorb, but who knew when she would factor everything out.

"I tell you what," I said, looking for a rise of some sort—a comment, an impression, something from behind those inscrutable black eyes that had been watching us all day. "Tell me what happened, and you'll make detective sergeant by tomorrow morning."

She smiled, a delightful expression that I'd learned she held in deep reserve. The smile didn't stay long enough, but faded as her eyebrows lowered in a frown. "I wouldn't know where to start."

I laughed. "Well, hell. *I* can come up with that much, Deputy Reyes. In case you *hadn't* noticed, you're going to end up clocking a dozen hours today if we don't knock off. That happens once in a great while—normally, our days are full of astounding boredom, and you'll have to develop your own system for not going insane." I pulled the car into reverse. "But in a case like this, we make hay when we can. The longer we dawdle around, the greater the odds that the killer will walk."

The LTD idled down Hutton…all right, *dawdled*. As far as I was concerned, the day was yet young. "I have a stop or two I want to make, but I'll be happy to drop you off at the office. "It's your call."

"You had mentioned coming up with a schedule for me…"

"Ah. I did. And of course, I haven't gotten around to it. *Mañana* isn't our motto for nothing, my friend." I watched Hutton creep by. "I'd like you to start out working dispatch days for a couple of shifts. You need to see how the organization works—or doesn't, as the case may be. Meet people, learn were the copier is, how the files work, how we manage the lock-up… just the whole ball of wax. It's not rocket science, and it's not a huge department." I shrugged. "So in about twenty minutes, you'll know all there is to know. Then we'll swing you around to four to midnight, and then midnight to eight. And then you'll dispatch, probably midnight to eight, with Ernie Wheeler looking over your shoulder. Fair enough?"

"Yes, sir."

"So what are your druthers for the rest of the afternoon? I plan to keep slugging along, and you're welcome to stick it out to the bitter end. I want to talk with the widow again, and then I'll need to refuel. That's the schedule."

"I'm fine, sir. I have a couple of things I need to get done before five, but otherwise, I'd like to see where all this is heading."

I grinned. "So would I. Let's sit down with Marilyn Zipoli for a few minutes." I rested my hand on the personnel folder. "She's not going to be thrilled with any of this."

"It's hard to imagine that she wouldn't know about the drinking."

"Yes, it is."

Marilyn Zipoli did not want to talk with us. We were a hundred yards away when she saw our county car approaching, and she wrapped up her sidewalk conversation with another woman abruptly. I saw her reach out a hand and touch her companion on the elbow, turning at the same time toward the house as if she'd heard the telephone imperative. The other woman said something, and morphed Marilyn's touch into a hug. They separated, and the woman crossed the street, heading for the house where the old yellow dog guarded the patch of shade by the garage. With an economy of motion, the woman stooped to pick up something on the sidewalk that offended her sense of tidiness, and entered the house.

Marilyn knew we were approaching—you can't disguise the squat, light-bar-decorated profile of a police car, after all. And she could guess that we might want to talk with her. Perhaps she even had a question or two for me. But by the time we pulled to a stop at the curb, it seemed to me that the neighborhood had drawn in on itself.

If Marilyn Zipoli was in no mood to deal with us, I can't say that I blamed her. We'd chosen a good time—the curb was empty of visitors, with only the daughter's little Honda in the driveway. Marilyn would be starting to feel the weight of the day, and the dreaded approach of another sleepless night. We wouldn't help bringing in all the dirt.

There were a myriad ways to offend her by being overly blunt or pushy—or even obsequious. We didn't need a hostile widow on our hands.

I fussed with junk that littered my rolling office, and Estelle Reyes waited patiently. Her hand had strayed to the door handle, though, so I knew that she *waited*.

"I'd be willing to bet a week's pay that Marilyn Zipoli is inside, watching us through the curtains," I said. "We want her to think that there's something specific that we're after, something specific that you and I have to discuss before getting out of the car. If there's some reason, however obscure, that our visit might put her on edge, we want to add to that tension." I smiled at my companion. "However innocently. What we *don't* want is for her to clam up. We don't want to make an enemy of her. That doesn't accomplish anything. All it does is force us to take the long way around."

"And if she's completely innocent of any…" Estelle paused, searching for just the right word. "Any nefarious designs, then what?"

I chuckled. "'Nefarious designs.' I like that. Estelle, I have every confidence that Marilyn Zipoli had nothing to do with her husband's death. She didn't hire a hit man. If we'd found him slumped in his truck, a bullet behind the ear, maybe I'd think differently. But not this way. So, that being the case…if everything in the Zipoli household is pure as the driven snow…then she *isn't* watching us through the curtains at this very moment. She has no reason to avoid us."

With a vigorous pull on the steering wheel to help launch my mass upward off the soft seat and out of the car, I almost beat Ms. Reyes to the pavement. Almost. As I rounded the left front fender to join her on the sidewalk, I said, "You see?"

"Yes, sir. She was at the south window."

"Unless their dog or cat stroked the curtain."

"A dog would be barking, and a cat wouldn't bother."

I smiled at that. As I stepped up onto the first concrete riser leading to the front door, I glanced at Estelle again. "It's nice to be as welcome as the plague." I pushed the doorbell, and heard no response from inside. I pushed it again, and that time heard footsteps padding toward us.

Marilyn opened the door wide, the way folks used to living in a small town do, rather than to the narrow little security slit favored by folks nervous about home invasions.

"Oh, hi." She didn't add the *it's only you* that her tone implied. She gave the screen door a push, enough for me to grab it easily. "Come on in. I'm right in the middle..." She waved a loose-wristed hand by way of explanation.

"We're sorry to intrude," I said.

"You do what you have to do, sheriff. I'm trying to deal with things that I just don't understand. Even my know-it-all neighbor across the street isn't of any help." She left us in the foyer with that comment, and walked off toward the living room. We could follow or not—who the hell cared. I carried Larry Zipoli's personnel folder, his records now encapsulated in one of our large manila envelopes—the legal kind with the string that winds around the closure doohickey. I hadn't decided how much to show Marilyn, if any.

Marilyn walked across to the impressive dining room table, a six place set now pressed into service as a cluttered office. She picked up a sheaf of papers and held them out to me. Even without my glasses, I could read the black, somber logo for Salazar and Sons—the oldest and now only funeral home in Posadas. The page included an unctuous paragraph or two about final parting, perfect ceremony, and lots of talk about "loved ones" and "memories." Nowhere did it discuss the ramifications of having a hole blown through one's skull while sitting in a county road grader. The rest of the document appeared to be a contract and listing of services—the cold, hard economics of death.

"In the first place," she said, and I could hear the anger in her tone, "I've known Art Salazar for *years,* sheriff. Just years. I've handled his accounts at the bank, I've…well, you know. This is a small town. Everybody knows everybody."

She picked up another folded document and handed it to me. *Estate Planning and You* was printed on top. The glossy folder was a handy guide for preplanning the disposition of a body when its owner had no further use for it. Inside were several photos meant, I suppose, to be soothing. I was just too cynical to understand why photos of wooded glades with muted sunlight should make me feel better about shuffling off my mortal coil, or the coils of those nearest and dearest to me. Would my relatives head for the forest to chat with my ghost?

"Maybe you can explain this to me," the widow said. "If you looked at that, what would you think?"

I skimmed the preplanning folder. Simple questions with blanks thoughtfully provided for the answers outlined the mortal one's wishes, and in this case, it appeared that Larry Zipoli himself had filled in the answers. "None," his blocky printing declared under *preferred religious services.* Cremation was checked, with ashes returned to family. Perhaps Larry wanted to rest on the mantle, his ashes participating in family gatherings. After *preferred memorial service,* he'd printed, a bit impatiently, "Whatever they want to do. Won't matter to me." What a touching sentiment.

The third page of the folder nailed the nitty-gritty of this process. *Total cost estimated for services* had prompted a flurry of printing, the ball-point pen pressed hard into the heavy stock paper. "Cremation services, $679.95." He'd checked the cost somewhere, or been offered a bid. Below that, he'd added, just in case there might be some shade of misunderstanding in the grief of the moment, "No other services. No embalming. No good wood to be wasted. No broke ground. No memorial stone no where."

No, no, no. Larry Zipoli made it clear—when it's over, it's over. He had signed and dated it two years previously. End of argument.

"He knew his mind," I said gently. That didn't assuage Marilyn much. The anger still flamed her cheeks, at the same time simmering the tears that gathered. "You were okay with this?"

"We talked about it back when Larry was facing his gall-bladder surgery, sheriff. We both knew how dangerous that can be, especially with someone whose weight is over the top like Larry's was. I got the forms from Mr. Salazar, and managed to corral Larry long enough so he would jot down some answers." She held up a hand. "I know, I know. It's hard to take something like this seriously. And I can tell you right up front, *Larry* didn't take it very seriously. But the whole process gave him the willies. I know that. The last thing he wanted was to be *embalmed*, Sheriff. He thought that was one of the most repulsive, pointless things."

"Most of us don't," I said. "Take it seriously, I mean. We leave relatives to clean up after us."

"And what a mess." She waved the document. "And none of this makes it any easier. Look, I know that he didn't want anything to do with a church service, or with any of that stuff. That's what he called it. *'Any of that stuff.'* Larry wanted his ashes scattered," she said. "You know what all this reminds me of?"

"What's that?"

"Remember that article about the car dealership up north? They'd take the customer's car keys—the keys for the trade in? They'd take them and not return them until the sale was made. Make the customer a captive audience. That's what this reminds me of. They have my husband's…" she paused and shook out a ragged sigh. "They have my husband's body because that's where the hospital sent it."

"I'm sure Art will work with you."

"Yes, he will." The determination in Marilyn's voice was hard. "And that's what I'll do. Larry loved the Butte, so that's where he'll go." She referred to Elephant Butte, the enormous lake that puddled the Rio Grande over by Truth or Consequences.

"Fair enough." I handed the preplan back to her. I noticed that it had been signed by her husband in November two years previous. I've always thought of November as a dark month—an appropriate time of the year for such sober thoughts. Things have to be damn sober to sit down and preplan the end of days.

Marilyn didn't bother wiping away the tears that coursed down her face. I could remember my own grandmother, a spare, hard-limbed old lady, saying to me after my childish blubbering was over and I had subsided into silent, persistent tears, "Billy, your eyes be leakin'." That was the case with Marilyn this time. No heaved sighs, no shaking voice, no huffing as she tried to catch her breath. Just leaking eyes.

Marilyn handed me the letter, the contract thoughtfully prepared by Salazar and Sons. "Now, this is what reminds me of the car dealer, Sheriff."

Cutting to the chase, I flipped to the last page. *Total Services* included an impressive figure well over twelve thousand dollars, including a 10C Sealtite coffin for more than four grand. A plot in Posadas Memorial Park took another chunk, with various other charges tacked on for this and that...even *grave closure* for $645.00. I was sure that Louis Trenton, who operated the backhoe at the cemetery, didn't pocket that.

"Now," Marilyn said again. "You're a detective. You tell me how we get from *this*," and she shook the preplanning folder sharply, "to *that*." She waited expectantly.

"Did you discuss this with Salazars?" None of this was within my province as undersheriff of Posadas County, but if Marilyn churned up enough rage at Art Salazar to shoot *him* through the eyebrow, it would be.

"*Discuss?* No, I didn't discuss it." This time, she sucked in a deep breath. "The body was taken to Salazar's after the PM, sheriff. Directly from the hospital. They asked, and I said, of course. Salazar's. Where else? They're the only game in town. Now, I know that I have to pay for that transportation, and I'm sure I'll be stuck for some outrageous figure that Larry's insurance won't pay. I called Salazar's to make an appointment to talk about arrangements, but Mr. Salazar said it would be easier for him to put together a preliminary package—that's what he called it—and bring it over to the house. I could look through it, and let him know. I mean, what's he doing…testing the waters?"

"Don't people usually have to select a coffin and stuff like that?"

"Oh," and she turned to glare at the table. "There's another brochure about them, too. Anyway, Mr. Salazar came to the house a little while ago and left this for me. Does he really think I'll agree to this?"

"I don't know what he thinks," I said. "As a businessman, I suppose it's to his advantage to encourage some rethinking of the final process."

Marilyn glared at me—well, *through* me—for a moment. Her gaze shifted to regard the silent Estelle Reyes, and what that young lady thought was anyone's guess.

"I want what Larry wanted," Marilyn said softly. "That's all. It has nothing to do with money at this point. I don't happen to *have* ten or twelve thousand dollars lying around the house, but I suppose I could get it. That's not the point. I know what Larry wanted. You know, I don't think anyone is ever prepared for this kind of earthquake, sheriff. None of us are going to die until we're a hundred and two. But that preplanning thing was serious. What he put on that form is what he wanted. Only that."

"So that's what he gets," I said. "It's as simple as Nicky Chavez here in Posadas trying his best to sell you a car. You want the basic model, but it's to his advantage to show you the luxury model, making you think that you'll feel better in the long run."

"Will I? Will I feel better?"

"No. You're not going to feel better for a very long time."

Her face softened, and she took a moment to mop up the tears. "I've always liked talking with you," she said. "The unvarnished truth. You went through this with your wife, didn't you."

"Yes." Accident or crime, no matter how the loss occurs, the questions linger.

She waited for a second or two to see if I'd elaborate, and when I stuck with unvarnished, she added, "They make me feel as if I'm somehow faulting my husband's memory by following his wishes." Marilyn laughed forlornly. "What the hell," she whispered and turned her back to us, still mopping her eyes. "You didn't stop by to listen to all my woes. What do you need to know?" She nodded at the envelope I held but didn't ask or reach for it. "The neighbors all have questions that they're afraid to ask. I can see it on their faces."

I needed to know who fired the bullet through Larry Zipoli's skull, but that didn't seem an appropriate question just then.

Chapter Twenty

"Would you like to sit down?" With a last disgusted look at the colorful and soothing brochures from Salazar and Sons, Marilyn Zipoli gestured toward the living room set—one of those matched things that sits empty most of the time waiting for a guest. I settled on the sofa and heard the wheeze of escaping air, I hoped from the cushion. Estelle settled like a graceful feather in one of the singles while Marilyn tried to make herself comfortable on the opposite end of the sofa, hands clasped in her lap.

"What have you found out?" There was no eagerness in her question, just resignation.

"We're closing in on a scenario," I said. Marilyn's eyebrows twitched. "We have a witness or two who heard the shot, and who might have seen something."

"*Something.*"

"And that's about as concretely vague as I can be just now." I held both hands out palm to palm, forearm holding the envelope on my thigh. "I spoke with Jim Raught earlier." She didn't respond. "I have to tell you, Marilyn, nothing in his attitude, nothing he said, leads me to believe that he might have anything to do with your husband's death. His version of the fence deal was that the whole thing was petty."

She drew in a long, slow breath.

"And it *is* Virginia Creeper, by the way."

"Oh, I know it is," she snapped. "For heaven's sakes."

"What actually happened with the fence?"

"What do you mean, what *actually* happened?"

"You said they argued over it, that Raught pulled it out of the ground. That eventually he threw it in the dumpster out in the alley. That's not what he said."

"The fence, the fence…" She looked heavenward.

"So…what's the deal?"

There seemed to be something fascinating about the wadded up tissue in her hand, since that's what she stared at for a long moment. "I would think it would be more important to find my husband's killer than to worry about a stupid little fence."

"Amen to that. We spent a good chunk of time interviewing Jim Raught based on what you told us, Marilyn. And you know as well as I do that it isn't the fence that concerns us. If the two gentlemen had called us to settle a property line dispute, we would have done so. A deputy would have talked with them both, and arbitrated a solution." I smiled a little. "Well, in the best of all possible worlds, that's what would happen. So the fence doesn't worry me. I'm interested in arguments that your husband might have had that could have led to this tragedy. Whether it's fences, or Virginia Creeper, or tiffs with the boss at work—whatever it might be, it's arguments that escalate that interest us."

"You've talked with Tony Pino?" She jumped at that opening to change the subject.

"Sure."

"And?"

"That's one of the reasons we dropped by, Marilyn." I rested my hand on the envelope. "Were you aware that your husband had nearly a dozen written reprimands for drinking on the job?" The soft friction of Estelle's pencil on her notepad seemed inordinately loud in the silence that followed.

"I don't understand how that's at issue," she said. "Are you saying that my husband argued with *Tony?*"

"It *isn't* at issue," I replied. "It's just an unpleasant fact, Marilyn. The evidence suggests that it was a common thing for your husband to take alcohol to work in his lunch cooler. Now, why his boss chose to do nothing about it over the years…well, that's another question."

She glared at me then, and as she worked to formulate either question or retort, I added, "A dozen written reprimands in the past few years, Marilyn. Several property damage accidents with county equipment. No one injured, but…"

"Mr. Gastner, do you seriously think…I mean seriously… that someone shot my husband because he's an alcoholic?"

"At this point, I'm not thinking anything."

That didn't sound just right, and sure enough, Marilyn actually laughed. "Oh, brother. This is the best we can do?"

"I'm open to suggestions, Marilyn. Was your husband involved in anything that might have led to…"

"Look," she interrupted, "my husband wasn't a closet gambler or something like that. He didn't associate with loan sharks. He didn't fence stolen cars. He wasn't into extortion, or blackmail, or whatever else." She had started to wind down, and the tears started to flow again. "I mean, isn't that the usual list? Isn't that what Hollywood has us believe? He wasn't having an affair, *I* wasn't having one, it was just life as usual. He went to work every day, and so did I. The kids are all out of the nest, and fighting their own battles now. So here we are."

"He argued with the neighbor?"

Marilyn's grimace was immediate. "Just forget about that," she said. "Just forget about it. I'm sorry I ever mentioned it."

"That's hard to do, Marilyn. If there was friction there…"

"There wasn't."

I looked at her in silence for a few seconds.

"So, you made that up? Is that the deal? Why would you do that?" I could guess some reasons, but Marilyn Zipoli just blushed, a nice, deep, guilty crimson, and that was answer enough. "Did you ever have occasion…" I hesitated, realizing that I sounded like a goddamn lawyer launching into his cross examination. What the hell. "Did you have occasion to talk with

Jim Raught during the past few weeks? You know, neighbor to neighbor sort of thing?"

"No."

"Not just in passing, maybe out on the sidewalk?"

"No. "

I hesitated for a fraction of a second. "You know, Jim Raught said that a number of years ago, you showed some interest in him...at least what he interpreted as interest." I saw her eyes go steely and guarded at my return to what was obviously a sore subject, but she said nothing, and that intrigued me. That doorway was still firmly closed and locked.

"Did you folks ever share backyard barbecues? Pool parties? Evenings in front of the hibachi?"

"It's not that kind of neighborhood, sheriff." She dabbed at her eyes. "At least, not those kinds of neighbors."

"So you really didn't know Jim Raught all that well...or any of the neighbors, for that matter."

"*Well*, as in quiet evenings with a glass of wine in front of the fire? No. Not even getting together for a weekend barbecue. Certainly not a nighttime tryst at the swimming pool under the hibiscus, if that's what you're thinking." Her smile was thin, and entirely without humor.

If there ever had been interest between Marilyn Zipoli and Jim Raught, I wondered who had done the refusing. At least she admitted to knowing about the pool.

"We see a lot of the neighbor kids," she added. "There's always an eager gang to go skiing or fishing, that sort of thing."

"You do that fairly often?"

"We spent a lot of time over at the Butte, sheriff. Like I said, that was Larry's favorite place, other than in front of the television, watching professional wrestling or boxing. Or golf. Or NASCAR. Or football."

"And yours?"

That drew her up short. "Elephant Butte is not my choice of paradise. Let me just put it that way. No matter what I do, I end up with a sunburn. I could spend the entire weekend in a sleeping bag, zipped toe to head. I'd still come home burned."

"But Larry loved it."

"Oh, certainly. That big ski boat out in the driveway? That was his passion. He'd be the first to tell you that it's got a 375 horsepower Corvette engine in it. He could pull four skiers at once."

"Kids would like that."

"Or one kid at a time, so fast that it brought out the worried mom in me. One of my nightmares was going to the Butte with five kids and coming home with four. Larry didn't worry about it. I mean, the Pasquale youngster was going to try barefoot next time we went out, if you can imagine."

"You're kidding. *Barefoot* water skiing?"

"He was almost there." Marilyn got up and walked to the bookshelf by the gas fireplace—a bookshelf that included just about everything but books. She retrieved one of those plastic flip-albums, and passed quickly through the pages until she found the photo she wanted.

Taken from the boat, it was crisply focused, like something out of a sporting magazine. The yellow ski rope drew the eye back to the skier, padded in his bright vest-preserver, balanced on the slalom ski while his bare left foot cut a narrow wake of its own.

I whistled softly and passed the photo across to Estelle Reyes.

"Who's the youngster?" I asked, even though I knew damn well who it was.

"That's the Pasquale boy. Tommy? His mom works at the dry cleaners? They live just up the street."

I drew out my notebook and found a blank page. "The kids who hang around most of the time. I'd like to have their names."

"They would have nothing to do with any of this…this horror. They couldn't."

"I don't doubt that, Marilyn. But one of them might give us a doorway. One of them might have seen something, or heard talk. You never know."

"A doorway? To what? I don't understand where any of this is going."

"Look, Marilyn," I sighed. "It's this painfully simple. Someone shot Larry while he was sitting in his road grader, engine idling. If there was an argument, there was no sign of it. Larry never had a chance to duck, to dive for cover, to swerve out of the way. I want the son-of-a-bitch who fired that shot. Larry might have had some faults, but he sure as hell didn't deserve that. And right now, I'm frustrated as hell, because we have *nothing* that's pointing the way. So we're going to flounder around, talk with every soul in Posadas if we have to, until something breaks. That's just what we do."

I held up a hand as she took a breath. "Let me tell you what I *don't* think happened, Marilyn. I don't think that some stranger from Lansing or Memphis or Dallas pulled off the interstate long enough to find a defenseless target to murder. I think the person who shot Larry Zipoli knew him. That's my gut feeling."

She regarded the floor for a long time, idly touching the edge of the carpet with the toe of her white trainer. After a moment, her eyes shifted up to the envelope on my lap. "And that?"

"Those are Larry's personnel records from the county."

"You brought them to show me? Is there some purpose to all that?"

"Actually," and I lifted the envelope a little, "I didn't want them out of my custody, Marilyn. I didn't want to leave them in the car."

Her sidelong glance at that was skeptical.

"How much did your husband drink at home?"

"Altogether too much, sheriff. The most common image I have of my husband is him in his bermuda shorts and flip-flops, an old T-shirt, and a can or bottle in his hand." It wasn't an affectionate image, nor said that way.

"Is this a recent thing?"

"No." She nodded at the folder of records. "And you know the answer to that."

"He took alcohol to work with him?"

"Routinely." That one word was soaked in bitterness, whether at the behavior itself, or her inability to do anything about it, I couldn't tell.

"You discussed the risks with him?"

"Not successfully, obviously."

"No ultimatums?"

"What's that mean, sheriff?"

"A decade-long problem never came to a head between the two of you? That's hard to believe."

Although swimming through a steady flow of tears, Marilyn's gaze was steady. She was really an attractive woman—as articulate, neat, controlled and polished as her late husband had been a drunken slob. Perhaps Larry Zipoli had been neat and polished at one time, but for the past decade it had been an attraction of opposites, if any attraction still existed.

"You talk with everyone," she said quietly, and nodded at the envelope of records. "I'm sure you'll eventually find out that I've filed for divorce. So yes—that's the ultimatum. That's where it all ends. Or so I supposed."

I've never been quite sure what to say to someone who announces that they've filed for divorce. "*Congratulations. You've dumped the bastard!*" Or, "*Gosh, I'm so sorry…*" Instead, I settled for the obvious. "You had informed Larry that you filed?"

"Yes."

"And you explained why."

"Of course."

"How did he take it?"

"He shrugged." I saw a flash of pain cross her face as if she had been clinging to some small hope that the announcement of her intended action would sink through her husband's fog.

"No big fight?"

"Larry likes to watch fights on television, sheriff. That's the extent of that." She had been watching Estelle Reyes as my young associate busied herself with talking notes. "You remind me of a court steno," Marilyn said as the pen paused. It wasn't a question, and Estelle didn't rise to the prompt.

"You've discussed the divorce with your daughter? With the other children?" I asked.

"Maybe they'll learn something from all this," Marilyn nodded. "That's the best we can hope for."

"The youngest...she's how old now?"

"Twenty-two. She's into her first year with one of the big banks in Albuquerque."

"I wish her all the best." I gave myself a few seconds to think, tapping my own notebook. "The neighborhood youngsters who knew your husband—we'll talk with them." A memory synapse popped somewhere in my head. "One witness recalls seeing your husband talking with a couple of kids over on one of the county roads yesterday morning. A couple of kids on bikes."

"That could be anyone."

"Let's start with the usual gang, then. The youngsters who came and went, the kids who tagged along on trips to the Butte. You mentioned Tommy Pasquale...who else?"

She ticked them off on her fingers. Matt Singer, Mo Arnett, Louie Zamora, Erik Zapia, Jason Packard. "Those are the ones who often go with us to the Butte," she said. "Jason and Louie come over to work on the boat. And sometimes Mo Arnett. Mo's folks are sort of hesitant to let him go to the lake with us, but he comes with us once in a while. Most of the time he seems to be with Jason. Maybe that's who you saw...both Jason and Tommy Pasquale ride bikes all over hell's half acre." She waited until I'd finished jotting down the names.

"They're nice kids, sheriff." She wiped her eyes. "If there's anything left that I loved about my husband, it's that. He spent time with them, more money than we could afford. I mean, you should see their faces when he allowed them behind the wheel of that boat. Just..." and she made a blossoming gesture with both hands. A drunk with a high-powered boat full of impressionable teenagers—just goddamn laudatory, I thought. Mo Arnett's parents had good reason for their reservation.

Marilyn obviously caught a fleeting expression that I wasn't able to poker face.

"Did your husband ever provide alcoholic beverages to any of these kids? During the trips to the Butte, or otherwise?"

Marilyn hesitated, an answer in itself. If Marilyn *knew* that her husband dispensed alcohol on those lake outings, that made her an accessory.

"That's why the divorce," she said flatly.

"He did this on more than one occasion?"

"Twice that I know of. He thought I didn't notice. But believe me, sheriff, you can't hide the smell. And the kids can't hide the guilty look."

"You confronted Larry about that?"

"Not in front of the kids. But when we got home, I tried to talk with him." The pained smile returned. "It's hard to compete with fifty-two inch projection TV and the interminable sports channels, sheriff."

"But you have a clear understanding of the risks that your husband was taking." Park police would have had a ball with the Zipoli clan—operation of a watercraft while under the influence, contribution to delinquency, endangering the welfare of a child, even the catchall of child abuse when prosecutors ran out of other ideas. And one thing was certain—with all that and the attendant publicity, Tony Pino might bury his head in the sand, but Marilyn Zipoli's boss at Posadas State Bank sure as hell wouldn't. Life as they knew it would grind to a painful halt.

"Of course, Sheriff. Of course I did. 'Look, my record's clean,' he'd say, meaning no formal DWI charges from the cops." She nodded at the envelope. "I don't call that clean."

A single rifle bullet had put an end to that whole messy scenario. It put an end to the agony of divorce proceedings, of dividing up house and chattel, even the nuisance of new addresses, new checks, new phone numbers. Marilyn Zipoli was vulnerable to all kinds of charges, and knew it.

That seemed to be a good time to let her stew for a while, and she let us go without ever satisfying her curiosity about her husband's personnel records. My guess was that she was beyond caring. I left a business card with her, in case something bubbled to the surface that we needed to know.

"I feel sorry for her," Estelle Reyes said as we settled into the car. The comment, a rare, unprompted observation, earned a perfunctory grunt from me.

"She could have stepped into the middle of this mess at any time," I said. "She didn't need to let the snowball roll for years." With the door wide open and the air conditioning turned up high, I finished with my log entry and keyed the mike. "PCS, three ten is ten-eight, Hutton and Sixth."

Dispatch acknowledged and I turned to look at Estelle. "What else strikes you?"

"You just sort of *cruised* through the interview, sir. I enjoyed listening to that."

"*Cruise.* Well, that's better than stumble or plod, I suppose."

"Earlier, when you said that you were going to talk with her again, I made up a list of questions," Estelle said, and turned her notebook so I could imagine seeing the tiny writing that filled the pages. "I would have started with the first one and gone from each to each."

"A dim recollection reminds me that the police science textbooks say something about 'controlling the interview.'"

"Yes, sir."

"And they're absolutely correct." I pulled the car into gear. "And one of the most important considerations is what we want the target's attitude to be the *next* time we have to talk with her. If we want cooperation, if we want information, then the bludgeon has never been my favorite tool. That's where the "control" comes in."

"It really doesn't matter how long it takes, does it."

I looked at the young lady with surprise. "No, it doesn't. If the target thinks that we've got all day to talk with her, that's a good thing. For a couple of reasons, but mainly because she knows she can't just wait us out." I reached across and tapped the edge of her notebook. "So, you listened to us yakking away. What did you learn?"

"Marilyn Zipoli is a most unhappy woman. I mean even before her husband's death."

"Indeed she is. With good reason. And that ain't rocket science, sweetheart. I want to hear astounding revelations and observations…things that crack the case before our very eyes."

"No matter what I imagine—even something as farfetched as Marilyn Zipoli's secret lover killing her husband—none of it squares with what Deputy Torrez has worked out about the murder weapon, or what we saw out at the crime scene."

"Her 'secret lover'?"

"Everyone has secrets, sir."

Chapter Twenty-one

I might not have been able to wear out my passenger, but I'd done a fair number on myself. I'd talked with nervous, apprehensive folks long enough that if I kept it up, I'd be next. What I really wanted was a dark hidey-hole where the phone wouldn't ring, where I could growl and prowl and ruminate, sheltered from the blistering, late afternoon sunshine. I could never guarantee the phone unless I unplugged the damn thing, but I could hope. A good green chile *burrito grande* at the Don Juan de Oñate would provide fuel for the rumination, gas for the prowling and growling.

Dispatch accepted my out-of-service announcement without comment. I noticed no particular eagerness on Estelle Reyes' part to finish her day, but I figured that she had her own thinking to do, including instructions to return in the morning for the dayshift with dispatcher T.C. Barnes. She'd had a hell of an introduction to Posadas County affairs, and dispatch would be a good change-up. Barnes was steady, happily married to Ethel, a young lady whose old-fashioned name had always tickled me. She was the only Ethel I knew. The two Barnes youngsters, Kit and Paul, enjoyed school to the point where I actually had an autographed Paul Barnes fingerpainting on my office wall, created nearly a decade ago. I'm sure the little kid had confused me for someone else—Santa Claus, maybe, but what the hell. The painting was a splash of color in an otherwise monotonous institutional scheme.

T.C. could be counted on to give the new hire a thorough orientation during his shift. He might not be entirely immune to having someone who looked like a damn movie star sitting at his elbow all day, but it would be a good test of his concentration.

By the time I finished my dinner and headed home, comfortably overfed and feeling sleepy, the village had settled into the evening.

Cruising under the street lights, I let the car barely idle along, ten, fifteen miles an hour on a four lane street that headed east, then took the intersection south on Grande. A handful of youngsters, all ready to face their first day of school, lounged in the parking lot of Portillo's Handi-Way. If they were bored before the *first* day, it was destined to be a long year. One of them glanced my way—Luis Fernandez, whose father Benny owned the Burger Heaven on Bustos—but the kid was far too cool to raise a hand in greeting or even recognition. Somewhere in that group of five teenagers there might be an interesting crumb of information, but at that moment I was too tired to pursue the opportunity.

I wasn't a fan of night lights. They played hell with my bifocals. With some relief, I headed south away from the commercial glitz of what passed for a downtown in Posadas, crossed under the interstate and a block or two south turned left onto Escondido Lane, then an immediate right after the Ranchero Mobile Home Park to Guadalupe Terrace. My own old adobe huddled secluded on five acres, nestled under a spread of old cottonwoods that blanketed out moon and starlight. The nearest streetlight was a single unit a hundred yards away over the trailer park's driveway.

Before getting out of 310, I found the house key so I wouldn't have to fumble in the dark. Closing the car door gently so as not to awaken all the spirits, I stood for a moment with one hand on the front fender and listened to the night. Traffic on the interstate was never light, but in this secluded spot it was far enough away that the noise blended into meaningless background that my tinnitus had no trouble covering.

At the trailer court, someone was being needlessly loud, and the voice drifted across, thankfully incomprehensible. I navigated the stone walkway around the garage by feel. The front door loomed in front of me, and I snapped on the tiny key-ring flashlight just long enough to find the keyhole.

The heavy, hundred year old hand-carved door—once gracing the entrance of a now crumbled Mexican mission—yawned open on noiseless hinges, and as my left boot touched the saltillo tile of the foyer, the damn telephone welcomed me home.

I didn't have an answering machine, having long ago decided that talking to a detached, electronic, soulless voice was an affront. Eight rings later, it was still ruining the silence, and I made it to the kitchen without breaking my neck over obstructions.

"Gastner."

A chuckle greeted that. "You always sound like you want to punch someone," Sheriff Salcido said.

"Not so, Eduardo. I just had a sumptuous dinner, the day wasn't an entire waste, and I'm drowsy enough to imagine that, if not interrupted, I might manage some sleep. What's up?"

He laughed gently again. "Us old guys march to a different drummer, no?"

"I'm too tired to march at all."

"It's been a long day. What's your impression of Reuben's niece after this? Grandniece," he corrected.

"Sharp kid. Not blabby, which is a blessing. She has some good ideas, but I damn near had to pry ten words out of her. I'd still like to know the real reason that she wants to work for us. With her background, her grades, one of the big metro departments would snap her up. Maybe even the FBI. Certainly the INS or the Border Patrol."

"Not everybody wants *grande*," Eduardo mused. "What you just said…I could ask the same thing of you, and look at where we are. Or me. Did I ever tell you that I was once offered the chief's job in Veracruz?"

"Is that a fact."

"Sometimes I wonder what would have happened if I had accepted."

"They'd have a chief who talked like a gringo."

"*Ay, caramba,*" he whispered. "I have to work on that." In point of fact, Eduardo Salcido never had to worry about being mistaken for a *gringo,* even in downtown Mexico. "So…what's tomorrow?"

"I have Ms. Reyes spending the day with Barnes in dispatch. She needs to familiarize herself with the home turf—records, communications, the lockup, the whole ball of wax."

The sheriff made a little humming noise as if something in all that didn't sound just right to him, but changed the subject without pursuing it.

"What did you think about the Deckers' story?"

I leaned my rump against the counter and closed my eyes. "Hugh heard a single gun shot at three minutes after two. Seconds later, he saw someone, a single person, walking west along Highland toward a parked vehicle. Hugh thinks the person was carrying something, but can't say what. He certainly couldn't say that it was a rifle. Maybe a walking stick. He didn't see Larry Zipoli, but saw the road grader."

"Three minutes after two," Eduardo whispered. "That's what he told me, too. Nice that he can be so exact." He sounded skeptical. "Tony Pino called me, by the way."

"And?"

"He wonders what's going to happen to Zipoli's personnel records."

"He does, does he?"

Eduardo's quiet chuckle followed that. "Our boy had trouble with the bottle, no?" Of course the sheriff knew.

"That's the understatement of the year, Eduardo. Larry Zipoli was a goddamn lush. Tony Pino should have fired his ass after the first incident ten years ago. Instead, Zipoli got a letter in his file. And more letters. And still *more.* What's with that? You know Pino better than I do."

"He's a soft touch, *Jefito.* Sometimes it's hard."

"Pretty simple, I would think. '*Take a hike.*' And then it's over and done with."

"Nothing is ever that simple."

"So tell me what I'm missing, Sheriff. What makes it complicated."

Silence greeted that. I could hear the Salcidos' television set faintly in the background. After a moment, rapid-fire Spanish followed as Eduardo only half covered the receiver. Juanita—I assume it was the sheriff's wife who cuddled in his lap—replied with a burst of her own. That went back and forth for a few minutes, and I made my way to one of the kitchen stools, propping my elbows on the counter.

Eventually Eduardo came back on the line, in English.

"You know Tony's sister?"

"His sister?"

"Well, he's got seven of 'em, I think. But Efita?" Another string of Spanish conversation with Juanita followed that. "My wife says it's not Efita."

"I'm glad to hear that."

The gentle laugh was either aimed at me or maybe he was tickling Juanita. I felt like a goddamn voyeur.

"Crystalita," Eduardo said finally. "That's who it was. Remember her?"

"Not a clue." Every once in a while I was surprised to discover that there were limits to what I knew about the folks of Posadas, New Mexico.

"She almost drowned in the arroyo down behind María. Let's see, I don't know. It would have been maybe fifteen years ago. Maybe longer."

"Was I here then?"

"I don't think so."

"Then it was more like eighteen years, Eduardo. Or longer." I admit that I was racking my brains for that memory. I took a good deal of pleasure in knowing history, and even something as common as an arroyo flood in rural New Mexico should have rung a bell. I could lead a tour for arroyo fans. I could show them cuts in the prairie a dozen feet deep and four times wider that had been cut in one night by one of our characteristic frog stranglers.

"Crystalita and her daughter." I heard more Spanish in the background. "The daughter. *That* was Efita, and I remember that she was only four at the time. You know, Crystalita was just nineteen, too. She was engaged to marry Hernán Muñoz."

"Him, I remember," I said. The Muñoz name was one of the ones engraved on the new veterans' memorial in Pershing Park, one of the Posadas contributions to Vietnam. I'd attended the dedication of the new memorial, and spent a few minutes reading every name. That's all it took to put some of the names into my selectively porous memory file. I could remember a name heard in passing a decade before, but not where I put my goddamn eye glasses.

"You knew him?" Eduardo asked incredulously.

"Just his name on the Pershing Memorial." By this time, I was regretting not turning on the coffee maker. Between Eduardo's storytelling pace and my own sympathy for history, this narrative could go on for hours. There was a fresh pack of cigarettes up in the cabinet above the fridge, but I wasn't that desperate yet.

"So," I prompted.

"You know that big arroyo just east of the power line down that way? It runs down behind María, and takes that turn to go under the highway. That's where Crystalita got caught. Dark, *por dios* it was dark that night, raining and thunder and lightning like I've never seen. Crystalita, she missed the little curve in the highway right there, then hit the bridge. That truck just *catapulted*, Bill. Down she went, and the water in the arroyo was already running high. *Hijo,* what a night."

"So she and the child drowned?"

"No, but so close. That truck was wedged by the water, cab nosed down, the water comin' up, the flood crushing that truck against the abutment. She couldn't get the little girl out of the child seat, you know. The way the cab was tipped, with all the water…and dark," Eduardo's voice fell to a whisper. I could imagine his wife lying there on the sofa, eyes huge as she listened to the memory. "With the truck lights out, the only *illumination*," and he damn made a melody out of those five syllables, "could have been the lightning, *Jefito. Ay.*" His sigh was huge.

"The first driver to stop was Larry Zipoli, Bill. Just seconds later, on his way back home from I don't remember where. And I don't remember if he saw the truck's lights go off the road, or what, but he stopped. First thing he does is slide down to the back of the truck. He sees it isn't going to be long before maybe the water is going to dislodge it. He can't reach either window, so he goes through the back. It's one of those sliding deals, you know."

"So he gets 'em out," I supplied.

"He does. You know, Crystalita wasn't very big. More child than a big woman. And the little girl, well, you know. She's like a little rag doll. So Larry's got one under each arm and there it goes. The water rips that truck right off the abutment, and they go under the bridge. How he saved them, nobody knows. A state trooper comes along and stops, and he finds Larry crouched on the concrete abutment just under the roadway, the water right at his knees. He's still got the two girls, one under each arm, trying to move against the water. They found the truck a quarter mile downstream the next day. Just a ball of useless metal."

"Tony Pino's *sister,*" I said. "And her daughter. Zipoli saved 'em both."

"That's right. Saved them both, *jefito.* There's all kinds of newspaper clippings about it, you know."

"I would think so." The rush of publicity would have been intense, but would fade with time just as quickly. And eighteen years was damn near long enough for a new generation who would never have heard of the rescue. The whole frantic, panic-filled night, with the roar of rampaging water and the bellowing of the storm, would become unimaginable, the stuff of old legends.

I had arrived in Posadas county the year after, and might have heard mention of the rescue, might have heard someone say, "Yeah, hell of a storm. Some guy rescued a couple girls down by María that night. Quite a deal."

Quite a deal, indeed. Larry Zipoli had taken a job with the county shortly thereafter, even before the grateful Tony Pino had become highway superintendent. Years floated by, and even when the man had grown into an irresponsible lush, Tony Pino hadn't been able to lift a hand against his behavior...behavior maybe even sparked by that impossible night. Larry Zipoli had certainly been a true hero, but his nightmares afterward—after he'd had time to think about it—might have been epic.

Larry and Marilyn had been married at the time, their youngest daughter maybe six years old. "Interesting that Marilyn didn't mention the episode to me," I said.

"That was a long, long time ago," Eduardo said, his voice soft like a good storyteller wrapping up a fable. "Maybe she doesn't like to think about what *might* have happened."

"Like her husband staying sober and fit after the incident, finding satisfaction leading the Fire Department's Search and Rescue Squad," I said without much sympathy.

"Or swept down the arroyo," Eduardo added, just in case I might not have thought of that by myself.

"So Pino sees his debt to Larry Zipoli as beyond settling. Is that what we're supposed to think?"

"That could be, *Jefito.*"

"Well, the debt's settled now. I'm sure Tony feels badly for Marilyn, but there's not much he can do for her. Where does Pino's sister live now, by the way?"

"Well, that's the sad thing. She got married to a fellow in Lordsburg. And this time it was a snowstorm over by Show Low. A semi jack-knifed on the interstate and burned, and that was that. She and her husband and the two kids. Along with a couple from Indiana. That was about five years after the night in María. Just a real sad thing, *Jefito.*"

I suppose that Tony Pino had his reasons to be uneasy when I walked out of his office with Larry Zipoli's records. Why people feel they have to do what they do is always a challenge to figure out, but it was obvious to me that Tony didn't want Zipoli's reputation smeared—nothing to overshadow that daring, self-less episode.

"Marilyn had filed for divorce, Eduardo."

"*Ay.* I didn't know that."

"Zipoli was providing alcohol to some of the local youngsters. Most of the time on the trips to Elephant Butte. Driving the boat under the influence apparently wasn't uncommon."

"And the park police never caught him, I guess?"

"Apparently not. It's a big lake, and not very many of them. He was lucky."

"And we never caught him either," Eduardo said philosophically. "Why didn't she just take the boat keys away from him?"

"One of life's great mysteries, Eduardo. Sometimes wives can't be that assertive."

He fell silent again. "So what now, *Jefito?*"

"I wish to hell I knew. There's an interesting connection that I want to check, but I don't hold out any great hopes. You know Mike Zamora?"

"Sure."

"He was the one who brought out the new hydraulic hose to Zipoli at the road grader. It's also interesting that Mike's brother Louis hangs out at the Zipolis from time to time, working on the ski boat. That's where I'll go with it tomorrow. Talk to some of the kids, see what little tidbits I can shake out."

"It's a small town, *Jefito.*"

"Well, maybe I can make that work for us. These little connections make me nervous, Eduardo. It's likely that Mike Zamora is one of the last people who saw Larry Zipoli alive."

The sheriff made a little humming noise. "That family has lived here for a long time, *Jefito.* The Zamoras."

"That makes a difference?"

Eduardo chuckled. "It's just the way it is, you know. They've been here a long time, lots of things happen."

"That's an interesting motive, Eduardo. *Lots of things happen.* I can hear the defense attorney telling a jury that."

"They'll hear some pretty strange things." He sighed. "I don't know. It's frustrating. You'll let me know what you find out?"

"Of course. How'd your day go?"

"Well, *interesting,* I guess." He fell silent for a moment. "I got this bee in my bonnet about that place, you know."

"What, out on Highland?"

"Sure. I got some little questions, and it isn't clear how to find out the answers, you know. You either got the killer driving around, looking for a specific target, or you don't…you got a chance thing. If he's *looking* for Larry Zipoli, how does he know where to find him? I mean, Zipoli works all over the county with that grader. How are you going to know, unless you have the county jobs schedule. I got to wonder."

"Someone like Mike Zamora would know, obviously."

"*Hijole,* I hate to think that. I tell you what…let me go talk with Mike come morning. Just sit down with him and see what he has to say. That okay with you?"

Eduardo Salcido hardly needed to ask my permission, but I could see the advantages. I made Mike Zamora's boss nervous, Eduardo didn't.

"Is there anything you want me to tell Tony when I'm out there?" the sheriff added.

"Not a damn thing," I said. Eduardo Salcido's roots were lifelong in the community, and like crabgrass, there was no way of knowing just where the tendrils went. "We need to know everything that Mike Zamora saw and said when he talked with Larry Zipoli out at the work site. If Zipoli seemed worried about anything—apprehensive, watchful, that sort of thing."

"I don't think he ever saw it coming," the sheriff said.

"Not until the last seconds," I replied. "That's what we have to wonder. Did he know why the trigger was being pulled."

For a few minutes after I hung up the phone, I wondered what it was that Sheriff Eduardo Salcido had actually wanted… other than trying to figure out what rocks I was turning over when he wasn't looking. But that was something I admired about Eduardo. He could accept almost anything with a philosophical shrug of the shoulders. I could imagine him arresting his own grandmother—were the wonderful woman still alive—and saying as he snapped the cuffs closed, "Well, *abuela,* I sure hate to do this."

It was easy to understand why Tony Pino had every reason to be upset and apprehensive. He would worry about that personnel folder and what I might do with it, and I doubted that it had anything to do with Larry Zipoli's memory, or with protecting the grieving widow. The superintendent himself would never survive an exposé in the *Posadas Register.* Tony's own gross negligence was clear in this case, and the superintendent knew it…enough so that he probably invented scenarios of me turning the records over to the local paper, even though that would never happen.

He should have fired Larry Zipoli years before. But if he thought that the sheriff would intercede on his behalf during an investigation, he didn't know the sheriff very well.

Chapter Twenty-two

I ground enough coffee for half a pot, and then wondered if I'd made enough. The aroma of Sumatran beans sent my hand to the cabinet, and I had the cigarette pack in my hand before hesitating. Just one butt, the narcotic habit coaxed. But the pack hadn't been unzipped, and I knew damn well that if I opened it, one cigarette wouldn't be the end of it. With a grunt of impatience, I tossed the pack back and shut the door. Maybe tomorrow, after breakfast.

While my seriously pokey coffee maker tried to figure out what to do, I stretched out on the old leather couch down in the library—my own personal rotunda, the circular architecture reminiscent of a kiva. The arc of cherry shelving was a pleasure to the eye and touch, loaded now with my comfortable collection that favored military history. Three volumes lay on the coffee table near at hand, bookmarks indicating that I hadn't finished any of them.

But my eyelids had concrete blocks attached, and the soft leather reached out and captured me. I tossed my glasses on the table.

This time, the telephone didn't awaken me. *Waiting* for it to do so kept sleep at bay. I'd drift off and then jerk awake, unsure whether it had rung or not, then drift off again. Why not just ignore it, one part of the mind suggested. I don't know what little break I was waiting for, or expecting. Mulling came easy, though, and mulling brought curiosity. There's at least one advantage of embracing the life of a hermit. Nobody held a clock to my head. The more I thought about the sheriff's story of the flood, the more my curiosity propped open my eye lids.

"What the hell," I said, admitting defeat. I heaved myself off the couch. Armed with a Thermos of coffee and proud of myself for leaving the cigarette pack in the cabinet, I left the quiet house. Settling into 310 seemed like the natural thing to do, and with the engine idling softly, I turned the police radio's volume up and listened to the silence for a few seconds. The county was typically quiet for the early morning hours of this Thursday. That would shortly change as school opened its doors for another season. I thought that the tradition of starting school with only two days remaining in the week was goofy, but they didn't ask my opinion. Maybe starting with a two-day week gave kids a little hope.

Avoiding town, I headed southeast on State 61. A dozen miles or so would put me in María, a tiny village of two or three extended families with the dubious distinction of having the border fence pass a few yards behind their back doors. The state highway was narrow, without enough traffic to mandate a huge re-engineering job. Little attempt had been made to flatten the road bed, and it followed the ocean waves of the desert. If you went fast enough, you could test the strength of your stomach.

Critter surprises were the norm. Crest a wave and see a family of javalina wandering across the pavement, or an enormous diamondback stretched out on the warm pavement, or a coyote fixed in place by the approaching headlights.

Something like that might have happened to Crystalita Pino that dark night eighteen years before as she approached María from the east. I slowed for the village, passing through the wash of light from the Taberna Azul, so named because of the saloon's blue door. Paulita Saenz , recently widowed by her husband Monroy's death from cancer, ran the saloon without fanfare. How she managed to keep such order was a mystery to my department. I could count on one hand the number of times we'd been called to a bar fight. On the other hand, it would take an entire legal tablet to record the number of occasions when illegals had relaxed there before hoofing farther down the road in search of paradise.

Five cars were parked around the building, at least one of them with Chihuahuan plates, a couple others with the characteristic white of Texas. Had I been an ambitious deputy, I might have paused and tossed some plate numbers to dispatch. But I was musing and mulling, and that calls for peace and quiet.

Wally Madrid's Texaco Station across the street was dark, and the scattering of houses behind it showed a light or two. It was hard to imagine a place much quieter, but a pounding thunderstorm would have dimmed the lights even more eighteen years ago. A mile beyond the village, the road humped up over a little rise, then immediately swung into the approach to the bridge across the San José Arroyo. With concrete buttresses and steel guardrails that left no room for shoulder, the bridge was certainly narrower than any current state standards, and when the traffic flow warranted it, would no doubt be replaced. Maybe they'd remember past fatalities and do something about the curved approaches.

The sedan's tires thumped on the tarred expander strips, and I coasted across the bridge, continuing on for a tenth of a mile before U-turning and then pausing on the shoulder. If Larry Zipoli had actually seen the girl's truck leave the highway, he could have been as much as a quarter of a mile behind her.

The concrete abutment showed a large, weathered scar on one corner, about eighteen inches above the ground—maybe from the Pino girl's truck, maybe from any one of a hundred accidents before and since. I stopped and planted the spotlight beam on the abutment. Somehow, the girl had drifted far enough to catch it with her left front fender. To do that, she would have had to wander completely off the pavement, perhaps asleep at the wheel. Brakes locked in panic, she would have frozen as the truck skidded and then tipped wildly.

Easing the car farther onto the shoulder, I turned on the four-ways and found my flashlight. The night was bright, cozy warm, a hint of breeze, every star ever lit now on display in the heavens, the half moon bright enough that the desert features took on some character.

The San José was a dry ditch. I stood just beyond the abut-ment and played my flashlight down, trying to imagine the roar of millions of gallons of chocolate water, all the floating crap caught up to be flooded into Mexico. Crystalita Pino would have had that view in full stereo as her truck plunged over the brink, sinking its headlights into the boiling soup.

I swung the beam up the arroyo. Twenty-five feet wide at the bottom, a dozen feet deep, the arroyo would have carried a powerful torrent. The noise would have been a cacophony. No one thinks in a situation like that. I turned the light to the bridge. The concrete abutments provided lots of ways to snag a vehicle before the water finally snatched it away. In the dry of late summer, a vast collection of tumble weeds and their kin had been stuffed under the bridge by the wind. Immediately under the highway, the concrete was sloped and smooth. I could imagine that the water could have flung Larry Zipoli and the two girls around the back of the tipping truck, and somehow he'd managed to scramble to a point where the water kept him pinned against one of the vertical pillars, waiting in desperation.

Hell of a hero, I thought. Hell of a hero. Even Larry himself probably couldn't explain exactly how the event had been cho-reographed. No thinking about how to do the impossible, he'd just *done* it, unthinking, in the best hero's tradition. Sometimes it all works out, sometimes not. This time, he'd won.

I snapped out my flashlight and trudged back to the car. The coffee smelled wonderful as it gurgled out of the Thermos, and hit the *Cigarette NOW!* switch really hard. Leaning on a conve-nient fender, headlights illuminating the bridge ahead of me, I contemplated and sipped coffee. Tires make a lot of noise, and I could hear the approaching eastbound car even before it slowed for the village. In a few minutes, it crested the rise and slowed when the driver saw the cop car on the shoulder. The cop himself made quite a picture, fat and lazy with a cup of coffee, leaning on the front fender and admiring the heavens.

"Taxpayer's money," the driver might have mumbled. I lifted a lethargic hand in greeting and watched his taillights fade off to the east before they disappeared behind a rise.

Someone so heroically wired that he could slam his own truck to a stop, then plunge down into a raging torrent to save two petrified girls, enduring the pounding of the water and the bruising of the concrete until yet another pair of hands helped him up the abutment—hell of a guy. And yet years later, Larry Zipoli, that incredible man of action, had sat in his road grader like a lump while someone walked toward him with a rifle and put a bullet through his head. No dive for cover, no hand raised in protest.

I refilled with Sumatra, thought about that some more. Eighteen years can force a lot of changes in a man.

Next time we enjoyed a thunder boomer that stretched from cloud to ground in an unbroken gray wall of rain, I was going to drive down to this arroyo and watch the water. Maybe I should write a letter to the right bureaucrat up in the State offices. New Mexico liked to name things after heroes, and might mark this the Larry Zipoli Bridge—provided that the memory wasn't smeared along the way.

Coffee drained from cup and bladder, I settled back in the car and saw that midnight had come and gone. I was as awake as if someone had blown reveille.

The Sheriff's Department needed convertibles...at least they needed to buy one for me. As a distant second best, I lowered all four windows and let the prairie waft through as I motored—dawdled—back toward Posadas. State 61 morphed into Grande Boulevard as I passed under the interstate, and as 310 drifted along under the ugly wash of the street lights, I wondered, for the millionth time, why the village wasted so much money trying to beat back the darkness. After all, any burglar worth the name could afford a good flashlight.

Grande T'd into Bustos, and I swung west, even though the Don Juan de Oñate at Bustos and Twelfth would be closed. North on Twelfth, up and over the steel bridge across the flood control ditch that once had been an attractive arroyo, and through the neighborhoods bordered by Hutton. In a few minutes I found myself drifting the car to a stop, lights out, at the intersection with Highland, right where J.J. Murton had been parked when I lifted his badge, and just about where another car had been seen by Hugh Decker earlier in the day.

I was sure that the southwestern breeze here carried a bouquet subtly different than down at the arroyo. On Hutton, the air picked up urban scents—diesel, ragweed, irrigated and mown lawns, full dumpsters, the dust from dirt lanes. For a moment, I considered my newly refined sense of smell a gift, a reward for abstaining from corrosive cigarette smoke for seventy-two hours. Or an imagination in high gear, fueled by the beans of Sumatra.

As I got out in the quiet of the night, I pushed the door against the latch until I heard the sharp click. It seemed important not to have to hear the rude slam of a door. The intersection was unmarked by a stop sign, just a dirt T scraped in the desert. I shot the beam down Highland. The road grader with the hole punched through the windshield had been driven back to the yard. Nothing remained to catch the flashlight beam, not even a curious coyote.

The rumble of a big V-8 drew my attention, and I turned to see the dim shape of the car approaching on Hutton, headlights off. The patrol car eased to a stop behind mine, and I ambled back to greet my visitor. Eddie Mitchell disembarked, nudging his own door shut without even the click. That reminded me why I liked this burly easterner who had adopted our county. He didn't talk a whole lot, but he seemed always in tune with his surroundings.

"Evening, sir."

"Spectacular," I said. I craned my neck back and looked at the heavens again, enjoying the vast spread until I felt the satisfying little pop of neck vertebrae relaxing into place. "Are you doing any good?"

"Some. There's a group of kids downtown who ought to be home by now."

I nodded across the field toward the nearest houses. "Hugh Decker claims he heard a single gun shot at three minutes after two, and then looked across his fence to see a car parked here, with a single individual walking back to it from the direction of the road grader."

"Two oh three, sir?"

"Exactly. He checked his watch when he heard the gunshot. He didn't recognize the person, though, or the car, or anything else. Just distant images."

"But a car, not a pickup?"

"That's what he says."

"Color?"

"Medium to dark." Just enough moon and starlight touched the young deputy's face that I could see the ghost of a smile. "Yeah, I know—it's the kind of vehicular description we all dream about," I added wryly. "But it's something. I don't know what the hell *what*, but it's something."

"Is the chick coming on board?"

The question shifted tracks so fast that I was left on the siding for a few seconds. "The chick?"

"Your ride-along earlier today."

"Ah. Miss Reyes. The *chick*. Yes, it looks that way. The sheriff offered her the job, anyway. Maybe after all this, she'll have second thoughts, although I hope not. She's one bright young lady." *Chick.*

"Interesting." His stony expression wasn't exactly aglow with approval, though.

"I'm sure that you had the opportunity to work with some female patrol officers in Baltimore. The *chicks*."

"Yes." The reply was flat and noncommittal.

"She'd be our first, other than in dispatch."

"She's workin' to be a patrol deputy, you mean?"

"Sure. I think it's about time that Posadas joined the twentieth century, don't you?"

"She's a little on the petite side," Mitchell observed.

"Maybe we'll put her on a weight lifting program to bulk her up a little. We'll find out how she does the first time that she has to respond to a bar fight." That earned a flicker of a smile.

"Her uncle's that old guy who lives out by the Torrance ranch?"

"That's him. Her *great* uncle, Reubén Fuentes." That Eddie Mitchell knew not only about Reubén but also that Estelle Reyes was his niece told me that either the deputy was most observant—which he was—but also that the staff had been discussing our new hire—and that didn't surprise me.

"The old man who wears a gun most of the time."

"That's him. You've met him a time or two?"

Mitchell nodded. "Tonight he was at the Handi-Way, coming out with a brown bag. My concern was more for the four or five kids in the parking lot, not him. He was walking steady enough. Warm as it is, he's still wearing gloves. He a closet cat burglar or something?"

I laughed. "There's no telling these days, Eddie. I can guess what was in the brown bag, though. And he'll be all right until he cracks the bottle. When he gets into that, we can all hope that he's safely at home."

"Might have been potato chips," Mitchell said.

"Oh, sure thing."

He shrugged and scanned the lights to the south. "The saloon in María is quiet tonight?"

"Like a church." I turned and smiled at him, amused that he'd known where I'd been. "Somebody reported me?"

"No, sir. I saw you heading south on 61. There's not much else down that way."

"I'm just out prowling, Eddie. I can't sleep, so I might as well do something instructive. It helps me think." I looked up at those wonderful heavens again. "And I think I'll burn some more of the taxpayer's gas. I'll be down in the southwest corner of the county if you need anything."

"Dispatch wants me central, so I'll be going in circles for a while."

"Cheer up, my friend. There are some village departments so tiny that the cop has a patrol beat about eight blocks long. He sees every cat and dog twenty times a shift."

"I'll take that over Baltimore," Mitchell said, and once more I wondered what his circumstances had been in that big city. His records, references, and reviews had been nothing but exemplary for the four years he'd been a flatfoot there, but he'd evidently generated no love for the place or the job.

"What time did you see Señor Fuentes at the convenience store?"

"Just a little bit ago. Maybe fifteen minutes. He's driving that battered white Chevy LUV."

"I'll head down his way, I think," I said, and beamed the flashlight across the open prairie toward Highland once more. "That'll give me time to think about all this. There's something we're missing here, Eddie. When you figure out what it is, let me know."

"Yes, sir," he said. And who knew. Maybe over the next seven or eight hours, some flash of brilliant intuition would light up his night sky.

Clear as the night was, what I really wanted to do was cruise along without headlights, enjoying the incredible star display as I drove south. Along State 56, there were long stretches where not a single modest porch light polluted the darkness, where I could see the loom of mesa against the heavens and the star-touched tawny of the prairie. With the windows open, what better elixir could there be.

But Posadas County didn't pay its undersheriff to spend his time ruminating on the state of the universe overhead, or the fragrance from sage, gramma and creosote bush. So I drove with my headlights on, the damn radio on, my thinking cap on.

Chapter Twenty-three

Reubén Fuentes was a crusty old fellow, seemingly indestructible, battered and brown and wrinkled, reminding me of someone from an earlier century. Some of his escapades south of the border were legendary, and why he wasn't currently rotting away in a Mexican prison was something of a wonder—except that the Mexican authorities who mattered turned a blind eye to this old guy who preferred to work on the Mexican side, where the language and the law came easy.

But he worried me a little, since in the modern age of mobile phones, computers, credit cards, and just too damn many people, Reubén Fuentes stood out in powerful contrast. He didn't bathe as often as someone standing next to him in the grocery store checkout might have wished, and the habitual revolver tucked in the ancient leather holster made folks nervous.

He lived with no telephone, no television, and a minimal number of what most of the rest of us considered necessary amenities. I'd had a cup of coffee at Reubén's place on more than one occasion, and knew that he still brewed the stuff in an old metal pot where the grounds just settled down through the water. Nice crunchy stuff. It complimented his well water, what there was of it, which was as hard as the granite sand through which it passed.

His grandniece had managed to live with the old man for two full years after coming to the United States to finish her high school career, a remarkable accomplishment for a teenager, even one such as herself who'd grown up in a tiny Mexican village with few amenities of its own.

It wasn't Reubén's usual day-to-day living habits that worried me. The old man didn't come into town often, and certainly not in the middle of the night. The drive from his small ranchito to Posadas was a fair chore for someone his age—rough two tracks down to the county gravel, then the miles north to Posadas on a sometimes busy state highway.

I knew the old man to be an early riser, often on the job with the dawn. The border crossing opened at six a.m., and if he was working in Mexico, he and his little white Isuzu-Chevy would be parked there ready to go, loaded with ladders, his battered wheel barrow, shovels, picks, and all the other accoutrements of his masonry. And by that time, he'd have sampled the brew, lacing his morning coffee. He tumbled into bed with the sunset.

His abrupt change of habit tweaked my curiosity. If I drove far enough southwest on State 56, I'd reach Regál, another tiny village nestled on the south flank of the San Cristóbals, within shouting distance of the border crossing that took Reubén to Mexico.

I didn't let the grass grow, giving 310 a little exercise. Mindful of the desert zoo, I played the spotlight down the shoulder of the road ahead of me, sweeping from side to side to catch the reflection of tiny eyes. They'd bolt, or maybe freeze in place, thinking that the inexplicable oncoming beast would pass harmlessly over their heads. Out past Wayne Feeds, a business that struggled as our county's economy collapsed, around the bulk of Arturo Mesa to the south and the remains of Moore, a three-family community long turned to dust north of the highway, I crossed the Salinas arroyo on a new state highway bridge that *was* entirely up to code, unlike the one I'd pondered earlier near María. I saw a set of taillights appear ahead, and overtook the little white truck before we'd covered another mile.

Reubén Fuentes drove like a man who wasn't sure exactly where he was—and no matter how sober he *might* be, twenty miles an hour on a state highway was too slow. The truck wobbled now and then, little jerky motions rather than the vague drifting of an inebriated motorist.

A car that comes up behind you like a rocket, then slows without passing, isn't apt to be your Aunt Minnie. Reubén figured it out without my having to announce my presence with a light display. In a mile or so, his brake lights flared and he pulled onto the wide shoulder. I did the same, keeping a respectful distance behind him when I turned on the flashers.

"PCS, three-ten will be with New Mexico Charlie Frank Nora triple eight, mile marker nineteen, State Fifty-six. Negative twenty-eight." Ernie didn't need to run a wants-and-warrant on the registration for me. I didn't see a current '89 sticker on the license plate, but the old man probably had it still in the envelope, stuffed in the glove box. Or perhaps not. Just then, I didn't really want to know. Reubén's license plate was worn and dented, and of course the little bumper bulb didn't work.

I'd chewed butt often enough with my deputies, reminding them that, no matter how innocent the circumstances, there was no such thing as a routine traffic stop. I'd told them that enough that I believed it myself. Only one head nodded in the cab, but who knew—an armed felon might be crouched in the passenger seat, waiting for my approach, or lying flat in the truck bed, shotgun at the ready. A little paranoia is a good thing.

"Ten-four, three-ten. When you're finished there, are you ten-eight?"

"That's negative."

"Ten-four." Ernie Wheeler sounded disappointed that I wasn't available for calls, as if he'd lined up a fair night's work for me.

By the time I made sure my vehicular office was secure and stepped out into the night air, Reubén had the driver's door open, propping it with one boot. As I approached along the shoulder, he turned, putting both feet on the ground and his right forearm on the door.

"Don't you ever go to bed?" he asked. His absolute calm and innocence might have been the old man's best defense when dealing with Mexican authorities. A true *viejo inofensivo,* I'd heard him called. No doubt when he crossed the border, he was a bit more discreet with the handgun.

"Reubén, how are you doing this fine night?" I watched as he pushed himself to his feet, staggered just a little and caught his balance by putting an elbow against the cab. Sure enough, Deputy Mitchell was right—the old man was wearing cheap cotton gloves, and he avoided touching them to the truck.

"Not so good, Sheriff. Not so good. I did a stupid thing."

"Really? I would have thought as old as we are, we'd have learned to stop doing stupid things."

Reubén laughed a silent little shake of amusement. "You'd think that." He leaned his forearms on the edge of the truck bed. "Can't even light a cigarette. Maybe I should quit." He reached up and touched his right wrist to his breast pocket, where the smokes were stashed. I didn't offer, since I knew what would happen.

"So what did you do to yourself?"

"Ay," he muttered. "I got lazy." He looked up at me as I joined him at the leaning post. Half my size, dressed in khaki shirt and trousers, he wore the aroma of sweat and wine the way modern man wears aftershave. With the back of his hand, he touched me on the arm, a substitute for a handshake. "We're working on the *iglesia*, down in Tres Santos."

"That's a tough job," I said. The little mission was ancient, adobe, and had suffered from lackadaisical maintenance over the years. Massive as adobe is, gravity eventually always wins.

He nodded with a philosophical shrug.

"How's Teresa?"

"She's good. She's good. She doesn't teach any more. Did you know that?"

"I did." I'd met Estelle Reyes' stepmother a couple of times, always in Reubén's company. I remember that she had long, iron-gray hair tied up in a bun, and snappy eyes with a mass of crinkles in the corners—a formidable boss of the tiny classroom.

"On that one wall, that's where the trouble is," he said, and I assumed he was referring to the church, not Estelle Reyes' stepmother.

"After two hundred years, we all crumble a little bit."

"*Ay,* that's true. We built a buttress—on both sides. That little church looks more like a fortress now." He chuckled.

"Who's working with you on that?"

He puffed out his cheeks. "Two of the Fernandez boys. You know them." I didn't, but Reubén continued on. "And Benny Orasco. He's got that big backhoe. He's got a couple of boys who work with him, on and off."

"So how did you hurt yourself?"

He sighed and regarded his gloved hands. "We're doing the plastering." His accent savored each syllable. He and Sheriff Eduardo Salcido probably enjoyed slow-talk contests now and then. "And the detail work around the windows on the east side. You know, make it just right." It would be, too, with Reubén's touch.

"They don't make good gloves any more," he added. "My hands got wet, and in that lime all day long…" He made a grimace. "There are places around the windows where only the hands can make the shapes. And now…*ay,* like fire."

"The plaster burned your hands, you mean?"

He nodded. "I had some *aloe verde,* but then I ran out. They don't make that like they used to."

"I see the word aloe on enough labels," I said. "Did you stop by the emergency room?"

"The hospital? No. Why would I do that? That's the big money, that place."

Reubén pushed himself away from the truck. "I found something at the store just now. Let me see if you think it'll work." He bent into the truck and I heard a groan unsuccessfully stifled. He backed out holding a bag between two fingers and extended it toward me. I pulled out the plastic bottle of hand cream and turned it so the headlights illuminated the label. *Clinical strength, healing formula,* bla, bla, bla. Whether it would sooth lime-burned skin was a stretch.

"Let me see," I said. "Can you slip one of the gloves off?"

He flinched at the thought. "I think I'll just take myself home," he said. "I got some aspirin, and I got this. That'll be okay."

And I knew damn well that wasn't all he had. "You're working tomorrow?"

He took a long time answering. "I don't think so. We'll see."

"So, now we get you home. You're not driving so good, Reubén, and you have a lot of miles to go, on the worst roads."

"I'll take my time."

"Nope. I don't think so. Tell you what, my friend. Let me run you home." I knew what Eduardo Salcido would say about a county taxi service, but what the hell. It was expedient. "We'll move the truck a little farther off the shoulder, and I'll have your grandniece come out in the morning to check on you and help you bring the truck home. How about that?"

"Estellita told me that she was going to work for you."

"For the county, yes sir. Quite a young lady she's turned out to be."

"Yes. She doesn't live with me any more." It was as wistful as I'd ever heard Reuben.

"I know she doesn't."

"I was hoping she would stop by tonight, but she didn't. Always in a hurry, that girl. She could live with me and still work anywhere in the county."

"Well, maybe so. That's between the two of you." I couldn't imagine it, but stranger things have happened. One of the major requirements of law enforcement is the long, hot shower, both to calm the nerves and to wash off the stink of nasty predicaments. Somehow, Estelle Reyes had managed to survive two years with her uncle—two years of high school with its peer pressures and other crap, while at the same time managing her personal life in her uncle's rustic paradise. Using the showers in the high school's girls' locker room must have served the purpose, but after that, a college dorm would have seemed opulent. I couldn't imagine her going back to the tiny cabin hidden among the piñons and junipers, sleeping on a sofa and looking forward to a nice hot sponge bath out of an enameled basin come morning.

"Let me give you a ride, Reubén. She'll be out first thing in the morning. We'll get those hands of yours fixed up."

He didn't argue. That told me how miserable he felt. I pulled his truck well off the highway. Now we had Jack Newton's Cadillac on one side of the county and Reubén's battered truck on the other. It seemed to me that things tend to go in series—a string of break-ins, a wash of domestic disputes, all the county's speeders congregating on the same stretch of highway. This happened to be geriatric alcoholic week.

Half an hour later, with the inside of my car smelling like old man, I pulled to a stop at the foot of a small mesa a mile or so off County 14. My headlights illuminated the squat adobe, rock, and log cottage, the back of the dwelling backed tight against a rock outcropping. A canopy of runty, gnarled trees found enough moisture in the cracks and crannies. An electric line ran along the two-track, and looped into the side of the building. At least there was that.

In 1930, when Spartan living was a way of life in the rural west, the place would have seemed cozy, even hospitable. Now, more than half a century later, with lives flooded with cheap luxuries, Reubén's home was an anachronism, damn near a tourist attraction.

Two dogs stood at silent alert, tails waiting, and when they saw—or smelled—my passenger, they did their dog-thing, becoming dervishes of greeting.

He hesitated, half in and half out of my car. "What am I going to do about my truck? My tools…"

"We'll get 'em back to you," I promised. That's the trouble with starting the taxi service, I would admonish deputies. One thing leads to another, and pretty soon you have a snarl. Good deeds rarely go unpunished.

"I guess I can take the old Jeep down. But I hate to do that." The 'old jeep' was just that, a topless old buggy with the seats showing springs in a dozen places. It was parked beside the house, its license clearly expired. I knew it was a '47, worth something now to a collector who might restore it. A bullet crease on the flat of the left front fender drew my eye. I knew how it had gotten there, and if either of the Hidalgo brothers were still alive, they'd probably welcome the chance for another try.

"Let Estelle help you with all this," I said.

"Maybe she'll stop on her way back," the old man said. "She went down to talk with her mother."

"Maybe she'll do that." What the hell. Dump all this on the young lady, who certainly had a full plate at the moment without worrying about her great-uncle. I left the old man safe in his own home with his aloe hand cream and bourbon, and by the time 310's tires chirped back onto the state highway, it was nearly 1:30 in the morning. When I saw Estelle at the office in the morning, we'd take care of the truck.

Chapter Twenty-four

Estelle Reyes appeared at the dispatch desk at 7:30 that Thursday morning looking well rested, well groomed, and just generally goddamned breathtaking, wide-eyed with interest for what the day might bring. For a moment, she seemed about 12 years old, eyes taking in everything and everyone.

She wore a conservative tan pants suit and a simple white blouse with one button open below the businesslike collar, with no jewelry of any kind except a wristwatch. Her shoes were sturdy black oxfords polished to a military sheen, the cuffs of her trousers breaking over the tops in a fashion that brought joy to an old sergeant's heart.

I stood in the doorway of my office, watching for just a moment as she chatted with Ernie Wheeler, who no doubt wished at just that moment that he was working days rather than the soon-to-end graveyard shift.

Estelle gripped a slender black briefcase, and I wondered what souvenirs she'd collected.

"Good morning," I greeted her, and Ernie looked disappointed. T.C. Barnes, already on deck, had been told that most likely he would be enjoying the young lady's company all day, and would present a comprehensive orientation. He was about to be disappointed, too.

"Good morning, sir."

"Change of plans, by the way," I said. "Come on in." She followed me into my office, but didn't take a chair. I waved her toward them, her choice, and she took the old wooden monstrosity to one side of the desk. "Before we get into anything else, I had a chat with your great-uncle early this morning. He managed to lime burn his hands at work down at the church, and he'd driven into town to find some ointment. He couldn't drive worth shit, and I took him home. His truck is parked along 56, just beyond the bridge."

"I saw it this morning on my way in," she said. "Ernie told me what happened."

"He'll be all right, I'm sure. And your mother? She's well?"

"She is." Estelle held the briefcase in her lap, one hand over each latch, her body English saying that she wanted to open the thing. Maybe her mother had sent up a serving of *galletas* for us. I didn't want to be sidetracked from the git-go, and handed the young lady a copy of the Simmons catalog that had been holding down the landslide of papers on the corner of my desk. "You'll need a rig," I said. A number of yellow tags marked various catalog pages. "We're going to need to order soon if you want to be outfitted for the academy." She hefted the catalog and tilted her head as she thumbed to the first tag.

"The deputies wear the line that starts on page nineteen. The one named 'Desert Tan', appropriately enough. You get the first three sets free, then two a year after that. Shirts, pants, shoes. The utility rigs are all on page twenty-eight, the line they call 'Borderland.' Stetsons are on page something. You'll find 'em. It's the off-white low crown."

I grinned. "In case you're marveling at my incredible memory, rest assured that I took a couple of minutes to look 'em up and mark 'em. Anyway, that's what you'll need for the academy starting in September, as well as a bunch of other things. Exercise sweats, that sort of thing. Barnes will walk you through the paperwork. Do it sometime today." She nodded and closed the catalog.

"One of these days when things slow down, Deputy Torrez and I will go out to the range with you and find out how much work needs to be done to make you safe with a three fifty-seven.

I have some reservations about that, since your hands aren't exactly hams." I regarded her critically. It's a hell of a note that someone's good looks can actually be a liability, but she'd just have to work to overcome the challenge. The uniform might help. I'd always thought that uniforms, especially with gun belts loaded with twelve pounds of crap, did a good job of ruining a trim line. With my girth, I favored civilian duds.

"You're going to have to be goddamn proficient with whatever weapon we find for you, because that's what you'll take to the academy. And that's what you'll have to qualify with for the department." I sat down heavily behind my desk. "Although I'm here to attest that a goddamn blind man can qualify."

The young woman absorbed all that without comment.

"And about the change of plans…there's all the time in the world for office orientation, but what the hell. We dropped you into the middle of something yesterday, and it's too good an opportunity to miss." I nodded at her outfit. "That's perfect, by the way. Looks sharp and professional. The sheriff wants you wearing a vest, so we'll see what we have as a stopgap until you can order your own." I looked at her critically again. Kevlar vests weren't made for comfort, especially for folks who were blessed with curves—and at the risk of sounding like a chauvenist pig, she had curves. She'd end up like a Joan of Arc, trying to look like a boy in her French armor.

"All right?"

"Yes, sir."

"Any questions?"

"As a matter of fact…" She snapped the latches on the briefcase. "May I show you two photos?"

"Of course."

The first, an eight-by-ten glossy surprised the hell out of me. I leaned back in the chair, examining the photo. "You took this when?"

"Yesterday at Raught's. You followed him into the kitchen, and I took the opportunity then. Yesterday afternoon, I made it in time to the one-hour photo in Deming and then to the Regál border crossing before it closed."

"Huh." The photo was clean, with no flash shadows, the *tres retablos* on Raught's fireplace mantel framed dead center, edge to edge. While I pondered the logistics of what the young lady had done, she drew another photo out of the case.

The similarity was startling, although the second photo captured three retablos far more primitive than Raught's, and it did so in a little, square instant photo of dubious quality. Raught's *El Jardin de los Tres Santos,* with gold leaf and startling detail, morphed into primitive folk art in the second photo, with faded colors, primitive technique, and chipped edges.

Estelle leaned forward and touched the second photo. "This is from the *iglesia* in Tres Santos, sir. Where my great-uncle is working. I didn't have time to take a quality photo and have it printed before the photo store closed, so I used the Polaroid."

"A common subject for a *retablo?*" I held the two photos side by side. "I don't claim to be an art critic."

"The *iglesia* in Tres Santos is named for the original mission in Veracruz, sir."

"So…"

She touched first one photo and then the other. "I took the second photograph at the *iglesia* in Tres Santos yesterday evening. The *tres retablos* are over the altar. My mother says that they've been there since the 1920s."

I glanced up at the clock. "Where are we going with all this?"

"*El Jardin* in Veracruz was painted in 1869 by Manuel Orosco." She touched a slender finger to the bottom edge of the eight by ten. "My mother says that he was one of the most famous religious and folk artists in Mexico."

"And this is a copy of the original that's hanging in Veracruz?"

"I think…I *think* that this is the original, sir."

"The original? How would that be?" The eagerness suffused her features, and I almost hated to throw a wet blanket on her enthusiasm.

"Actually, that's not true," she said. "I don't know enough about art to tell an Orosco from a..." She floundered for a name and gave up. "*I* don't know. But my mother does, sir. First, I took her to the *Iglesia* in Tres Santos last night. I wanted to make sure that my memory wasn't playing tricks on me. I remember the *Jardin de los Tres Santos* there from when I was little. I remember always wondering why the saints looked so miserable." The ghost of a smile touched her features.

"I had the same thought earlier today," I said.

"When I was sure my memory wasn't playing tricks, I showed *mamá* the photo of Raught's *retablo*. She looked at it for a long time, sir." She touched her face under her left eye. "And then the tears started to roll."

"Teresa knows about the one in Veracruz well enough to recognize it? After all these years? How many times has she actually seen the Orosco piece?"

"Half a dozen over the years."

"And you?"

"I've seen it once, sir. When I was twelve."

"So there's an obvious question here." I handed the photos back to her.

"Yes, sir. What's interesting is that the original Orosco was stolen four years ago. Thieves hit significant art in three Veracruz locations, major places with showcase religious art. One of them was *Los Jardins.*"

"Now wait a minute. Have some mercy on my poor, slow brain, sweetheart. You're claiming that you knew about the Veracruz theft, one that happened four years ago, before we went over to Raught's home? You knew about the theft and recognized the piece?"

"No, sir. My *mother* knew about the theft, had heard about it, especially because of the emotional link with the church in Tres Santos."

"You've got to be kidding me."

"No, sir." She looked puzzled.

"You're thinking that Raught stole the piece?"

"I don't know, sir. *If* it's the Orosco in the first place. In all these years, it might have wended its way to a dealer in the states…or in Mexico. Mr. Raught has been in both places, sir. He worked in Verzcruz at one time."

"And in Ohio," I added. "This was an emotional tug for your mother, then."

"Yes, sir."

"So explain to me how she thinks this is the original deal. How can she tell that from a photograph?"

Estelle looked down at the photographs, brows knit. "I don't see how she could, sir. Except that the level of skill, the level of art? If it isn't the original, it's certainly a powerful copy."

"This kind of thing gets *copied?* I can see copying a Picasso, maybe. Or a Rembrandt or the ear guy…Van Gogh. I mean, there's millions at stake there. But this?"

"It's of significant value, sir." Estelle reached into the briefcase and brought out a yellowing newspaper clipping.

"Yes, uh huh," I said, and handed it back. I didn't read Spanish, but could see that the clipping was dated four years previous.

Estelle flattened it out on my desk, skimmed quickly, and stopped at the third paragraph. She pointed out the figures. "*Los Jardins* was valued at more than two hundred thousand."

I whistled in appreciation. "Signed?"

"No, sir. My mother said that Orosco used to say that all of his religious works belonged to God, not to him. That they were done by God's hand, not his."

"That makes it a tough nut."

"Except the piece is *well* documented, sir." By now I was expecting a rabbit, but she pulled a manila folder from her briefcase. "*Los Jardins* is in at least two art books that my mother owns. I have the books in my apartment, but these are fair copies that Ernie Wheeler did for me just this morning."

"You must have been first at the border gate," I laughed.

"As a matter of fact, I was."

I examined the best photocopy side by side with the eight-by-ten. My uneducated eye said they could be the same, but what the hell did I know.

"The proverbial can of worms," I murmured. After another minute of looking, I handed the material back. "It'll be interesting to hear what Mr. Raught has to say. If he greets us this time and says, 'Hey, come back with a warrant,' we're toast. What we have is the contents of your briefcase, and what your mother thinks that she remembers." I smiled at her. "That isn't much to chase an international art thief with."

"But we're not saying that Mr. Raught *stole* the original," Estelle said. "There may be a significant possibility that he now *owns* the original somehow."

I took a very deep breath and let it out in a loud, long hiss. "So, back on earth..." I slid my notebook toward her and tapped the page. "These are the kiddos that Marilyn Zipoli told us about—the Zipoli skiing and boating club. We want to talk with all these little bastards, and that's a hell of a challenge. We'll be over at the high school and that's *another* challenge. You've met Glenn Archer?"

"Yes, sir. My last year at the high school was Mr. Archer's first. He was teaching biology that year."

"And now he's superintendent and principal of the high school, both jobs rolled into one. Glenn is a good guy, and an ally. But the issue is cops interviewing minors," I said. "Fortunately for us, the school operates *in loco parentis,* and Archer will be sitting in on any interviews that we have. We don't need the parents there, but regardless, we need to be circumspect. For one thing, anything we talk about, we talk about with a blabby kid. His or her version of events is going back to all his friends."

"It's interesting that Mr. Zipoli attracted a fair crowd of kids on occasion," she said.

"Well, a fast boat and a set of water skis will do that. It's also interesting that a couple of kids were talking with him over on County Road 19 the day before the shooting. We don't know who that was, but it's a connection that we need to explore. I mean, if you're grading a ditch and someone rides or drives by, the usual thing might be a simple greeting—a nod or a friendly wave. I'm surprised that Zipoli stopped what he was doing to shoot the bull." I sighed. "And we need something, Ms. Reyes. We have nothing but blind alleys so far." I rapped my ring on the desk. "And now we have the list of kiddos. It'll be interesting to run them past Jim Raught." I smiled at her. "No ulterior motives, of course."

I watched her face for a moment as she appeared to examine a smudge on my desk top. If she thought any harder, her brain synapses would start smoking.

"What?" I prompted.

"It's difficult for me to believe that Mr. Zipoli didn't share his stash with youngsters," she said quietly. "The opportunities were obvious."

"You think?" I laughed. I would have liked to have heard something a little less obvious than that. After all, I'd had that same thought, and I hardly qualified as a forensic Einstein. "So on this occasion, some homicidal kid asked him for a beer, and he refused?"

"Most likely not that," she said soberly. "I can't imagine someone being shot over a can of beer."

"You'd be surprised how little motivation is needed sometimes." I snapped the notebook closed. "How's your great-uncle, by the way? On your way in from down south, did you take a moment to check on him?"

She nodded. "He was sleeping soundly. His truck was still parked on the shoulder."

"And what time was that?"

"Not long ago. I suppose it was almost six-thirty." I tried to picture her as a teenager living with her great-uncle, getting ready for school with only a rude sink and sometimes hot water. But for him to actually ponder what his great-niece might *need?* Not Reubén. I liked the old man, but talking with him was always about Reubén, and what Reubén was doing. He was the solid center of his own universe. A wife would have murdered him long ago.

"Anyway, we see what the kiddos have to offer today," I said. "The Zipoli gang. If there were regulars hanging out with him, then we want to know about it. They might have heard something, seen something…who the hell knows in what ugly direction that might lead." I shrugged. "Or maybe not. It occurred to me sometime last night that we might be chasing just some random thing—some trigger-happy bastard who lets fly with a rifle without a clue about what he's doing. Like those nitwits who shoot at highway signs." I glanced her way as I hefted my own briefcase and headed for the door. "In a lot of years in this business, I've never caught one of them at work. Don't know anyone who has. How often does someone call in to report the murder of a stop sign?"

I didn't add that it was probably a good thing that taxpayers didn't know how little crime went unreported, uninvestigated, and unpunished. Most of the time, crime *did* pay, and sometimes handsomely.

A moment later, we settled into the car and Estelle watched me as I updated my log, called in the mileage to dispatch for *his* office log, and reviewed the few questions I had jotted down the day before. None of the other deputies used 310, so the car remained my private mobile office.

It's possible to drive from the Sheriff's Department parking lot to Posadas High School in thirty seconds and never break the speed limit. I made it in something under five minutes. I don't know what I was looking for, but a couple of nagging thoughts kept playing their loop. When that happens, my pace slows as my gaze drifts into every crack and corner. I drove with the windows down, elbow on the sill, chin propped in my hand, my mind trying to rush in two directions at once. Would Larry Zipoli recognize an Orosco when he saw it? Nah. Not a chance.

Estelle Reyes patiently endured our idle-along until we parked in front of the school in the *No Parking—School Bus Loading Zone*. A minute or so later, we sat comfortably in Glenn Archer's office, and he took a great deal of care in closing the door, standing there with one hand on the knob, the other on the jamb as if making sure no one was going to sneak up and put an ear to the wood. A dapper fellow who took off the prissy edge by favoring comfortable corduroy trousers and a baggy cardigan, Archer had always welcomed a comfortable relationship with the Sheriff's Department. We provided officers—with the help of Chief Martinez and the village department—for sporting events, tried to be gentle when we had to arrest one of the teenagers who fell into hard times with drugs or alcohol, and offered a sympathetic ear when we arrived on the parents' doorstep at 3 a.m. to change lives forever. He seemed reasonably calm for the morning of the first day of school.

Once satisfied with his office security, Archer turned back to his huge desk. A box of tissue graced each front corner, within easy reach of our chairs. Another rested on the bookcase behind my head. I wasn't planning on breaking into sniffles, but I'm sure such was routine for kids about to be flogged.

"So…the first day of school, and here we are." His smile was strained. "I was hoping you'd come today to arrange a series of public service programs for the kiddos. Or maybe talk during our assembly later this morning. But maybe not." He paused and glanced at the door again. "Ms. Reyes, I'm delighted to see you." He looked sideways at her, figuring something. "Refresh my memory. What year?"

"Eighty-four, sir." I knew from her application that Estelle Reyes had not yet celebrated her twenty-second birthday. Still, it must have seemed like centuries ago that she'd been plowing through the required reading in Mrs. Hammerman's American History class, or smelling the mid-morning aroma of the cafeteria.

"Time flies," the superintendent said. "You're going to be with this gentleman's outfit now?" He nodded toward me.

"We hire only the best and the brightest." I slipped a page out of my notebook. I handed the list of names to Archer, and he studied it as he circled his desk to sit down in the huge leather swivel chair. The throne.

"Arnett, Packard, Pasquale, Singer, Zamora, Zapia." My list wasn't in alphabetical order, but Archer's mind was. He found a convenient category for the six. "Good kids, all, Sheriff. What are we fishing for?"

"Glenn, I'm interested in what they might be able to tell us about Larry Zipoli." I would hesitate about mentioning a case to ninety-nine percent of Posadas County residents, knowing that gossip made a prairie wildfire seem sluggish. But Glenn Archer had never given me reason to doubt his discretion. His frown was immediate.

"What a mess," he whispered. He read the list again, then looked up at me, tapping the little piece of paper against his thumb. "I have to hope that none of these kiddos are in any way involved with that."

"We hope not."

"Specifically you need..."

"Whatever you can tell me," I said. "It would be convenient to chat with each one. We can do that off school grounds, but this will save us some time."

"Can you tell me what direction you're headed with this?"

I sighed. "Just preliminaries, Glenn. That group of boys has spent time with Zipoli in the past. Recreational trips over to the Butte, that sort of thing. At this stage, we're just scouting the options. Fishing, like you say."

"I heard Mr. Zipoli was killed in cold blood? While he was working?"

"The victim was minding his own business, grading a county road. Somebody put a bullet through his brain and left him sitting there in the sun."

"My God."

"Right now, we're touching bases with anyone who knew Zipoli, who spent any time with him. Maybe it'll lead somewhere. Maybe it won't." I shrugged. "These six were in his circle, so there we are. Until something better comes along, we talk with everyone we meet."

Archer pivoted just enough in his chair that he could reach his computer keyboard. He stared at the screen as the program woke up. "We never know, do we." I didn't know just what he meant by that, and didn't ask. "Arnett and Zapia are seniors, the others are juniors. Well, all but Louis." Archer glanced across at me. "Louis Zamora? He's a sophomore this year."

He frowned at the screen again, then relaxed back in his chair. "They're not a group here at school, if you know what I mean. Not like it's the 'gang of six.' That's interesting. I mean, Tommy Pasquale and Matt Singer hang out together some." He smiled at Estelle. "I'm sure you remember how it was, Estelle. There's friends," and he held his arms out wide, encircling a large, imaginary beach ball, then brought his hands together to palm a basketball, "and there's friends, and then," he clasped his palms tightly, "there's *friends*. Best buds. Go to class together, eat lunch together, hang out at the Handiway together, go to parties together." He leaned forward and tapped the list. "I'd put these six in the first category." He spread his arms again.

His fingers danced on the computer keys, and he leaned his chin in his left hand as he read the results. "And would you believe this…of the six, *four* are AWOL today." Archer turned just enough to catch my eye. "Can you believe that? First day of the first week of school, and there they go." He shrugged philosophically. "We expect absentees, really until next week. But still…"

"Which ones didn't make it today?"

"Pasquale, Zamora, Arnett and Packard." He frowned. "Zamora surprises me. He didn't miss a single day last year, when he was a freshman. And if my memory serves me, he was a star in middle school, too…perfect attendance. Jason Packard is junior, just barely. You probably know him."

"The Packard ranch up by Newton," I said.

"That's it." Archer grimaced. "And caught right in the middle. Jason lives here in town with his grandmother, and I won't even begin trying to explain the mess that family's in. Suffice to say that I don't think we offer a whole lot that's of interest to the boy. He's a ranch kid at heart, regardless of how often his stepfather tries to beat it out of him, so there's no telling what's keeping him away from school today."

Estelle Reyes' black eye brows narrowed a bit at that. She'd learn soon enough that ninety percent of the criminal cases that the Sheriff's Department dealt with blossomed first as a family dispute of some kind. And most of the time, kids were caught painfully in the middle.

"Jason lives and breathes 4-H, and we have fairs coming up. He could be busy with that, although how he does it caught between two places is beyond me." Archer smiled gently. "That's one of the amazing things about kids, sometimes. They can bounce back from the darnedest things." He nodded at the computer. "Now Maurice 'Mo' Arnett? There's no telling. He's a senior, and I'm proud to report that he has an early admission at the University of New Mexico. He'll be leaving us in January, and I know he's pretty excited about it. He's signed up for R.O.T.C., with a military career in mind. Military might be just what that kid needs. He's one of those rascals who is seventeen going on eight, if you know what I mean. Some military discipline will do him good. Now," and he scrolled the computer display to another screenful, "Mr. Thomas Pasquale? Again, who knows. He's a junior, and if it has an engine, Tommy is operating it."

"Let's start with the other two," I said. "The ones *in* school. Matt Singer and the Zapia kid. Two birds in the hand."

"We can do that. Hang on just a minute." He rose and left the office, this time leaving the door open.

I leaned closer to Estelle. "Something to watch. The Zamora kid? His older brother is Mike, over at the Highway Department. The one who worked directly with Larry Zipoli."

Chapter Twenty-five

In the next few minutes, we learned little from Matt Singer and Eric Zapia that we didn't already know. Both boys certainly knew Larry Zipoli, and had taken part in various recreational outings with him. There was no formal arrangement, no calendaring of events. Their participation was a spur of the moment thing. Eric Zapia's folks hadn't been thrilled with his taking part in the excursions over to Elephant Butte, and I got the impression that Eric was kept on a pretty short leash.

Still, Zipoli didn't actively recruit these boys from around the neighborhood. It appeared that he was a kid magnet whether he wanted to be or not. Fancy truck, fast boat, not the least bit circumspect about supplying the odd can of suds now and then…and his youngest attractive daughter who was home often enough to inspire lust in teenaged minds.

During the brief interviews, Estelle Reyes kept her own council. She watched each kid, each twitch of the hand, each squirm in the chair. Matt Singer tried to ignore her for the first few minutes, then ended up talking directly to the young lady, despite the questions coming exclusively from me. Had the opportunity presented itself, he probably would have asked her out on a date.

Watching the interplay between the two young people— and it was a one-way attraction, obviously—was fascinating. When he'd first come into the room, Matt Singer had been a bit stooped, affecting that backpack induced posture so many teens suffered, but now he sat with shoulders square, trying to add a couple of years of maturity. He had a nice smile, and apparently had decided during a session in front of the mirror that a slight Elvis curl of the lips added to his charm. He tried several versions of that on Estelle, all to no avail.

For his turn, Eric Zapia impressed me as a harmless airhead, a kid who'd spent too long with the earphones cranked up to ten. It took him a while to find the superintendent's office, and he sort of sidled through the door as if concerned that he might be entering the wrong room. I didn't care what he wore, or how ridiculous his spiky hair looked, but *he* certainly did, and I think he hoped one of us would say something. His favorite word was, "whaaa?" as if either his hearing or his comprehension had headed south. Our interview with him didn't last long—he was either dim-witted or a consummate actor. Apparently he enjoyed the lake outings because of the "chicks," the parading laker groupies.

We left the school with one little tidbit of information that pointed us toward something we already knew. Eric Zapia didn't ride a bike—I'm not sure his reflexes were sharp enough for that, but he fingered two who did. Both Tom Pasquale and Jason Packard—two of the students enjoying hooky—were cyclists of some repute, and Larry Zipoli had been seem talking to cyclists sometime during his last hours on earth.

In a world where the automobile was God, here were two kids who still pedaled. Jason missed his horses, I would guess, and Tommy Pasquale would have preferred something with a V-8. But according to Eric Zapia, both Pasquale and Packard were rabid fans of the professional teams—enough so that they wore the bright racing jerseys from time to time, even wore them in *public,* risking the scorn of peers. They had proposed a bike club at school, and were greeted with underwhelming enthusiasm.

Riding bikes didn't seem a likely thrill for either of them. Maybe some of the roads on the side of Cat Mesa were sufficiently vertical that they could reach escape velocity. Adrenalin junkies, both boys must have loved Larry Zipoli's boat, with its rumbling V-8, chrome-plated air cleaners, and ear-busting exhaust stacks.

"What do you think?" I asked Estelle as I eased the county car out of the school's circle driveway. "Did that little session at the school bring back memories for you?"

"In what regard, sir?"

Well, of course she wasn't going to babble on about her own high school experience, regardless of how recent it might be. I was coming to learn that Ms. Reyes' reticence wasn't just a passing phase. Most of us humans took some small delight in chatting about ourselves. Somebody tells us a yarn about their adventures, even if it was just a flat tire on the way to Walmart, and we respond with our own version, usually flavored with a little one-upsmanship. "Why, I had *two* flats last night in the middle of the worst electric storm of the century."

Estelle Reyes apparently didn't feel even the slightest need to chat about her high school years, challenging as they must have been. I had no doubt that her thoughts were focused on *El Jardin de los Tres Santos,* but she didn't continue her suppositions about that, either. She'd spoken her piece, displayed what little evidence there was, and got on with her day. And I liked that, from the very start. She kept her focus on the job at hand. That didn't mean some small room in her brain wasn't reserved for the welfare of the three saints.

"Schools are a culture all their own," I said by way of explanation.

"Yes, sir."

I chuckled at that. "Who do you want to find first?"

"The cyclists," she said, cutting to the chase. The radio crackled, and I slowed and nodded at the mike. Sheriff Eduardo Salcido's voice sounded tired.

"Three ten, ten twenty."

Without a fraction of a second's hesitation, Estelle unclipped the mike and replied, "Three ten is just leaving the high school, eastbound on Piñon."

"Stop for a minute at Handiway."

"Ten four."

I could see the sheriff's vehicle at the convenience store before the young lady had racked the mike. "He sounds as if he spent a long night," I said.

The sheriff leaned against the fender of his unmarked county car, arms folded across his chest, boots crossed at the ankles. He didn't shift position as I drove up, but surveyed 310 critically.

"When are we going to get you a new car?" he greeted as I pulled myself out of the low-slung LTD.

"Any decade now," I replied, and patted the faded front fender. New vehicles, when they infrequently arrived, went to road deputies. "Old men get old cars." Salcido smiled at that, and raised a hand to tip his hat at Estelle, who had remained in the car.

"How is she getting along?"

"Just fine. She's a thinker, Eduardo. I like that."

Salcido nodded, but it wasn't the talented young lady whom he had on his mind. "Jack Newton died early this morning."

I felt the same pang that most folks my age—or the sheriff's—feel when someone near our own demographic dies. Mortality is a melancholy thing. "I'm sorry to hear that, but it's not surprising, I guess. He was in a bad way."

"That's what Nicky said. It was coming, he said. The old man was just lucky that he didn't drive that big Caddy into somebody first." Salcido pushed himself away from the car. "Ay," the sheriff added, and shook his head. He straightened his shoulders, and I heard weary bones pop. "Bobby is working with George Payton this morning."

"What's George got for us?"

"I don't know. Bobby thinks he's got a lock on the bullet make, and that sent him off, you know. He wanted to paw through George's stuff."

I frowned. "And George?" Payton owned the only gun shops in town, a nifty, memento-filled little place with more inventory than most shop five times its size. And the shop was *his* turf.

George Payton didn't let anyone forget that. I couldn't imagine George opening his books to the cops, no matter how well he knew Bobby Torrez, or me, or Eduardo.

"I think we're going to need a warrant," Eduardo said. "Bobby said no, but you know, I'll be surprised if George opens his books to us. I was thinking that maybe you need to talk with him."

"What's Bobby hunting?"

Salcido pushed his Stetson back on his skull, and he rubbed his eyes wearily. "He's sure now that the ammunition used was .30-30. And he thinks that he knows the brand of bullet."

"No one found a shell casing, Eduardo."

"No, no. Not the casing, *Jefito*. But the *bullet*. He says he's sure it's a Mountain States brand."

"Millions of those around, I suppose. He thinks that George Payton might have sold it originally?"

Salcido's shrug was deep and expressive. "Maybe he did."

"Or mail order. Mountain States has been in business for years."

"But it's something, you know. If the ammunition was hand-loaded, rather than just off the shelf..." He shook his head slowly, gazing off into the distance. "This is a bad thing. A bad thing."

I nodded. "And any little bit is going to help." I understood what had piqued Bobby Torrez's curiosity. A box of loaded ammo, bought from the store shelf, would have generic bullets, either made by the ammo brand company itself, like Winchester or Remington, or purchased from a major bullet supplier, like Sierra, Speer, or Hornady. Mountain States was a smaller company, catering to handloaders rather than manufacturers.

"You were at the school this morning?"

"You bet. We talked with two of the kids—Matt Singer and Eric Zapia. The other four are ditching school today."

"Ditching." Salcido savored the syllables. "I used to enjoy that. Maybe too much. Didn't get me anywhere, though." He flashed a smile. "You're going to talk with them this morning?"

"I'm curious, is all. Two of the kids are cyclists, and with weather like this, I'm not surprised that the bikes hold more attraction than school. We'll start there. The Pasquale kid and Jason Packard."

Salcido bent and looked into my car. "What do you think, señorita?"

"I'm curious to hear what they have to say, sir."

"We're curious, all right," he smiled, and looked across at me. "All this is *muy curioso.* You'll have time to stop by George's place? Bobby's there right now."

"We'll make the time," I said. "Where are you headed?"

"Home, I think. You know, I didn't sleep so good last night." He rubbed his chest over his breastbone. "This whole thing with Zipoli…" He shrugged helplessly. "It's a bad thing, this not knowing. Something like this happening right in our own back yard."

"We'll figure it out, Eduardo." I saw my last chance to fill him on the *Tres Santos,* but he didn't look as if he needed more weight on his shoulders.

He held up a hand, and turned back to his car. From the avalanche on the front seat, he rescued a manila folder. "We got this late yesterday." He handed it to me, and I flipped the cover. The application was generic, filled out in large, block letters that would have been appropriate for a ten year-old.

"Jerome Jesse Murton. Not a chance, Eduardo," I said, and snapped it shut. "J.J. Murton shouldn't even be working for the village. Chief Martinez should have his head examined for allowing it."

Salcido's smile was gentle. "He might fit into dispatch all right. He's dependable, you know."

"J.J. Murton is an illiterate moron," I snapped.

"In three years with the PD, he's never missed a day of work. That's what the chief tells me."

"Whoopee. That means he's a *consistent* illiterate moron. There are enough ways for a deputy to step into trouble without someone like Murton at his back in dispatch. Don't do it, sheriff. You want my advice, don't do it. Hell, if we get short, *I'll* sit dispatch if it comes to that."

I handed the folder back. "Anyway, Miss Reyes can step in to dispatch as soon as I finish up some orientation."

"You sounded good on the radio," the sheriff said to Estelle and straightened to pat me on the shoulder. "I guess we have her caught up in the middle of things, no?"

"And that's the way it is," I replied. "It's good for her to see how all this works. There'll be plenty of time to swim in all the paperwork later."

"But then she goes to academy, and we won't have her on staff for eight weeks. Maybe more. I was just thinking…"

"You'll get into trouble doing that, Eduardo. You want my advice, don't do it."

The sheriff wobbled his head, neither a yes nor a no. "Let's sit down this afternoon and see where all this is leading us," he said. I didn't want to spend five more minutes thinking about the Sleeping Beauty, but it was Salcido's call. I appreciated that all employers faced the same conundrum—finding employees who showed up for work when they were supposed to, without going missing during the holidays or finding excuses on Monday mornings and Friday afternoons. But critical jobs deserved more than just a warm body.

Chapter Twenty-six

We could have jogged over to George Payton's modest shop in less time than it took to mount up, turn the LTD around, and cross traffic on Bustos to the little avenue behind Pershing Park. "Cross traffic" meant pausing for a second while Mimi Sloan drove through the intersection in her Oldsmobile.

Deputy Torrez's new Bronco was parked in front of Shooters' Supply, taking advantage of a scraggly elm for a spot of shade. I swung in behind the Bronco.

"You've met George Payton before?" I asked Estelle.

"No, sir. I know who he is, that's all. I've heard Reubén talk about him now and then."

"I'm not surprised," I said. "Where else would Reubén find ammo for that antique of his."

"There's a partial box of cartridges on the mantel above the fireplace," Estelle said. "The dust on them is about this thick," and she held her fingers an inch apart. "They haven't been touched in a long time."

"And let's hope they stay that way." I perused the junk on the seat for a moment, wondering what I had forgotten. "You want to call us in? Leave us available, though."

She did so without fanfare, putting us ten-eight at 101 Baca. General Pershing was honored by the whole park and facing street named for him, while Elfego Baca's memory was noted with a short cul-de-sac, more of an alley than a street.

The front door of the shop opened with a single squeal, and George Payton looked up from the large book and brochure that engrossed him and Deputy Torrez. The deputy's black briefcase rested on the counter.

"What the hell do you want?" George's warm, affectionate greeting was par for the course, and didn't actually mean that he was an abrasive old son-of-a-bitch, which he was, or that he didn't want to see us—which he probably didn't. He squinted at me through his coke-bottle glasses. Diabetes was killing him just as surely as high blood pressure and arteriosclerosis were likely killing me, and he leaned his heavy body against the counter, taking the weight off his ballooning ankles. His gaze locked on Estelle as she gently closed the door behind us.

"Showing your granddaughter around the big city, Billy?" Payton was the only person in the world who still used a nickname that had rested mercifully dormant since the days of Mrs. Lewis, my third grade teacher.

"George Payton, this is Estelle Reyes."

"Yeah, yeah," George said ungraciously. "I know who she is." He nodded at Estelle, but didn't offer a hand. "How's the old man?"

"He's fine, sir," Estelle replied.

"So, what, you're thinkin' of workin' at the funny farm now with these guys?"

"Yes, sir."

He glanced at me, rheumy blue eyes twinkling, then back at Estelle. "You know, they never come in here unless they want something. And it sure as hell ain't never to *buy* anything." He pulled back a little, surveying the row of handguns on the top shelf. He selected one boxed specimen, pulled it out, and slid it across the glass to me. "Got you one," he said. "Came in with a collection yesterday." The stainless Smith and Wesson Model 66 four-inch appeared flawless, but I didn't dare pick it up, knowing the instant it nestled in my hand, I'd have to own it.

"I'll be back to talk with you about that," I said.

"Got about eight other people who want that one," George said.

"Well, go ahead and sell it to them, then," I said. "I'd hate to barge in and cut my place in line." That earned what passed for a smile.

"Are you doing any good?" I asked Deputy Robert Torrez. He towered over the three of us, darkly handsome, and most of the time overly serious. His face could stand a little smile cracking now and then if he expected a Hollywood talent scout to pay him any mind. He and Estelle would make a hell of a couple, but nature didn't need any help, or even suggestions, from me.

"I was just telling the deputy that I don't sell much Mountain States inventory," George Payton said before Torrez had a chance to reply. He put the Model 66 away, and then slid a colorful brochure toward me with the Mountain States logo prominent across the top. "This was in my slush pile. They keep sendin' me junk, even when I don't order nothin'."

"There's always a chance," I said.

"Hell, they got a good lineup, but I don't sell five boxes of their stuff a year, all of it special order. And what's the point of that? All a guy has to do is call their 800 number and order it direct." He reached out and made a circle around the image of the 170-grain thirty caliber Mountain Slam flat-nosed bullet, just about in the middle of their product line-up. "The young fella is right, though." He spoke as if Deputy Robert Torrez wasn't standing right there at the counter. "That's what you have."

"Not popular, or what? Just pricy?"

Payton shrugged as if he was loathe to sound as if he knew something. "Expensive, mostly."

"So who's likely to use these?"

George shrugged. "They're goin' after some of the cowboy action shooters, maybe. Some of them get pretty serious. Maybe some of the more serious lever-action metallic silhouette shooters who want a bullet just a bit heavier than average." His finger drifted down the row of illustrations, and stopped over a long bullet labeled for the .38-55 Winchester. "Not too many folks making this one commercially. Or the .40 caliber either." He swept his finger all the way to the end of the line-up. "How many companies you think make the big .50? You got a handful of folks loading the .50-110, but not many. Now, if you're going to hand load for some run-of-the-mill old rifle like a .30-30, like what you're talking about, what's the point of using premium, custom bullets?" He laughed a sort of choked-up *huff, huff.* "Especially when you're going to go ahead and shoot the stuff out of the wrong gun."

"Some folks like the best, maybe?"

George scoffed. "Hell, if I was handloading for an old .30-30—well, I wouldn't do that anyway—but if I did, I'd just buy some cheap Winchester bulk stuff. That'll shoot better'n me or the gun, either one."

"As I remember, you're not required to keep records of cartridge component sales."

George shook his head and grimaced. "And even if I was..." he left the rest to our imagination. "That's what this one was asking," and he jerked his big round head toward Bob Torrez.

"So...what did you think of Robert's experiment with the two rifles?"

"There's easier ways to shoot somebody," George said. "You really think this went down that way?"

"It's beginning to look like it."

"Well," he said philosophically, and shrugged again. His eyebrow cocked at me.

"George, it might be helpful if we knew of any recent sales that might fit this pattern."

George looked pained. He made his way to the battered swivel chair behind an amazingly cluttered desk and relaxed back in it, hands folded over his belly. "If you think that I'm going to turn over a list of all my customers, you're nuts. I don't care how much paperwork you bring over from old man Smith."

"That's not what we're asking for." I hadn't even seriously considered the notion of a warrant from Judge Everett Smith.

"Well, that's good, sheriff. Because I'm not going to list everyone I know who shoots a .30-30, or a .32 Winchester Special. I'm not going to give you a list of every Tom, Dick, and Harry who reloads his own ammunition, or who buys components." His large head shook sadly, as if we'd asked him to trade his soul. "That just isn't going to happen."

"You wouldn't be giving us much, George. For a village the size of Posadas, what are we talking about—ten people at most?"

"One's all it takes, Billy. Word gets around that when you buy something from old George Payton, your personal information is handed over to the cops...I might just as well close the doors right now. Nope, I don't see that as my job."

I wasn't in the mood to argue the point with George. Anytime someone purchased a firearm, the buyer filled out the yellow form required by the ATF, but that form stayed with the dealer. Other than that, nothing. Minors were prohibited from buying ammo or the like before sixteen or so, but no records were kept of sales.

"That's not what we had in mind," Deputy Torrez said, his voice just a notch above a whisper.

"Yeah, I could name a couple of guys who own Winchesters, including you and myself—and I suppose you could get a warrant and look through my books for recent sales. It ain't going to tell you nothing. Trust me on that. You got something screwball going on here, that's what I think. And by the way," and he tapped the edge of his desk with his heavy ring. "The last lever gun I sold was a .444 Marlin, and that was months ago." He caught Torrez's trace of a smile and nodded with smug triumph. "And yeah, *you* bought that."

"Did you know Larry Zipoli very well, George?" I asked.

"Nope."

"At all?"

"Nope." Apparently he realized how obstinate he was sounding, because he shrugged helplessly. "Look, if I knew something about all this, maybe I'd find a way to let you know. But I don't. The whole thing is screwy, if you ask me. Nobody is going to intentionally put the wrong ammunition in a rifle. Just maybe in this case it was a dumb mistake that happened to have worked."

"Well, we'll figure out a way to track it," I said.

"I suppose you will," George Payton said helpfully. "Best of luck to you."

While we were jawing, Estelle had drifted over toward the overloaded shelves of boxed bullets. Customers who hand-loaded could assemble their own favorite brew, selecting primers, empty casings, propellant and finally bullets. And George was right. With the attention that careful hand-loading required, it was improbable that the finished product would then be stuffed—intentionally—into the wrong gun.

Maybe that was what the young lady was thinking. Her perusal took her over toward the window, and she stopped by a small bulletin board that was papered with notices and 3 x 5 cards advertising the stuff of shooters and hunters. Some of the notices and ads had been tacked there for so long that they imitated parchment.

Leaving the deputy to pack up his show-and-tell and make peace with George Payton, I joined Estelle as she jotted notes from the bulletin board.

"What's up?"

"I was wondering what a three-gun match was, sir."

"That would be something where they use three guns," I said helpfully, and saw the aging flyer that held her interest. I turned so that the old man could hear me. "George, how does a three-gun match work?"

"All sorts of ways," he said.

"Like how? Name me one, you cantankerous old bastard."

He chuckled with delight. "Maybe long range silhouette with the heavy guns, then the short range course with center-fire pistol cartridges and a third round with .22s. Usually like that."

"By long range, what do you mean?"

"Starts at fifty meters, with the last stage out at two hundred."

"That doesn't seem so far."

George huffed. "You try it."

"Scopes?"

"Hell, no."

"Can I use a rest. Off a table for support?"

"Nope. You just stand there and wobble."

"Ah. So a competitor needs a variety of hardware," I said more to Estelle than anyone else. She had placed a finger on the flyer, and tapped gently. I leaned closer so I could read the faded print. "Huh." She turned her little notebook so I could see the page she'd been working on, and I nodded.

"George, does Mark Arnett still run these matches? He's the contact person, or what? I'm talking about this three-gun they had down in Cruces last…" I moved a couple notices to one side to reveal the upper right corner of the flyer and the date. "Last summer."

"I'm not sure whether he does or not," George replied unconvincingly. He knew damn well what Mark Arnett did. He turned toward the door as it opened to allow in a grizzled fellow as huge as two of me, along with an over-weight golden retriever who instantly made a dogline for Estelle, tail flailing.

"Dodie, get back here," the fellow snapped. The dog ignored him, and the man grinned at Estelle. "He sure likes the ladies. Just ignore him."

She did, and after a quick snuffle of her pants suit trousers, Dodie gave up.

"Mark would be the best one to check with about future events, though?" I asked, and George looked sideways at me.

"I guess maybe."

Wilbur Haines, never bashful about becoming part of the conversation, thrust out a huge paw toward me.

"Mornin', Sheriff. Hey, Bobby." He pumped hands all around, including Estelle's. I introduced them, and Wilbur's beard bounced as he first nodded and then shook his head. The dog tried to wag himself into a big yellow ball.

"Wilbur, you'd know," George said.

"What would I know?"

"Does Mark Arnett still run the silhouette matches? I know he did for a while, there."

"Well, sure he does," Wilbur said, and found himself a chair. I knew Wilbur was one of the morning Geezer Group that gathered at the shop. In another few minutes, two or three more old guys would arrive at George's shop, and the coffee and donuts and tall tales would start to fly. "Sure he does." Wilbur looked up at me. "You lookin' to get into competition, Sheriff?"

"Been thinking about it," I said. "The idea appeals to me."

Wilbur nodded eagerly. "You bet. Arnett's the one to talk to on that, all right. He generally posts the schedules." He twisted and peered across the small room at the bulletin board, then grinned again at Estelle. "You can arrest me anytime, little lady." His impression of John Wayne lacked something, but another thought jarred Wilbur loose from his ogling of the little lady. "He's been trying to pry some land loose from the county for a decent shooting range, you know."

"I knew there was some interest along those lines."

"Oh, sure. Other than the gravel pit, which isn't open all the time, there's no good, close place for us to go. I mean out on the prairie, or up on the mesa, sure, but nothing real close or real handy. We've been figuring the county has lots of space out north of the airport there, against the mesa. Hell, that's only seven miles from town."

"Seems logical," I said. Deputy Torrez was already at the door, and I didn't want to linger. "You gents have a good day," I said. George muttered something, and Wilbur grabbed the dog's collar. We made our exit before the chitchat locked us in for another hour. I promised George that I'd take him to lunch in the near future, but his "Yeah, yeah" didn't sound as if he was holding his breath waiting.

"You want me to go talk with Arnett?" Torrez said as the door closed behind me.

"No. Let me." I stood in the sun for a moment, letting it bathe my pulse back down where it belonged. My car's passenger door closed, and I saw Estelle was already settled in.

"Good eyes," I said as I slid into the seat. She'd opened a door for us that I'd missed.

"I didn't know if Mark Arnett was related to Mo," she said, scanning her notes.

"Oh, he's related, all right. Indeed he is. Mark, Mo, and little sister Maureen. Mom is Mindy." I thumped the steering wheel as the LTD cranked into life. "Cute, eh?"

Chapter Twenty-seven

Talking to Mark Arnett would have involved a trip to Deming, where he was estimating a roofing job. Mom Mindy was in her office at the rectory of St. Mary's Catholic Church, and I wasn't in the mood to confront her. She ran the church with an iron fist, leaving Father Vince Carey free to save souls. Mindy knew everything about church operations, about every member of the congregation. But first, I was interested in what young Mo had to say without mom hovering over his shoulder.

We cruised around the block to north Fourth. No one appeared to be home at the Arnett *casa,* and I parked just around the corner on Blaine with a clear view of Zipoli's place and the various neighbors, including Jim Raught's address. A short stroll took me across the street, and I knocked on front, side, and back doors of the Arnett's trim little place. Nothing. The garage was closed and dark.

As I recrossed the street, I was close enough to the office to use my handheld on car-to-car, where there were fewer eavesdroppers. "PCS, three ten."

"Go ahead, three ten."

"PCS, find out what vehicles are registered to Mark or Mindy Arnett." I spelled the last name for him and provided the address. Deputy Robert Torrez's oldest sister was manager of the local Department of Motor Vehicle office, and on several occasions she had made investigations a whole lot easier than us trying to stumble through the computer's innards to find what we wanted.

"Ten four, three ten."

Back in the car, I dug the Posadas phone book out of the center console. Rebecca Pasquale was listed at 313 South Tenth, just a few blocks south of Bustos, the main east-west drag through the village. She worked at one of the dry cleaning establishments, and her ex-husband Manny tried his best in Las Cruces. The last time I had seen Manny, he was selling newspapers at one of the major intersections near the plaza.

But it was the Pasquales' cycle-riding son, Thomas, who interested me at the moment.

I'd like to claim that brilliant detective work located the kid. Not so. We were rolling across the old irrigation bridge, headed for the intersection of Twelfth and Bustos, when I saw the bike rider. Dressed in bumble bee Spandex, with helmet low over his eyes and hi-tech riding glasses reflecting the sun, the kid blew through the stop sign, weaved around first one car and then another, and sprinted across Bustos, taking the right hand lane westward. I was sure he didn't see us—by that time, my county car had drifted into the shade of the Don Juan de Oñate restaurant.

As he passed directly in front of us, I recognized Tommy Pasquale, focused on the highway in front of him, oblivious to traffic from the side roads. Maybe his peripheral vision was gecko-sharp. He didn't look my way, but powered west. Bustos eventually left the village and became the pothole studded state highway 17, heading westward out of Posadas County.

"One of our boys," I mused, and watched the kid crank up to speed. Traffic was light, of course—other than a few ranchers or lost tourists, there was little reason to take this particular route. A high school kid playing hooky might head out to the desert for some personal reflection. Maybe. I had had intimate experience with four teenagers when my own brood worked their way through the impossible years, and deep reflection wasn't a common course of action. Tommy Pasquale was riding as if he needed to burn out the kinks.

When the certified speedometer in the LTD touched twenty-one miles an hour, I was pacing the kid, holding fifty yards behind him. Twenty-one may not seem like light speed, but young Thomas was burning the calories. I'd read enough sporting magazines to know that maintaining anything over twenty miles an hour on the flat and level—and with a hint of head wind—took conditioning and muscle. How long this kid could keep it up was anyone's guess, but his whole body spoke determination.

The young man never looked behind him. He hunched into the breeze, hands down on the drops, pumping like a machine. Keep that up, and in an hour, he'd be in Arizona.

"Let's see what he has to say," I said, and reached for the switch on the radio console. I waited a moment until an oncoming pickup truck towing a stock trailer rumbled past east bound, and then waited again until a long stretch of guard rail slipped by. I lit the roof rack and touched the siren's yelp mode for a single whoop. That won the cyclist's attention. His rhythm broke and he cranked around on the saddle to look at us.

I pointed at the shoulder, and he collected his balance again and paid attention as he slowed without turning off the pavement. In a moment he twisted his feet sideways to pop the pedal clips and drifted to a stop. He hopped off and lifted the bike from the macadam onto the grass-dotted shoulder, setting the machine down as carefully as if it were made out of glass.

The county car's tires crunched off the pavement, cutting through the grass, goatheads, broken bottles and all the other crap that lines our nation's highways. No wonder the kid was so careful. I lifted the mike.

"PCS, three ten is ten six with a bicyclist, mile marker 34, State 17."

"Ten four, three ten." T.C. Barnes didn't ask what I was doing, but the ten-six request meant we wouldn't be interrupted unless a storm broke loose somewhere in the county.

"Always," I said to Estelle Reyes. "No matter how inconsequential, no matter how innocuous. Always keep dispatch

informed, especially when you're going to be out of the car."
Do as I say, not as I do. There were many times when I was loath
to blab over the air the details of what I was up to but a rookie
didn't need to start out that way.

Tommy Pasquale watched the performance, standing on the
shoulder side of his bike, one hand on the bars, the other on the
saddle, probably wondering what he'd done to warrant a traffic
stop. I turned off the roof rack, leaving the four-ways on. As I
stepped out of the car, he took off his helmet and dark glasses,
a courtesy that impressed me.

"Good morning, sir," he said carefully, and that impressed
me even more.

"It is that," I replied. "You apparently haven't heard that the
minimum vehicular speed on all paved roads in the county is
now *twenty-five* miles an hour? I clocked you at twenty-one." His
face went blank, and I laughed. "Just kidding, Mr. Pasquale."
I stepped far enough off into the bunch grass that I could keep
an eye on traffic, should there be any. I let the kid wonder how
I came to know his name.

"This is Estelle Reyes, new with the department. We're doing
a little tour this morning, and when I caught sight of you back
there crossing Bustos, it reminded me that we had wanted to
chat with you."

He reached out a gloved hand and shook hands with Estelle.
"Yes, ma'am," he said. A husky, powerfully-built kid already
breaking six feet tall, Tom Pasquale ran a hand through his
rumpled, sandy-brown hair as if concerned that the attractive
young lady might catch him at something less than his best.

"Thomas, I wanted to talk with you about Larry Zipoli," I
said, and the kid grimaced, his hand stopping at mid-skull for
a second.

"Aw, jeez," he said, sounding like a teenager from 1955. He
dropped his gaze to the grass around his fancy cycling shoes.
"That is *so* bad."

"You knew Mr. Zipoli pretty well?"

"Sure. Mr. Z was cool." He glanced at Estelle as if her ears might be too tender for all this. "Well, sort of, anyway."

"Why 'sort of?'"

"Well, you know." I waited for him to finish the thought and could see the march of conflicting emotions across his face. He looked back toward town.

"When was the last time you talked with him?" I prompted.

"Well, it ain't been too long."

I smiled. "Up on the mesa the other day?" He looked puzzled at that, so I added, "On the county road out of town?" The light dawned.

"Yeah, me and some of the guys…talked with him for a few minutes. He was workin' the bar ditch. And he had some trouble with the grader. That old thing leaks like crazy."

"Some of the guys?"

"Yeah. You know. A couple of us were takin' the hill."

The hill. Only an attraction for the young, I thought. Pump up the mesa for five miles, even the paved portion of County Road 43 so steep that the effort threatens to explode your heart, sweat drenching the Spandex, tires cutting groves in the hot asphalt. What fun. Of course, if you were a teenaged adrenalin junkie speed-freak—and I don't mean the chemical—then maybe the trip down the hill was a fair trade. Glorious wind roaring in the ears, wheels a blur, that patch of sand maybe strategically placed at the apex of a corner…

"Who was with you?"

"Just some of the guys."

"Just *some?*"

"Like a couple of the guys."

"But today you're solo."

He ducked his head and glanced back toward town again as if the truant officer might be hot on his trail.

"I'm surprised you'd miss the first day of the first week, Thomas. Kinda tough to slip behind from the get-go, don't you think?"

"Not much going on, sir." He made a face. "I was going back this afternoon to catch Spanish and metals." He shrugged.

"Anyway, nobody does anything these two days. Except in Spanish and metals."

"They hit the ground running, do they?"

"Yes, sir."

"When you talked with Mr. Zipoli up on the mesa road, did he mention any kind of troubles he might have had with anybody? Any arguments? Anything like that?"

"No, sir."

"He didn't seem worried or apprehensive to you?" The youngster shook his head. "How long did you guys spend there?"

"Just a few minutes. Mr. Z was finishing up something he had to fix on the grader. I think he had a leak somewhere in the hydraulics that was getting worse. We just shot the breeze for a few minutes."

"Did he have any refreshments with him?"

"Sir?"

"Did Mr. Zipoli offer you anything to drink? It was a hot day, after all."

"No, sir." The two words were simple enough to say, but Thomas Pasquale had trouble with them, and his eyes flicked toward Estelle, as if maybe there'd be an ally there. The kid wasn't a practiced liar.

"What, a can of beer or something like that?"

Pasquale took a deep breath. "Yes, sir."

I let that answer hang in the bright sun for a moment. "You're starting for the Jaguars this year." I knew the starting line-up, and knew that as a ninth-grader two years before, Thomas had warmed the varsity bench for the first few games, then played a little, and then, the previous year as a sophomore, had hit pay dirt. Big and husky for his age, he loved the tackle business.

"Practice this afternoon, right?" I added.

He nodded. "I won't miss it, sir."

"I'm not concerned that you might," I said easily. "Of course, if Coach Page had driven by while you were hitting the suds with Mr. Zipoli, you wouldn't have to worry about it, would you?"

The stricken expression on the boy's broad face gave me a surge of satisfaction. Maybe he'd think a little, now and then. I took a deep breath, head tipped back, examining the kid's face through the lower choice of my bifocals. "You know, son, at this point, I just don't care about whether or not you and some of your pals shared a brew with the county road grader operator. Now, if *I* had driven by while that was going on, Mr. Zipoli would be facing all kinds of charges. At the very least, he'd have lost his job. Maybe even faced some jail time. You understand that, don't you?"

"Yes, sir." The words came out as a strangled whisper.

"But Mr. Zipoli is dead." I reached out and tapped the boy gently over the left eyebrow with an index finger. He didn't flinch. "Somebody put a rifle bullet right through the windshield of his road grader and blew his goddamned brains all over the inside of the cab." An exaggeration, of course, but it had the desired effect. "*That's* what interests us at the moment."

The kid's face paled several shades. "I don't know anything about what happened, sir. I really, really don't." His gaze didn't waver.

"I don't guess that you do, Thomas. But we'll talk with every soul we can think of who might have crossed paths with Larry Zipoli just before he was killed. Right now, the list is damn short, son, and you and your friends are included. Who were you riding with the other day?"

"Just the guys, sir."

I grinned. "Look, son, I know you don't want to rat anybody out, okay? I understand that. And I already told you…at this point, I don't care if you guys had a goddamn orgy up on the county road, and wobbled home stinkin' plastered. You follow me? We already *know* that Mr. Zipoli had beer with him… maybe some of the hard stuff as well. We already *know* that. So." I sighed. "I don't care what you and your buds did—or did not do—for a few minutes up on the mesa yesterday. But I *do* need to know who else was there that afternoon. I need to talk with them, but they won't know you're the one who gave me the names." I reached out a hand, made a fist, and thumped him gently on the shoulder. "One way or another, Thomas. And it'll save a whole lot of valuable time if you'll tell me what you know." I thumped him again, just a bit harder.

"See, the thing is, Thomas, the killer is still out there somewhere. Now, exactly why he or she pulled the trigger, we don't know. But we *will* know, Thomas. I guarantee you that. Larry Zipoli showed you guys some good times. You owe him for that."

For a long moment, Thomas Pasquale occupied himself with a bit of loose handlebar grip tape. He smoothed the frayed end in about eight directions, but his mind had no idea what his hands were doing.

"Jason and Mo," he said finally. "It was just the three of us."

"Jason Packard and Mo Arnett?"

"Yes, sir. Just the three of us."

"Mo and Jason…they're into this as much as you are?"

Thomas grinned, showing a chipped tooth he'd probably earned sometime when he'd taken up aviation with his bike. "Jason more so, Mo hardly at all. We're trying to get him on the team. Me and Jason."

Jason Packard, a junior classmate of Pasquale's, looked like a cyclist—medium height, not an extra ounce of pudge, hair cropped short, a thin, hatchet face that would split the wind. I didn't know the boy very well, other than being able to pick him out of a crowd when reminded of his name. I knew his stepdad, Lance Frank, a man who was joining the legion of unemployed as Consolidating Mining collapsed. Frank had fallen for Jason's mother, decided that ranching was the life for him, and made a hash of the whole affair—alienating Jason at the same time.

Mo Arnett had made it to his senior year without drawing the attention of the Sheriff's Department or the village police. I could pick him out of a lineup as well, but that was the extent of my background on him. A little on the pudgy side, but medium everything else, as I recalled. Medium height, looks, intelligence…nothing to make him a standout. The latest page of my memory had Mo Arnett lighting M-80's, or cherry bombs, thrilling his neighbors.

"Of the three of you, who's the fastest?" I asked.

"Jason," Thomas replied without hesitation. "I can outsprint him for a little bit, but not for any distance. And on hills, forget it."

"How's Mo do?"

"He's…" Thomas paused and made a face. "He doesn't try very hard. But his bike sucks, so that's part of it. He's got this old Schwinn three-speed that weighs a ton."

"Not a hot rod, eh."

"No, sir."

"How often does he go out with you?"

"Just a couple of times."

"He's not in school today, Thomas. I'm surprised he isn't out with you."

"I don't know where he is, sir."

"You didn't talk with him this morning?"

"No, sir."

"You'll see him this afternoon?"

"Hmmm…might."

"Where were you guys headed the other day when you stopped to chat with Zipoli?"

"We were thinking of the mesa top, but Mo was walking more than he was riding. Jason was way out ahead—he said he'd wait on top. So me and Mo were just makin' it work. I was going to try and take Jason on the hill, but then Mo couldn't keep up, and I didn't want to just take off and leave him. I knew Jason wouldn't wait, 'cause him and Mo…" He stopped, as if embarrassed by this gusher of information.

"Him and Mo what?"

"They don't get along so good any more. They used to, I guess, but…"

"So you were riding with Mo, trying to coax him along."

"Yes, sir. And then we came around that corner there above the old drive-in and Jason was stopped, talkin' with Mr. Zip."

Mr. Zip, your friendly circus clown. "For how long?"

"Just a few minutes."

I leaned back and rested my rump on the front fender of the county car, crossing my arms over my chest. "He offered you guys some refreshment?"

"Yes, sir."

"You accepted?"

That prompted a long, uncomfortable silence. Self-incrimination wasn't Tom Pasquale's favorite sport.

"I guess," he said finally.

"What, a beer or two?"

"Me and Jason shared a beer. Mo didn't."

"Really." That was interesting, peer influence being the superpower that it was.

"No, sir. He was workin' on his bike, and rode on up the road a few feet. Something with his chain, but I don't know what. I mean, what's to go wrong with a chain? It's either on or it isn't."

"What did Zipoli talk about?"

"Oh, just stuff, you know. He wanted to know if I was going to get a job with the county when I graduate."

"And are you?"

Pasquale frowned in disbelief. "No, sir. I don't think so."

"And that's it?"

"He mentioned that he'd be taking a trip over to the Butte with the boat some Sunday comin' up. That'd be cool."

"Indeed. So no mention of any arguments? Nothing like that?"

"No, sir."

"And then you went on up the hill."

"Yes, sir. Mo went on ahead some while we was talking, working on his bike, but it only took us about ten seconds to catch him."

"You went all the way to the top?"

"Me and Jason did. Mo turned back at the intersection with the paved road. That's a nice coast back down into town."

"And the two of you—you and Jason—went on to the top of the mesa."

"Yes, sir."

"Was that the last time you saw Mr. Zipoli?"

He nodded silently and then shook his head. "Is there anything I can do, sir?"

"You're doing it," I replied. I fished a business card out of my shirt pocket and handed it to him. "If you think of something else, don't hesitate to call me. If you remember something that Zipoli said to you, or you hear some rumor at school. Any little nugget." I pushed away from the car. "We're in the information business, Thomas."

He tucked the card into a nifty little plastic container that took the place of a wallet.

"And stop ditching school," I added. "That's a given. If I need to talk with you again, I want to know where to find you."

"Yes, sir."

"Jason's not with you today either? You're flying solo."

"He had to go to Cruces with his grandma for an eye appointment."

"And Mo? You don't know where he's at?"

Thomas shrugged. "I haven't seen him since...Tuesday morning? When the three of us went riding. If I saw him today, I was going to talk with him about a great bike deal for him. Jason's got this older Peugeot he wants to sell. It'd be a whole lot better than that heap he's got."

"Maybe it'll work out." I turned to Estelle. "Anything you need to know?"

She'd been working with her notebook, and now regarded Thomas Pasquale curiously. I didn't expect a flood of questions, but maybe one or two. She snapped the book closed. "I don't think so, sir."

"Then we're off," I said. "Pedal safe, son."

"I'll try to remember the minimum speed," he laughed.

"And stop signs," I added. "*Stop* actually means just that. Even for bikes."

"Yes, sir."

He lifted the bike back onto the pavement, and by the time Estelle and I were back in the car, Thomas Pasquale was already a hundred yards down the highway.

"So, there we go," I said. "Tell me what you think."

"Well, that's twice," Estelle said, and didn't amplify the thought as I keyed the mike.

"PCS, three ten is ten eight."

Dispatch acknowledged and went back to sleep.

"Twice what?" I asked.

"When Mo Arnett was having fun with the fire crackers, he made himself scarce when Larry Zipoli came home for lunch. No chit-chat, no greeting. According to Mr. Raught, Mo ran and hid. This time, the three boys come upon Mr. Zipoli out in the country, under relaxed conditions. Two of the boys stay and chat, even share a beer. Mo makes himself scarce again, heading on up the road while he monkeys with his bike."

I regarded the young lady carefully, damn impressed. "There could be dozens of explanations for that," I said. "Or not."

"Yes, sir."

"If we assume that Mo Arnett was uneasy in Larry Zipoli's company, then it would be interesting to find out why. Who knows what goes through a kid's mind."

Chapter Twenty-eight

The Arnetts owned three vehicles, one of which was parked in the driveway on North Fourth. A yellow late-model Jeep CJ-7 was parked in front of the two car garage, and records showed it was registered to Mark and Mindy Arnett. Little Maureen might be waiting until she was old enough to drive that little yellow gem to school.

Mo would have his choice. He could walk to school, all of ten minutes. He could ride the Schwinn. He could—maybe—drive the Jeep. Fat chance. He'd catch less flack from his peers on the Schwinn, although half of his pals wouldn't admit that they'd kill for the Jeep, yellow or not.

Dad Arnett would be driving the dark blue three-quarter ton Ford crew cab, somewhere at the moment between Posadas and Mark's potential roofing job in Deming.

That left mom's car, a gold late model Pontiac Grand Am, license Charlie Lincoln Thomas four niner niner. The Arnett home was six blocks from the Catholic Church on Bustos and Third. Would Mindy drive to work? Of course she would. The Pontiac was either hidden in the garage or over at the rectory.

I parked a couple of houses down from the Arnetts and walked to the front door. No one answered my knock or the bell, and I could hear the dingdong echoing through what sounded like an empty house. I took my time, rapping and ringing again, then sauntered back toward the county car. As I passed by the side of the house, I saw the heavy Schwinn bike resting against the side of the house in front of the garage.

Back at the car, I sighed. "Let's pay a visit to Mindy Arnett."

In a few minutes, Estelle and I entered the side door of the rectory, under the modest little sign that announced Father Carey's office, and walked a couple steps down a polished, dark wood hallway to the office doorway.

I earned only the briefest glance from Mindy Arnett, but she leaned to one side for a clear look at Estelle Reyes as we entered.

"Mindy, this…"

That's as far as I got with my introduction. Mindy nearly bounded to her feet, and skirted the big desk with astounding agility for a woman of such matronly build, arms wide. "For HEAVEN's sakes!" she cried. "Look who's here!" She enveloped Estelle in a hug, then pushed her away, a hand on each shoulder. "Just look at you. Teresa's little girl is *all* grown up!"

That outburst earned Mindy Arnett a warm smile from the girl, all the encouragement Mindy needed. "The *last* time I saw this young lady was at baccalaureate, I do believe." I never had been able to keep such meticulous track of acquaintances, but Mindy had no such trouble. "Of course, I see Teresa *almost* regularly, don't you know." She leaned well into Estelle's airspace, but the young lady held her ground. "We all hope that one of these days she'll move to Posadas, you know. I mean, Tres Santos is *so* picturesque, but still…" She took a quick breath. "I *do* hope you'll be joining us now that you're with the county. You know, *I* think that's so exciting. I mean, have we ever had a woman deputy? I don't think we have. And it's long overdue, don't you think so?" That was my cue to fit a word in edgewise, but I was slow on the uptake.

I hadn't told Mindy that Estelle had joined us, but the grapevine was efficient. And what I feared would happen was in full swing. Unless I could clap a hand over her mouth, Mindy Arnett would continue to gush. Certainly, Father Vince Carey had long since figured out how to manage the woman, but my strategy simply had been to ignore her.

Mindy dropped her hands and reached across the desk to poke keys on the computer's keyboard, then took me by surprise. "Now, did you want to visit with Father? I think he's in his office this very minute." Her face softened with concern. "And *such* a tragedy with Larry Zipoli." Her hand drifted up to cover her mouth. "I just can't imagine…"

"Actually, I need to chat with you, Mindy," I said, and toed her office door closed. "Do you have a moment?"

"My word, of course I do." She looked at me warily as she slid back into her chair. She waved toward two straight chairs that nestled tight against floral wall paper. "*Such* a tragic week we've had. First Mr. Newton passing away, then that *awful* thing with the Zipolis. Just awful. And I suppose you knew Miriam Archuleta?"

I didn't, but Mindy rattled on. "She had *just* gone to live with her son in El Paso, and died with the pneumonia, of all things." She shook her head. "Such a *wonderful* woman she was." Mindy folded her hands, either about to run down, or settling in. In her mind, apparently, Larry Zipoli's murder was in the same category as a death from old age or pneumonia.

"Mrs. Arnett, we're in the process of talking to anyone who might have spent some time with Larry Zipoli just before his death."

"Well, I should *think* so," she responded quickly. "You know, I haven't talked with either Larry or Marilyn in quite some time." She leaned forward and lowered her voice a bit. "They aren't our most regular members here at the church, you know. Once in a while, I have the opportunity to chat with Jim next door to them." She looked conspiratorial. "We're always concerned with shepherds who stray, you know."

I didn't know, and didn't care. I kept my tone pleasant as I said, "Actually, I wasn't concerned with you, Mrs. Arnett." I held up a hand as she took a breath, winding up to begin another roll. "There's a group of kids who hang out at the Zipolis at various times. On several occasions, they've gone to the lake with the family. Water skiing, that sort of thing."

Her right hand drifted to her mouth. "Oh, my, are you saying that one of the kids had something to do…"

"Nope, I'm not saying that, Mrs. Arnett. I'm saying that several youngsters, your son Mo included, had occasion to spend time with Larry Zipoli—most often over at the lake, or working on the boat at his home."

"Mo and…"

"At the moment, I'm concerned with Mo," I nodded. She wanted the whole list, of course, but that wasn't going to happen. "He's not in school today, I understand."

"He most certainly *is* in school," Mrs. Arnett said, and some steel crept into her voice, reprimanding me for making such a silly mistake.

Her eyes narrowed when I added, "And I can understand that, the weather being what it is. A grand day for a little hooky."

She turned and regarded the telephone console. A call to the school would clear things up, but there lay the risk. Without making the call, Mindy Arnett could rest comfortable in the notion that I was wrong, and that her son was in fact sitting at an uncomfortable desk, listening to a litany of all the work the school year held in store, overlaying the assurances of all the *fun* he was certain to have.

"Go ahead," I said gently. "You'll want confirmation, Mindy."

She sat back and looked at me. "Do you know where he's been?"

"No. That's why we're here."

"I don't understand, then. You sound as if he's involved in something. Since when did you folks become truant officers?"

"Since never," I said with a chuckle. "As I told you, we're in the interview process. Now, it's our understanding that Mo and some of his friends frequented the Zipoli *casa,* and even took some recreational trips to the Butte. The kids might not have a damn thing to tell us. Then again, we never know. They might have heard or seen something that could be a help." I shrugged. "That's the sum and substance of it."

"Let me," she said, and picked up the phone. In a couple of minutes, she settled the receiver back in its cradle, clearly distressed at what the school secretary had reported. "All day today." She dialed another number, and the phone at her home rang ten times before she gave up. With the efficiency of a practiced secretary, she punched in another number. "Is Mark back from Deming yet, Julie?" She listened in silence for a moment. "All right. What's that number?" She jotted, broke off the call, and dialed again, this time long distance.

We waited patiently while she tracked down her husband. Finally, after the usual back and forth of greetings and explanation, she asked with visible relief at having someone she trusted to talk with, "Mark, is Mo with you?" Obviously he wasn't. "He's not in school today." She glanced at me. "Well, I'm not sure where he is. The sheriff is here and wants to talk with him." I couldn't hear Mark Arnett's voice, but his tone was such that Mindy didn't interrupt him. After a moment of nodding, she said, "No…it's Bill Gastner. Here, why don't you talk with him?"

I took the receiver. "Mark? Bill Gastner. How are you."

"What's the deal, sheriff?" In the background, I could hear traffic, and at least one piece of heavy equipment, its exhaust bark close by.

"We'd like to chat with Mo about when he might have talked last with Larry Zipoli."

"Shit."

Exactly what Mark Arnett meant by that was unclear. "Just some things that we want to clear up," I added.

"Like what?"

"When Mo last saw Mr. Zipoli, for example. Or if he heard Zipoli talk about any…what, issues that he might have had with anybody? Things like that."

"Why Mo? He's not the only kid that hangs out over there."

"No, he's not. He's one of several. We've started the process of talking with them all."

"Huh. So what's the deal, anyway?" He didn't sound terribly concerned.

"Just that. We want to talk with anyone who happened to see Zipoli recently."

"Well, Mo ought to be in school. That's all I can tell you, sheriff." He barked a short laugh. "He's not the most motivated little bugger, I'll tell you that."

"Any particular place that he likes to go?"

"Nope. I mean, other than in front of the damn video games. Just out and about with his buddies. One of the kids has been trying to get him interested in ridin' bikes. That'd be a good thing. He's got the old Schwinn out and oiled up."

"Who does he hang out with, generally?"

"Oh, you know…the Pasquale kid. Tommy, I think his name is. Once in a while with Louis Zamora or Jason Packard. Him and Packard used to hang out together a lot, but not so much any more. You know how those things go. His sister might know."

I took a slow breath. Of course—a fourth grader, in this case little Maureen Arnett, would know where her brother was if the folks didn't.

"Did Mo take the Pontiac today, do you know?" Even as I asked that, Mindy Arnett was shaking her head vehemently.

"Damn well better not have," dad said. "Why, did you see him in it?"

"I thought he might have taken a trip to the city or something," I said. "So you folks haven't noticed anyone or anything unusual in the neighborhood these past few days? Strangers, that sort of thing?"

"Hell, no. 'Course, I ain't home most of the time. And you're right. The kids would have seen or heard more'n me. Them or Jim Raught across the street. Hell, *he's* always home. Meditating or some damn thing."

"Look, thanks, Mark. We'll touch bases with Mo later today sometime. No big deal. If you see him before I do, you might have him give me a call."

"You got it."

"And one of these days, I need to talk with you about an estimate on my old *casa*. I've got a couple of leaks that I can't find. "

"You got it. Let me bend Mindy's ear for a minute."

I handed the phone to her, and after a moment, she stopped listening and hung up.

"Now what happens?" she asked. "You know, our hearts just go out to Marilyn. Such a loss for her."

"When we cross paths with Mo, we'll have a chat," I said, and it sounded as if I didn't really care one way or another. Mindy Arnett relaxed a little. "Kids these days, eh?"

"Oh, my," she sighed, and turned her attention to Estelle. "Will we be seeing more of you now?"

Estelle replied with a gentle but noncommittal smile. "I'll tell *mamá* that we spoke, Mrs. Arnett. She'll be pleased to hear that things are going well."

"You'll bring her by the next time she visits."

"I'm sure."

I stood up abruptly, a clear signal that we were on our way. "The Pontiac is in the garage?" I asked, and Mindy was caught off guard by the question.

"The Pontiac?"

"Yes. The little gold one."

"Well, sure it is. I've been walking to work the past few weeks, trying to lose a little of the *avoir dupois.*" She patted her hip, then frowned. "Now, Mark is real strict with Mo about when and where he drives. *Never* to school. *Never* at night. And *never, never* with a carload of friends. In fact, most of the time, all he gets to drive is the truck when he rides with his dad. Not the Jeep or my car."

"Driving will consume his time soon enough," I said. "Mindy, we'll get out of your hair. Thanks for talking with us." I fished out one of my cards and handed it to her. "If you see Mo before we do, have him give me a call."

"The garage is open, sheriff. If you need to satisfy your curiosity about the car, it's parked right there. You're welcome to look."

"Thanks, Mindy. We may do that." Once outside, I took a deep breath to rinse out the stale, perfumed air of the rectory. "You know," I said to Estelle as we settled into the car, "I have four kids. They've been out of the nest for years and years. And I can't remember when I stopped checking on their whereabouts every minute of the day." I looked at her, but knew I was talking a foreign concept. She was four years out of school herself, and I'm sure there were a myriad of times when her mother had to trust in her abiding faith that this daughter was safe and well in the United States. Great-uncle Reuben, on the other hand? The concept of reins would never enter his old head.

"I mean, when they're little, you keep your eyes and ears sharp, even the eye in the back of your head. Then they hit middle school, and it seems easier just to shout, '*be home by eight!*' without a clue about where they really are or what they're really doing. And high school? Forget it. We just start trusting 'em and hope that they survive the experience."

"Most do, fortunately," she said.

"Yep, they usually do." I turned back toward Fourth Street and nosed the county car into the Arnett driveway. Sure enough, the handle of the garage was turned sideways to the unlocked position. And sure enough, after I got out of the car and rolled the heavy door up, all that remained of the Pontiac were vague scuffs on the garage's concrete floor. I stood there, both hands on the door over my head, trying to believe that there was a simple explanation for all this. Estelle had gotten out of the car as well, but stayed a step or two behind me.

"And so much for that," I said. "Mom is right…the little bastard never drives to *school.*" I glanced back at Estelle as I eased the door downward. "But where else remains the question." She was leafing through note book pages, but I could have told her that her memory was correct—Hugh Decker, with his 20/200 vision, claimed to have noticed a small, dark, innocuous sedan at the intersection of Highland and Hutton with a single occupant.

For a long moment, I stood in the sun in front of the door, looking down at the concrete at my feet. "What makes me sick with all this is that it fits," I said. "A kid sneaks away for a little hooky—a little R & R before school settles in for the duration. He takes mom's car—hell, she won't know. She's at work, and dad's out of town. Sis is at school, where she's supposed to be. Mo takes the car, maybe takes one of dad's rifles, and on impulse takes a wild shot at a parked piece of county machinery."

I checked that the garage door was secure and made my way back to the car. I didn't pull it into gear, but just sat there like a lump, musing. "Fits, doesn't it?" I said finally.

"Almost," Estelle Reyes said. Her voice was so soft I cocked my head.

"Almost?"

"I don't understand it as a wild impulse, sir. Not a wild shot like one of the highway shooters taking a pot shot at a road sign. It appears that the killer got out of the car and walked some distance *toward* the road grader, sir. That's if Mr. Decker's testimony is believable. And then he saw a figure walking… not running…walking back to the car." She fell silent, and I prompted her with a beckoning motion of the hand. "I agree that with the afternoon sun on a dirty windshield that it would have been nearly impossible to tell if the grader was occupied."

"The killer would have heard the grader idling, though," I said.

"He possibly could have, if he walked close enough. If the wind was right."

"So what are you saying, then?" Estelle hesitated, and I added, "I'm serious. I want to know what scenario makes sense to you. You're saying that you see a definite intent in all this? Not just senseless vandalism?" Anyone who had been thinking as hard as she had been should have had *some* notions, and at this point, I was open to suggestions, even from a sub-rookie. Something in that quiet, analytical manner of hers impressed the hell out of me.

"I find it hard to believe that it was an accident, sir."

"That's what's been giving me nightmares for the past couple of days." I spun my index finger beside my skull, mimicking an old film projector. "I keep playing out the scene, and that creates more questions than answers. If some guy had a serious grudge against Larry Zipoli—I mean something that would drive him to murder—then I wonder why he took the shot from fifty or sixty yards away…when he would have had difficulty making out the target through a grubby windshield? Why not stalk right up to the grader, maybe have time for a word or two, a curse or two, and then *bang*. Right through the open door."

"Fear of confrontation, maybe?" Estelle said. "And maybe we're supposed to think it was an accident—what's been mentioned since day one. A moment of vandalism gone wrong."

"Fear of confrontation." I echoed, and gazed at Estelle thoughtfully. "You're goddamned right about that. It takes a special kind of cold son of a bitch to look the victim right in the eye before the shot. So he takes it from a safe distance. If the shot misses, and Zipoli comes charging out of that machine to pound his lights out, then maybe he can sprint back to the car in time."

"Why not just take another shot?" Estelle asked.

"Why not indeed. A miss gives him time to reconsider, maybe. Shoot and run is one thing. Trying again is another kettle of fish. Shoots and run. That's what makes sense to me." I pulled the car into gear and backed out into Fourth Street. "Shit," I muttered. "And that's what fits. So where did the little bastard go?" I reached for the mike, and in a moment dispatch was handling a BOLO call—be on the lookout for a little gold Pontiac, license CLT 499. I was loath to add the armed and dangerous advisory, but wishful thinking wasn't going to make anyone safe.

Chapter Twenty-nine

Jason Packard had found better things to do than attend school, and it didn't take a BOLO to find him. The door of his grand-parents' garage was open wide, and Jason was working at the bench in the back, under the light of a fluorescent fixture. He wasn't alone. Tom Pasquale had had enough lung busting. He had circled back to town, and now he and Jason were deep in conference over a bicycle wheel that was suspended in some form of vise. A tiny dial indicator mounted on the side of the vise measured the wheel rim's wobble in thousandths.

Years ago, one of my sons had tried to true the front wheel of his bike, spinning it in his hands, squinting with one eye closed, then wrenching on the heads of the spokes. He didn't know what he was doing, and when he gave up, his wheel wobbled just as much or more than when he started. Packard's approach, with Pasquale kibitzing, appeared far more scientific.

While Tom Pasquale was ruggedly built, broad through the shoulders and already starting to put on the padding that prom-ised him as a real bruiser as an adult, Jason Packard was a typically thin and wiry ranch kid. He could probably throw bales of hay off a tractor-trailer for hours without breaking stride. That his mom and stepfather couldn't find some common ground with this hardheaded boy was one of those senseless tragedies that always left me shaking my head in puzzlement.

The two kids didn't stop work when the county car slid up to the curb, although they certainly saw us. As Estelle and I walked up the driveway, Jason stepped back from the wheel and let fly with a string of profanity as he tossed a wrench onto the bench. I suppose the obscenities were for Estelle's benefit.

"Mr. Packard, Mr. Pasquale," I said pleasantly. "How goes the truing?" A flicker of surprise touched Jason's face. Geezers who knew about truing bike wheels? Jeez, what's the world coming to. Leaning against the workbench was the gold and blue racing bike that Pasquale had been riding earlier, minus the front wheel. "Hit a curb?"

Tom grinned sheepishly. "Yes, sir. That's exactly what I did."

"It jumped into your path, did it?"

"I got cut off," he said. "You know, some lady wasn't watching and cut me off when she turned right."

"You okay?"

"Yeah." He glanced down as he shifted his weight, and I saw a scrape just above his ankle. "I didn't dump it, but came close."

"Did she stop?"

"Ah, no, sir." The kid grinned. "She waved, though."

"Well then, that makes it all right." I stepped closer and peered at the wheel. "May I?"

"Sure."

I nudged the wheel gently and watched the little dial indicator as it flickered only a thou-and-a-half through a full revolution. "Hell of a good job." Packard didn't reply, but he looked pleased. "So. Have either of you two seen Mo around lately?"

"No, sir." Pasquale's answer was immediate, but I saw a twitch of expression on Jason Packard's narrow face that told me he'd rather talk about bike wheels.

"Jason?"

"Nope."

"But he's been riding with you lately?"

"Well…some, I guess. He can't keep up, the wuss."

I laughed. "You set the blistering pace, do you?"

"He don't have a decent bike," Jason said. "And he won't work on getting in shape."

"But he'd like to?"

Jason frowned, not sure how to answer. He settled for a noncommittal shrug.

For a long moment, I regarded the wheel in the vise as the hub gently drifted on perfect bearings. "So you haven't seen him around today or yesterday? It's unusual that the three of you all ditched school today. You were all planning a ride or something?"

"Just got things to do," Jason said. He glanced at Tom Pasquale, probably wondering what else his cycling friend had told me during our earlier conversation. I couldn't imagine that Tom *hadn't* mentioned his traffic stop out on NM17, or my admonition that stop signs applied to cyclists. I jumped right into the issue at hand, hoping for a little shake-up value.

"What do you think about what happened to Larry Zipoli, Jason?"

It was one of those stupid questions in the same category as those asked of catastrophe survivors by television reporters. Before either young man had the chance to cook up a response, I added, "Did either of you ever hear arguments between Zipoli and anybody else?"

"No, sir," Tom Pasquale said, and his expression added, *"What arguments?"*

"Arguments with the neighbors? Fence encroachment, unkempt lawns, the boat leaking oil, kids hanging around at all hours, maybe dealing marijuana…"

Jason Packard's frown was dark and stormy, and he glared at me incredulously. "Jesus, mister, where'd you dig up all that shit?" Obviously he wasn't a kid easily intimidated, by stepfathers, school staff, or cops.

"None of it's true?"

"I don't know about any of that."

"You ever have the chance to pass the time of day with Jim Raught next door?"

"No. I seen him once in a while. He keeps to himself."

"Did you overhear any arguments that Mr. Zip might have had with him?"

"No. That ain't any of *my* business what they do." He touched the wheel so that it coasted another turn.

"You guys shared a beer or two from time to time with Mr. Zipoli?"

"Sure. Why not?" I glanced sideways at Tom Pasquale. He couldn't suppress the fidgits, and his T-shirt armpits were wet.

"About a hundred reasons." I picked a tiny piece of something off one of the wheel's yellow spokes. "So let me ask you both something you *do* know about." I regarded Jason thoughtfully. "The other day, the three of you apparently stopped up on the county road to chat with Larry Zipoli—just up past the old drive-in. But one of our witnesses says he saw just the two of you there. Not three."

"Yeah? So?" Jason's tone was wary. Tom Pasquale studiously examined the concrete floor, since he knew what he'd already told me.

"Were was Mo? Wasn't he out riding with you that day?"

"Yeah, he was on that wreck of a bike of his."

"He lagged behind, or went on ahead while you guys talked with Zipoli? Is that it?"

"He went on ahead a ways. He said he was havin' trouble with his chain." Jason shrugged expressively. "What's to go wrong with that thing? He's always comin' up with something like that. Always some lame excuse."

"A lame excuse for what? For talking with Zipoli? For sharing a brew on a hot day? Does this Mo guy have an issue with Zipoli somehow?"

Jason almost laughed at that. "This Mo guy," he repeated. "Not no more issues now, I guess."

"He did have, though?"

"Mr. Z picked on him sometimes," Tom Pasquale offered.

"Because?"

The boy shrugged. "Just 'cause. Mo was kinda clumsy. Kinda chubby."

"And Zipoli wasn't?"

"I'm just saying." Tom smiled. "Mo couldn't ski…I mean he tried, but he couldn't stay up more'n a hundred yards. He made it up once, and Mr. Z spun the boat around in a real tight circle, and that dumped him." The young man laughed with delight at the memory. "The only time Mo got up, and he gets dumped."

"That made Mo angry?"

"Well, Mr. Z did that with all of us," Jason said. "I mean, it was just part of the fun." He drew circles in the air. "You know, you drive the boat in a circle tighter and tighter, and pretty soon the skier can't keep the slack out of the tow rope and you just kinda sink. If you're paying attention, you can hand-over-hand some of the ski rope slack, but that don't work for very long. Anyways, Mo couldn't do that. Stayin' up was his big accomplishment, and then he got dumped."

"Well, big fizz," I said. "The kid can't take a little horseplay. Is that what you're saying?" I had no idea where all this was headed, but the two boys were talking then, and I didn't want it to stop.

Jason nodded. "He got mad last week 'cause Mr. Z bet him a buck that he couldn't take me."

"What do you mean, he couldn't take you?"

The lad looked pained. "We rode out on Highland a little bit. I was trying to sell him my old Peugeot," and he turned and nodded at a well-worn ten-speed that hung from the wall. "Just a little test ride. Mr. Z was out there that day, too. He was workin' on the grader. Seems like it was broke down more than it worked."

"And you stopped to visit?"

"Yep. Just to shoot the breeze for a minute or two."

"Any refreshments that day?"

Jason smiled slyly. "No." He looked sideways at me to see just how gullible I was.

"And this 'take you' business?" I prompted.

"Mr. Z kinda poked Mo in the gut, you know. He was just joking around, but he's always after Mo, every chance he gets. He'd say, 'When's the baby due?' or shit like that."

"There's an old adage about a pot and a kettle," I said. "Did Mo ever give back as good as he got?"

Jason shook his head slowly. "He's just not too good at that. He just gets mad and goes off by himself."

"That's what happened that day?"

"Well, sort of. Mr. Z is all into boxing, you know. He was always saying that he wanted to get a club started in town. And then he kind of stepped back a little, standing there like a referee or something with his hands on his hips. 'Winner gets the buck,' he said. 'Hell, make it five.'"

"Winner? He wanted you and Mo to fight, you mean?"

"Sure. *I* knew he was jokin'. But I don't think Mo did. I pretended to get set." Jason held up two fists, fighter like, and glowered over his knuckles. A good glower, too. I would have been convinced.

"What did Mo do?"

"Well, he kind of got all flustered, sort of. And then I got to thinkin' I could use five bucks. No big deal. I was thinkin' we could play around some, you know. Pretend boxing. I poked him up here," and Jason rubbed his own cheek near the jaw line. "Nothin' hard or anything. Just like they do in Hollywood. But Mo, he didn't lean back and I kinda hit him maybe a little harder than I wanted."

"You connected, you mean."

"Not hard or nothin', but yeah…I connected. It looked kind of funny, you know. We all cracked up, 'cause he lost his balance and stumbled backward. Well, Mo was pissed, and he ran back to the bike and took off. Mr. Z thought that was pretty funny."

"And you got the five bucks?"

"'No fight, no money.' That's what Mr. Z said. I knew it was just a joke, anyway. Funny thing is that big as Mo is, if he got himself into shape, he'd probably be a pretty good boxer. Got real big hands."

"You saw Mo after that? What did he have to say?"

Jason shook his head. "He dumped the bike back here, right in the front yard. I guess he just went home."

"When did you see him after that?"

"Just when him and Tom and me went for a ride this past week. Tom invited him along, not me. Mo wasn't talkin' much. He wouldn't say shit to me. Still mad, I guess."

"He was," Tom Pasquale added. "He wondered what would happen if sometime he dropped one of those M-80's he's got down the fuel tank of Mr. Z's road grader. See how *he* likes it. That's what Mo said."

With a gentle tug, Jason set the bike wheel in motion again. "You're not saying that Mo might have had something to do with the shooting, are you, sir?"

"Nope...we're not saying that." Jason heard the 'we' and glanced across at Estelle, who true to form had remained silent through the whole chat. "Do either of you happen to know where Mo went this afternoon? Did he stop by here?"

"No, sir," Tom Pasquale said. "I haven't seen him."

Jason shook his head, then smiled, an expression that would have been charming if someone had taken care of his dental needs when he was a squirt. "He's probably still mad at me. He'll get over it."

"Maybe so." I wasn't sure I believed that.

Chapter Thirty

Estelle Reyes picked at her chicken taco salad while I indulged my broad streak of gluttony with a green chile burrito that would no doubt give my ailing gall bladder fits. But what the hell. The person I most wanted to interview was seventeen year-old Maurice 'Mo' Arnett, but he'd played his wild card.

Small as Posadas was, there were a myriad places to hide, and my inclination was to think that's what Mo had done. I couldn't see him taking off cross-country. South of the border wouldn't appeal to him, a pudgy gringo who didn't speak ten words of Spanish and for whom the vast northern Mexican desert would yawn as an endless threat.

"So, where did he go?" I said around a mouthful of fragrant cheese and chile slices. "If you were seventeen and on the run, where would you go? You have a stolen car…well, a *borrowed* car. He can't hide that very well. That's a ton of metal that we're going to find eventually."

"Relatives out of town?" Estelle toyed with a tiny slice of chicken.

"No doubt. But how's that going to work? Auntie sees Mo on her doorstep over in Calcutta, Texas, and what's she going to do? Call Mindy and Mark, is what. And then it's over. He can't hide with friends, because he doesn't have any. And I have a hard time believing he's the sort of independent kid who could go to a strange place and just settle in. Not many kids are self-reliant enough to do that."

Before she could answer, my radio, standing like a sentinel beside the salt and pepper shaker, squelched to life.

"Three ten, PCS. Ten twenty-one." Baker's voice held no particular urgency, but good dispatchers are like that. The world can be collapsing under them, and the voice on the radio is calm and mellow.

I reached across and pushed the transmit button. "Ten four." I shoved my plate forward a bit and pushed myself out of the booth. "In a minute," I said, and made my way toward the front of the restaurant. A phone nestled under the short counter by the cash register, and I dialed the Sheriff's Department. Barnes picked up on the first ring.

"What's up?" I leaned on the counter, looking down through the scratched glass at the tempting array of small cigars.

"Sir, Mark Arnett is here and wants to talk with you. Hold on a minute, and I'll get him."

"No, no, don't bother with that. We'll be back in the office in ten minutes. If he wants to wait, make him comfortable."

"Yes, sir."

"Well, that was quick," I muttered as I hung up. Arnett had pounded the pavement home from Deming without delay, and that told me that the standard issue parental denial might not be the case here. I could make it back to the office in three minutes, but what the hell. A burrito was waiting back at the table, steaming and fragrant, and who knew—with the way the day was going to hell, the opportunity to eat might be as elusive as Mark Arnett's son. A dozen pairs of eyes were now looking for Mo Arnett, and they didn't need me for a few minutes.

When I returned, Fernando Aragon, the restaurant's owner and chief chef, was leaning against the back of the booth, hands clasped over his generous belly as he chatted with the department's newest recruit. He laughed at something Estelle said, and looked up at me as I approached around the waitresses' island.

"Hey, Sheriff!" He thrust out a hand. His grip was strong, but his hand felt bloated, damp, and smooth from all the hot water, detergent, and hand cream. "You know, I met this young lady when she was this high." He held his hand a couple of feet above the well-worn carpet. "What do you think of that?"

"Small world," I said. "How's business for you?"

"Ay." He straightened up and moved so that I could slide in to my seat. "You know, with the mine closing, we're going to be facing some lean times."

I wagged my eyebrows while readjusting the precise position of my plate. "I'll always do my best to help." I glanced at my watch. "I hate to eat and run, but we need to get back to the office." Fernando took the hint—one of the many things I liked about him—and headed back to his kitchen, leaving us to our gastronomic delights.

I shoveled two mouthfuls of burrito, and then paused. "So, your fiancé…you said he's the only member of his family living in the United States? How did you two meet?"

She thought about that for a piece of chicken or two. I was amused at the level of thought she gave the opening of each doorway into her personal history. "His aunt is a lawyer in Veracruz. She knows my mother. From years and years ago."

Teresa Reyes, Estelle's stepmother, lived in Tres Santos, a miniscule hamlet south of the border and a scant fifty miles from where we now sat. Veracruz was a long, long trip south, on the east coast of the country a stone's throw from the Yucatan—about the same distance from Posadas as Cleveland, but with no nifty interstates between to eat the miles. I made a mental note to pursue how an attorney in Veracruz had come to know a school teacher in Tres Santos—a school teacher who owned neither car nor telephone nor a long list of life's other comforts.

"Ah," I said, and let it go at that. "The reason I asked about Francis is that one of the most interesting things that we end up doing in this crazy business is talking to parents, Estelle. Mom, Dad…that's if the subject in question is lucky enough to have both, and both functional."

I speared another section of burrito, and worked at keeping the cheese from sagging down my shirt front. "I did my time as a parent—two sons, two daughters," and I spread my hands.

"Scattered all over the country. And," I chewed thoughtfully for a moment. "I'm acutely aware of some of the mistakes that I made. Hell," and I waved the fork. "I have a son who won't even speak to me...how stupid is that? I also have a daughter who won't *stop* speaking to me. That's almost as bad."

Estelle listened politely, without comment or question. She absorbed information like a sponge. I wondered how well she'd be able to jump into an interrogation. The bad guys weren't going to confess all just because it was the right thing to do.

"The phone call just now was Mark Arnett, father of Mo. He's at the office and wants to talk to us, about what I don't know. Mom Arnett is all bustle and control and whatnot, but did you get the feeling that she isn't in touch with her son very much?" I didn't give her time to answer. "Did she know that he wasn't in school? No. Does she know that he has her car? No. Will she have a clue about where her son might have gone? I bet not. So...bossy, controlling, *and* clueless—a poor combination. And that brings us to Dad Arnett."

I held up a hand as I chewed. "I'm willing to bet that he'll be defensive, that he'll be ready to take the belt to his son...or at least he'll make a big show about *saying* that he will. Lots of dads are all talk, no action." I shrugged. "I'm not saying he is, but the odds are there. He doesn't know Mo is pitching M-80's around, or if he does, hasn't done anything about it. The folks aren't wild about Mo going on the Elephant Butte trips, but don't prevent it. You see how it goes?" That earned a nod. "And I'm also willing to bet that he'll be angry with *us.*" I chuckled. "That just comes with the turf. We generally end up as hated messengers."

Estelle nodded as if my lecture had made sense. I put both hands on the table. "Think about this, Estelle." And she *was* thinking, I could see, her thick black eyebrows knitting to practically meet over her slender, aquiline nose. "A guy and a gal get married," and I drew two imaginary circles on the table, then produced a third one between them, "and along comes the kid. Now, we have a triangle. Who controls the household? Who is the absolute authority? When there is a problem, what are the dynamics between family members? We know it's not always dear old dad. He may be an authority figure, or he might be a wuss. Ditto for mom. And the kid? If the parents have given up and let him run things, well then. It becomes our business when the law is involved. The trick," and I pushed my empty plate away, "is that when all the dust settles, for us not to have made things worse. And the *sad* thing is, that can't always be helped."

I gazed across the restaurant at one of the waitresses as she chatted with a family of six about to have every sense assaulted with the best chile in the world. I envied them, since I had finished my treat and now had more mundane things to do, while they had the whole menu to explore.

"Let me end the lecture by adding that I tell my deputies that how they respond to a domestic disturbance at 11 p.m. will determine what kind of ruckus they'll have to return to a second time at 3 a.m. So we'll listen to what Mark Arnett has to say without landing on him with both feet, without making him feel desperate. We try to keep him on an even keel, and then we wing it from there."

"Yes, sir."

"Yes, sir," I echoed. "And we can hope that in the meantime, someone stumbles across their son, alive and well and ready to come home."

"When you spoke with Mr. Arnett on the phone the first time, did he indicate that he was coming right home?"

"Nope. Maybe he thought of something we need to know. We can always hope." Her frown hadn't relaxed, and I'm sure it wasn't the remains on her modest plate that fascinated or perplexed her. "What?"

She cocked her head, still regarding the plate. "Mrs. Arnett said a curious thing."

"Curious how?"

"When she was talking about James Raught, sir. She referred to him as a shepherd who strayed."

"Vaguely I remember that, but I think she was referring to the Zipolis."

"When church people talk about shepherds, they're referring to the priest—or pastor, or whatever." Her tone was one of musing, not correction, and I waited for the rest of the thought. "Mrs. Arnett might have been referring to Larry Zipoli, leading the kids around. I suppose that could be what she meant."

"You're still thinking about *Tres Santos,* aren't you."

She shrugged helplessly. "I heard that one word, sir. *Shepherd.* The connotation of that is so strong to me, growing up where I did. And all of Raught's art, his obvious interest in *religious* art—the icons of it all."

I sat back in the booth, both hands folded where my plate had been. For a full minute, we remained in silence. Estelle neither fussed nor elaborated. She was as comfortable with the silence as I was *uncomfortable* with her suggestion.

Finally, I said, "You want to talk with him again?"

She nodded. "My mother was going to talk with Sophia today."

"And who the hell is Sophia?"

"My fiancé's aunt, sir. The lawyer in Veracruz I mentioned."

"Ah." To have a twenty-one year old memory again. "Tell me about this."

"Sophia Tournal is *acusadora*—a prosecuting attorney, sir. She was involved with the original *Tres Santos* case. At one time, they thought that they had arrested one of the suspects in the theft. But no."

"Poor bastard is probably still in the can, though," I said. "I wondered how all this got around to your lovely mother."

"My mother was going to ask Sophia for some details, sir. If there are any identifying marks, characteristic things, that could help identify the *retablos* that Raught has in his home."

"Your mother has no phone. How is she going to accomplish all this?"

"The Romeros, just down the lane."

"All right, then. Let's see how it all washes out. You want to talk with Raught again?"

"Yes. After I hear from my mother."

"Fair enough. In the meantime, we have a man waiting. A *nervous* man. Let's not keep him waiting." I stood up, intercepted the lunch ticket from the waitress, and folded it around a twenty. "Thanks, Jana Lynn."

Mark Arnett's white three-quarter ton was parked in one of the two visitors' spaces at the county building. Enough junk was loaded in the back to make it squat. But Mark wasn't inside the truck, giving his son a tongue lashing. They weren't sitting together, having a heart-to-heart father-son talk. Mo Arnett wasn't slumped in an emotional heap on the front steps of the Sheriff's Department building.

Dispatcher T.C. Barnes looked up as we entered the employee's entrance behind dispatch. "Sir, Mr. Arnett is waiting in conference."

I nodded and skirted the dispatch island. "Conference" was a grand term for the small room across the hall with a six-place table and a small cabinet that held the coffee maker, cups and such, two tape recorders that often didn't work, and a video camera mounted on a tripod. Across the room was a small copier/fax that worked in the best of times.

We had no fancy one-way observation glass like they always use in the movies, no place for an audience to stand and watch the interrogation process. Most of the time, deputies used the room as a spacious office and lounge, or a non-threatening place to interview minors whom the state's Children, Youth and Families outfit wouldn't let us just throw in the lock-up—although that approach would have done some kids a world of good.

The conference room door opened soundlessly, and we caught Mark Arnett in a relaxed moment. He was seated in one of the side chairs at the table, leaning back, one boot up on the corner of the table. His chin rested in his hand pensively, elbow propped on the arm of the chair. Across the room, a four-by-five foot map of Posadas County was framed on the wall, the surface dotted with an array of colored pins, one of Sheriff Eduardo Salcido's projects to visualize the pattern of every motor vehicle fatality in the county.

Arnett swiveled his head just enough to see us, but otherwise remained motionless as we entered. A burly, powerful man used to hard labor dawn to dusk, Mark Arnett was likely forty years old or so but looked fifty-five, his broad face baked into lines and wrinkles by the sun reflecting off the roofs on which he worked.

With exaggerated care, he swung his boot down to the floor and rose from the chair. At six-one, he had me by two inches, but I outweighed him by fifty pounds—all pork.

"You made it," he said, his implication clear that the twelve or so minutes he had to wait had been too long. He eyed Estelle with interest. "And who's this?" He gave her hand a perfunctory, single pump as I introduced them. "You don't look like your average cop." His smile was tight. It wasn't a question, and sure enough—Estelle Reyes' only response was the hint of a smile of her own.

"Thanks for coming in." I took the offered hand. "I know this isn't the easiest thing."

"Goddamn right." He slumped back down in the chair, and I took the one to his left at the end of the table. It would have been easy, in one of those mini-moments of control, to assign Estelle to a seat, but I made no motions or suggestions, curious about the little things in human behavior. She selected the chair to Mark Arnett's right where she'd have a side view of his face, able to watch the flushes work on his neck, or the expressions touch the side of his mouth. To look at her, he'd have to twist in his chair…or he could just ignore her.

"Okay, Mo is screwing up," he said. "Goddamn kids. He took his mother's car, the little shit." He rapped the table sharply with the heavy class ring on his right hand. "He *knows* that's not going to fly."

"Has he ever done this before?"

"Hell, no. He *knows* that if he takes the car or any other damn thing with a motor, his ass is grass."

"Some troubles in the past?"

"Nah. Not really. For one thing, he's skippin' school, and that gets my goat. The last thing I want is him drivin' around town with a carload of his buddies. You know how they are. Tomorrow is Friday, and that's party time—even if they haven't done a goddamn thing to deserve it."

"I suppose." I regarded him long enough that he dropped his gaze and studied the class ring. "So tell me...when Mo was over at Larry Zipoli's place, or off with him and the rest of the kids on one of those skiing trips, how did you feel about that?"

Mark shifted in his seat, and the damn ring rapped again, this time a nervous little drumroll. "Look, Larry Zip is one of those guys who lives and breathes his boat, his beer, his football. You know, he's just one of those guys. Kind of reminds me of that fat neighbor in the Sunday funnies...the one who's always sittin' in his recliner with a brew in his hands. Now, I've heard that he gives it to the kids sometimes. You know, a can now and then. I guess that's no big deal." He glanced up at me to see if I agreed that it was no big deal. "But there's other things I wish Mo would do with his time."

"Who does he hang out with mostly?"

"Oh, I don't know. The Pasquale kid, some. He used to be pretty tight with Jason Packard, but they don't see so much of each other any more."

"Friendships come and go pretty easily," I said, and Arnett nodded.

He leaned forward, both elbows on the table, hands raised. "Look, is all this somehow related to that thing that happened to Larry? Is that what you're gettin' at?"

That thing. "We're talking with everyone who spent time with Zipoli in the past few days or weeks, Mark. Somebody out there saw something, heard something. Even a rumor at this point would be welcome. Mo was riding his bike with the other two boys—Tom and Jason—on the same day that Larry was killed. Maybe just hours before. So." I shrugged. "And our curiosity grows when Mo takes off, when he goes missing without leaving word with his folks." I leaned against the table. "Look, I'm a parent too, Mark. If my kid took off with the family car and I didn't know where the hell he went, I'd be upset too."

"Shit," Arnett muttered, and twisted around to look at Estelle. He looked her up and down and then turned back to me. "Can you tell me exactly what happened with Larry?"

I shrugged and replied, "It's pretty simple. He was sitting in the county road grader, and someone put a rifle bullet through the windshield." I touched my left eyebrow. "It keyholed and hit him right there. He never had a chance to move from his seat."

"Jesus. Who the hell would do a thing like that?"

"That's a good question. If one of those kids is in danger, for instance…"

"Why would they be?"

"We don't know. We don't know who saw what."

He bit his lip. I imagine that his thoughts just then were agonizing. "What do you know about the weapon used?"

"Rifle, thirty caliber. The bullet is a 170-grain flat point."

He cut right to the chase. "How the hell did you recover it?"

"During autopsy."

"Come on, now. It had to have been fired from a hell of a distance not to blow right on through his skull," he said. "What's Bobby say?"

"Deputy Torrez tells me that in all likelihood the shot was taken from about fifty paces."

"That close? Shit. A thirty caliber high-powered rifle would have blown his skull all to hell, and then just kept on going."

"Seems likely, doesn't it?"

"That's all you know?"

I smiled gently. "I know that we *don't* know where Mo is right now, Mark."

"He's probably home by now, if he knows what's good for him. But look, you're implying that he had something to do with all this? Is that what you're saying?"

"That's not what I'm saying," I said. "I want to talk with him. That's all. If he saw something, that's one thing. I'd hate to think that he was in danger somehow. Do you mind if we follow you over to the house?" I didn't tell him that his little bastard was the center of interest for a BOLO.

"Hell no, I don't mind." He rose quickly. "Right now?"

"That would be good." I held out a hand toward Estelle. "Do you have any questions for Mr. Arnett at this point?"

"No, sir. We've talked to the neighbors and some of the other youngsters, so the sooner we can hear what Mo has to say, the better." Maybe Mark Arnett felt a little better thinking that his son wasn't flying solo.

"What's Raught say?" Mark asked. "Hell, right door-to-door like that, he's got to know what's goin' on."

"One would think," I said, cutting off that avenue.

"Odd duck, that guy."

I didn't pursue that comment, but held the door for Arnett as we left the conference room. "We'll be along in just a minute, Mark."

"You want to talk with the wife again? I can stop by the church and pick her up."

"I don't think that's necessary, but suit yourself."

He nodded and made for the front door. I leaned on the dispatch counter. "Find Bob Torrez and have him meet me at the Arnetts'."

Barnes looked blank for an instant. "Bobby doesn't come on until four, sir."

I glanced up at the white board on the wall behind the dispatcher, where all the little magnetic roundels on the calendar, one for each deputy, showed how desperately shorthanded we were. Perhaps T.C. didn't think that I paid attention to the duty schedule when I made it up each month.

"Have him meet me at Mark Arnett's ASAP," I said gently. "And then call the sheriff and ask him to swing by as well."

"I think Sheriff Salcido went to Las Cruces, sir."

"All right. Have him reach me as soon as he comes back, then." The sheriff hadn't told me that he was heading out of town, but then again, he didn't need to. In fact, one of the things

I liked about Eduardo was that he let me work without reins. I didn't have to explain to the sheriff where I was or what I was doing every moment of the day. I extended the same courtesy to him.

"He had a doctor's appointment," Baker added.

I nodded, and my hand drifted to where my gall bladder was currently trying to tell me something. Some things just have to learn to be patient.

As I pulled the county car to the curb by Arnett's driveway, we saw Mark Arnett standing with both fists balled on his hips, garage door agape. He swiveled to regard us, his anger index escalating toward the top of the charts. The little Pontiac was still conspicuously absent.

Chapter Thirty-one

I retrieved a small plastic evidence bag from my briefcase.

"At what point do you have to call for a warrant?" Estelle asked.

"When our friend," and I nodded toward Mark Arnett, who apparently believed that if he glared long enough, the Pontiac would reappear, "decides not to cooperate. I'm hoping that won't happen." I made gloving motions. "So, kid gloves." I counted her question as great progress.

With the car door open, a heavy, throbbing exhaust note attracted my attention, and I looked down the street to see Bob Torrez's pickup cruising toward us. A '69 Chevy 4x4, it had been battered, bruised, and wrung out by a string of contractors when he had rescued it a couple of years before. He'd scrounged various parts here and there, and referred to the truck as his "junk yard dog." He'd been on the team for a drug sting in Cruces the year before, and the truck had gone undercover with him.

Torrez eased the pickup to a stop behind my unit. A half a dozen lengths of PVC pipe were lashed to the headache rack and hung back over the tailgate.

Mark Arnett approached us, hands now hidden in his back pockets. "What do you want to do?" He nodded at Torrez as the deputy joined us. "Bobby, how's it goin'?"

I handed the plastic evidence bag to Arnett, and he examined it for a second or two before asking, "What's this?" He looked up at me. "I mean I know *what* it is. What's the deal?"

"That's the bullet that killed Larry Zipoli, Mark."

"You're shittin' me." He turned the bag this way and that, then donned a pair of half glasses and examined it some more. "Looks like a Mountain States," he offered. "Didn't come apart, did it."

"Nope." I was impressed that someone could just look at a projectile—not even an entire cartridge—and make an educated guess about its manufacturer. Bobby Torrez could, of course, but his gunny knowledge was legendary.

Arnett pushed his glasses up on his nose and squinted. "This son-of-a-bitch don't have rifling cuts." He looked up quickly, a little disappointed when he saw that he wasn't telling us something we didn't know.

I asked, "You use these?"

For a long moment, Mark Arnett didn't answer, then he handed the bag back to me. "I use 'em in silhouette matches from time to time. Expensive as hell, for one thing. But they shoot tight, and I like the extra weight. What's with this, anyhow?"

"You want to show us the ones you use?"

He frowned at me as if I had threatened him with a cattle prod. "Now wait a minute. What are you saying, sheriff?"

"What we're trying to do is find out as much as we can about the circumstances of Mr. Zipoli's death, Mark. To do that, we go to the experts whenever we can. Nobody in Posadas knows more about ballistics and the shooting sports than you do, so here I am." I shook the bag a little, hoping that flattery would get us everywhere. At this preliminary stage, I didn't want to waste time with a warrant, but I knew that in all likelihood, that was on the horizon.

"I want to know as much as I can about these little bastards, Mark." I poked a finger at the evidence bag when I said that, and then shook it for emphasis. "I want to know about this. What can you tell me?"

"Other than that each one costs about half a buck? Not a whole lot. I mean, you got what you got, except I don't understand why there's no rifling marks." He peered at the slug again, rolling it this way and that under the plastic. "Not even a scuff."

"Worn out barrel?"

He scoffed. "Had to be damn near a shotgun, then. And that wouldn't give the kind of accuracy you're talkin' about—unless the whole thing was some kind of gross accident."

"We weren't thinking along the lines of accident," I said.

Mark regarded me for a long moment, then jerked his head toward the door. "Well, come on inside and let me show you." He started to turn toward the house, then stopped short. "But none of this is going to find my boy, Sheriff. That's what's important to me right now, not some damn bullet. I need to find his ass before he gets himself into a round of trouble."

"I can't argue with that," I said. "We're going to find him, Mark. Take my word on that. Zipoli's death has upset a lot of youngsters…neighbor kids, family friends, neighbors, you name it. Right now, Mo doesn't know what to think. When he's done chewing it all over, he'll be back."

Mark nodded dubiously. "I got the feeling that you know more about this than you're telling me, Sheriff. You guys are looking for my son. Is he involved somehow? Is that it? Are you going to tell me what I need to know?"

"I wish I could, Mark. I wish Mo was standing right here, right now, explaining himself to you. But he's not. So we do what we can."

Arnett sighed and shrugged. "Come on in." We trooped into the house after him, taking the side door from the driveway. A steep stairway plunged down from the first landing, another shorter one angling up to the kitchen. We headed down into the basement.

A pool table sporting a rich green cover occupied much of the floor space, with a stereo system mounted on one wall that looked as if it was capable of busting windows. A selection of chairs, a rack of pool cues, an apartment-sized fridge and a variety of other toys jammed the basement—not a bad haven for a contractor after a day simmering on a hot roof. I skirted the stereo and eyed a CD case lying on a shelf. I flipped it over and saw that the recording included Frankie Lane's "Mule Train," along with a selection of other favorites.

"Is this Mo's?" I glanced down the table of contents. "'Liberty Valance,' 'High Noon'…this is all good stuff."

Arnett's laugh was immediate and disgusted. "Hell no. If you can understand the words, it ain't his. Borrow it if you want." I put the CD back, making a mental note that such wonderful things existed and that I should own a copy. Arnett reached up to the top of a door frame at the far end of the room and found a key—one of those magical hiding places that no one could possibly discover—and unlocked both knob and deadbolt.

When he snapped on the light, I saw a neat room about a dozen feet square, with a large safe in one corner. The safe was concreted in place, sunken up to its ankles, not about to be hauled away by some ambitious burglar. It must have taken Mark Arnett and a crew of friends a lot of sweat and several cases of beer to install the unit.

Twisting at the waist, I took the opportunity to scan the room, fascinated. Arnett's inventory of ammunition reloading components was neatly organized on shelves above the work bench, and revealed a significant investment in this hobby. A series of reloading presses were bolted to a three-inch thick laminated table top, and on the opposite side of the room, three steel wall cabinets were mounted at a convenient height.

I bent slightly and examined a wooden loading block on the bench that held a hundred cartridge cases, little pudgy bodies that necked down sharply to a small caliber bullet. Of the hundred cartridges, thirty were finished. Bob Torrez glanced at them and knew exactly what he was looking at. I looked at the ammo, not recognizing a damn thing.

"I have a bench rest match next week," Arnett explained. "Up in Ratón." He saw the puzzlement on my face. "Those are six millimeter PPC's. That ain't what you got from Zipoli." He reached past me. "This is what you want to see." The unopened red box of Mountain States bullets that he slipped off the shelf featured a fifty-six dollar price tag from George Payton's shop.

He split the tape and opened the box, setting it down on the counter. I lifted the slip of paper that covered the bullets and regarded the shiny array of brass-jacketed slugs, each with a crisp lead tip. "Just like you got there, sheriff. 170-grain flat point, .308 caliber."

I picked one out of the box, fumbling, then caught it before the slippery little thing skittered across the counter.

"Moly coated," Arnett explained. "Fancy stuff."

I nestled the brand new bullet on the plastic bag that contained the recovered slug. A microscope might disagree, but to my eye they were identical—or had been before glass, bone and brain ruined the one's aerodynamic shape.

"Three Ten, PCS on channel three." The damn radio was so loud it startled me. I hauled it off my belt.

"Three ten."

"Deputy Reyes has an urgent phone call. Ten-nineteen."

I glanced across at the young lady and saw the excitement in her eyes. This wasn't the time or place to ask how many other roads she was planning to investigate all by herself, the ink of her contract barely dry on the dotted line.

"Ten four. It'll be a few minutes."

I heard a jingle of keys, and turned in time to see Deputy Torrez extending his hand toward Estelle. "Take my unit," he said. I nodded agreement. Maybe she understood my expression as permission, but in fact it was amusement at the image of this slip of a girl behind the wheel of Torrez's rusted, battered heap. She left the basement.

"You thought some about the gun involved in this shit?" Arnett watched Estelle's backside as she ascended the stairs, but his question was clearly directed at Deputy Torrez.

" Some." The deputy's voice wasn't much more than a whisper, and I guessed that his reticence was an issue of rank. We hadn't had time to discuss who was going to say what to potential witnesses, so his natural inclination was to let me spill as many beans as I saw fit.

"You got the shell casing?" Arnett pressed.

I didn't hedge my answer. "No, we don't have it. But I can't see why the rifle would be anything other than something with a tubular magazine. Winchester, Marlin…some lever action like that? I mean, what would be the point of using flat-nosed bullets like these," and I patted the red box of Mountain States slugs, "in something *other* than a gun with a tubular magazine?"

"Or in a smooth bore. No point. No point all." Mark's reply was immediate and emphatic. "That's the weakness for lever action rifles, sheriff. I'm sure Bobby told you all about that. 'Cause the cartridges sit nose to tail in the magazine tube, the tips of the bullet need to be flat so they don't strike the primer of the bullet ahead during recoil."

"That could ruin your whole day."

"Damn straight. But that flat nose also means the long-range ballistics aren't worth a shit—like pushin' a brick through the air."

"So we're left with a major conundrum," I said. Mark Arnett didn't know about Bob Torrez's extensive session out in the gravel pit, or the conclusions we had already reached. "Why no rifling marks? How does that happen?"

"Beats the shit out of me." He turned to the safe, punched in numbers and twisted the handle. The door opened to reveal a neat row of a dozen long guns, with a half dozen handguns hanging by their trigger guards from rubber-jacketed hooks.

He selected a rifle and hefted it out of the safe. "My dad bought this at a Sears store in Cruces in 1939." He jacked the lever open and peered into the empty chamber, then held the rifle out to me. "First rifle he ever bought."

"A Winchester," I said.

"Just a plain old Model '94," he said. "There's millions of 'em on the planet, but this one means a lot to me."

Holding the rifle gingerly by the butt plate and the barrel just shy of the muzzle, I turned the Winchester to read the caliber stamped on the barrel just forward of the receiver. ".30-30," I said. Arnett snapped on a bore light and held the curved tip of the little flashlight into the rifle's open chamber.

I angled the rifle so that I could peer down the bore. The sharply-cut spiral grooves of rifling winked in the bright light. They'd slice nice crisp tracks in any bullet headed outbound. "Sweet," I said, the old gunnery sergeant genes tweaked by seeing a nice clean weapon. Shifting my grip on the rifle, I took the bore light from him and turned it this way and that, examining the bore more carefully. "Not a speck, soldier. Outstanding."

"That Winchester has won a bunch of matches for me," Arnett said. "Sixty years old, and look at that rifling—still crisp and sharp."

I stood silently, holding the rifle, enjoying its classic lines. Every movie goer who ever enjoyed a western had seen some version of this gun. After a moment, I eased the lever closed, pulled the trigger and lowered the hammer with my thumb. I wasn't looking closely at the rifle, though. My gaze was locked on the open safe behind Arnett. The row of rifles, all good soldiers standing in line, included a couple of semiautomatics, and at least four bolt-actions. Four other lever actions, three of them short enough to be carbines, rounded out the row.

"The other levers?" I asked.

Before answering, Arnett accepted the .30-30 Winchester and put it back in the rack. He put a finger on the muzzle of one rifle and tipped it forward a little, not offering it to me. "Marlin .45-70. I bought this big old bad boy for an elk hunt up north in Montana." Shifting his finger to the muzzle of what was obviously another Winchester, he explained, "This one is a later model '94 carbine in .32 Winchester Special. I use it during the long range portion of the three-gun matches. That and this little jewel for the twenty-two event." He tapped the muzzle of a slender lever action .22 caliber rifle, then moved on to a fancy little number that showed a lot of brass and an octagon barrel. "I picked this up just this summer." He hefted it out of the safe, but by then my attention was elsewhere. I knew the rifle that he held was a more-or-less repro of a '66 Winchester, a gun that wouldn't come close to accepting the cartridge size we were interested in.

He held the replica long enough that he could see I wasn't much interested. "What?" he prompted.

"Tell me about the .32," I said.

"Yeah, so?" He slid the replica back into place, and reached for the .32 Special, picking it out of the safe rack with a one-handed grip on the fore-end wood. "A late one. 1959," he offered. "It's a good solid gun. George Payton had that in his shop, and I couldn't pass it up."

"Ah, George," I said. My fingers were tingling.

"He's got another one right now," Arnett said. "Priced out of my league, but he's got it. Made before World War II."

I didn't mention that the specimen from Georgie Payton's inventory had been in Deputy Torrez's possession out at the gravel pit, blasting the wrong sized bullets down range. At the moment, we were far inside without a warrant, and Mark Arnett had been the proud owner, enjoying showing some friends his collection. That might change in a heartbeat. But what the hell. I drew the slender ballpoint pen out of my pocket, reached out and slid it down the barrel of the .32.

"Mind?" I said, and again, with one hand on the butt plate and the other using the pen as a handle, I hefted the rifle, not adding my finger prints to the rifle's collection. Torrez was on the same page. He snapped on a pair of surgical gloves, and that earned a frown from Arnett.

"I got the lever," the deputy said to me, and as I held the rifle, he opened the action.

"Shit," Mark Arnett said, and I could imagine how he felt. We weren't old friends any longer, enjoying a collection. If he was smart, he'd stop the whole show now and tell us not to let the door hit us in the ass on the way out. If he was smart, he'd tell us to fetch a warrant and in the next breath, he'd call his attorney. But he knew us, and I could flatter myself that he trusted us. So he did none of those things. "You want the bore light?"

I nodded. Arnett held it in the action. With Torrez supporting the rifle with his gloved hands, I removed my pen from the bore and peered inside. For a long time, that crisp, bright bore held my attention. When a cartridge is fired in a rifle, it's a contained symphony. About forty grains of gun powder ignites in this particular version and burns in a microsecond, creating an incomprehensibly huge cloud of brilliantly hot gasses. Contained in a brass shell casing that is in turn contained in the chrome steel chamber of the rifle, the erupting gas seeks exit. By moving the projectile, the 'plug', forward, there's relief, and the whole mass of gasses propels the bullet down the tube and out the muzzle, on the way to the target…in this case, Larry Zipoli's forehead.

"Do you always clean your firearms after a session?"

"Absolutely. Sometimes several times *during* a match."

"Always?"

"What's your point, sheriff?"

"I think you can probably guess, Mark." He knew—far better than I—that even a single round, a single symphony of burning powder and brass projectile hustling down the barrel, would leave its mark on the bright steel. Turning the bore light, I could see the haze of powder residue. I could see a fleck or two of unburned powder just forward of the chamber. Closing my eyes, I bent my head and inhaled slowly and deeply through my nose. Even as a mending smoker days removed from my last cigarette, I could smell the sweet aroma of burned powder.

Chapter Thirty-two

"That rifle was thoroughly cleaned after my last match," Arnett said, but he sounded distant.

"When was that?"

He glanced across the room at the large wall calendar over the bench. "July eighteenth."

I tipped the gun toward him. "That smell fresh to you?" I pushed the rifle away when he reached for it. "No touch. Just smell."

He did so, and stepped back. "It's been fired." He reached around to put the bore light in place and examined the bore for himself.

"You recall doing that? Firing it a few times? Maybe to try out a new load?"

"No." He hesitated for a moment. "I've been shooting the same load in that rifle for years. If it ain't broke, don't fix it. I gotta tell you, I don't like the way this is goin'. You're telling me that somebody used this rifle to shoot Larry Zipoli?"

"I'm telling you that I have questions, Mark. We all have questions. Look, what do you think would happen if you fired a .30-30 round in this rifle?"

I decided at that moment, watching Mark Arnett's face, that he was a pretty sharp fellow, even though flooded with emotions he didn't know how to deal with. My question out of left field drew him up short, and his eyes narrowed. It was obvious to me that he wasn't just pondering an interesting question—he was putting two and two together now. I held up the plastic evidence bag containing the fired slug. "What do you think?"

"I think it wouldn't shoot for shit," he said flatly.

"Might not even leave rifling marks on the bullet, would it."

"There's about fifteen thou difference in bore diameter," Arnett said. "So no. The rifling wouldn't have much to grab on to." He opened the box of new .30-30 slugs, selected one, and motioned for Torrez to change his grip on the gun. I took the pen out of the muzzle, and he dropped the shiny new bullet down the bore of the .32. With a little clink at the end as it hit the bolt face, it dropped through slick as can be.

"And the bullet's most likely going to keyhole, besides," Arnett added.

The room fell silent. Arnett looked as if he wanted to say something, then thought better of it. Maybe he was mulling the warrant/attorney suggestion.

"So now you know where we're at," I said. "Are you going to let us take this rifle for a little while, or do you want us to get a warrant?"

"Shit, take it," he said without hesitation. He reached into the corner and hefted a plastic rifle case. "Do what you got to do. You got a shell casing for comparison? I mean, what good, otherwise?" I finished putting the Winchester in the case without upholstering the smooth surface with my fingerprints.

I would be quickly paddling out of my depth if I tried to answer his questions, and I nodded at Bob Torrez. Anything I said would be bullshit, and Mark Arnett would know it. A shrewd guy himself, Deputy Torrez could figure out for himself how much we wanted to reveal.

"There'll be burned powder residue imbedded in the base of the bullet." The deputy's voice was almost a whisper. "That can be chemically matched to the residue in the rifle's chamber."

"Horseshit," Arnett scowled.

"When you crimp the cartridge casing around the brass bullet," Torrez added, "there are characteristic scuff marks…

nothing like rifling cuts, but microscopic marks that we can compare."

"Do *you* think this is what happened with all this shit? A .30-30 fired from a .32?"

Torrez nodded. "I tried it."

Arnett gazed at the young man in disbelief. "You got to be shittin' me."

"Nope."

"Why would anybody *do* that?"

"Don't know, Mark."

"And if you think Mo is involved somehow, you've been smokin' that funny tobacco," Arnett said.

"We didn't say that he was involved, Mark," I said.

"You don't got to. Look, the last time that rifle was out of this safe…the last time…was when *I* shot it in a match. You think any other way, it's bullshit. Look."

He opened one of the cabinets above the bench. "Look. Here's a box of .32's," he said, and pulled out a large plastic ammo box that hit the counter with an authoritative thud. He fumbled the latch and opened it, revealing a hundred bright cartridges, nose down, the fresh primers facing us. "I got four of these boxes. You want to check all four hundred rounds?"

"We might."

"Well, then," and he hauled all the storage boxes out. When he was finished, he said, "Satisfied? And I got five boxes of thirty-thirty." He hauled one out and opened it. "This one ain't full, but the others are." Sure enough, there were forty-nine loaded cartridges, their headstamps bright, announcing the caliber and the manufacturer. In additon, there were thirty-seven fired rounds, with fourteen unoccupied slots. The empties were inserted in the box mouth up, the powder residue obvious around the necks and case mouth.

With bifocals, my vision was pretty good, but not as good as Bob Torrez's. He could see that the mouth of one fired case was larger than it should be. Arnett, intimately familiar with the reloading process, familiar with measurements and quality control, familiar with what it took to win shooting matches, moved faster than the deputy...perhaps because Mark wasn't thinking about latent finger prints. Before we could react, he snatched the last empty round out of the box.

He read the headstamp, or tried to. His eyes were blurring. Even I could see the tears forming at the corners—rage, grief, frustration, all of the above. "Ah, come on," he whispered, and shook his head. He clenched his eyes hard, and the veins on his neck bulged. With a hard snap, he hurled the empty shell casing across the bench. It struck the wall and skittered into a corner.

Without another word, he turned and headed for the door. This time, Bob Torrez was faster. He blocked the passage, but it didn't appear that Mark had a clear idea where he wanted to go. He turned half a circle and pounded the table with his fist.

"Mark, use some judgment," I said.

"You won't even need to talk with that little fat bastard when I finish with him," he said between clenched teeth. His vitriol took me by surprise.

"Not going to happen, Mark," I said. "This isn't about taking the belt to his butt and then grounding the kid for a couple weeks. The boy is scared out of his mind and on the run. That's what it looks like to me. If he pulled that trigger on Larry Zipoli, then you're going to need to help us, Mark."

He made a strange gurgling noise, as if he was choking on his own spit. He sagged back against the safe, both hands on top of his head.

"Have you ever made that mistake?" I asked gently. He shook his head without moving his hands. "Ever reach for the wrong box? I mean, the guns are similar—the *ammo* is similar." I reached across the bench and retrieved the empty casing by slipping my pen down its mouth. Sure enough, the head stamp in the brass base announced .30-30 Winchester.

"No."

"Did you ever run short of .32 cases and blow out a few .30-30's to get you by? I mean, you could do that." I was no reloader, but knew enough folks who did, and knew that they were always experimenting with this and that, fashioning cases that couldn't be purchased commercially. He shook his head again. "Ever loan these guns to someone who might do that?" There was that chance, of course—the chance that somehow, Mo Arnett was innocent as the driven snow.

I reached out a hand and rested it on Mark's shoulder. "We need to talk with your son, Mark. We need to talk with Mo."

"You better find that little shit before I do," he threatened again, the only thing he knew how to do just then. He was of the old-fashioned beat-the-crap-out-of-the-kid school of child rearing—a school that sometimes had my sympathy. But sometimes that mentality just wasn't enough.

"No, that's not what's going to happen, Mark." My grip on his shoulder rocked him a little, ameliorating the sharpness of my words. "Let me tell you what *is* going to happen. One of the deputies will be back with a warrant. We'll use that whether you think one is required or not—and let me tell you. We appreciate your cooperation. But we'll have a warrant. Then, this room will be sealed off, inventoried, all that happy shit. The two rifles will be taken into evidence, along with all the ammo for them. We'll have photos up the whazoo. Prints on everything. Interviews, depositions. You know the drill. Between now and the arrival of the warrant, that door," and I turned and nodded at the entry that Deputy Torrez so effectively blocked, "will be sealed with a Sheriff's Seal. You won't come in here. None of your family will. Not until we're finished.

"And if we're wrong in all this, and Mo walks through the front door in five minutes with a hell of a perfect alibi, with a hell of a good reason for touching your rifles, I'll be the first to show up and grovel with an apology, Mark." I smiled at him. "I'll buy you a case of beer . Whatever the apology takes." Safe promise, I thought. But it sounded good, and I saw Mark Arnett wilt a little.

"What do I do?" The stuffing had been knocked out of him, the umbrage diluted. We were making progress.

"First, we want Mo found, we want him safe. So go fetch your wife. Then decide what attorney you're going to use, and get him over here to assist you, to assist Mo. Trust me on this… if he's charged with anything, you're going to need all the help you can get. So start early."

"He's just a *kid*, for Christ's sake."

"Yep, he is. Or was." I opened the safe again, touching it gingerly by one corner of the massive door. "Are you missing any guns?"

Mark Arnett's glance was perfunctory. "No. Everything's there."

"Small thanks for that, at least."

"There was one in the center console of the Pontiac," Arnett said. His face had drained of color. "He don't know anything about that one."

"You better hope he doesn't," I said, not the least bit optimistic. "What was it?"

"A .45 Springfield."

"Loaded?" Why would it be there if it wasn't?

"One loaded magazine. Nothing in the chamber."

I groaned inwardly as Mo Arnett's slippery slope clicked a few degrees steeper. Someone, most likely Mo, had used the not-so-thoughtfully hidden key to the gun room. Why he'd decided to take a shot at the grader—and maybe the operator in it, I certainly didn't know. If the kids' stories were to be believed, Mo was humiliated by Larry Zipoli. Most folks could take a little humiliation. But now, *someone* had managed to open the safe, unless dad was so careless that he left it unlocked. That someone was now fleeing in his mother's car. And we could add the 'A and D' to the BOLO.

Chapter Thirty-three

Estelle Reyes held out the photograph, and I took it reluctantly, standing just inside my office door with about thirty other things that demanded my attention at that moment. The last thing I wanted was to be sidetracked by a treatise on religious art. Who the hell knew where Mo Arnett was at that moment, or what the kid might do next. Jim Raught's saint panels weren't going to fetch the boy home. But I could tell by the look on the young lady's face that she'd been captivated by *that* puzzle, if in fact it was one. Maybe the muse of the three saints had grabbed her attention.

"The attorney is sending us a photograph of the original *retablo,*" she said. "A good series was taken for a magazine article not long before the theft. It shows," and she leaned forward to point out a neat circle she had drawn with an orange hi-liter around St. Ignacio's left sandal. "That margin is a portion of the gold leaf. And you can see where it's been mended at one time."

"I can?" One gold leaf looked pretty much like another to me, but I could see some small fracture lines that appeared to interrupt the flow of metal.

She persisted. "Sophía Tournál is sending an enlargement, but from her description, I would guess that this is much the same."

"Sophía…"

"My fiancé's aunt. The lawyer."

"*Much* the same? It damn well better be more than that if we're going to make time for this."

"Yes, sir." She drew another photo from her briefcase. "This is the enlargement Ernie made for me from the art book. The damage to the gold border is quite clear in this."

I glanced, compared, nodded, and looked at my watch. Time was on Mo's side. The saints could wait.

"More important is that the work is *attributed* to Orosco on the back," Estelle persisted. "The three *retablos* were actually framed as one unit in 1919, and the framer documented Orosco's artistry by writing his name in India ink on the back, just beside the new frame."

"Okay."

"The original *retablos* disappeared in the art theft with several other important pieces four years ago. No trace since."

I handed the photos back to her. "I'm impressed, although not with the timing of all this. Look, we've got a missing kid, maybe armed and dangerous. The saints can look after themselves for a little while longer."

"Did Mr. Arnett have any notions?" Her easy change of subject suggested that she was easy with relegating the saints to the back burner.

"None. So we start digging. Are you ready for that?"

"Yes, sir."

"I'm not suggesting that we're going to forget all this." I waved a hand at the photos she was sorting back into her briefcase. "But right now, the good judge is signing a warrant for us, and that's where we're headed…to take Mo's life apart and see what we can find."

She nodded, almost eagerly sure enough, but I could see the resignation just the same.

A few minutes later, with a fresh warrant in hand, we talked with his parents, now sitting hand-in-hand on the living room sofa while officers upset their household. Mark had given up blustering and promising a punch, and now had deflated a couple of sizes. We talked with Mo's little sister, and finally elicited from fiesty little Maureen the evaluation that Mo was decidedly "a creep." Of course, to a fourth grader, most of the world was full of creeps. Mindy 'Mom' Arnett's favored expression was, "I just don't understand this."

We discovered that Mo's life *wasn't* an open book. That was scary. Mo Arnett was truly a stranger in his own house. We had heard lots of helpful gossip from others.

"He'll find shelter with a friend or relative."

"He'll retreat to a favorite private spot—a hide-a-way."

"He'll try to cross the border."

"He'll find a quiet place and kill himself."

"He'll…"

No one, including his immediate family, could give us an intelligent guess about the boy's intentions or location. As far as we could discover, Maurice "Mo" Arnett wasn't buying into any of the neighbors' predictions. While every available eyeball was looking for a gold Pontiac, license Charlie Lincoln Thomas four nine nine, we kept plugging away closer to home.

A sweep of the boy's room showed us nothing beyond a nest for a surprisingly neat teenager, and that in itself made me uneasy. Mo Arnett had a love affair with the Chevrolet Corvette and old steam locomotives. A lad of contrasts, for sure. His choice of art included sixteen framed photographs of Corvette models from the car's clumsy introduction in the early 50s to the latest heart-thumping twin-turbo version. To compliment those, six photos of huge late-vintage steam locomotives were gathered in framed elegance over the head of his bed.

The clothes in his closet were orderly, and there was nothing hidden under the socks and underwear in his bureau. If he'd left with no intention of returning, it wasn't clear what he might have taken with him.

A student desk nestled under one window with a view out across the street. Sitting at it, I had a clear view of the Zipolis' to the right, and Raught's to the left. Did Mo sit here and stew, watching the fat man go about his home chores, beer can habitually in hand? Did he watch the other kids gather when it was time for a boating and skiing expedition? Did he watch Jim Raught grubbing among the cacti?

The desk drawers yielded nothing beyond the usual—pencils, pen, a calculator, a tiny teddy bear apparently hibernating for a while, a broken ream of printer paper. I sat in the straight-backed chair and regarded the modest computer and its accessories. I was willing to bet that there would be no secrets there, either. "You know how to run this thing?"

"Yes, sir."

"Turn it on for me."

She did so, and in a few moments I could see that the list of files appeared as innocuous as everything else in the room. "We'll want to take this with us and do a thorough search of the drives," I said. "Dollars to donuts says we won't find anything, but we have to look."

A single four-shelf bookcase held a couple dozen slip cases for video games—a conservative collection that leaned toward auto racing—a handful of books that ranged from fantasy to those study guides that students use so they won't have to read the entire novel, and a modest collection of magazines, again leaning heavily toward muscle cars but with a few model rail-roading issues thrown into the mix. And true to motif, one shelf showcased a plastic model of a late 70's era 'Vette, its hood up to show the chromed engine. At the shelf's opposite end, sitting on a twelve-inch section of track, was an HO gauge steam locomotive bearing the Santa Fe logo.

We found no journal, no diary, no stash of documents illuminating a teenager's secret life, no little notebook full of sinister plans or names on a hit list, no Polaroid snapshots of either victims or intended victims. I stood at the end of the double bed, surveying the room. "How sad."

Estelle looked up from her inventory of the closet. "Sir?"

"This place reminds me of a motel room," I said. "I think about my own kids and the nightmare my wife or I faced when we ventured into their rooms. I mean, the life of a kid is a messy thing."

She slid the closet door closed gently. "This closet is where they store their Christmas ornaments," she said.

"And it should be stuffed with *his* stuff." She stepped to one side as I slid the closet doors this way and that, double-checking for myself. I pulled a shoe box down off the shelf and opened it to find a pair of baseball shoes, spikes clean and new. "At least there's a little something," I said, and tapped each shoe to dislodge anything that might be stashed inside.

"Sir?"

I turned and glanced at Estelle. She reached out with a toe and touched a drawer pull just showing from under the hem of the bed spread. Flipping the spread up, I saw there were actually two brass pulls a yard apart.

"Isn't that slick," I said. The "drawer" was actually a piece of three-quarter inch plywood on drawer glides, and it slid out easily. The HO gauge model train layout on the plywood base was neat and organized—nothing fancy, but large enough that the train would be able to negotiate the twists and turns. The thoughtful builder had even engineered two short folding legs on the front edge for further support when the layout was pulled out. I wondered, at the time that Mark Arnett was building the table for his son, if there had been a spark of warmth and camaraderie there.

Estelle dropped to one knee and leaned on the bed with an elbow, taking a closer look. "Not much use," she said, and reached out to nudge a dust bunny that threatened to block the track.

"He's not really here, is he." I glanced at Estelle. "It reminds me of a kid's room who's away at college or something. Neat, clean, and unused. A shrink would probably have a field day. God damn sad."

Another hour was no help in figuring out the enigma that was Mo Arnett, and after Deputy Tom Mears arrived and collected the computer, we left the house. Estelle had been perfectly willing to remain with the Arnetts, or take on any task that I assigned. Her argument was a good one—there was no point in wasting a certified officer as a babysitter for the family. Nor her either, I reminded her. And I sure as hell didn't want Miss Reyes driving around by herself, in her own private vehicle, playing cop. Badly as we needed personnel, she'd have to be content to sit and watch.

I stopped the county car at the intersection of Bustos and Grande, and in the rearview mirror watched a small group of kids—maybe ten year olds—trooping out with fists full of junk food.

"Where did he go," I mused, not expecting an answer.

"Assuming he's not in a shallow grave somewhere," Estelle said, and I looked at her in surprise.

"I don't think so." I didn't *want* to think that. Larry Zipoli's loss needed to end this tangle. Still, Estelle was right. Mo Arnett might have seen someone fire the shot, and been seen in turn. All the firearm evidence weighed against that, but we'd have to wait on some complex lab analysis by the state lab. I was half certain that Deputy Robert Torrez had been blowing smoke when he said the powder residue in the rifle's chamber could be matched to the residue welded into the base of the bullet. *We* sure as hell couldn't do that.

What we *could* do, however, and Bob Torrez was working on the task at that very moment, was compare the firing pin impressions—the face of the firing pin itself, compared to the dent in the cartridge's primer. No two firing pins were microscopically alike, nor were the dents that they left.

Of course we could do that, but what difference did it make? What mattered was the bullet that the coroner had pulled from Larry Zipoli's skull. *It* had to match a weapon for us to make progress. I wasn't sure we could do that, but I sure as hell didn't want anyone to know I had doubts.

"What?" I prompted. Estelle's black eyebrows were furrowed in ferocious concentration. She leafed through her notebook as if she'd misplaced something now suddenly become important.

"I was wondering when Mo took off. What's his head start?"

"Zipoli was killed Tuesday," I said. "*If* Mo pulled the trigger, he drove home, dumped the shell casing back in the box, put the rifle away—didn't clean it. One swipe with a patch would have thrown a good roadblock in our path, but he didn't do that. I gotta wonder—but maybe he was just spooked. Or confident. That's what it seems to me. I mean, why return the shell casing? Clever kid. He's thinking." I touched my forehead. "But he doesn't know that he used the wrong cartridges. How about that. Clever, but dumb as a box of rocks." I ticked off finger tips with my thumb. "He didn't go to school, but his parents didn't report him missing. They probably didn't know. They didn't pay attention to where he was on Wednesday during the day, but they *think* he was home on Wednesday night. He ditches school today, unbeknownst to mom and dad. Sometime today, he takes the car, bound for who the hell knows where."

"He would have had to leave after his parents both went to work," Estelle said.

"Certainly, unless the Arnetts were so numb they didn't bother to check the boy this morning—or open the garage to see that the car is gone. I think it's likely that he left after they did, though. Mom and Dad go off to work this morning, and the boy is home...we assume."

There's a limit to how long you can park at an intersection, even when it's a cop car. I pulled 310 out of my lane and idled to the curb. Two cars—what amounts to a traffic jam in Posadas—slid by, both drivers looking over at me curiously. Or perhaps my passenger.

"It's now five forty-five," I added. "To guess at an answer to your question, the boy could have a nine or ten hour head start. How scary is that. He could be..." I shrugged. "You name it. He could be anywhere."

"I'm wondering why he waited so long before taking off."

"Well, think about it. For a while, maybe he thought he'd pulled it off. Keep mum, just like a school kid. He didn't even have to say, '*I didn't do it!*'." I shrugged. "There's also the possibility that he didn't *know* what he did, that somehow, he didn't even *see* Larry Zipoli inside that grader. He didn't walk over to check, and later in the day, when he heard what happened, he's petrified. He doesn't know who knows what. We started talking to his buddies *today,* right? This morning, in fact. We stopped Tom Pasquale out on West Bustos. What time did we do that?"

Damned if she didn't know right where that particular notebook page was. "Nine fifty-five, sir."

I reached for my aluminum clip board and scanned my own log for verification. She was right.

"You think young Mr. Pasquale called Mo? I mean, he got stopped by the cops—that's news, right? That's good stuff. Call a friend and tell 'em you got stopped for rolling a stop sign on a bike. How cool is that. But Tommy didn't say that he reached Mo this morning, or that he talked with him."

"Very likely, sir. If he knew that Mo had not gone to school either."

"Well, shit. There's that." I frowned. "But regardless, by Thursday morning, Mo would have to be living under a rock not to know about the death. Time to split. Time to run. Five or six hours ago, maybe. Sixty-five miles an hour in that Pontiac, and he's three hundred miles away."

"To where, sir?"

I laughed. "That's why we need your woman's intuition, sweetheart." I didn't know Estelle Reyes well enough to excuse calling her "sweetheart", but what the hell. I was impressed. Let her sue me.

Back at the office, we spent fifteen minutes with Sheriff Eduardo Salcido, who looked like shit after his doctor's appointment. He wanted nothing more than to go home to bed, and I encouraged that very thing. I would have done the same if sleep was my friend. He listened as I filled in the informational chinks.

"He's only seventeen," Eduardo observed. "He's not going to get far."

I didn't argue, since there was no predicting *what* the kid would do, and history had proven that teenagers could accomplish all kinds of things, nefarious or otherwise.

At 7:15 p.m., we were assisting State Police Officer Mark Adams with a roll-over accident on the interstate seven miles west of Posadas. Life goes on. Just because we had a mess on our hands with Zipoli's killer, the rest of the world didn't slip into suspended animation. The rolled car was totaled, but four occupants inside, including two little kids, were just shaken. It took some soothing to convince them that their luck *hadn't* run out. The family all rode in one ambulance to Posadas General for a check up. The two little kids needed Teddy Bears, and Adams had only one. I don't know why Estelle looked surprised when I hauled another out of 310's trunk.

Adams and I made sure the family had arrangements at the Posadas Inn via a courtesy car from the motel, and I left them with my card and assurances that the Chavez brothers at Chavez Ford-Lincoln Mercury would take care of them the next morning.

I was jotting in a log notation before I left the hospital parking lot when one of the county Broncos pulled up beside me. I hadn't seen the vehicle turn in off the street, and it stopped with a jolt after circling to approach head on, driver to driver.

"Evening, sir," Bob Torrez greeted. "You all set here?"

I nodded. "Nothing serious except a totaled car. The family is going to spend the night at the Inn. Did you see the sheriff?"

"For a little bit. He headed home. He said the doctor wanted to admit him, and he refused."

"That's smart," I scoffed, feeling a sympathetic twinge. "What did you find out?"

"Mears and me worked on the computer and the case match." He managed a small grin—hysterics by his standards. "The firing pin and bolt face of Arnett's .32 Winchester Special matched the impressions on the base of the blown out .30-30 casing." Torrez sounded as if he were reading a prepared statement. "It's all packed up to go to the FBI tomorrow morning for confirmation."

"Of course it matched," I grumbled. "It was Arnett's gun, and Arnett's shell casing. The kid was careless and grabs either the wrong rifle or the wrong ammo. It's a long shot that Mark would make the mistake himself." I thumped the steering wheel. It was one of those things that we needed to know for sure, but

I would have been astonished and flummoxed and stuffed in a quandry if it *hadn't* matched. "A cartridge taken from Arnett's ammo box, fired in some *other* gun, and then returned to the box? Not damn likely, Bobby. What else do you have?"

"Nothin' on the computer. I mean nothin' we need to know." Torrez pulled two large black and white photos from an envelope. He handed them across to me, and it took a while for me to recognize what I was looking at. Enlarge something umpty-ump times, and it loses some focus. The cannalure—that criss-crossed channel around the circumference of the bullet into which the shell casing crimps—showed clearly enough. The body of the bullet was a mass of fine scratches, dings, and dents—almost microscopic marks most of which could be explained by the manufacturing process.

"That's the slug from Zipoli's brain," Torrez said.

"I see that." The hugely distorted tip ran off the right side of the photo margin. I held the second photo just above the first. The second photo was a different bullet, one that still showed some distortion from firing. "Where'd you do this?"

"They got a water tank over at maintenance," Torrez said. "Kinda messy, but it works to trap the bullet."

"Nice photos." I lined up cannalure to cannalure. "What am I supposed to see?" I held the photos so Estelle could see them, although the car's lame dome light made it difficult.

"The scuffs where the shell casing crimps the bullet are in exactly the same place," the deputy said. Sure enough, they were.

"Meaning?"

"Meaning that in all likelihood the same reloading die reloaded both bullets. What are the odds that two different people set two different reloading dies so that the crimps are identical?"

"I have no idea. And in all likelihood, that's what a defense attorney is going to question." I looked across at Torrez. "What do you think?"

"I think the bullet in Zip's head came from one of Arnett's cartridges, sir. I think that's obvious."

"We *think* it did. What did the sheriff say? You told him all this?"

"Yes, sir. He said to keep after it."

"And that's what we'll do. *Somebody* somewhere knows where Mo Arnett might have gone. His parents say that he has a credit card that he's not supposed to use. If he's smart, he won't."

Torrez looked disgusted. "If they don't want him usin' it, what's he got it for?"

"They say he got it as part of a school civics project. How about that?" I shook my head. "Times have changed, that's for sure. And I wouldn't presume to understand his folks," I said. "And they're not missing any cash, so he's not flush in that respect. He might have been able to scrape together a couple hundred bucks. He had time to visit the bank. You want to work on Tom's brother?"

Deputy Tom Mears' twin brother Terry was a vice president at Posadas State Bank.

"Find out if the kid made any withdrawals from his college account or whatever…whatever he's got. If Terry wants a warrant, go ahead and bother the judge again. And do it tonight, Bobby."

"Gotcha."

I sat for a moment, trying to climb into the kid's mind. About the time Torrez's brake lights flared as he reached the end of the parking lot, I turned to Estelle.

"Everyone needs a place to go," I said. "Everybody. Even Mo Arnett. Most of us just go home. What the hell does he do?"

Chapter Thirty-four

When the phone rang, it just about put me into orbit. I'd finally fallen asleep in that huge, maroon leather recliner down in my den—my place to go. The nearest telephone was up on the kitchen counter, its location one of my quirks. I didn't want the thing in my inner sanctum, competing with the solitude of my library. But as a result, it took a while for me to reach the kitchen without breaking my neck.

The phone was patient, its insistent ringing imperative.

"Gast…" I coughed and tried again. "Gastner." The stove clock blinked, which told me the power had been off. I looked up at the clock over the counter and saw that it was close to midnight.

"Sir, this is Marcus Baker," my swing shift dispatcher said. No doubt my fine diction told him I'd been blowing z's.

"Sure enough," I managed ungratefully. I had collapsed into my chair after dropping Miss Reyes off at her modest little apartment behind the school. I hadn't bothered to promise her a normal day tomorrow…today, now. Who the hell knew what would happen. I'd managed to read half a Chapter about Chichamauga, then dropped off, book in my lap, pages rumpled.

"Sir, they found Mo Arnett's car up in Albuquerque," Ernie reported. "In the long-term parking lot at the Sunport."

"Well, son of a bitch."

"Yes, sir. Do you want me to call the sheriff?"

"No, I don't," I said quickly. "The Pontiac, but no Mo?"

"No, sir. It's a Sergeant Patterson who called from the APD. Would you like his numbers? He said he'd be available until two."

"Absolutely." I copied the number, thanked Ernie for calling, and dialed. In a moment, Patterson's light voice came on the line. He sounded as if he were twelve years old.

"Airport security made the identification," he acknowledged. "None of the flight manifests show your subject boarding any flight within the last twenty-four hours."

"Shit," I said, and Patterson chuckled.

"Security made a sweep of the airport. Mr. Arnett doesn't appear to be on the premises."

"Any corners he can hide in?"

"I don't think so, sheriff. Of course, it's a big place."

A big place, indeed. The high school photo we'd included with our bulletin showed Mo as he was the year before, and he happened to have been particularly scruffy in that portrait... long hair, with what passes for a teenage beard, not as pudgy as he was now. He could blend in with a family, or sit in a quiet, dark corner of the restaurant, waiting for his flight.

"But no hits on the manifests," I repeated.

"No, sir. But we'll keep after it. We have the car. A teenager isn't going to stray far from his wheels."

"We can hope not." But with this particular teenager? Who knew where he'd stray.

"By the way, sarge, there was a handgun in the glove compartment. I need to know if it's still there."

"I'll get back to you on that. The vehicle was locked, and it's going to be a few minutes yet while they process it."

"I need to know if the kid has the gun with him. You sure as hell do too. And it'd be nice to know if there's a body in the trunk."

He laughed. "I hear ya."

"We never know."

"Well, according to the ticket on the dash, it was in the hot sun all day, and nothing smells. But I'll get the team on that

ASAP. He hasn't boarded a flight, and he sure as hell wouldn't try carrying a gun on board."

I was skeptical about that, but didn't burst the sergeant's bubble.

With the sleep driven away by the phone call, I stayed vertical and brewed a fresh pot of coffee. By the time I took the first sip, wondering where my cigarettes were before recalling that I was trying to quit, the clock had ticked to twelve fifteen.

Parked in the Sunport, but not on a flight. Airport Security said that Mo Arnett wasn't on the premises, but I didn't believe that as a given. It's easy to hide in a huge facility, easy to slip here and there, away from prying eyes. If that was the case, what was the boy waiting for? The sooner airborne, the better, if he was on the run. If he hadn't grabbed a flight, odds were good he was still in Albuquerque, a place that must seem incomprehensibly huge after the tiny confines of Posadas.

With a full mug of coffee, I left the house, enjoying the quiet of the village. Lights from the trailer park down the street and from the interstate interchange ruined the view of the star canopy overhead, but I could see a few being squired around the heavens by Orion. No wind, mild—a magnificent night.

The middle of the night is a cruel time for the cops to show up on the doorstep, but I knew that the Arnetts wouldn't be asleep. They deserved to know that the Pontiac had been found in the big city, and that information might jog their memories. And sure enough, they lived on a block where they weren't alone with their worries. The lights were ablaze in the front rooms of the Arnetts, and across the street at the Zipoli residence. A bright light drifted out from Jim Raught's back yard. Maybe they'd all joined forces to find the errant Mo.

I parked in the street half a block down from Arnetts' and sat for a bit with all the windows open. The lights might have all been blazing, but that was the extent of any activity I could hear. I cracked the door and when I swung my boot out and planted it on the asphalt, it was as if I'd grounded a faulty connection, throwing a switch on my car radio.

"Three ten, PCS. Ten twenty."

Home in bed, I almost said, but the graveyard dispatcher, Ernie Wheeler, already knew that wasn't true. He would have called the house and chatted with my answering machine. And he knew my habits, habits fueled by a persistent insomnia that most of the time I found both useful and pleasant.

"PCS, three ten is ten eight on Fourth Street."

"Ten nineteen if you're not busy."

"Ten four." I'd already said I was ten eight, or in service... hence "not busy." I swung the door shut and started the car, leaving the neighborhood to its own thoughts and worries. As soon as I swung into the Sheriff's Department parking lot, I saw the little sedan tucked into a spot between two department cruisers. Estelle Reyes hadn't listed insomnia as one of her virtues.

I trudged inside using the side entrance, and saw the young lady over in the lobby, hands thrust into her pockets, gazing at the huge county map that was framed in walnut. The six foot square map had been prepared by Enuncio Baca, a county assessor and artist, based on the most recent data at the time. The "time" happened to be 1936, which meant that the map was now functionally useless, but a historical treasure. I had a long list of questions to ask Enuncio, history being one of my passions. But Enuncio had died in 1951, so my questions would have to wait.

Estelle turned as I stepped into the dispatch island. Ernie Wheeler, tall and lanky and one of those guys who looks thirty going on sixty-five, nodded toward the young lady.

"She has a question for you," Ernie said. "I think that she wants to use the phone."

"Our phones are restricted now?" I asked, puzzled. "She doesn't need to ask permission from me."

"She wanted to talk with you first, sir, but then went ahead and used the one in the conference room."

Not more saint stuff, I almost said, but instead held up my now empty coffee cup. "Anybody fueled the pot?"

"Fresh an hour ago," Ernie said, and I beckoned to Estelle as I headed for the work room.

"Good night's sleep?" I asked as she followed me into the room. "We need well-rested staff, you know." If I successfully managed a touch of amused reproof, she didn't acknowledge it. Besides, she appeared fresh and well-rested. Even her tan pants suit was wrinkle free. Did she own a rack of the damn things?

"I got to thinking, sir."

"Uh oh. You need to know, by the way, that they found Mo Arnett's car in Albuquerque International's long-term parking lot. No Mo yet."

That brought no response, and I glanced at the young lady as I snapped off the coffee flow. I held up the cup, offering her some.

"No thank you, sir. His car was at the airport?"

"Correct. APD and airport security are following up on it for us. I was just heading over to the Arnetts' for a few minutes to let them know. Maybe news of finding the car will jar something loose."

Her eyebrows furrowed. "He hadn't taken a flight?"

"Not yet, at least. And they're continuing a sweep of the airport. If he's there, they'll find him." I watched her face as she mulled all this. "What's your concern?"

She took a deep breath, and I got the strong impression that she was trying very hard not to be too forward with her opinions. "I'm surprised that he didn't consider the train."

"Ah. Amtrak."

"He loves trains, sir. I'm just surprised that he was at the airport. There wasn't a single model or photo of an airplane in his room."

"Well, that's true. Old steam engines, yes. He also loves Corvettes, but as far as we know, he didn't steal one."

"He's too smart for that."

"I'm not convinced of *that.*"

"He got rid of the Pontiac right away, and parking it at the airport was good thinking. Even if the car was discovered promptly, it makes us think he was planning on air travel."

"That's a possibility. A conniving little bastard, he's turning out to be. So what's he do? Take a taxi down to the train station?"

"That or a shuttle or city bus, sir. No I.D. required. Or he could walk. It's not that far."

I gazed at her with interest, enjoying the way the excitement of the chase made her dark, almost Aztecan features glow.

"Train four eastbound was more than two and a half hours late, sir," Estelle offered. "It left Albuquerque northbound at two fifty six. Train three westbound was nearly four hours late. They said that they had a medical emergency near La Junta, Colorado, with one of the passengers. It should have left Albuquerque at 4:55 p.m., but didn't actually pull out until 9:27 p.m. Albuquerque is a fuel stop, and that put them even further behind."

"Nine thirty, then. Okay."

"Security on both the bus and the train is lax, sir. You can even step onboard and pay your ticket after the train is in motion. I've done that."

"The Southwest Limited goes north out of state and then swings east to Kansas City," I mused. "And then the route ends in Chicago. There are connections all along the way to God knows where."

"Yes, sir. And the westbound train heads out to Flagstaff and finally Los Angeles. Even though it was late, eastbound left the city first."

"Which way, then. If he jumps east, he's out of here at two yesterday afternoon. In Kansas City by mid-morning. Or he could wait around for the west-bound…hell of a wait until 9:30 last night. It all depends, I suppose. Does he have a particular destination that makes him choose a train, or is he just jumping on board the first one that shows. Just the two trains each day, right?"

"Yes, sir."

I dumped the remains of the coffee into the utility sink. "Let's see where this leads us." Ernie Wheeler was on the phone with someone when I reappeared, and he leaned forward, nodding, trying his best to cut off the conversation.

"Dogs," he said, and scanned the roster. "Just what Miracle needs." I didn't interrupt as he forwarded a radio call to village unit 327, requesting that part-time officer J.J. Murton respond to a barking dog complaint over on Llano del Sol.

"We need a copy of Mo Arnett's photo faxed up to Amtrak security in Albuquerque," I said. "We want to know if he boarded either east or westbound, and if there's a destination on his ticket."

Wheeler nodded, excited at having something worthwhile to do. "They have a seat manifest?"

"I would think that they do." Then again, I thought, who knows. I hadn't ridden a train in a long time. I had picked up a passenger once in Albuquerque not too many years before, and it seemed to me that the platform had been a disorganized flood of people, a swarm. Any nimble person could have slipped on or off without much notice. And someone familiar with trains would know where to hide to avoid the conductors.

Buses didn't keep track of anything but the gross number of passengers, making them the absolute best public transportation for those wishing to stay under the radar. It was entirely possible that Mo Arnett might be handing us a fast one as he boarded a friendly Greyhound.

"And mention to both rail *and bus* security that the subject *might* have a firearm…" The telephone hand buzzed again, and Ernie took the call. As he listened, he raised a hand toward me. I waited, and in a moment he covered the receiver.

"No gun, nothing in the trunk." He held the phone toward me. "You want to talk to the sergeant?"

"Nope. That means Mo likely has the gun with him, unless he got smart and ditched it. Tell 'em to be careful."

"Yes, sir." He turned back to the phone.

The only safeguard the transportation folks had was sharp-eyed conductors, agents or drivers who might recognize a nervous passenger when they saw one. Hopefully a pudgy kid, sweating with strungout nerves and trying to conceal a big .45, would trigger their radar.

Chapter Thirty-five

"Sorry for the hour," I said when Mark Arnett answered the door, and I spoke before his blood pressure had a chance to spike. I held up a hand. "Some developments," I said matter-of-factly, making sure that he heard me. "May we come in?"

He nodded and held the door for us. "We're in the living room." Mindi was sitting in a padded rocker, her hands clasped in her lap. She rose as we entered, her hands remaining locked together. None of the office-boss spunk stiffened her shoulders now.

"Mr. and Mrs. Arnett, Albuquerque police have found your vehicle in the Albuquerque airport parking lot. There's no sign of your son yet. The handgun is not in the car."

Mark gestured toward a couple of chairs. "You mean he just *left* the car?"

"It would appear so." I settled on a stout, straight-backed chair, all leather straps and heavy wood. Estelle took the end of the sofa an arm's length from Mark. "The car was locked when they found it in the long-term lot. Nothing in the trunk, but the gun was taken. We don't know if Mo still has it, or if he chucked it somewhere. Maybe in a garbage can or something."

"Why the hell would he do a stunt like that?"

"Maybe he didn't want it taken from the car if someone broke in. Maybe he took it, then found it too hard to conceal. Maybe he just got scared with it. We don't know."

"So where did he fly to, then?" Mark's question was blunt, still carrying the tone of voice that promised *"an even worse lickin' when he gets home."*

"APD is surveying the flight manifests right now, double-checking. Depending on when he actually got to Albuquerque, he could have had several choices, but right now, it looks as if he didn't take a flight at all. I mean it doesn't take long to check computer manifests." Mark appeared ready to sputter something, but I held up a hand. "You saw him at breakfast, was I correct in hearing you say that?" Mark looked across at Mindi, a silence between them about a mile wide. I felt like saying,

"Okay…who's going to lie first?"

"Did you see him at breakfast?"

"No, I didn't," Mark snapped. "I had to leave early. I left before he was up."

I looked questioningly at Mindi. "You saw him at breakfast?"

"I told you that I did," she murmured.

"Refresh my memory," I said pleasantly.

"I made sure that Mo was up…he loves to sleep in, you know. I told him that he needed to come down for breakfast. I had it all laid out for him."

"And he did that?"

"Certainly."

"You physically saw him enter the kitchen?"

"I…" Mindi came to a embarrassed halt. She glared at me, some of the spirit coming back now that she had a convenient target. "Listen, *I* had things I needed to do. Mo is perfectly capable of getting up in time for school, fixing his breakfast, and…you know."

"So you didn't sit down to breakfast with him."

"No. I told you I didn't."

"When you left the house, it was your assumption that Mo was up and about."

After a grudging pause, Mindi said, "Yes."

"And you haven't seen him since."

That brought tears from Mindi and a concrete set to Mark's jaw. I sighed. "If Mo was going to fly somewhere, where do you think it would be?"

"He wouldn't fly," Mark said instantly. "He gets airsick just looking at an airplane."

"Is that right."

"That's right."

"He'd take a train or bus?"

"Train. He loves 'em. You know that already. He wouldn't take a bus. He thinks only vagrants travel by bus."

"Who does he know that he'd visit? Let's say up north, or off to the east. If he took Amtrak, he might be heading toward Kansas City, maybe Chicago. Or connections beyond. Or west to Flagstaff? Kingman? L.A.?"

"Look, how can we know that?" Mark asked. *How can we know that?* The absurd question needled my blood pressure a couple of clicks upward. "He don't have many friends anywhere. Neither the wife or me has any relatives out of state."

"I have an elderly aunt who lives in...it's Cleveland, I think," Mindi said.

"We haven't seen her in a dozen years or more," Mark snapped. "Hell, Mo wouldn't even know who she is."

"So in a nutshell, if Mo boarded Amtrak, either west or east-bound, you wouldn't have any idea where he's headed."

"Shit, I don't see how we could," Mark said. He glanced sideways at Estelle, who was regarding him thoughtfully. "You know how kids talk. 'I'd like to do this, I'd like to do that.' It don't mean a whole hell of a lot."

"For instance?"

"For instance what?"

"When Mo talks about what he'd like to do..."

"Well, shit. He wants to go to Sea World, that place out in San Diego. He thinks that he wants to go out in a boat and do something or other with whales. That whale talk stuff." Mark grimaced. "All talk. He'd probably get seasick. He says that he'd like to go to New York and be a stock broker, for God's sakes. Hell, you got kids. You know how it goes."

"Where was he planning to go after graduation? Has he decided?"

"Damned if I know. I've tried to talk him into working for a year or so with me. Get some of the kinks out. Get some fresh air and some muscle on his bones." He shrugged. "Or see what the service has to offer. Do him good." He glanced at Mindi, who had frowned and shifted position as if someone had poked her in the butt with a hot poker at the mention of military. "The wife don't think much of that idea," Mark added.

"Well, either direction, east or west, if he's on the train, there's a good chance he'll be found," I said. "If. If he *didn't* take the train, it's still anybody's guess. If he had a chance to visit the bank, how much money would he have with him?"

"Couple hundred bucks, maybe, I don't know."

I sighed, liking Mark Arnett less and less. We were spinning our wheels with these people, and every moment we spent here was a moment farther away from Posadas for Mo.

"You'll let us know?" Arnett said as we made for the door.

"Of course."

"What'll happen now?" he asked, almost as an afterthought. "I mean, Mindi said that he didn't even take many extra clothes."

He won't need them when he's wearing jailhouse orange, I thought, but I kept the unkindness to myself.

I looked at Mark, wondering what made him tick. "If Mo took plane, train or bus, we'll find him. Unfortunately, we have to assume now that now he's armed, and that's a complication. What was the weapon you left in the car?"

"Just a beat up .45 ACP Springfield I've had for a while."

"Loaded, I assume?"

"Full mag. We didn't keep one in the chamber."

How goddamn thoughtful. "If police are able to arrest him without incident, he'll be returned here for questioning and in all likelihood, arraignment."

"Damn right he'll be questioned." He didn't ask me what the other side of that *if* was, but he had to know. I gazed impassively at him. "He'll be questioned by us, Mr. Arnett. Then we'll see."

Outside, the air was fresh relief.

"They're glad that he's out of the house," Estelle said.

"That's my impression," I grumbled. "Was it Robert Frost who said that home is the place, that when you have to return there, they have to take you in? Something like that? Mo's going to have a hard time coming home." I shook my head wearily. "Once the justice system is finished with him in twenty years or so."

"Do you suppose that he knows that? Mo, I mean?"

"Probably not. My experience has been that kids aren't fundamentally believers in reality. Whatever gremlins that might be lurking out there, teenagers believe that the bad luck doesn't apply to them."

Estelle remained silent for a while, but I could see her dark eyebrows furrowed in thought. "How do we go about getting him back?" she asked finally.

"I wish we had an easy answer for that. We can hope that he's jumped on Amtrak. In a way, that would be a good thing. It doesn't matter where the container goes. He's inside, bottled up. If the rail security can locate him, they've got a captive audience. As long as he doesn't do something stupid."

"His track record isn't good in that regard," she said soberly. "And if he has the gun with him?"

"Then all bets are off. It depends, of course, what he does with it, but I'm optimistic that he's not in a hurry to be found. Nothing will bring the wrath of the law down on his head faster than trying to use a weapon. I hope he knows that, and I hope that he took the gun in the stress of the moment, and ditched it the first chance he got. If he's smart and just blends into the woodwork, we're going to have a hell of a time finding him."

Chapter Thirty-six

Maurice "Mo" Arnett tried his best to blend, but at 1:19 a.m., night dispatcher Ernie Wheeler reached out with the radio.

"Three ten, PCS. Ten twenty."

I was standing in the middle of the street, and for about the third time that day, planning to walk across to the Zipoli home. Estelle Reyes, who was well on her way toward earning her night-owl wings, had accompanied me. Three cars were parked on the curb and every light in the house appeared to be ablaze…Marilyn was not being left alone with her thoughts. I had planned to chat with her again, specifically to find out if she'd heard her husband mention Mo Arnett by name, or if she'd heard her husband and the boy talk about hopes, dreams, plans—anything to give us an edge.

Ernie's clipped voice on the radio stopped me in my tracks. I returned to the car and leaned in to grab the mike.

"Three ten is on Fourth Street. Ten eight."

"Three ten, Amtrak says they have your boy. Ten-twenty-one ASAP."

My pulse shot up through the roof. "On my way," I said, and whistled sharply at the young lady, who had continued moseying toward the Zipoli address. She jogged back, and I threw 310 into gear even as her butt touched the seat.

"They've got him," I said as I pushed the sedan through the first corner way too fast, accelerating hard toward Pershing. "And you were one hundred percent right."

"East or west, sir?" She didn't sound triumphant, just interested in what might come next.

"We'll know in a few minutes."

And sure enough, Lieutenant Leo Burkhalter answered on the second ring. His voice was a little scratchier than it had been five years before when I met him during a Joint Task Force waste of time...a JTF *exercise.*

"About goddamn time," Burkhalter rasped when I introduced myself. "How's life in the fast lane?" he chuckled. His county in northeastern Arizona, so huge that dinky Posadas would be forever lost in one remote arroyo, presented a whole catalog of challenges that we never faced—massive forest fires, for one, along with distances that made me tired just looking at the map.

"I'll be perfect if you tell me that you have one of our errant teenagers in custody, Lieutenant."

"Maw-reese Arnett. Ever heard of him?"

"Indeed I have. What's the deal?"

I heard papers shuffle. "Well, this is a mess. And on the day that my daughter is about to give birth to my first grandchild, you drop this in my lap, Undersheriff. Look, rail dispatch called us with word that they've got this Arnett kid on the manifest... or at least a kid who fits the BOLO you sent out. They're just a few minutes out of Winslow, and without security on board, they played it pretty smooth. He's contained in the observation car, along with one of the attendants. The engineer is takin' it slow, headed for the first siding that comes along."

"Why didn't they take him off the train at Winslow? The city PD would have done that."

"That would be Amtrak's call. I suppose because they didn't want an incident at the station. That's right in the middle of that old hotel in the middle of lots of people. If this kid is armed, if he's a fruitcake, we could have a real incident. It's a whole lot easier to just isolate him out in the middle of the goddamn desert, and take him out at our leisure."

"So he's still on the train, still unsuspecting?"

"As far as we know. The rail folks know who he is, and he's contained with an attendant who apparently is really skilled at making up stories about why the train is going so slowly. But I'm not there, so I can't say for sure. All I know is that they say the situation is secure for the moment. What's your call, Undersheriff?"

"I need to be there."

"Damn right. So get your old carcass out here. We'll get rail dispatch to stop the train where we can reach it by vehicle. The rail freight traffic is hellacious on that line, so Amtrak isn't about to let their passenger train just sit in the middle of things. They'll want off the mainline. Who'd this kid kill, anyway?"

"A county employee."

"No shit."

"I'll tell you all about it when I get there. Look, I'll be coming into Winslow airport. You can have a deputy there for two of us?"

"You got it."

"And get me two hours. Patch through to Amtrak and tell them *status quo* is just fine until we show up. It isn't like the passengers aren't used to it."

"Doing nothing is my specialty, Bill. Like I said, Amtrak doesn't have armed security on the unit, so they're more than happy to have us take care of it. They'll wait."

When I hung up, Ernie Wheeler leaned forward expectantly, his hand reaching for the phone. He'd heard Winslow airport mentioned, and knew that Southwest Airlines didn't have a direct flight from Posadas planned any time soon.

"Call Jim?"

"Tell him he's got two for Winslow. And then wake up Schroeder and have him start on the extradition paperwork with his Arizona counterpart." Our District Attorney, Dan Schroeder, might occasionally serve as president of the Procrastinator's Club, but he was capable when conditions warranted.

"Burkhalter will work his end. And you might as well wake up Ruth Wayand and give her a heads up." I took a deep breath to slow down. "The kid hasn't broken any Arizona laws yet, beyond being underage while carrying a firearm on a train. I'd think that the Arizona cops will be happy to get rid of him. Just hope to hell that he doesn't pull the trigger and change all the rules."

We dashed out to the car and blasted out of the village, taking the state highway toward the airport.

"This is where it gets sticky," I said to Estelle. "Ruth Wayand is with the state department of Children, Youth, and Families. See, the catch is that Mo isn't eighteen yet. So technically, we have a juvenile on the run." I took both hands off the steering wheel and held them up toward heaven, then shrugged and paid attention to my driving for a moment. "And that just adds all *kinds* of shit to the mix, sweetheart."

The Posadas Municipal Airport was seven miles beyond the village on State 76, and other than the security light over the apron, was dark as a closet. I parked beside the hangar where I knew Jim Bergin's plane to be, and tried to be patient. But in two minutes I gave that up.

"PCS, three ten." I drummed fingers on the steering wheel while Wheeler found a moment to respond.

"Go ahead, three-ten."

"Is Bergin on the way?"

"Affirmative. He said you should go into the FBO and start the coffee."

I laughed. I glanced at my passenger. Estelle Reyes was as composed as usual, as if flying off into the desert in the middle of the night was a usual activity. I realized that I hadn't given her even a moment's notice to gather personal items—I hadn't bothered, and it hadn't occurred to me until now that she might like a scant travel bag at least.

"You all set?"

"Yes, sir."

On the still night air, the howl of Bergin's late model pickup truck carried to us, and he had to brake hard for the airport gate. His GMC slid to a stop behind 310, the dome light came on, and I could see him shuffling papers, cigarette between his lips, eyes squinting against the smoke. He found what he wanted and climbed out, crushing the butt under foot.

"What's wrong with a sunny morning for this sort of thing?" the airport manager grumped. A short, lithe man with an old-fashioned buzz cut left over from his military days, Bergin had taken over the manager's job two years before, and we'd become good friends from the get-go. I admired his ambition... he seemed to be able to make a living at an airport where on a busy day, air traffic could be counted without resorting to double digits. He nodded at Estelle as I introduced them, then beckoned us to the enormous hangar door.

"As long as you're here, give me a hand with this son of a bitch," he said, and we all leaned against the door and pushed it to one side against the drag of cranky, squeaky rollers. "One of these days, I fix it," he muttered, and found the light switch. Racks of florescent fixtures blossomed in the cave-like hangar. I'd ridden in Jim's Cessna 182 RG a few times, enough to know that flying held no thrill for me, and considerable gastric anguish for my stomach. It was parked square to the door, with two other aircraft crammed in the hanger behind it.

"Go ahead and board," he said. "Damsel in back."

"You want help pulling it out of the hangar?"

"Hell, no."

By the time Estelle and I had squeezed inside and found all the seatbelt connections, Jim had finished a cursory walk around. "Not even cooled off from the last flight," he said as he slipped inside with considerably more grace than I had managed. A twist, a pull, and a few other gyrations, and the big engine fired, settling into a ragged idle. Lights, camera, action. About that fast, Jim finished up with the switches, dials, and controls, released the brakes and eased the Cessna out of the hangar under its own power, wing tips clearing the door frame with a foot on each side.

"Winslow?" he shouted, and I nodded. "Whoever would want to go there?"

"Us," I shouted in response.

"I hear ya," he said, and then ignored his passengers. The run-up thing that pilots do was accomplished on the way out to the taxiway and then a final prop cycle and check at the donut at the runway end. Even as he steered out onto the asphalt runway, he radioed his plane's I.D. and intentions out into the disinterested night, and then we were gone—blasting down the pavement for about a thousand feet before heading for the heavens, wheels tucking up into the plane's belly, prop settling into fast cruise once we were safely clear of the ground, the cacti, and the mesa.

We tracked northwest, and even though two hundred miles isn't far in a speedster like the Cessna, it was altogether too long for me. The air had quieted down to nighttime velvet, and it was like sitting in a noisy, vibrating arm chair for an hour and a half. There wasn't much point in trying to carry on a conversation, so I sat there and tried to think of a hundred ways out of the scenario waiting for us in Winslow.

Chapter Thirty-seven

Arizona is a wonderfully picturesque state, but at two in the morning, all I could see were swatches of lights here and there. Leaving New Mexico, we could see Silver City tucked behind us at the foot of the Gila Wilderness with a scattering of tiny communities around it, and then ahead Springerville, Arizona in the middle of the great black void with Show Low off to the west. Snowflake finally showed itself after too long wondering where the hell Jim would land 592 Foxtrot Gulf should the engine quit. He wasn't sparing the horses. About the time Holbrook and the daisy chain of lights on I-40 hailed into view, I could also see what had to be Winslow in the distance to the west.

I had no idea where Winslow-Lindberg was, but that didn't matter. Jim Bergin did, and a genteel approach wasn't in the books. He peeled off from altitude and did a steep approach, flaps hanging down from the wing's trailing edges like great shaking doors. All the while he talked on the radio, and part of the conversation included the terse instructions, "And make sure the deputy is parked where we can see him."

Even as our tires kissed the pavement, I could see the cop car well off to the side, red lights flashing. We fast taxied in and Jim cut the engine, the prop windmilling to a halt as we coasted the last few feet.

"You probably want a ride back," he said laconically.

"Yep. But I don't know when. Do you have something to shackle to? We may have a prisoner with us."

Bergin looked skeptical.

"Just a kid," I added, but Bergin could read my expression. As far as I was concerned, Mo had taken himself out of the "kid" category about the time that he squeezed the trigger of his father's Winchester. Kids' advocate Ruth Wayand might disagree, but she, the D.A., and the judge could fight it out. I hoped only that Mo would survive to take part in the negotiations.

"Ah. Seat frame works for that. Done it before. Look, I'll grab a ride to the railroad hotel and finish the sleeping that you so rudely interrupted. Give a holler when you're ready to go back. How's that work?"

"Outstanding." I held out my hand. "Thanks."

I slid out of the plane, followed by Estelle. The Arizona deputy tried not to do a double take when he saw the young lady, then introduced himself as Willie Begay. Not sure of the protocol, he held the Suburban's back door for Estelle while I climbed into the front.

"It's about twenty miles," he announced. I tightened my seatbelt, because I knew what was in store. Young men and powerful engines bring out the best. We wailed out of Winslow onto Interstate 40 and kept to the left lane for enough miles to make me nervous. We dove off an exit and hit the dirt paths that pass for secondary roads in that part of the state, and sure enough, out ahead of us like an illuminated snake, the Amtrak Santa Fe Chief train #3 was parked on a siding. The approach was a rail access road that turned the Suburban into a bucking bronco.

Just off the tail of the train's last car, a fleet of six police units had congregated. Had he been able to look out and see them from where he sat five cars forward, Mo Arnett might have felt proud of himself for generating so much attention. But he was isolated from a rear view, with only the black desert out the side windows.

Deputy Begay turned at the last moment and tucked the Suburban in behind an unmarked Dodge SUV. A huge individual broke away from the circle and headed toward us.

"Damn good thing," he greeted. "We're out of donuts." Leo Burkhalter hooked an arm through mine as if he were escorting an old lady, nodded a greeting at Estelle, and then led us toward the rear door of the last rail car. He paused with a hand on the passenger rail. His head oscillated as if he had a loose bolt in his neck.

"This is what they tell me," he said. "He's at one of the four-top tables at the front of the observation car. The door's locked now, and the attendant apparently spun a tale that it's all part of whatever problem they're having. With the train being delayed for hours up north, it isn't much of a stretch to believe there's more trouble."

"You have communication?"

"The attendant has a radio, but they've played it cool, man. The kid hasn't heard a thing. Every once in a while, the attendant walks back to make a show about trying the door. Gives her a chance to communicate a little bit."

"Her name?"

"Iola Beauchamp. Forty-four year old mother of six. Home is Chicago."

"We need to get her out of there. Is she the one who I.D.'d the kid?"

Burkhalter exhaled loudly. "I tell you what, sheriff. I wish to hell that woman worked for me. She said Arnett was sleeping, head down on the table. I guess her motherly instincts kicked in, and she went to find him a blanket. When she got back, she went to put it over him, and that's when she saw the gun. He had it in his pants on the right side, near the small of his back."

"Not the smartest move he's ever made," I said. "She couldn't grab it easily?"

"Not a chance."

"Just as well that she didn't try."

"He's zonked out, and Iola takes her time. That time of night, there were only two other folk at the far end of the car. Iola discreetly gets 'em gone, then calls for the door lock. And there she is, one on one with your fruitcake. He hasn't tried to explore the train, which is a good thing. Just a matter of time, though. I don't want Iola having to confront him to keep him in place. Doors are locked, but you know…"

The door above us zipped open, and a tall, trim conductor looked down at us.

"This is Bruce Hammer. He's the boss," Burkhalter said. "Sir, this is Sheriff Bill Gastner from Posadas, New Mexico. The suspect belongs to him. This young lady is one of his deputies."

"Sir," Hammer said, and extended a huge hand. His grip was powerful. He tipped his gold-edged cap in an old-fashioned salute to Estelle. "I don't need to tell you all that what we want to avoid is any kind of disturbance. I want this young man off my train, and I want it done so quietly and quickly that the rest of the passengers never know what happened." He stepped down so he was looking me in the eye. "It's our understanding that he's armed."

"One forty-five caliber pistol," I said. "At least that."

"And he's killed once already?"

"Yes. We're not sure of the circumstances," I replied. "Lots of pieces to the puzzle are still missing. But he's not a psychopath," and I had reservations about the veracity of that but didn't voice them. "He's not a serial killer. He's not a bank robber. He's a scared kid who made a bad mistake. We're not even sure of the circumstances of that mistake." I saw the lieutenant grimace at that.

"He's on the lam, he's got a gun, he's cornered," Burkhalter said.

On the lam, I thought. Machine-gun Mo Arnett, on the lam. "So let's just take him out with a sniper rifle shot through the window. Why the hell not." Burkhalter looked as if he wanted to agree with me, despite the heavy sarcasm.

Hammer regarded me for a moment. "One of my employees is in that car, sheriff. My chief concern is her safety."

"My concern as well, sir. Her safety comes first, then ours, then *his.* That's the mess he's put himself in. So let's do this. Let's get her out of there, right now."

"She's had that opportunity, and chosen not to take it," Hammer said.

"She'll come to the door if you request it?"

"I'm sure she will, but she won't leave the young man by himself, locked in the car. He's suicidal?"

"I really don't know," I said. "But Iola probably called it right. Let's see what we can do." I turned to Estelle. "You get to stay here."

"Yes, sir." She didn't sound happy, but I had already worked out a scenario in my mind, and there was no role in it for her. I turned back to Burkhalter. "Let me tell you what I want to do."

Chapter Thirty-eight

The three of us, Hammer, Burkhalter, and I, made our way forward through the cars. I suppose he had his reasons for not walking outside, through the gravel and desert wildlife along the side of the railcars. The passengers sprawled this way and that, finding a way to sleep or read or, in the case of a couple of teenagers, snuggle, the wildlife on board the train.

One middle-aged lady looked up, saw Hammer, and reached out a hand.

"Are we *ever* going to get to Flagstaff?"

"Yes, ma'am. We'll be underway in just a few minutes."

She glanced at Burkhalter and me, both obviously cops, but she didn't ask.

The dark aisles passed one by one, each car packed with warm, smelly bodies, some a good deal smellier than others. Legs and other body parts crowded the aisles, and we maneuvered carefully. Each door at car's end snapped open like a good sentry coming to attention.

Hammer led us through several cars before holding up a hand. "The car beyond this next one." He palmed his radio and pointed with the antenna through the door ahead. I saw a snack bar of sorts taking up the bulk of the next car. A television up in the corner was harshly bright, showing an early morning western. The door snapped open and as we entered I saw a hirsute young man curled in the corner with a heavy knapsack, sleeping over a copy of *Les Miserables*.

The complication was simple. Just as we could look through the sliding door into Mo Arnett's car, he could see us. I wanted him to have no advantage—none whatsoever. We took the absurdly narrow stairs down to the lower level where Hammer opened the exterior door.

"You'll want to stay close to the side of the car," he warned, and we sidled along, shoulders brushing the aluminum. At the far end of the sleeper car ahead of Arnett's observation unit, we re-entered and made our way up to the second level. As long as the boy remained at his table, we'd enter behind his back.

"All set?" Hammer whispered.

"Tell the engineer that all we need is a couple of bumps... nothing spectacular. Just enough to make the kid think we're underway again."

"You got it." He handed me a radio unit. "So you can hear what's goin' on," he said, and wagged a finger at both of us, a warning that if we put any holes in his train, we'd be in deep shit. With the conductor gone, I punched the door release, and it hissed open. The sealed landing between cars was wide enough for both of us to remain clear of the entry. I eased forward toward the door's window, but the bulkhead prevented me from catching a glimpse of Mo.

The radio barked a triple blast of squelch, and Iola Beauchamp's must have done the same. She heard it and made her way toward the rear door. She was a large woman, easily capable of snapping Mo Arnett into little pieces. But she was smart enough to know that size didn't matter to a .45.

"We're about to get underway," Hammer's voice said. "Let me know if all the doors are secure."

Iola acknowledged with a quick, "You got it." At that moment, the train lurched—not much of a bump, but for folks who had grown used to sitting still in the middle of the night, it must have felt like an earthquake. There was no reason for Mo Arnett to think anything amiss. He knew that the train had been delayed for hours before he'd boarded, and another delay wasn't unimaginable. And, out in the desert under cover of darkness, he might have felt secure, safe from his Posadas troubles.

At the far end of the car, Iola's door snapped open, and she turned toward Mo with a broad smile, playing her part to perfection. Hammer appeared, and she touched the conductor's arm as she passed him. The door hissed shut behind them, and Mo was alone in the car.

I activated my own door just as Mo came out of his burrow in the corner. It's hard as hell to make snap decisions in the groggy wee hours, especially when you've alternately been sitting and snoozing the hours away. Mo saw me and for just a fraction of a second, his face went blank. Mo and I didn't know each other well—not face to face, anyway. Under other circumstances I might recognize him on the street among a gaggle of other teens, the events of the last few hours made it seem as if we were lifelong acquaintances.

He might not have been able to recall my name, or for sure place that big old face, the fat belly, or the salt and pepper stubble that passed for my haloed hair-do. He sure as hell could recognize cops when he saw them, especially since Leo Burkhalter was in uniform and the lieutenant's face was set in that expression that all bad guys, even neophytes, recognize.

Mo hesitated for just a fraction of a second, then tried to scramble around the table, Iola's courtesy blanket wadding around his legs. He sprawled out into the aisle, now thrashing in four-wheel drive, making for the back door. The gun went skittering, and he grabbed it just about the time I reached his ankles.

I had stared down the bore of a .45 ACP pistol a good number of times, but always while cleaning the damn thing, never while a live round might be nesting in the chamber while a nervous nitwit's finger shook against the trigger. Mo now lay in the aisle on his back, eyes the size of dinner plates, the gun held awkwardly in both hands, pointed squarely at me.

Well-tempered bravery washed over me, brought on by the various patents that John M. Browning, arguably the greatest firearms designer who ever lived, had melded into the model

1911 semiautomatic pistol. Mo Arnett had been carrying the heavy, old-fashioned handgun stuffed under his belt. I ducked my head and saw that the hammer was not cocked. In that condition, the gun was about as useful as a boat anchor.

"Mo," I said, "why don't you give me that thing before someone gets hurt."

I held out my hand. Unconvinced, Mo dropped one hand from the gun and tried to push himself backward down the aisle. "Where are you going to go?"

His eyes had teared so that he couldn't focus either on me, or the hulking figure of Burkhalter behind me. And the lieutenant's weapon *was* cocked.

"Mo, I can understand why you ran. When you found out that there had been someone in that grader after all, well, hell... who can blame you?" I held out my hand again. "Here. Let's see if we can salvage something from this mess, Mo. Give me the gun."

Mo didn't give me the gun. He jerked around, trying to get up, trying to untangle himself from the blanket. Keeping my bulk between the squirming kid and the lieutenant behind me, I stepped forward, grabbed his right arm and yanked it out from under him, driving his face into the railcar's flooring. With my left, I palmed the .45, twisting it from his fingers and tossing it backward between my legs. Mo let out an anguished howl as I snapped a set of cuffs on his right wrist. With a yank, I pulled his left arm behind him as well, and in seconds he was helpless, belly down in the aisle. Burkhalter had holstered his gun, and now handed me another set of long-chained cuffs for the boy's ankles. With the final click of the stainless steel locks, I straightened up. Glancing toward the back door, I saw conductor Bruce Hammer standing with Iola Beauchamp, their faces grim. I gave them both a little salute of gratitude.

As Burkhalter led the hobbled Mo down the stairs, out into the cool, fresh desert night and finally to one of the county Suburbans, I took a brief statement from Ms. Beauchamp. The Amtrak folks wanted their train to roll. They were in no mood to chat. Although she was clipped and all business, in her eyes I could see a touch of sympathy for Mo Arnett.

She explained succinctly how she had seen Mo sleeping at that four top, an enormous puddle of *drool* leaking onto the table. "I mean, he looked just plain worn out, you know. I felt sorry for him, and there's plenty of blankets, so I fetched him one," she said. "That's when I saw the gun in his waistband." After that, the decision to isolate and call the nearest police had been simple enough. The Coconino Sheriff's Department had received—and thankfully read—the BOLO.

After I finished with the Amtrak folks, with names and addresses and the like, they didn't waste any more time. Train #3 had been delayed long enough. I saw plumes of diesel shoot upward from the two engines, and the Santa Fe Chief started to roll, spooky quiet. In the back of Burkhalter's Suburban, Mo Arnett twisted his head around to watch—whether as a train aficionado or a sorrowful fugitive wishing he were westbound, I couldn't tell.

"What were you going to do out in California?" I asked as Mo settled back awkwardly.

"I don't know," he managed, not sounding like much of a fan of anything.

Chapter Thirty-nine

As it turned out, The Great State of Arizona did not want Maurice "Mo" Arnett. They were entirely satisfied that I had conducted the arrest, nailing a fugitive from New Mexico's justice. Our DA and theirs chatted, no doubt made promises, and the great wheels of the legal system turned and groaned and spat Mo out in record time. As the tires of Jim Bergin's Cessna cleared the runway at Winslow, heading home to Posadas, the sun was working on its zenith, burning ferociously through the Cessna's tinted Plexiglass. I managed a wonderful cat nap, Estelle sifted through notes, and I doubt if the miserable Mo even shut his eyes.

Mo sat in the left rear, directly behind Bergin. The boy was a sorry sight, wrists cuffed and then along with his ankles chained to the seat frame now that we were airborne. Since I'd slapped the cuffs on him, he hadn't bothered with a song of denial. He hadn't sung—or said, or sobbed—a word. He slumped in the crowded little seat, now and then snuffling snot and leaking tears. He held a barf bag between his knees, but hadn't used it. He was so fatigued and stressed that he didn't take any pleasure in rubbing hips with Estelle Reyes. Perhaps her own quiet presence only served to remind Mo what he was going to miss for a long, long time.

Jim Bergin did the talking, and although the day was clear and the air smooth, he filed IFR. The FAA certainly knew 592

Foxtrot Gulf's location every step of the way. About 90 minutes later, I awoke with a jolt, looking down to see the western hip of Cat Mesa outside of Posadas. Taking care not to yank a muscle out of true, I cranked around and looked back first at Mo and then at Estelle. She almost smiled, and except for a trace of dark circles under her elegant eyes, she didn't look the worse for a sleepless night. Mo wouldn't return my gaze, but kept his eyes locked on the rugged terrain below. I'd have given a lot to know what thoughts were roaming through that young brain.

"You got yourself a welcome party." Bergin pointed.

I looked down and saw the airport with two police cars parked on the apron, lights flashing. As we turned into the downwind leg for runway 28, I saw another vehicle as well, a white pickup truck tricked out with contractor's tool boxes and headache rack.

"Oh, that's just what we need," I muttered. I felt motion behind me, and watched as Estelle unlocked Mo's ankle chain. I had explained to her in Arizona that the prisoner was to be free of restraints that locked him to the aircraft during both take-off and landing—and I hadn't needed to mention it again. That was a marvel to me, since my own memory was as full of holes as a garden colander.

"Posadas Unicom, Cessna five niner two foxtrot gulf is down-wind, two eight." Jim's greeting was enunciated clearly, and I'm sure boomed out of the outside speakers above the door of his FBO. For ordinary civilians unused to the world of aviation, there's something official about the landing process for an air-plane. A car just slips into the driveway and stops. But it always seemed to me that airplanes have this ritual, this governmental procedure that gives them some kind of mystique.

We banked steeply into base, and then final approach, Jim announcing our presence again so that some other airplane didn't try and share the same bit of airspace. The fat tires touched the asphalt a hundred yards beyond the threshold so gently that the transition from flight to ground was seamless. Jim had plenty of time to brake for the first intersection to the taxiway.

"Posadas traffic, niner two foxtrot gulf is clear the active," Bergin radioed, and then glanced at me. "Stewardess service is shitty, but we made it." He taxied to the far side of the pumps, well away from the reception committee, and shut down. As the prop ticked to a stop, he jerked a thumb rearward. "Best to exit toward the rear." He nodded ahead. "Even if it ain't spinnin', it's a bitch to crack your skull against that prop."

Airplanes aren't my choice for graceful exits, but I made it without bruise or laceration. Without being asked, Estelle had a secure grip on the chain leading to Mo's handcuffs, and she handed the kid off to me. I got rid of the chain, leaving Mo with just cuffs behind his back. I slipped an arm through his.

I guessed that this was the moment the boy had been dreading the more than any other—stepping out of the plane, his life essentially over by his way of thinking, but still having to face mom and pop.

Mom Mindi remained in the truck, but Mark Arnett had joined Deputy Robert Torrez and Sheriff Eduardo Salcido. Salcido was firm on both feet, so apparently he'd come to an understanding with his doctors. I didn't have to worry about Bobby saying more than he should to Arnett. He'd honed his taciturnity to a fine art. The sheriff, and I loved him like a brother and respected his judgment in most things, could be chatty.

As the prisoner, Estelle, and I left the airplane, the sheriff moseyed forward. He wasn't concerned about Mark Arnett, but Bob Torrez was. The tall deputy circled behind the sheriff to within easy arm's reach of Mo's father. When fifty feet separated us, Salcido stopped abruptly and turned, blocking Mark Arnett with a hand on his chest. "Give us some space," he said, and then removed his hand and motioned to Torrez, who remained with Arnett as the Sheriff then continued toward us.

"Any troubles?" the sheriff asked.

"None whatsoever," I replied. "Mo was cooperative every step of the way." *Well, almost.* "I appreciate Schroeder clearing the way for us so promptly."

"You bet," Salcido mused, but he was gazing at Mo Arnett with interest. "Have things been explained to you, son?" The boy said nothing, but managed a slight nod. "Do you understand them?" Another nod. Salcido pushed out his lower lip, still regarding the boy. "Okay, then." He glanced at his watch. "The arraignment is set for four o'clock this afternoon. That gives us a little time to clean him up and get the paperwork in order. Schroeder said he'd be with us this afternoon with Ruth Wayand."

"Hey!" Mark Arnett had used up all his patience. He managed three paces forward when Bob Torrez grabbed both his arms, but the man twisted away. Backing away from Torrez, Arnett couldn't have missed the deputy's next move. Handcuffs appeared in Torrez's hand, and Arnett held up an index finger in the big deputy's face.

"Now you just back off," Arnett barked. A husky, strong man with a short fuse, he wasn't used to confrontation. "I got the right to talk with my son."

I didn't want to take time explaining to Mark Arnett that, no, he *didn't* have that particular right at that particular moment.

"There's no cause to be leadin' him around like some goddamn convict," Arnett shouted, but turned his attention to the three of us. With one hand held out to fend off Torrez and the other stretched out toward me, Arnett took a couple more steps. The deputy shifted with the cuffs, but Salcido stopped him in his tracks with the slightest of nods.

Arnett advanced to within a dozen feet. The sheriff intercepted him, forcing Arnett to look around him to make eye contact with his son. A quick glance, and then Mo continued his examination of the asphalt at his feet.

"I got to know," Arnett said to the boy. "These men said that you shot Larry Zipoli. Is that true?"

I could imagine Mo Arnett's public defender cringing at that moment, but what the hell. Maybe Mark Arnett *did* deserve to hear the boy's answer, but father and son's days would be filled with more court proceedings than either could now imagine.

"This is not the time or place," I said, tightening my grip on Mo's left arm.

"No, you *tell* me." Arnett's face was an interesting shade of purple. "You go draggin' our name through the mud, son... now you're bein' led back home in Goddamn *chains,* for Christ's sakes."

"We'll take my car," I said, and started to steer Mo that way.

"No. I got a right to know. I got the right to talk with my son," Mark shouted. What had started as wet eyes became an uncontrolled gusher. He started to push past the sheriff, but that was like trying to walk through a brick wall. "You tell me what you did!" he cried.

Mo had started to walk between Estelle and me, but he hesitated and looked one more time toward his father. "It was an accident," he whispered.

That wasn't the answer that Mark Arnett wanted to hear. He slashed an arm to fend off Deputy Torrez. "How the *hell* can something like that be a goddamn *accident?"* he choked.

"Give us some time," I said, but Mark Arnett was in no mood for platitudes.

"Goddamn time?" Arnett almost laughed as he waggled a finger in my face. "You'll get goddamn time. I'll be talking to my goddamn lawyer, is what's going to happen."

"That's the best idea you've had so far," I said.

Chapter Forty

I agreed with Mark Arnett about one thing. How could a kid take a Winchester from his father's gun safe, grab a cartridge or two, then stalk Larry Zipoli, finally shooting him where he sat in the cab of the road grader, placing a bullet squarely through the brain, and then say with a straight face that it was all an accident? Trial lawyers were going to have a field day.

A small room full of people interested in that very question gathered an hour later in the conference room of the Sheriff's Department—not because the boy was being granted special comforts, but because that room was the only one large enough for more than a handful of participants.

District Attorney Dan Schroeder, looking and smelling as if we'd interrupted him from a family barbecue, shuffled papers for five minutes before he clasped his hands together, leaned forward, and fixed his watery blue eyes on what was left of Maurice Arnett.

"Mr. Arnett, you are being charged with the unlawful death of," and he glanced down at his notes, "one Lawrence C. Zipoli, a resident of Posadas, New Mexico, by rifle shot. You've been advised of your rights?"

"Yes, sir," Mo whispered.

"You understand them?"

"Yes, sir."

"Do you want an attorney present?"

"No, sir."

"Do you understand that you may very well be charged as an adult?" At the corner of the table, Ruth Wayand sat with her various notebooks, looking uncomfortable. Ruth and her Children, Youth, and Families outfit were present to guard Mo Arnett's possible status as a juvenile. By the set of Dan Schroeder's face, I knew that wasn't going to fly. And I knew and respected Ruth, too. She'd fight for what she truly believed was right.

"Yes, sir."

"When is your birthday, Maurice?"

"Next week. September third."

"And how old will you be?"

"Eighteen."

Schroeder nodded and glanced across at first the sheriff and then me, indicating that it was now my turn.

I sat on the edge of the table just to Mo's left. "So, tell us how this miserable event happened," I said.

Mo whispered something inaudible, and Schroeder reached out and tapped the tape recorder with his pen. "You'll have to speak up, son. This gadget can't read your mind."

"I took one of my father's rifles and a few cartridges."

"How many?" I asked.

"Five."

Five. The kid rode out to do his work with a pocketful of ammo. Some accident. "And then?"

"I borrowed my mom's car and I was going to go out on the mesa and pop some cans." He hesitated. "Then I saw where Mr. Zipoli had been working."

"You went out specifically to find Mr. Zipoli?"

"No, sir."

"But you knew that he had been working out there?"

"I...guess that I did."

"How did you know where that might be?"

"Because earlier I saw him driving the grader out that way. And he'd been out there the day before, but the grader broke." Mo's voice had taken on a drone, as if he might be reciting a script. Maybe that's what he'd been thinking about during the flight home.

"What time was this?"

"I don't know. Early afternoon, I think."

"Why wouldn't you know for sure?"

Mo shrugged.

I asked, "Closer to one or closer to two?"

"Maybe one."

"Maybe. Where did you park the car?"

"Just off the road. By the intersection."

"Intersection of what?"

"Highland and Hutton."

"Where were Mr. Zipoli and the grader?"

"The grader was parked a ways down Highland. Half way down the block, at least."

"You saw him?"

"No, sir."

"Did you think that he was in the vicinity?"

"No, sir."

"Why not?"

"I couldn't see him in the cab, and his truck wasn't there. I mean, I didn't *see* his truck. He sometimes tows it behind the grader."

"What did you do?"

"I walked toward the grader a ways, and when I was sure I could hit it, I tried to shoot out the windshield."

"How many shots?"

"Just one."

I straightened a little to relieve my spine. "Now why would you do that? You had how many cartridges with you?"

"Five."

"Why not fire five times?"

Mo shut his eyes, but that didn't stop the tears. I reached across and slid the box of tissues within his reach.

"Why not five times, Mo?"

"It was really loud, you know." He opened his eyes and looked up at me, just a quick glance. "'Cause I didn't have ear phones or nothing. I thought someone might hear the shots and see me if they looked over that way. So I chickened out."

"Chickened out? Too bad you didn't chicken out before that first shot." I stood up, kicked the chair out, and sat down, leaning my elbow on the table. "So you shot once. One time only."

"Yes, sir."

"Was the grader running?"

"Yes, sir."

"Did you hear it running, or see exhaust from the stack, *before* you fired the shot?"

"No sir. Only when I walked closer."

"How close did you get?"

"Maybe…I don't know."

"A hundred yards? The length of a football field?"

"No, sir. Not that far."

"A hundred feet then? Fifty feet?"

"Somewhere around there."

"And before you fired, you did not see Larry Zipoli sitting in the cab, watching you approach with the rifle?"

A strangled sob shook the kid, and I paused as he dropped his head onto his arms.

"Did you see him?"

"No, sir."

"I find that hard to believe, son. From a hundred feet away, you couldn't see him, sitting there in the cab of the grader?"

"No, sir. I mean, *after* I shot, I walked a little ways off to one side. For a second or two, I was thinkin' of putting one through the engine block."

"Why would you do that? Why through the engine?"

Mo shrugged helplessly. "Just 'cause."

"But you were afraid someone might hear you."

"I was thinking that."

"But…"

"Then I saw Mr. Zipoli in the cab."

"What did you do then?"

"I left. I drove home, put the gun and shells away, and threw up."

"Threw up?"

"Yes, sir."

"I suppose when all else fails, that's the thing to do," I said. I confess I was having trouble feeling a whole lot of sympathy for this kid. "When your parents came home, they didn't notice that anything was wrong?"

That wonderful shrug answered the question.

"Why did you decide to run?"

"I heard that you were talking to some of my friends. I figured it was only a matter of time before you got to me. So…"

"Why did you park at the airport, Mo? Were you thinking of taking a flight?"

He shook his head quickly, as if the very thought of flying gave him the willies. He'd been a quiet passenger in Jim's Cessna, but that happens. Folks can trust a puddle jumper, but not a Boeing at 36,000 feet. "Just 'cause."

"You thought that might throw us off?"

Shrug.

"Where did you think you could go?"

Shrug.

"Is there someone out on the coast whom you know?"

"No, sir."

"Where were you going to live?"

"On the beach."

"Ah, the beach. Have you ever been out there, Mo?"

"No, sir."

"So let me ask you," I said after a pause that stretched so long Mo looked up to see if I'd fallen asleep. "Why, Mo?"

"Why what?"

"Why shoot Larry Zipoli, Mo?"

Down went the head again, his voice muffled against the table's mahogany veneer. "I didn't see him."

"You've said that. Why shoot at his road grader?"

Shrug.

"What did he ever do to you that prompted that kind of vandalism, Mo?" *Vandalism.* That word sounded goddamn odd in the context of that room at that moment. "You wanted to scare him?"

Shrug.

"I think we should take a short break," Ruth Wayand observed. *She* was tired? She should have come with us to spend an interminable night and a worse morning in Arizona, fussing with paperwork and phone calls.

"Do you know Jason Packard, Mo?" I asked, ignoring Ruth's suggestion.

"Yes, sir."

"A friend of yours?"

Shrug.

"Did Mr. Zipoli encourage the two of you to fight at one point? On a bet?"

After a long hesitation during which Ruth played various tattoos with her pencil eraser until I shot an annoyed look at her, Mo murmured something.

"Say again, son?"

"Yes."

"Yes, what?"

"He did that. Mr. Zipoli did. He loved the fights, and he thought it was a great joke, trying to get me and Jason to go around."

"And you two guys fought for him?"

"No."

"What did you do?"

"I left. I…I ran away."

"And you were angry with Mr. Zipoli for that? Enough to punch holes in his road grader?"

Shrug, then Mo added, "That wasn't the only time. He was always on my case."

"In what way?"

"Just stuff."

"Stuff like what?"

Shrug. Mo had that reply down pat.

"Was Jason willing to fight?"

"Sure. He'd get a dollar."

"A dollar. That was the purse?"

"Yes, sir."

"You're older than Jason, Mo. Bigger, too. But you wouldn't do it?"

"No." Probably a wise choice, I thought. Wiry, tough Jason would jangle Mo's chains.

"Were you two friends before that? You and Jason?"

Shrug. "Sort of."

"And after?"

That earned a shake of the head.

"Let's take a short one," I said. "Then we'll go through this again."

Joints cracked as five of us got to our feet. I beckoned to Ruth, and she, Sheriff Salcido, District Attorney Dan Schroeder, and Estelle Reyes followed me from the room, down the short hall and to my office. I made sure the door closed tightly behind us.

"Ruth, this is Estelle Reyes, a new hire," I said, and didn't bother explaining why a new hire would be stuck to this case like a burdock. A hell of a ride-along the girl was taking, and as far as I was concerned, she might as well stick to the end.

Mrs. Wayand was fiftyish, stout, and what euphemistically might be called plain. I knew her to be a powerful advocate of children without going all gooey on us, and I hadn't seen any great wash of sympathy on her face during Mo's initial interview. The young man deserved every consideration that the law would allow, but there was nothing the least bit cuddly about this kid. That he'd seen nothing wrong with fetching a rifle to use against someone because of some vague personal slight indicated to me that we were damn lucky to have Mo Arnett in custody after a single fatality. I wondered who the other four cartridges had been meant for. I didn't believe for a moment that he had taken the rifle for a practice session.

"I see no chance that Judge Smith is going to let this go through as a juvenile case," she said without preamble. "I mean, you folks might unearth *something* that might change my mind, but at this point? I don't think so. He'll be eighteen in just days. I think he'll take the full ride."

"He'll be tried as an adult," the district attorney said flatly, even though we all knew that decision wasn't his to make. "I want one piece of information before I proceed, though. I want a perfect photograph of that road grader's windshield, taken *in situ,* at the time of day in question. I want to see the reflection." He smiled without humor. "You'll get that for me?"

I nodded. "You bet. We have it photographed already from every direction, up, down, and sideways."

"But at that precise moment when Mo fired? Do we know what the light conditions were?"

"Bright sunshine all day. But we don't *know* the precise time yet."

"But we will. Best guess, anyway. Maybe a sequence, taken every fifteen minutes starting at noon and continuing through the afternoon. That would be the way to do it."

"We can do that."

"I'll bet dollars to donuts that this is going to go through as murder two, with unlawful flight to avoid prosecution thrown in as a kicker. But if it turns out there's any chance at all that the kid could see the victim before pulling the trigger, then it's a different ball game."

We spent another two hours running Mo Arnett through the grinder, with Sheriff Salcido and the D.A. each taking a turn. If we expected a clear explanation, we were disappointed. I'm not convinced that Mo actually understood his own motives. He clearly hadn't liked Larry Zipoli much, but joined in on some of the trips because that's what the kids were doing. And after each trip, I guessed, Mo arrived home feeling just a touch humiliated…teased beyond friendship, the butt of jokes, an easy target.

At four o'clock, Maurice 'Mo' Arnett was arraigned before District Judge Everett Smith. His father attended the arraignment, his mother did not. Mark sat stony-faced through the whole thing, shaking his head in disgust each time his son answered one of the judge's questions in that quiet, snuffling voice.

Mark Arnett obviously felt the public defender was entirely adequate, and the elderly fellow, Lucius Salazar, did his best. He didn't have a lot to work with. The plea for the boy's release into the custody of his parents fell on deaf ears. Judge Smith refused bail, leaving Mo as the county's guest until after the Grand Jury deliberations. I wouldn't have left Mo with his parents either.

The ball was now in the District Attorney's court as he prepared his case, and our job was simple enough—provide Schroeder with whatever he asked for.

As we left Smith's chambers, Estelle surprised the hell out of me by touching me on the elbow, obviously intent on initiating a conversation.

"I'll be happy to shoot the photos for you, sir. We can get that done tomorrow."

I smiled at her serious enthusiasm. "That would be wonderful, except for one thing," I said, and saw one of those black eyebrows lift a fraction. "You can't testify about the photos. Well, you *can,* but even old Lu Salazar for the defense would shoot us out of the water if you did. You aren't certified, you haven't any established expertise—no matter how talented you might be. In point of fact, you haven't even been officially *hired* yet, as far as county paperwork is concerned." I lifted my shoulders in a helpless shrug.

"What I want you to do is take some time to get yourself some rest, then meet me tomorrow at high noon on Highland Avenue. I'll shoot the photos." I smiled. "It'll be your finger on the shutter, all right, but with me at your elbow, there's no chain of evidence problems. Will that work?"

For the first time since she'd walked into my office, Estelle Reyes smiled broadly, a heartwarming burst of sunshine.

Chapter Forty-one

Late the next morning, Deputy Howard Bishop drove the county road grader from the Quonset hut in the corner of the maintenance yard the several blocks out to Highland Avenue. He parked facing west, the cleats on the machine's massive tires settling into the exact spot where it had originally rested with the dead Larry Zipoli slumped at the controls.

Mo Arnett, seeing cooperation as his best defense, marked a site photo for us, the little 'x' indicating where he remembered standing when he pulled the trigger. Using that and Deputy Robert Torrez's best guestimate of yardage, we set the heavy camera tripod so that the camera lens would match Mo's eye level, five feet three and one half inches off the ground.

The department owned a fleet of junky little cameras, one aging but high quality reflex, and a Polaroid. I settled for Estelle's elegant new Nikon F, and I was impressed when she chose a 70mm lens because it was the closest to matching the image seen by the human eye. I hadn't thought of that, and it made me feel like a Neanderthal. That, I reflected, is why we hired young people. I felt an uncoplike, parental stab of pride from the git-go.

The grader's windshield, sporting a messy bullet hole beside the wiper blade, was heavily veiled with red dust and years of grime from diesel smoke and oil fumes. How Larry Zipoli could have seen clearly enough to blade the damn road was a mystery. With the sun slanting on it, it was impossible to see through the dull silver slab of glass.

As the afternoon wore on well past any likely time for Mo to have fired the shot, right up to when I first spoke with the shaken Evie Truman, matters only got worse. Mo Arnett had been telling the truth. It was unlikely that he could have seen even the vague outline of the victim inside the cab. Nervous, apprehensive, probably about ready to piss his pants, Mo had not looked closely enough. The grader was parked, the door open, and no one evidently around. So he took the shot. Bookmakers might have said the odds were against him, having grabbed the wrong ammo, the bullet wandering down the barrel to wobble and wander, finding its lethal way. But despite the odds, Mo had managed one perfect shot.

"I think that's all Schroeder will need," I said to Estelle at three o'clock. Conditions hadn't changed except for a pesky breeze.

She dismantled the camera from tripod, rewound the film and dropped the thirty-six exposure canister into my hand. "Schroeder will be disappointed?" she asked. "He's hoping for murder one?"

I shook my head. "We don't hope for one thing or another, Estelle. What is, is. Our job is to find out just that, and Schroeder's job is to make the punishment fit the crime." I chuckled at that little bit of sanctimonious wisdom. "That sounds pat, doesn't it? But that's the way it *should* work."

"I can't imagine Mo in prison," Estelle said, and I grimaced.

"Let me tell you, by the time they're finished with all the psychobabble about the influence of a thoughtless, domineering father, a numb mother, and all of Mo's other troubles with every relationship he's ever had since birth? I'll be surprised if the kid lands anything beyond three or four years in some rehab center."

"Are you okay with that, sir?"

I looked at her in surprise. "I'm okay with that. There are a lot of things I could *wish* for, but wishing isn't going to make them so. So I do what I do and don't stew about it. Mo Arnett made his choices, we catch him, and now it'll be interesting to see how he turns out. We can hope that we don't end up chasing him again."

"I suppose that happens," the young lady mused.

"We hope to get there before he pulls the trigger next time. That's something to wish for, I guess...that we could get there before that happens, whether with Mo Arnett or someone else." I shot the legs of the tripod in and folded it to fit the black bag. "That's a rare thing. And that's job security, I suppose."

We settled back in the car and watched the grader trundle away, bouncing rhythmically on those big donuts as Deputy Bishop guided it back to the county barns. Despite years of being operated with a windshield full of cracks, it would be changed out now, removed with great care and entered into evidence, bullet hole included.

"Tomorrow I'll have a dispatch schedule for you." I made an entry in my log. "And *that* will be a challenge for you. Sitting dispatch for eight hours when nothing much is happening? *That'll* be a challenge."

I looked across at her just as she frowned, her expression telling me that for the first time she might be ready to question the scheme of things. "And you understand that *nothing* about this case is to be discussed with anyone other than the sheriff, me, or the district attorney. Nothing." Her nod was impatient. "You did extraordinarily well these past two days. I want you to know that."

"Thank you, sir."

"There's a lot of work now, keeping Schroeder happy with the evidence. But part of the heat is off. We got the bad guy off the street. And that always makes me *really* hungry." I held up the canister of film. "I'll give this to Deputy Baker so he can make a set of prints for the D.A. In the meantime, may I buy you something at the Don Juan?"

Estelle made a face that I couldn't translate. Disappointment, distaste, impatience, maybe a potpourri. "How will we pursue the Orosco, sir?"

"The what?"

"The *tres retablos,* sir. The more I examine the photographs from Veracruz..."

Despite what the young woman might have thought, I hadn't forgotten Jim Raught's treasure, and the various possibilities they offered. Stolen art? A cunning copy? A lucky—and legal—purchase, or the tip of an iceberg that might lead to who knew what depths of international art theft. And I knew what Estelle Reyes wanted just then.

"The best thing to do," I said judiciously, and hesitated as I frowned at the steering wheel, "is to hand this over to Tom Mears to handle. He's careful, thoughtful, thorough…" I stopped there, amused at the expression on Estelle's dark face. Deputy Mears *could* handle the art case thoroughly and efficiently, and, I was willing to bet, the young lady would bite her tongue and go with it. But she didn't know me well enough yet to realize my suggestion was in jest.

"You really *don't* want to sit dispatch, do you," I laughed. "Any excuse at all."

"I'm looking forward to it, sir. It's just that…"

"All right, then, what do you want to do? What do you think your next step should be?"

Her relief was palpable. "At least we might talk with Mr. Raught again, sir. I want to know how he acquired that artwork."

"And if he chooses not to tell us?"

"I think he will, sir. He's too proud of it not to."

"Ah." I nodded. "And if it's an innocent fake, acquired legally?"

"I'll apologize to him for wasting his time, sir."

"And if it is, in fact, the original Orosco?"

"Then it needs to be returned to its home in Veracruz."

"If you're tied up with dispatch tomorrow," and I glanced at my watch, "that means we should go after this today."

"Yes, sir." She managed not to sound too eager.

I sighed. "There's always something else on the horizon in this job," I said. "All right, we'll go see Jim Raught. After some dinner, we'll pay the gentleman a visit." Estelle Reyes looked down and smoothed the leather cover of her soft brief case, forcing patience. "That's one thing you'll learn as you go along, sweetheart. When a few minutes present themselves to enjoy a green chile burrito, you take 'em."

A special note of thanks...

I'd like to extend special thanks to B.J. Eiland, who provided two Model '94 Winchester lever-action carbines, one a .32 Special, the other a .30-30 Winchester, for a series of tests, the results of which were as described without modification in Deputy Robert Torrez's experiments in *One Perfect Shot*.

And, as always, to Kathleen, whose compilation of the *Posadas County Mystery Series Index* made the writing of this prequel possible.

To receive a free catalog of Poisoned Pen Press titles, please contact us in one of the following ways:

Phone: 1-800-421-3976
Facsimile: 1-480-949-1707
Email: info@poisonedpenpress.com
Website: www.poisonedpenpress.com

Poisoned Pen Press
6962 E. First Ave. Ste 103
Scottsdale, AZ 85251